A Vision of Battlements

MANCHESTER
1824

Manchester University Press

The Irwell Edition of the Works of Anthony Burgess

Series editors: Andrew Biswell and Paul Wake

Anthony Burgess (1917–93) was one of the most prominent novelists and critics of the twentieth century. He wrote thirty-three novels, twenty-five works of non-fiction and two volumes of autobiography. Pursuing a parallel career as a classical composer, he wrote a symphony, a piano concerto, a violin concerto for Yehudi Menuhin, and more than 250 other musical works.

The Irwell Edition takes its title from a collected edition outlined by Anthony Burgess himself in the 1980s but never achieved in his lifetime. Each volume in the series presents an authoritative annotated text alongside an introduction detailing the genesis and composition of the work and the history of its reception.

The Irwell Edition of the Works of Anthony Burgess

A Vision of Battlements

Edited with an introduction and notes by
Andrew Biswell

Manchester University Press

Published by Manchester University Press
Altrincham Street, Manchester M1 7JA

www.manchesteruniversitypress.co.uk

British Library Cataloguing-in-Publication Data
A catalogue record for this book is available from the British Library

ISBN 978 1 5261 2203 2 hardback

First published 2017

Typeset in 10/13.5 Stempel Garamond by
Servis Filmsetting Ltd, Stockport, Cheshire
Printed in Great Britain by
CPI Group (UK) Ltd, Croydon CR0 4YY

Contents

General Editors' foreword   *page* vi
Acknowledgements   viii

Introduction   1

A Vision of Battlements   19

Appendices
  1 Anthony Burgess, Introduction to the first British and
    American editions   197
  2 Anthony Burgess, 'Gibraltar'   200
  3 Anthony Burgess, 'Rock of Ages'   211
  4 Anthony Burgess, 'Everyone's Free … Except Me: One
    Man's View from the Barrack Room'   214
  5 Anthony Burgess, 'First Novel'   218
Notes   223

General Editors' foreword

John Anthony Burgess Wilson (1917–93) was one of the most prominent novelists and critics of the twentieth century, but for many years much of his work has been unavailable. A graduate of Manchester University, he wrote thirty-three novels, twenty-five works of non-fiction and two volumes of autobiography. Pursuing a parallel career as a classical composer, he wrote a symphony, a piano concerto, a violin concerto for Yehudi Menuhin and more than 250 other musical works.

The Irwell Edition of the Works of Anthony Burgess is the first scholarly edition of Burgess's novels and non-fiction works. One of its purposes is to restore 'lost' novels to the canon of available work. The edition will include stage plays, musical libretti, letters and essays.

The Irwell Edition takes its title from a collected edition outlined by Anthony Burgess himself in the 1980s but never achieved during his lifetime. Each volume is edited by an expert scholar, presenting an authoritative annotated text alongside an introduction detailing the genesis and composition of the work, and the history of its reception. The appendices will make available previously unpublished documents from the Anthony Burgess archives held at institutional libraries in Europe and North America, in addition to rare and out-of-print materials relating to Burgess's writing.

The Irwell Edition is designed for students, teachers, scholars and general readers who are seeking accessible but rigorous critical editions of each book. The series as a whole will contribute to the ongoing task of encouraging renewed interest in all aspects of Anthony Burgess's creative work.

Andrew Biswell
Paul Wake
Manchester Metropolitan University

Acknowledgements

Assembling a scholarly edition is inevitably a collaborative process. I am pleased to acknowledge the institutions and individuals who have supported this book in one way or another. The Harry Ransom Center at the University of Texas at Austin and the Andrew W. Mellon Foundation awarded me a short-term fellowship which gave me time in which to think and write. The archivists at IMEC (L'Institut mémoires de l'édition contemporaine), McMaster University and the Special Collections Division at Washington University in St Louis have accommodated visits or requests for information. My colleagues at Manchester Metropolitan University had the kindness to leave me alone so that I could get on with the job. Simon Johnson tracked down Burgess's wartime service record and shared it with me. Dr Graham Foster helped with capturing the text at an early stage. Matthew Frost and Paul Clarke at Manchester University Press showed enthusiasm for publishing the Irwell Edition which has been echoed by the Press's anonymous readers. Georgia Glover at David Higham Associates has proved herself to be the best and most sensible of literary agents. The writer Nicholas Rankin, who knew Burgess and interviewed him for the BBC World Service, shared his extensive knowledge of Gibraltar during the Second World War and kindly allowed me to read his unpublished work. Jonathon Green's monumental *Dictionary of Slang* has been my constant companion in this and other adventures.

Anna Edwards, the archivist of the Anthony Burgess Foundation, located books, notebooks and other objects from the collection. Paul

Boytinck sent copies of reviews. Will Carr provided a sympathetic ear whenever one was needed. Jane Stevenson and Peter Davidson generously put their knowledge of the classics at my service. Jeremy Huw Williams helped me with the Welsh dialogue. My father, Alan Biswell, was a valuable source of information about Army slang. William Dixon and Yves Buelens have never flagged in their support and encouragement. Dr Paul Wake, my fellow general editor of the Irwell Edition of the Works of Anthony Burgess, has been a loyal friend, and I am in his debt for casting an expert eye over the text and the notes. Any errors which remain are probably mine.

I am especially grateful to the International Anthony Burgess Foundation and its trustees, both past and present. Without the fore-sight and generosity of the Foundation's benefactor, the late Liana Burgess, this Irwell Edition would have remained a distant hope.

Andrew Biswell
Manchester Metropolitan University

Introduction

Genesis and composition

The earliest surviving fragments of the novel which became *A Vision of Battlements* are to be found in Anthony Burgess's notebook from 1940, now in the collection of the International Anthony Burgess Foundation, Manchester. This is the blue hardback notebook in which John Burgess Wilson, as he was known until he began publishing fiction in 1956, drafted the undergraduate dissertation on Christopher Marlowe's *Doctor Faustus* which he submitted for his BA degree in English at Manchester University in the summer of 1940. Burgess was conscripted into the British Army in December of that year, and he kept the same notebook with him throughout the Second World War. It was still in his possession when he lived in colonial Malaya in the mid-1950s: the latest entries in the notebook are a series of calligraphic exercises in Jawi (the Arabic form of Malay) and many pages of calculations in Straits dollars.

At an indeterminate point between 1943 and 1945, Burgess sketched out two sections of an untitled story about life in the army:

I am the Barracks. I am circled with brick walls and garnished with barbed wire. My mouth is my sole orifice and I clamp shut with iron at midnight. My stomach is an asphalt square and my limbs spread out in redbrick married quarters. My veins and arteries are little streets, my brain has its will in the Commanding Officer's office and memory in the

Orderly Room. I take in shovel-loads of civilians and digest
soldiers.

My memory is longer than yours. I have seen a multitude
of regiments. I have seen bandboys become bandsmen. I have
seen the rookie become a tyrant. I have seen the drafts out with
bands, and the spewed out without bands.

This first-person narrative in the voice of 'the Barracks' is the first
known example of Burgess's fiction-writing after he had graduated
from university, and it demonstrates how far he resented having to
serve in the Army. In part one of the story, Burgess wrote (and later
crossed out): 'I munch the raw stuff to a bolus and shit digested soldiers.' This deleted line tells us a good deal about the extent to which
he was irritated by life in the military.

The second section of the story approaches the territory of *A
Vision of Battlements* more directly. It concerns a character called
Regimental Sergeant Major Creswell, an Army Education instructor, who is bored with his work and longs for the day when he can
leave the army and return to composing music in civilian life. On
the desk in his office is a silent metronome. Like Richard Ennis, the
fictional composer in the later novel, Creswell also has a hatred of
physical exercise. He contemplates with evident distaste the gymna-
sium which exudes 'heavy body smells', the 'thugfaced corporal' who
presides over the compulsory regime of running on the spot, and the
'sweating herd' who willingly surrender themselves to such activities.

It is possible to date these two short story fragments from their
context in the notebook. The first part appears immediately after a
page which is headed 'Notes on Cultural Reconstruction' – the subject of one of the lectures that Burgess delivered while working for
the Royal Army Education Corps in Gibraltar between December
1943 and May 1946. After these two short and inconclusive exper-
iments with fiction, Burgess temporarily abandoned the idea of
writing a novel about his life in the Army, and there is no evidence
to suggest that he returned to the subject until the end of the decade.

One reason for valuing this notebook from the 1940s is that, apart
from an article about poetry and a handful of short film reviews, very

little of Burgess's other wartime writing has survived.[1] More than twenty years after peace had been declared, he published a number of his Second World War poems, reattributing them to the poet Francis Xavier Enderby in *Enderby Outside*, and he included a number of other war poems in *Little Wilson and Big God*, the first volume of his autobiography.[2]

Publication history

A Vision of Battlements emerges from an uncertain period in Burgess's personal history. Having been demobilised from the army in 1946, he spent the next four years undertaking a variety of short-term teaching jobs at Brinsford Lodge, a residential college near Wolverhampton, and at Bamber Bridge Emergency Training College near Preston in Lancashire. It was not until 1950 that he succeeded in finding a permanent teaching post at Banbury Grammar School in Oxfordshire, where he remained until 1954. Burgess wrote music and poetry during this period, and he was involved in directing amateur theatre for the Banbury Players and the Adderbury Drama Group. In 1951 he completed his first stage play, a verse drama in the manner of Christopher Fry titled 'The Eve of St Venus'.[3]

If there has always been a certain amount of doubt about the novel's date of composition, this is partly because Burgess himself offered a number of misleading statements about it in his published writings. In *Little Wilson and Big God*, he claims to have written the novel in the winter of 1953.[4] In his introduction to the first edition of 1965 he states that 'I wrote it in 1949, three years after leaving the scene where it is set'.[5] In another essay first published in the *Observer* in 1993, Burgess claims that the book was written in

1 For further detail on these publications, see Andrew Biswell, *The Real Life of Anthony Burgess* (London: Picador, 2005), pp. 99–100.
2 See Burgess, *Enderby Outside* (London: Heinemann, 1968, pp. 239–43); and Kevin Jackson, *Revolutionary Sonnets* (Manchester: Carcanet, 2002).
3 This dramatic work, which forms part of the Burgess collection at McMaster University, is distinct from the novella published under the same title in 1964.
4 Burgess, *Little Wilson and Big God* (London: Heinemann, 1987), p. 362.
5 Burgess, *A Vision of Battlements* (London: Sidgwick & Jackson, 1965), p. 7.

1953.[6] Both of these dates are incorrect. A reference in the text to Jean Cocteau's film version of *Orphée* (p. 165), released in September 1950, indicates that the novel cannot have been completed before that date; and a memorandum discovered in the Heinemann archive states that *A Vision of Battlements* was 'originally offered to us in 1952 and rejected'.[7] The available evidence points to a period of composition which began in the second half of 1951, following the completion of 'The Eve of St Venus', and continued into the autumn of 1952.[8] Burgess submitted the novel to Roland Gant, the senior fiction editor at Heinemann, who declined to publish it but encouraged him to embark on a second novel, *The Worm and the Ring*. Heinemann also rejected this second book when they read a draft of it in 1954, and Burgess moved abroad to take up a new teaching post in Malaya, where he became a published writer with the appearance of *Time for a Tiger* (the first volume of his Malayan trilogy), completed in 1955 and published by Heinemann the following year. Unfortunately no other editorial papers, readers' reports or publishing contracts relating to *A Vision of Battlements* have so far come to light.

Some time after the novel had been rejected by Heinemann for the second time in 1961, Burgess's agent, Peter Janson-Smith, offered it, in the summer of 1964, to Peter Dawnay at Sidgwick and Jackson, who planned to revive the Victorian or Dickensian tradition of publishing illustrated novels. Sidgwick and Jackson had already published *The Eve of St Venus*, rewritten as a novella and adorned with illustrations by Edward Pagram, an Australian-born artist then living in London. Pagram, who had become a personal friend of Burgess and his first wife, was once again recruited to provide seventy black-and-white illustrations, a title page and a colourful dust jacket for the novel.[9] The dust jacket copy in the British

6 Burgess, 'Great Expectations' in *Observer*, 28 March 1993, p. 4; reprinted as 'First Novel' in *One Man's Chorus*, ed. by Ben Forkner (New York: Carroll & Graf, 1998), pp. 270–3, 270.

7 James Michie, internal memo dated 17 May 1962, Anthony Burgess papers, William Heinemann archive.

8 For more detail on this point, see *The Real Life of Anthony Burgess*, p. 101.

9 For more detail on Edward Pagram, see Colin Wilson's introduction to

edition emphasised the novel's comic content, to the exclusion of its darker qualities:

> This novel has many claims on the attention of lovers of comic fiction. The setting is Gibraltar, a place rarely visited by novelists; the theme is not the frustration of a wartime garrison so much as the pain of looking forward to re-building, re-adjustment at war's end. But it is still gloriously comic.[10]

In the United States the book took a very different form. It was acquired by Eric Swenson, Burgess's regular editor at W.W. Norton in New York, who took the decision to publish the text without any of Pagram's illustrations. The dust jacket makes it clear that Norton saw varieties of tone and meaning in the novel which seemed to have been overlooked by its British publisher: 'The theme of this novel is serious: the pain of adjustment to the war's end and to the prospect of building some new kind of life [...] Whatever Ennis touches turns to muddle. His teaching is chaotic and bad for discipline. His love affairs are inconclusive and unresolved.'[11]

Writing about the novel a few months before his death in 1993, Burgess expressed a strong opinion about which version of the book he regarded as canonical: 'My novel appeared with comic illustrations by Edward Pagram. This turned out not to be a good idea: the text was diminished by the drawings and the book not taken seriously. It was never paperbacked and so failed to reach a genuine reading audience.'[12] He added that, in the United States, *A Vision of Battlements* had been a commercial and critical success and 'ended up as a subject for university dissertations' (p. 273). The decision not to include Edward Pagram's illustrations in this critical edition has

Pagram, *A View of London* (London: Hamish Hamilton, 1963). See also *The Real Life of Anthony Burgess*, pp. 281–2.

10 Burgess, *A Vision of Battlements* (London: Sidgwick & Jackson, 1965). Dust jacket copy.

11 Burgess, *A Vision of Battlements* (New York: Norton, 1965). Dust jacket copy.

12 'First Novel', p. 272.

been taken in line with Burgess's stated preference for having a text in circulation which would stand or fall on the merits of its writing, without the distraction of images.

Background and contexts

The novel takes its title from an entry in *The Illustrated Family Doctor*, a popular reference book of the 1930s. In the section which lists the symptoms of migraine, we find the following: 'Warning of an attack may be given by tingling sensations in the limbs, impairment of vision, flashing lights, a vision of battlements, noises in the ears, mental depression or other phenomena.'[13] Such visual hallucinations are a well-documented feature of migraines, memorably described by the neurologist Oliver Sacks as the 'classical zigzag fortification pattern'.[14] Burgess, who was predisposed to migraine and had experienced these visual phenomena since his teenage years, blamed his migraine in Gibraltar on 'the heat of the sun, the stress of duty, above all sexual frustration'.[15] He intended the title to carry a certain amount of metaphorical weight. The 'vision of battlements' represented by the Army is itself a kind of illness or an 'impairment of vision', and the novel encourages its readers to think of the Second World War and the ordinary sufferings of soldiers as aspects of an unappealing collective hallucination. On a more straightforward level, the title might also be thought to refer to the situation of wartime Gibraltar as a fortified zone of military activity, from which most of the civilian population had been evacuated.

One of the most important literary contexts of *A Vision of Battlements* is its indebtedness to Virgil's *Aeneid*. The extent of Burgess's borrowing is clearly signalled in his introduction to the 1965 edition (reprinted as Appendix 1 below). He indicates that

13 Anonymous, *The Illustrated Family Doctor: A Guide to Essential Medical Knowledge and the Maintenance of Good Health. By a General Practitioner* (London: Amalgamated Press, 1933).
14 Oliver Sacks, *Migraine: Understanding a Common Disorder* (London: Duckworth, 1985; revised and expanded edition, Picador, 2012), pp. 273–4.
15 Burgess, 'First Novel', p. 271.

a one-to-one correspondence exists between certain figures in Virgil and the major characters in his novel. Aeneas becomes the utopian lecturer and composer Richard Ennis; his faithful companion Achates is Julian Agate, a dancer who once met Stravinsky and Diaghilev; Dido is Concepción, Ennis's former student and deserted lover; Iarbus is Barasi; and the warrior Turnus becomes Turner, an Army instructor whose cult of the physical body is at odds with Ennis's belief in the primacy of art and music. Other characters, such as Major Muir and Mrs Carraway, stand in for Virgilian figures such as Jupiter and the Sybil. Lavinia appears under her own name.

Although the catalogues of Burgess's private libraries are available and searchable, very little research has been done into his intellectual formation as a reader. The collection of his books on deposit at the University of Angers includes two student editions of Virgil's *Aeneid*: Book 6, edited by J.T. Phillipson; and Book 8, edited by A. Sidgwick.[16] The ownership marks and dates within these books ('John Burgess Wilson, 1934') indicate that they were the texts Burgess studied at Xaverian College for his Higher School Certificate examination in 1935. Given his close familiarity with these particular sections of Virgil's poem, it comes as no surprise to discover that most of the Latin quotations and other specific Virgilian references within the text of *A Vision of Battlements* are taken from Books 6 and 8 of the *Aeneid*. For example, Chapter 20, in which Richard Ennis and Julian Agate visit Mrs Carraway the fortune-teller, is closely modelled on Aeneas's encounter with the Sybil in Book 6 of Virgil's poem.

Like James Joyce before him, who had used Homer's *Odyssey* as the basis of his novel *Ulysses*, Burgess took the skeleton of a classical epic in order to furnish his work with a strong story and a set of mock-heroic characters. His critical writing about Joyce is instructive when it comes to understanding how *A Vision of Battlements* relates to the epic Latin poem on which part of its meaning depends. In *Here Comes Everybody*, the first of his commentaries on Joyce's works, Burgess draws substantially on the work of Frank Budgen,

16 Virgil, *Aeneidos: Liber Sextus*, ed. by John Tindall Phillipson (London: G. Bell, 1922; reprinted 1933); Virgil, *Aeneidos Liber VIII*, ed. by A. Sidgwick (Cambridge: Cambridge University Press, 1926).

whose book *James Joyce's Ulysess* had informed his thinking about Joyce's response to classical epic. In particular, Burgess took from Budgen the idea that *Ulysses* is a schematic work, carefully planned and written according to a principle of 'extreme accuracy', in which Joyce 'followed the Homeric precedent of carefully arranging his data [...] and imposing on them the rule of a severe logic'.[17] Burgess was so impressed by Budgen's book that he lifted its schematic tables (the lists of organs, arts, colours and symbols, which had been given to Budgen by Joyce himself) and redeployed them without acknowledgement in *Here Comes Everybody*.[18] In his commentary on *Ulysses*, Burgess notes that Joyce had taken liberties with the structure of Homer's *Odyssey*, reducing the number of chapters from twenty-four to eighteen; Burgess, working with the example of Joyce in mind, adopts a similarly cavalier approach to Virgil's *Aeneid*, expanding the number of sections from twelve to twenty-three (including the prologue). When it came to modernising Virgil in this, his first completed novel, Burgess always had Joyce's book in mind, and he acknowledges his debt to *Ulysses* by deploying a few lines from it as one of his epigraphs.

Another significant deviation from Virgil is that the action of *A Vision of Battlements* does not follow the order of the *Aeneid*: the death of Turnus, which Virgil places at the end of Book 12, occurs much earlier in Burgess's updating of the story; and the taxi race around Gibraltar, corresponding to the funeral games in Book 5 of the *Aeneid*, takes place in Chapter 5 of *A Vision of Battlements*, whereas the descent into Hell which follows in Book 6 of Virgil is delayed until Chapter 21 of Burgess's narrative.

One of Burgess's difficulties in trying to forge a twentieth-century novel out of Virgil is that the *Aeneid* is incomplete: the poem falls away after the defeat of Turnus in Book 12 and never reaches a decisive point of resolution. Burgess navigates this problem by making Ennis's departure from Gibraltar the final episode of the novel.

17 Frank Budgen, *James Joyce's Ulysses*, revised edition (New York: Vintage, 1955), p. 82.
18 See, for example, 'Ways into the Labyrinth', in *Here Comes Everybody* (London: Faber, 1965), pp. 83–7.

Whereas Aeneas had looked forward to the founding of imperial Rome, Richard Ennis can anticipate nothing more glorious than a new standardised era of the common man, in which the serious music he proposes to write will probably never be heard. Julian Agate sums it up for him: 'A new world, I believe. Wide boys, drones, a cult of young hooliganism. State art. Free ill-health for all. Lots and lots of forms to fill in. The *Daily Mirror's* increasing circulation' (p. 191). Among other things, Agate's vision of the postwar future anticipates the wide-boy hooliganism of *A Clockwork Orange*; but whether this new world will also be able to accommodate an idealistic artist-figure such as Richard Ennis is by no means a certainty at the novel's end.

After *A Vision of Battlements*, Burgess wrote nothing of substance on the subject of Virgil, but he included a reference to the *Aeneid* in a lecture on censorship delivered to the Malta Library Association in June 1970, and subsequently published as a pamphlet titled *Obscenity and the Arts*:

> I have never yet dealt in 'blow-to-blow' accounts of the sexual act. I am not interested. I am much too concerned with living my own marital life. I do not want to live it as it were vicariously […] I find Virgil's reference in Book IV of the *Aeneid* to the 'known flame' far more appropriately inflammatory […] than any 'blow-to-blow' account.[19]

Burgess returns to this theme in the typescript of an unpublished article written in 1985:

> The best writing about sex is in Book IV of the *Aeneid*, where Virgil describes the orgasm, and everything leading up to it, as either *nota flamma* or *flamma nota* – the conflagration you all know about. I've tried to follow Virgil; in doing so I've achieved a diffidence open to bizarre interpretations, of which necrophily and bestiality may be one.[20]

19 Burgess, *Obscenity and the Arts* (Valetta: Malta Library Association, 1973), p. 15.
20 Burgess, 'On Having a Book Written About One', unpublished typescript,

Readers of Virgil will search in vain for this description of *'nota flamma'* or *'flamma nota'* in Book 4 of the *Aeneid*. In Book 4, line 23, we find 'agnosco veteris vestigia flammae', where Dido speaks about feeling a spark of the flame of her former love. But the passage that Burgess has in mind occurs in Book 8 (lines 387–392), immediately after Venus has spoken to Vulcan:

Dixerat et niveis hinc atque hinc diva lacertis
cunctantem amplexu molli fovet. ille repente
accepti solitam flammam, notusque medullas
intravit calor et labefecta per ossa cucurrit
non secus atque alim tonitro cum rupta corusco
ignea rima micans percurrit lumine nimbos.

(The goddess ceased, and as he falters throws her snowy arms around him and fondles him in soft embrace. At once he felt the usual flame; the familiar warmth passed into his marrow and ran through his melting frame: just as when at times, bursting amid the thunder's peal, a sparkling streak of fire courses through the storm clouds with dazzling light.) (Virgil, *Aeneid VII–XII*, trans. by H. Rushton Fairclough, revised edition (Cambridge, MA: Harvard University Press, 2000), pp. 88–91)

It seems more than likely that Burgess has confused Dido's flame in Book 4 with the flame of Venus in Book 8. He is also incorrect in supposing that 'flamma nota' or 'flammam notusque' would translate into English as 'known flame'. Virgil's known flame in the above passage is 'solitam flammam'. 'Fiamma nota' in modern Italian would mean 'well-known flame' but it would sound odd to a native speaker. In both the lecture and the article, Burgess appears to have back-translated himself into Latin via a literal piece of Italian.

This apparent lack of familiarity with his original source text raises the question of whether Burgess was reading Virgil in Latin

International Anthony Burgess Foundation, Manchester, Journalism Box F, p. 3.

or in English translation. Although it has been established that he studied Books 6 and 8 of the original poem when he was at school, a copy of the standard Penguin translation by W.F. Jackson Knight survives in his book collection, and he may have owned other translations. It is reasonable to suppose that he knew some sections of the poem in Latin and other sections in English. One other possible source is Cecil Day Lewis's radio version of the *Aeneid*, which was broadcast on the BBC Third Programme between September and December 1951 (the year in which Burgess began to write *A Vision of Battlements*) and later revised for publication.[21]

Army Education during the Second World War provides another important context for the novel. After fourteen days at sea, Burgess arrived in Gibraltar on 24 December 1943 to take up a new post in the Royal Army Education Corps. His main task in Gibraltar was to deliver 'British Way and Purpose' lectures, known as 'BWP', to members of the British armed forces and Italian prisoners of war. 'The British Way and Purpose' was a programme of civic education, established in November 1942, when the Army Council decreed that every combatant was to be released from other duties for up to three hours per week of instruction in 'citizenship'.[22] Burgess taught the third sequence of the lecture course, which dealt with questions such as the wartime economy, the consequences of the falling British birth rate and the anticipated transition from wartime to peace. He was also required to lead discussions on 'The Idea of Empire', 'Education for the Colonies' and 'Building a Durable Peace'. BWP looked forward to the creation of a welfare state and a new system of national insurance, state pensions and health-care, along the lines proposed in the Beveridge Report of 1942, titled *Social Insurance and Allied Services*. In many respects BWP was a liberal and forward-looking educational programme, which foresaw a post-colonial time when territories such

21 The first part of *Vergil's Aeneid*, translated by C. Day Lewis and produced by Basil Taylor, was broadcast on the BBC Third Programme on 17 September 1951; the final part on 6 December 1951. For the published text, see *The Aeneid*, trans. by C. Day Lewis (London: Hogarth Press, 1954).
22 See *The British Way and Purpose* (Directorate of Army Education, 1944), pp. 1–2.

as India would begin to govern themselves. Burgess's discussion of the colonial status of Gibraltar in *A Vision of Battlements*, which is mobilised through the voices of Spanish and Gibraltarian characters, emerges from his involvement in Army Education work. These dialogues also anticipate his later writing about Malayan independence in the novels *Time for a Tiger* (1956), *The Enemy in the Blanket* (1958) and *Beds in the East* (1959). Gibraltar provided an ideal location in which to consider the status of Britain in relation to its dominions and colonial territories.

Burgess's reservations about BWP arose from its total silence on the question of cultural reconstruction after the war. He articulates these doubts through the exchange between Ennis and his commanding officer, Major Muir, in Chapter 5, where Ennis argues in favour of 'the full life, sir, the total sensibility. Values, civilised living, the contact with the bigger reality'. Muir's position is solidly utilitarian: 'Education is a *useful* thing; we must never forget that. The world has to go on. 'Ouses have to be built, trains run, busted pipes repaired. All the rest is really trimmings. I know it is very nice to read poetry and look at paintings, and I would never deny the value of music. I am fond of it myself' (p. 61). Ennis, through his artistic activity as a composer, shows himself to be a utopian who is trying (like Virgil's Aeneas) to build a new city based on civilised values. Burgess's 1940 notebook reveals a similar urge at work. In his 'Notes on Cultural Reconstruction', he gestures towards a plan for postwar life which will address the cultural silence of the BWP lecture course:

> Programme of Reconstruction after the War may remedy many pre-war ills in housing and town-planning. People however will continue to carry their own slums with them. Sooner or later it comes about that reform must be induced from within. The ego exists apart from the id. Environment is not a free conditioner of character. Programme of Cultural Reconstruction must come about. What are we fighting for? It seems negative things – absence of tyranny etc. What is 'liberty' but a negative thing we occasionally bolster up by positive talk of national heritage? Collectively we have nothing to gain in war

except the maintenance of the laissez-faire weaknesses of status quo. Individually we have everything to lose. Life is collective. Material needs end with the family – cultural needs with the society. This in the widest sense: the family system cannot support culture. Culture requires the traditions of a society.[23]

Burgess's release from the British Army was delayed until 24 May 1946, by which time he was already twenty-nine years old. Like many young men of his generation, he felt that the Army had interrupted his education and his wider ambition to embark on an artistic career as a writer or composer. Speaking about this sense of frustration in relation to the anti-heroic attitudes of Richard Ennis within the novel, Burgess aligned himself with the so-called 'Angry Young Men' of the 1950s:

> My first novel did have an anti-hero in it, but I've often felt that the anti-heroes of Kingsley Amis and John Wain and so forth came very late. It was during the war and especially in the services that young men began to feel that they were being fed a great deal of ... a lot of ... about the future, the great future that lay ahead, that didn't really exist, and this quiet stoicism began to develop.[24]

Given that Kingsley Amis's first novel, *Lucky Jim*, did not appear until 1954, Burgess seems to be making a claim here for *A Vision of Battlements* as an early manifestation of the spirit of 'quiet stoicism' and anti-establishment rebellion which was later identified as having been characteristic of the Movement generation of British writers.[25]

23 Burgess, 'Notes on Cultural Reconstruction', 1940 notebook, Burgess Foundation. See also his review of *Friends of Promise: Cyril Connolly and the World of Horizon* by Michael Shelden: 'Connolly's decision, sustained every month, to promote literature as part of the war effort, proved to be not only courageous but correct.' Untitled typescript dated 9 February 1989, Burgess Foundation archive, Journalism Box G, p. 1.

24 Burgess, *Desert Island Discs* (radio interview with Roy Plomley), BBC Home Service, broadcast 28 November 1966.

25 For more detail on this point, see Blake Morrison, *The Movement: English Poetry and Fiction of the 1950s* (Oxford: Oxford University Press, 1980), pp. 10–54.

He reiterates this point in the preface to *Little Wilson and Big God*, where he suggests that his autobiography 'may stand for a great number of my generation – those who were dimly aware of the muddled ethos of the twenties, were uneasy in the thirties, served their country in the forties, and had some difficulty in coming to terms with the postwar world – the peace or prolonged truce that is still with us' (p. viii).

Critical reception

The British edition of *A Vision of Battlements* was published by Sidgwick and Jackson in September 1965. Reviews from the London papers were mixed, with frequent reservations being expressed about the difference in tone between Edward Pagram's illustrations and Burgess's text. The longest and most considered review was by A.C. Cockburn in the *Times Literary Supplement*, who noted that it was not necessary to know anything about the *Aeneid* in order to understand Burgess's story. Cockburn compared the novel unfavourably with Aldous Huxley's *Antic Hay* and *Lucky Jim* by Kingsley Amis, but he stated that 'The trouble with the book really is that not enough happens'.[26] There were also misgivings about the overall structure of the novel and the briskness with which it proceeds from one comic episode to the next:

> With Turner's end the reader notes with some surprise that there are forty pages to go. Vignette follows vignette in the rambling tones of a soldier recalling the war on television. Ennis suffers from premature ejaculation with his wife, Concepción and Lavinia. This malady extends to the novel. Too many of the effects are consummated with premature and bootless speed; which presumably is why it went back in Mr Burgess's bottom drawer, till he had acquired greater control and direction.

26 A.C. Cockburn, 'The Ennead', *TLS*, 30 September 1965, p. 850.

Cockburn also complained that 'The illustrations do not really give the reader's imagination much of a slash across the rump, and do not appear to be well executed either'.

Peter Vansittart wrote in the *Spectator*: 'Time is not wholly kind to this tale, a Virgilian symbolism is too deeply buried to be noticed, but there is left much genial mockery of war-time militarism, tourist clichés, official attempts at moral uplift, together with a sideglance at colonial poverty, sardonic but compassionate.'[27] Jocelyn Brooke wrote in the *Listener*: 'The passage I admired most was one in which [Burgess] starts off a chapter with a rhapsodic tribute to Spain in the best (worst) sort of travel-agent prose, then switches abruptly to the real thing: the drabness, the squalor, the vomiting drunks, the beggars, the used french letters in the gutters.'[28] Writing in the *New Statesman*, Christopher Ricks made useful comparisons with Burgess's other novels, such as *Honey for the Bears* and *The Wanting Seed*. He described *A Vision of Battlements* as 'consistently entertaining and observant,' and admired Burgess's 'great ear for barrack-room talk'.[29] His major reservation concerned the use of the *Aeneid* as a structuring principle:

The framework of the book is a flop, as Mr Burgess more or less admits. He planned parallels with the *Aeneid*; they have no good effects and some bad effects. (For example, they let us know that the character Turner will get killed.) But the myth-manipulating can easily be ignored, and one is left with a vivacious truth-telling at which memory will appropriately flinch. Added to which, there is the double interest of its date. For one thing, the novel shows (not 'in embryo', but aptly subordinate) all the concerns which have dominated the later books. There is the matter of the epicene, important here, and kindly seen, but less interestingly handled than in *Honey for the Bears*. And the idea that 'all artists are hermaphrodites.'

27 Peter Vansittart, 'Rebels and Officers', *Spectator*, 1 October 1965, pp. 424–5.
28 Jocelyn Brooke, 'New Fiction', *Listener*, 30 September 1965, p. 505.
29 Christopher Ricks, 'Rude Forerunner', *New Statesman*, 24 September 1965, pp. 444–5.

And that America and Russia are 'both the same.' Then there are those famous interpenetrating opposites Yin and Yang [...] And there is Pelagianism, as in *The Wanting Seed*, that comic primer of modern heresy.

The most favourable British review came from Martin Shuttleworth in *Punch*: 'Here it all is: the drunken, browned-off soldiery of the democratic world; dumb society gearing itself in the dark for peace; the individual, baffled in his search for pattern and shape in his own life, finding consolation and oblivion in the comicality of present surfaces – a novel, in short, of wit, shape and importance, perhaps *the* novel of those years.'[30]

The American edition, published by Norton towards the end of 1965, was much more positively received. Conrad Knickerbocker wrote in the *New York Times*:

The postwar world is a mess, and the novels of the English writer Anthony Burgess grind our face in it. His cosmic sense of pain and baroque gift of language hammer down the lid of the garbage can. Only the size and blackness of his wit make the despair barely bearable [...] In his later novels he unabashedly owes much to Joyce, but his ideas are his own. His commentary in the *Spectator* displays one of those prolific, encyclopedic talents that England manages to produce in fair abundance and America almost never.[31]

Knickerbocker's assessment of Burgess's first novel is that 'What began in the books as a private pleasure evolves into a public point of view – fierce, voracious, pitiless humor. Life, Mr Burgess obviously discovered as he wrote, responds to language, and one does not have to compose music to be an artist. His forces thus massed, he sallied forth a strong man.'

Charles Wheeler wrote in the *New York Times Book Review*:

30 Martin Shuttleworth, 'New Novels', *Punch*, 20 October 1965, p. 588.
31 Conrad Knickerbocker, 'Variations on an Antiheroic Theme', *New York Times*, 1 February 1966, p. 33.

'This is an Army novel, without the foxhole or stockade, that suc-
ceeds in conveying a humanity where others dig into mire. The
author's failing but never failing musician-sergeant (so obsessed by
creative energy that even in the midst of a foolish philandery he
"worked out a passage of double fugue") is as fallible as the brass.'[32]
Wheeler found continuities between this novel and Burgess's
Malayan trilogy: 'The grating between dull English and more exotic
cultures appears here in an apt first form.' As a satire, he concluded,
A Vision of Battlements succeeded because 'There is laughter here
but no scorn. And there is an unmistakable love for the human race
despite its faults.' Finally, the American essayist John Gardner wrote
in the *Southern Review*: 'The language in *A Vision of Battlements*
is not as ingenious as in the later Burgess novels, but it is sufficient,
often very funny, rich in images which are at once clever and grimly
appropriate.'[33]

Although *A Vision of Battlements* has been out of print for
more than forty years, its publication in the Irwell Edition allows
us to reconsider Burgess's earliest work of fiction in the light of
his better-known later books. This 'lost' novel about the Second
World War and its hangover is a brilliant piece of early Burgess.
Despite the apologies Burgess made for it in his autobiographical writing as a mere piece of apprentice-work, it deserves to
be regarded as a fully formed fictional statement. The figure of
Richard Ennis, the thwarted composer, anticipates many of the art-
ist-protagonists of Burgess's later novels, such as the poet Enderby,
Shakespeare in *Nothing Like the Sun*, John Keats in *ABBA ABBA*
and Christopher Marlowe in *A Dead Man in Deptford*. Burgess's
anti-heroic or mock-heroic war novel can also be seen to be the-
matically engaged with the other books he went on to write in the
1950s. It foreshadows his analysis of the peacetime status of art
and education in *The Worm and the Ring*, and of the imminent
collapse of British colonialism in the three Malayan novels and

32 Charles Wheeler, 'Intrigue on the Rock', *New York Times Book Review*, 30
   January 1966, p. 32.
33 John Gardner, 'An Invective Against Mere Fiction', *Southern Review*, vol. 3,
   no. 2 (April 1967), 444.

Devil of a State. By investigating and dramatising these aspects of the new, post-1945 reality in *A Vision of Battlements*, Burgess was already mapping out the territory of his future creative work.

A Vision of Battlements

—What year would that be about? Mr Bloom interpolated. Can you recall the boats?

Our *soi-disant* sailor munched heavily awhile, hungrily, before answering.

—I'm tired of all them rocks in the sea, he said, and boats and ships. Salt junk all the time.

Tired, seemingly, he ceased.

– *Ulysses*, James Joyce

'... Warning of an attack may be given by tingling sensations in the limbs, impairment of vision, flashing lights, a vision of battlements, noises in the ears, mental depression or other phenomena.'

– *The Illustrated Family Doctor*

Prologue

'A.V.C.C.', said the big blonde Wren. 'I don't think I've ever seen them letters before.' Her huge feet firm against the rolling deck, she marched round Ennis, examining curiously his left shoulder, then his right shoulder, then his left shoulder again.

'The Army calls these numerals,' said Ennis.

'Then the Army's daft,' said the Wren. 'Numerals is numbers. Letters is what these are. Come on, tell us what they mean.'

'Arma Virumque Cano Corps,' said Ennis, teasing. And then, seeing her look blank, 'Army Vocational and Cultural Corps.' But she looked no less blank. She said:

'Aw, come on, tell us in plain words.' She began to wriggle her upper body gently and seductively at him. Ennis said:

'Well, it's to prepare for the future, you see. It's to get the men ready for when this lot's all over. To teach them how to build a new world.'

'Aw, teaching,' she said, disappointed. 'You mean you're like a teacher?'

'I,' said Ennis, erect, 'am a musician. If I'm a teacher, I'm a teacher *malgré moi*. Just as I'm a soldier *malgré moi*.'

'You do talk funny,' giggled the Wren. 'But it's nice, really. Educated. And you don't look like a soldier, somehow. My sister got engaged to a fellow who looked a bit like you. He was a piano player and had long hair. He was allowed to have the long hair because he was in munitions.'

'Well,' said Ennis, a little angrily, 'even though I don't look like a soldier – Ah, never mind. What I was going to say was that I've done my share of fighting.'

'I'm sure you have, love,' she soothed.

'Dunkirk,' said Ennis, 'and then Crete. They wouldn't let me carry on in a combatant outfit. That's why they transferred me to –'

'That's all right, dear,' she said. She was a very pink girl with a Roman nose but very little teeth.

'As long as we're absolutely clear about that,' said Ennis. 'We had a terrible time at Crete.'

'Yes, yes, that's all right.' And then she said, with unexpected viciousness, 'But you're alive, aren't you? Not like my cousin Ron.'

'If you can call it being alive.'

'Blown up at sea, Ron was. Fighting on dry land's one thing. You ought to try it at sea, fighting and spewing up and then there's U-boats and mines. Ron was in the Merchant Navy, Ron was, bringing food and fags from Yankland for the likes of you.'

'We've all got to take our chance.'

'Do you good, it would,' she said, 'to have all that lot to cope with. U-boats and thunder and lightning and right big waves a couple of miles high.'

'Don't tempt Providence,' said Ennis.

'Do you all the good in the world it would. You're just like that piano player my sister got engaged to, you are. You've got just his eyes. He upped and left her and took the money she'd saved up and all. Some men are just like beasts. Beasts is all you can call them. Men,' she said, big, blonde, nastily.

'Are you readah?' called the epicene captain of artillery. He was the producer. They were rehearsing for the ship's concert. 'Very well, then. On stage, all who should be. Now, Judy,' he said, putting his arms round the big blonde Wren, 'let's have no fluffing this time, hm? And try to make it a bit more, you know, refined.'

'June my name is,' said the Wren. 'Judy's more the name for a lady dog.'

'Yes, yes.'

'I reckon I can talk refined. I can talk as high society as what he can.' She glared at Ennis. She had taken, for some reason, a really strong dislike to him, hardly explicable in terms of drowned Ron and the absconding piano player. In her billowy curtain robes she bounced up the steps to the stage.

'Tabs,' called the captain of artillery. 'She's awful really,' he confided to Ennis, 'but she looks right, you know. All that pink flesh.' Ennis, piano player, sat down at the piano. He waited for green floats to glow sickly on the closed curtains, then flung himself into a storm of diminished sevenths. The curtains jerked open and the big blonde Wren was disclosed on an empty stage. She yelled coarsely above the music:

'Ocean, be calm! Storm-winds, do not affright!
For we have got this concert on tonight.'

'Watch those vowels, dear!' called the captain.

'Æolus, we require a steady stage,
So shut your mouth and cool your senseless rage–'

Ennis and his keyboard went down, down, down, like a cinema organ and organist. Then came back up again, to no applause. A scream rang offstage. The big blonde Wren fell, cursing. 'Oh, dear,' wailed the captain. The storm-god had heard; the storm-god was going to let fly.

The rehearsal was abandoned. The world burst noisily asunder. The North Atlantic's black back cracked. Howling sea-ghosts scrabbled at the rigging. Soldiers lurched along the troopdecks, howling also, slopping tempestuous mess-tins of tea. Over the decks salty knouts of broken sea lunged and sloggered. Acres of frothing marble leered monstrously, as though Rome had melted. Riding the bitter uncertain ranges, the troopship soared and plunged in agony. A dry ship (haha, dry!) with nightly lemon squash drunk, like a ghastly parody of drinking, in pint mugs, and now the decks struck at one, unprovoked. Men tottered and spewed and were heaved into their bunks and hammocks without the satisfaction of knowing they had brought it all on themselves. It was not fair. Sweating and groaning in his bunk, the Nonconformist chaplain (more of a Unitarian really) felt his nausea churn in him like a sermon (terrible aboriginal calamity; sin grows wild, as God-made as an apple).

Ennis, Sergeant Richard Ennis, A.V.C.C., lay in his hammock on the sergeants' troopdeck, shaping in his mind, behind his closed eyes, against the creaks and groans of the heaving ship, a sonata for violoncello and piano. He listened to the sinuous tune of the first movement with its percussive accompaniment, every note clear. It was strange to think that this, which had never been heard except in his imagination, never even been committed to paper, should be more real than the pounding sea, than the war which might now suddenly come to particular life in a U-boat attack, more real than himself, than his wife. It was a pattern that time could not touch, it was stronger than love.

No! That was heresy, He remembered the last days of embarkation leave in London. They had clung together at night in the narrow bed of her tiny room, while the sky shook with the rhythm of aerial express trains, the approaching sickening thuds set the walls quivering. The two of them had seemed stronger than death. The sinister lights of distant burning illuminated her face ghastily, but there was no fear there. Death did not seem all that terrible, their love seemed a Troy that a ten-thousand-year siege could not shatter. This separation was incidental, something they tried to see already as a past thing to be joked about.

Think of *Nazi* lipsticks,
Gestapo cigarettes,
And children cuddling toy
S.S. men in their beds.

But on the last night, when it was time to report to the transit depot at Marylebone, the flood mounted and broke. Twice before he had had to report to transit depots before going overseas, but not then as a man in love and married. They stood in the bombed-out Soho street and he cursed, screamed, shook childish impotent fists at his enemies. He cursed the whole pantheon in a foul stream of obscenity

that frightened even the steel-helmeted special constable who came
to see what the trouble was. Ennis, in his ecstasy of execration, could
not tell who the enemies were, but a number of faces had coalesced
into a single image – the destroyer, the anti-builder, a Proteus capable of being time, the sea, the state, war, or all at once. It wanted cities
down, love broken, music scrambled. Ennis the builder cursed and
wept in the ruins.

But was love the same as music? Already adjustment was beginning, adjustment to something even so transitory as a voyage. He
thought uneasily of Troilus and Cressida, classical lovers remade
by the Middle Ages, eternal symbols of the war-sundered grown
unfaithful. Was love less important than the urge to build cities?

The storm died down, and there was already in the clearer air the
smell of a warmer climate. The rolling English drunkard had come
to the Mediterranean by way of the Viking whale roads. The ship
woke to life again, the decks were busy with arms drill, P.T., a succu-
lent drawled lecture on venereal disease. Wrens, dapper in flapping
bellbottoms, provocative with Sloane Square vowels and wagging
haunches, minced up and down. But the big blonde hater of Ennis
was, it was said, in the sick-bay with a wrenched hip.

'Now,' said Lance-Corporal Cheney, the historian, 'we approach,
in effect, our home, our mother, the middle sea of Noah's flood
and Deucalion's. Our voyage in itself is a symbol of the course
that English history took, rejecting the dark world of the northern
brine and the crude heavy gods. Here are wine, logic, the city-state,
Aphrodite's frank smile, the Arabs discussing Aristotle on the colon-
nade of an Iberian university, and, above all, the sun, our indulgent
father.'

Only a few bodies still lay prone and supine, rejecting the hard-
boiled breakfast eggs and the lyrical call of life. As to some faun-fife
or Triton-horn, the colleagues of Sergeant Ennis rose from their
beds, back to perpetual games of solo, and their harsh vowels cut
the mellow cultured flutings of the Intelligence Corps contingent.
Though the vowels of Sergeant Agate, ballet-dancer, one-time
Petrouchka praised by Stravinsky and patted by Diaghilev, were far
from harsh. Agate had made friends with an infantry lance-corporal

of good family. Ennis, looking eastward over the taffrail, heard them pass on their circular morning stroll.

'But everybody said he would be unfaithful. Reggie was quite distraught with the worry of it all. Coming back at all hours with the most disgusting little sluts.'

'He should be happier now, though, dear. If what I hear is true, this little Cypriot should be very very good for him. A bit brainless, I know, but that's sometimes all to the good. Makes them most accommodating –'

Agate was, Ennis had to admit, a cut above the other A.V.C.C. sergeants. Williams and Evans, fluent at scolding each other in thick Northern Welsh, were slow at English. Welsh Nationalists, haters of the *Saes*, would they, in their civics lectures, be able to flush matters of local government with the *hwyl*? Williams looked like an egg perched on a loosely stuffed battledress, Evans was red-haired, wiry, truculent. And then there was Bayley the craftsman, tall, big-nosed, lugubrious, worried about his wife, who was expecting in a month's time. Ennis was aware of this gestation as of another ship, pounding forward with a quiet throb of engines. Lastly, there was Tomlinson. He, with respirator spectacles glinting above bad teeth, found time to create a myth. The ship was carrying dockyard maties and dark colonial civilians back from visiting their evacuated wives. Among these, alleged Tomlinson, were saboteurs, enemy agents, home-rulers. He had seen, he said, some of them hanging round the engine-room.

'You noticed, boy,' he said, 'the other night, the ship stopped dead, without warning. They know all about it, but they can't do a thing. You mark my words, there's something queer happening, something brewing. It won't be long now. Just before we left London I saw a swaddy salute an officer just by Marylebone Station. He clenched his fist just as he brought his hand up to his head. And, by God, the officer returned it!'

Things were going to happen, he said. This was no time for committing oneself to opinions. Back home he had stuck to facts in his talks to the lonely gunsites. 'Gentlemen,' he had said, 'it is a fact that there is a House of Lords. It is a fact that there is a House of

Commons. Beyond that I will not go. Now I ask for your views on the matter.'

Someone had said, 'I think the House of Lords is a bloody anachronism.' Tomlinson had said, 'That's a point.' Someone else had said, 'Why do the Yanks get more pay than what we do?' Tomlinson had replied, 'That's a point, too.' On one occasion a bold bombardier had ventured, 'I think you're a bloody fool, Sergeant.' Tomlinson had said, 'That also is a point.'

With some pride he stated that he had been known as That's-a-point Tomlinson. 'By Christ, it's coming,' he asserted. 'The long knives. You'll remember what I told you, you mark my words.'

Life went on. The concert at last was given to a large audience robust with purgation, tickled by approaching warmth. And the big blonde Wren, arisen for her prologue perceptibly pinker and plumper, did not hate Ennis any more. After the show, on an empty stage in a property armchair, she said:

'I think you're quite nice really. I don't know what got into me that time. If we was both going to the same place I could be your girl. But I'm going on to Cyprus.'

'You're returning home in a way.'

'How do you mean?'

'Venus came from Cyprus.'

'Oh, that's an awfully nice thing to say,' she said, after a few minutes. 'That's like a real compliment.' And so, hopelessly, his bridges burnt, Ennis was made free of her warm pinkness. It happened at the right time, for, the next afternoon, Africa lay basking on the starboard side, lavish in the sun. There lay her northern portals, there her woods and mountains and, behind, a whole hinterland of tawny lions. Open-mouthed, the troops gawked over the rails. But Ennis had passed this way before. He smiled when Sergeant West, an instructor on his circuitous way to the Falklands, said:

'Down here on the messdeck it's still England, still Avonmouth, and hence still the past. Up there it's Africa and the future. On trains, you remember, when one asked what time lunch was served, one was told, "Just after Reading". Time is really space after all.'

So now, with the approach of the new life, many clung to their past, they snuggled into the dark of their bunks, they feared the new big daylight in which the ship rode calmly. And, as this age of transition from the known to the unknown assumed the quality of a real memorable past, the other past, the past beyond (wives, familiar pubs and chairs, children) became very remote, like somebody else's past – in a word, history. But Ennis pushed his wife farther back, beyond history, to myth. It was the best thing to do; it would ensure a kind of fidelity.

Christmas Eve. They awoke with a shock to find their future was upon them. It had appeared suddenly in the night, the giant threatening rock, the vast crouching granite dragon, the towering sky-high sphinx, its forehead bathed in the mild sun. It brooded, an incubus, but also their bride and mother. In Ennis's head the winding line of his sonata lost sonority, faded to a bat-squeak, and the heavy brass, the horns, the skirling flutes and fiddles took over. Like Andromeda, he thought, chained to this rockface till time should send the deliverer, they now had to learn the great gift of patience. No ill-wind Germans would dislodge them from here.

Patience. The waiting for orders, the helplessness as, static in straps and packs and haversacks and respirators-at-the-alert, they stood around, their throats parched, their palates foul with many cigarettes. They were lumpishly stuck, arms and men, among milling officials with orders in triplicate, majors with Movement Control brassards, worried platoon commanders. Like a disenchantment was the raising of that backcloth of sea and sky, the sight of reality in the gantries, the grey dockyard, the slow coming-on of a land evening. Slowly the drafts moved down the gangways, heavy-booted, stumbling, to the waiting tumbrils. Finally it was the turn of the A.V.C.C. draft, the smallest. The six minced clodhoppingly down to the unfamiliar feel of stone underfoot. The Rock was twinkling to life, lights in tier after tier. The distant haze of the town hummed in the violet evening.

'This is it, then,' said Evans. Nobody said anything. There seemed to be nothing to say. They waited, with something like the apprehension of children who fear they are lost, but also with a quite irrational half-formed hope. Perhaps nobody wanted them, perhaps they could go home? Arriving in a theatre of fighting had not been like this: fighting was different, fighting got you somewhere, even if only kicked out and home. At length a truck arrived, and from its cabin emerged a cadaverous hatchet-faced warrant officer. There was no welcome. He merely said, 'Two of you for the Engineers' Mess, two for the Pay Corps, two for the Second Wessex. Sort yourselves out into pairs. Remember, you're here for the duration. This isn't a two-year station any more, so you'd better choose someone you can stand the sight of. But don't take all night over it.' They eyed each other shyly. From the promenade deck of the troopship came a call.

'Yoohoo!' The big blonde Wren was waving. Ennis waved back. She blew a kiss. 'Look after yourself! Don't do anything naughty!' Ennis blew a kiss back then climbed aboard. The truck moved into the future that was now the present. The past lay well behind them, a sheer hulk stripped of its freight of human society. And behind that? None of them wanted to think.

I

'But I do love you,' protested Ennis, 'if that word has any meaning at all.'

'You don't really,' complained the flat voice from the bed. 'You wanted me for one thing. You as good as said so. Twelve months here, you said, without even speaking to a woman.'

Ennis looked through the lattices at the hot noon in crowded Main Street. In one or two cafés tinny orchestras were striking up. He saw naval uniforms, khaki drill, white civilian suits, heard the giggles of schoolgirls who, at fourteen, were as nubile as they would ever be. Heat pressed on him from the low ceiling, sweat rilled down his chest.

Concepción sat up in bed, her blue-black hair framing reproachful eyes. 'It wasn't for this,' she said, 'that my father asked you to come here. It was to give me guitar lessons.' Then she wept.

'Paolo and Francesca,' said Ennis. He grinned wearily: she hadn't read Dante. He turned back to her and took her in his arms. The musk of the dark skin, the tang of sweat in her hair, the faint residuary breath of garlic whetted a compassion in him that was near to love. 'I do love you,' he said again. 'I do want to be with you all the time. You mean so much, especially now.' In his shirt pocket, on the chair, was the airmail letter he had received that morning. Fragments passed through his mind: 'Still nobody like you – shall always think – better this way perhaps – he wants to marry –' Paolo and Francesca. Troilus and Cressida. One man could be many heroes; a woman was just what she was. 'Tell me,' he said, stroking her dark-flued forearm, 'what did you feel like that time? When you lost your husband, I mean.'

She didn't reply at first. Then she said, 'I felt bad. Then I realised it never meant much to me. It was my father's idea. He thought it would be a good thing. A daughter is a big responsibility here. So many men go over the border for their wives.'

'But Pepe went over the border for something else.'

'He was a fool. Their politics was not his affair. And he was too old to go fighting other people's wars for them.'

Ennis lay back drowsily. This was an absurd time for making love. The whole liaison was difficult to conceal, anyway, something that would reveal itself through random cracks and chinks. Popular opinion ready to be stirred up, a new pretext for attacks on the morals of the garrison, the Christian Brothers ready for lip-licking, her own father, most of all the bad-toothed greasy businessman Barasi, heavy with rings, each finger in too many pies, his smugly honourable intentions towards Concepción, his too many friendships on both sides of the border.

'You still love her,' said Concepción fiercely. 'If you didn't, you'd do something. You could take me back to England. Everybody says the war is going to end soon.'

'It's you I love,' said Ennis. 'As for the other thing, well – *yo también soy católico*.'

'That's what I hate!' she raged. 'You'll do this, and this is a sin, we're both damned for it. And you don't go to mass, you haven't been to confession for sixteen years – you told me so – and yet you argue so smooth to those others about God. It's all lies. How can you expect me to believe you when you talk about love?'

She sobbed, and he tried to comfort her, and the comforting begot appetite. When he looked at his watch the sweat started again and his heart (the musical direction *martellato* came unbidden) hammered. He should now be lecturing at the Detention Barracks. Prisoners assembled prompt at twelve-thirty in the little fortress twenty minutes' climb away. Twelve-forty by his watch. The R.S.M. would by now quite certainly have telephoned the Vocational and Cultural Office to ask what was going on. Could he pretend to have been taken suddenly ill? No, there was the business of having to report sick. His watch, that was it, his watch had stopped. Feeble perhaps, but it would have to do.

He kissed Concepción a good smack of finality and then got dressed. As he walked quickly into the fierce heat, through the knots of workmen sitting with their bread and garlic by the Library steps, past jolly jacks and undulantly sauntering gobs (U.S.S. *Benjamin Franklin* in port), he realised that it was useless to worry. What was there to lose, after all? The Russians were driving fast to Berlin, the release group scheme would soon be operating. But this panic could not be reasoned away. The Army was rather like the Church, conditioning one to sweat with wholly irrational fears: Army crimes were like sins. And hell existed; hell lay on a map in Major Muir's office. The other units of the Rock, whose specialist officers were also regimental officers, had the easy gift of quick expiation – the charge sheet, the trifling punishment. But Major Muir, officially delegating discipline to the units to which his instructors were, 'for all purposes', attached, could invoke eschatological sanctions. There was the case of Sergeant Tomlinson, who had become 'bloody-minded'. That term and a new slogan of Tomlinson's – 'All I want, sir, is a fair crack of the whip' – had become the themes of a complex subterranean fugue. Tomlinson had asked for a posting. Obscure machinery had been started, and now Tomlinson was a private soldier in Burma. With Major Muir it was hell or nothing.

Outside an air-raid shelter that had, custom begetting law, become a public urinal, Ennis saw his small Spanish protégé, Juanito. A wise urchin of eleven, son of a washerwoman, he leered up at Ennis, whining:

'*Penique, penique, maestro.*' Ennis handed all his coppers over, saying:

'Have you been up at the office?'

'Oh yes, they speak they make bloody hell with you.' Ennis nodded. He said, handing over a piece of chalk:

'You go now to sergeant-major's billet and draw dirty things on floor and wall. You make sure you not be seen.'

'*Oqué, maestro.*' And, filthy, his breeches-behind out, he needled off. A useful boy.

Ennis climbed Castle Steps and turned right at the top. The letters A.V.C.C. shone out above the Corps sign – the hammer of vocation, culture's lamp. Controlling his breathing, he marched into the outer office. Gregg, the hatchet-faced warrant officer, looked up shiftily at Ennis, his sharp chin resting on his hand, the fighting cats on his forearm peering too, and said:

'The Major wants to see you.' Ennis said:

'I want to see the Major.' Gregg shambled into the inner office. There was a rumble of talk within, then Gregg reappeared, holding the door open. Ennis closed his mouth tight, filling the space between teeth and lips with air; he then forced this air out vulgarly in a shrill brace of whistles. He marched in, halted, thrust out his right arm in a fascist greeting, then brought his hand trembling to his brow in an orthodox salute. Major Muir pretended to be immersed in an A.C.I.

Major Muir was a regular W.O. 1 with a First Class Certificate of Education. Wounded early in the war, he had been commissioned as a lieutenant in the Army Educational Corps, then transferred, with promotion, to this newer organisation. He had delusions of grandeur and had invented many fantasies about himself – the many books he had written, the many universities he had attended. He spoke often ungrammatically, with a homemade accent in which Cockney diphthongs stuck out stiffly, like bristles. His ignorance was a wonder. But he had power, pull, in high places, nobody knew how. He was twisted in body, perpetual pain burning out of deep-set rather beautiful brown eyes. These he now raised, turning them full on Ennis. He said:

'The R.S.M. at the Detention Barracks rang me up.'

'Sir.'

'Apparently this is not the first time this has happened.'

'Surely –'

'Wait till I've finished. It happened two weeks ago, or something as like it as makes eff-all difference. The men were assembled, and you dismissed them after five minutes. They were sent back to their cells. Also, the week before that, you told the N.C.O. in charge to wait outside, and then you started handing fags round.'

'That's a lie, sir. I admit I smoked myself, but –'

'You had no right to. I'm not at all satisfied about the way you're carrying on. Your duty is to give these men a forty-minute talk every week. It is part of their training programme. You have violated instructions. Fragrantly.'

'Sir?'

'Fragrantly.'

'Look, sir. The only prisoners up there at the moment are Italian Pioneers. The only Italian I know is musical Italian. You can't make a lecture out of *andante* and *lento ma non troppo*. I tried giving a talk in English about Mussolini, thinking that at least they'd recognise the name. They started cheering, and the meeting was broken up. It's absurd.'

'It is your duty,' said Major Muir, 'to obey instructions. If I tell you to lecture a squad of Hottentots, then you must do that. What have you got to say about this morning?'

Ennis indicated his watch. 'This let me down, sir. That's what I came along now to tell you. These things will happen. I just honestly mistook the time.'

'What were you doing when your watch stopped?'

Here it was, then. 'I was giving a music lesson, sir. To Mrs Gomez. You know about that.'

Major Muir fixed the penetrating hot eyes on him. 'Yes, I know about that. I know *all* about that. I know every single little thing that there is to be known about that, Ennis. You watch your step. Because if there's going to be any trouble, Ennis, by God, I'll make you wish you was never born. Because it's me who gets the ballocking from the Governor and then from the Warbox. It's me who has to be responsible for the way you buggers carry on. Like young Burton, for instance.' Burton was the red-haired orderly who had got one of the Governor's serving-maids into trouble. 'I'm ordering you to stay away, Ennis, I'm not having civilians coming to me and making complaints about the carryings on of my instructors. You're not to give any more of these guitar lessons or whatever it is you call them. And that's an order.'

'With respect, sir, you can't give me that sort of order.'

'Can't I, by Christ? By Christ, you'll see whether I can or I can't. I'll put the whole bloody Rock out of bounds to you, by God I will.' He flashed fires at Ennis. 'I'm going to have a real unit here. I'm not having one of those halfbaked all-boys-together outfits like what they have in the Educational Corps. You'll soldier, by God Almighty you will, and if you won't soldier with me, well, then, there's other places.' He paused; the ghost of Tomlinson seemed to beat at the window. 'That's all,' said Major Muir. 'Now get out.' He turned wearily back to his papers. Ennis saluted, saw Muir's eyes looking down, so rolled out a couple of inches of valedictory tongue at him. He walked out, crossing his eyes at Gregg, then sought the astringent sunlight of the courtyard. The *hombre* who did odd jobs was eating a lunch of fried air, as the troops called it: a coat of batter covering nothing. And there also was Barasi, fat and sweating in a well-cut white suit. He showed a mixture of gold and black teeth in greeting. He said:

'You are well, Sergeant Ennis? And Concepción?'

'Mrs Gomez?'

'She is Concepción to us. That is a very beautiful name, Concepción. Many of our names are beautiful.'

Ennis boiled, then boiled over. 'I suppose it's you who's been spreading the dirt,' he said. 'You lousy bastard.'

'Dirt? What dirt? Of dirt I know nothing.' He beamed, holding out his hands as to show how clean they were. 'You sometimes talk very funny, Sergeant Ennis.'

'*Cabrón*,' said Ennis. 'Dirty big he-goat. Ah, never mind.' Barasi beamed and bowed him off, wobbling. The sun flashed in the mirrors of his thick glasses. Ennis, raging, climbed too quickly for health up the white sunbeaten road to Moorish Castle. '*Naranjas*,' offered a parchment crone, squatting with her basket full of sour Sevilles. 'Ah, hell,' said Ennis.

He entered the high-set barracks where the Second Barsets dwelt. Ennis and Bayley were attached to whatever infantry battalion was in residence: first it had been the Second Wessex, then the First Loamshires, both now broken on foreign fields, spewed home to their depots. The Second Barsets had been line-of-communication troops in Catania, and they still seasoned their speech with a few drops of Italian – *bonner, molto bonner, bonner sarah, see.* The N.C.O.s were ancient and mostly looked forward to early release. As Ennis crossed the training area to the sergeants' mess, he passed a bent corporal in his sixties, grey but spry, wonderful for his age. Before entering the ante-room, Ennis looked out over Spain; the mess clung like an eyrie to the Rock, commanding a magnificent panorama – the border town, the distant sierra, a bullring like a lost coin. Toiling up from the Casemates by steps set in the rockface, sergeants panted, cursed, near-expired. Ennis went in to the smoke, coarse talk, click of billiards. At the bar he said:

'Quadruple whisky.'

'Sarge?'

Ennis held up four fingers. 'You can't count,' he said. 'Single, double, treble, quadruple. Another lesson this evening.' He carried his drink over to the nest of old men's chairs. Bayley came from examining the flagged map on the wall; Ennis picked up the *Overseas Daily Mirror.*

'It won't be long now,' said Bayley. 'The Russians are moving in fast. Oh, God.' He flopped in the armchair next to Ennis. 'Roll on the boat.' In his mournful eyes, over the long nose and sucked pipe, was the ever-present vision of his wife Doris and the child he had not yet seen. Ennis looked up from 'Live Letters'. ('We old pair think that much good comes out of evil – the example set by all our brave boys – never forget –') Poor Bayley had not been very lucky. Sent out here with a narrow and deep specialisation, his hand happy only with plane or chisel, he had been turned into a teacher of book-keeping. Orders were orders. And he brooded on his wife, performing unequivocal rites to her memory after the lights had been put out, when each lay sundered in his lonely bed.

'Home,' he murmured now. 'I can see Doris's face when she opens the door. It's not fair to us married men.'

'No,' pondered Ennis.

'It's different for you, though,' said Bayley almost reproachfully. 'You don't seem to feel it like I do. You don't even talk about your wife now. You've forgotten.'

Ennis was irritated. 'Oh, for Christ's sake,' he said. 'There are other things to think about.'

Bayley turned slow mournful eyes on him. 'Never,' he said. 'Never.'

They went in to lunch. There was tinned M. and V., with dehydrated potatoes over-reconstituted; as always, a tin of curry powder rested on each trestle-table. One old man cried and streamed with sweat, spooning it on, mashing it up, forking it in. The air was close and rich with spice. Afterwards there was a heavy duff, cloaked in sluggish custard.

'Bugs is something chronic again,' said a sergeant in denims. 'Marchin' over the ceilin' last night they was, real proper formation. Real good squad drill, like.'

'Not like in Alex, though,' said a pickled quartermaster-sergeant. 'Turn the light on and there they was, about turnin', right back to where they'd come from, behind the pillow. It's the stink I can't stand, though,' he added, and spooned custard into his leathery old mouth. 'When you squash them, the blood that pours out, all over the wall. Like a bloody massacre.'

Bayley pushed away his plate.

'You finished, chum?' asked a flame-headed Cockney sergeant, younger than most. He ravished the almost-untouched portion of duff. 'The 'eat, I suppose. Takes some blokes' appetites away. Not me, though.' His teeth churned away with relish, visibly. Ennis took out his worksheet and found that he had to walk to a Catalan Bay gunsite, there to lecture on the subject of 'Economic Recovery After the War'. Everything was going to be all right: improved industrial techniques, American aid, plenty of jobs. God, what a city they were going to build!

2

'Mister Murillo infirm. Maybe he get dose in Tangier. He now in house all day. Most best you not go there.'

So little Juanito had reported and Ennis had not visited the house in Irish Town for nearly a fortnight. Love, he knew, should be all impetuosity and defiance of the law, but not when a father was around. It was comforting to know that he was staying away from Concepción not because of Major Muir's interdict but in a pure spirit of Southern prudence. And now came another reason for reconsidering this liaison – a surface-mail letter from his wife completely reversing the theme of the last air-letter. Ennis sat in a small teashop on City Mill Lane, reading and re-reading, Bayley was there, too. He had received ten long letters from Doris, written on consecutive days, and a deck of photographs of the baby. His pipe puffed jubilant smoke.

'Darling,' said Ennis's letter, 'what I wrote last was very, very foolish. Life is so difficult here, what with the V-2s, that it makes it seem almost wicked to plan ahead. But they all say it can't go on much longer, and then you'll be coming home, or rather – Well, that brings me to another point –'

'What do you think of that?' said Bayley with pride. 'Every time the little beggar sees a soldier he says "Daddy".'

'You see,' read Ennis, 'he had money if he had nothing else. He's planning to go to India at the end of the war, and he wanted me to go with him. But he wasn't much good in other ways. I'm fed up with life here, it's so cold and dismal and things are so short –'

'This is him here in the garden,' said Bayley, showing a snapshot. The snapshot showed a fat infant clinging defensively to his straight-haired spectacled mother. 'I made that swing there on embarkation leave.'

Ennis read: 'Can't you perhaps get a job out there for a time? You must have contacts after all these years. Or perhaps you could sign on with a commission. You remember Sam Brayshaw? He was only a corporal when you left but he's a captain now at Uxbridge, expecting his majorship, or whatever you call it, any time now –'

'This,' interrupted Bayley, 'is a studio photograph Doris has had taken.' 'Very nice,' murmured Ennis. Glasses, no bosom, a front tooth missing. 'A good-looking girl,' he added. 'Good-looking?' said Bayley, indignant. 'She's beautiful. She's a flower, she's like a lily.' He frowned up an instant at the two teashop girls, Spanish, not at all like lilies, then went on hungrily with his solid reading.

Ennis read: 'I'd give anything for a bit of sunshine. I often think of you out there with your cheap cigarettes, short as hell here, and whisky. And there's lovely bathing, isn't there? And then there's Spain and Morocco and bullfighting and exotic little bars –' She was telling him all about it, wasn't she? Come to sunny Gibraltar where you already are. Ennis skimmed over the letter's peroration: '– Do try, darling – Push yourself a bit more – There must be lots of people useful to you – My clerk's husband has just been promoted to wing-commander – Love – Always thinking about you – Your loving wife, Laurel.'

So, thought Ennis, the idea was that he should join the Rock raj. The perils of hypergamy. She would not be at home in filthy teashops like this. The Rock Hotel, rather, cocktails with the moustaches and synthetic public-school accents. Ennis the success, with his charming wife. Still, if she wanted it that way. And that would definitely be the end of poor little Concepción. 'I'm off now,' he said to Bayley. 'Got to lecture to the Dockers.' But Bayley hardly heard, breathing hard over some wholesome erotic passage. Ennis said, in Spanish, to the teashop girls, 'This *señor* will pay.' Then he left.

Ennis shut his eyes an instant, walking down Main Street, and tried to see himself transformed into a worthy consort for Laurel. It was not easy. And yet he desperately wanted conformity, stability. There was no lack of offers: the Army said, 'Do try to be a good soldier'; the Church said, 'Come back'; Laurel now came along with 'Elevate yourself to my world.' The trouble was, of course, that his art got in the way.

'But I'll try,' he said aloud. A denimed soldier said:

'That's right, Sarge, you do that.' The point was that he loved her, he was quite sure of that. He even worshipped her like some spring goddess who would only return after the winter of war. It was still winter, despite the heavy golden warmth that beat from the empty sky, radiated from the huge crouching Rock.

He walked on, greeted by various grinning troops. It comforted him to think that there was something like affection in these greetings. It was affection won by a kind of hypocrisy, for in most of his talks to the units he deliberately made himself a mere mouthpiece for the inchoate feelings of the many inarticulate. The talks were called 'bolshie' – delightful old-fashioned word – but they were not really political. He invoked a vague golden age to come (they all, speaker and audience, knew it would never come) when wrongs would be righted, wives no longer seduced by the stranger in the land (Pole, Free French, American), work plentiful and beer cheap. It was all an opiate, but perhaps even a kind of poetry in which the act of expression meant everything, the content nothing. '– And so perhaps we can look forward to an age when real equality will be possible, when we workers will no longer be spat upon, spurned like so much offal, when the mighty will be brought low and the humble raised. Democracy a reality, no longer a pious shibboleth.' Such perorations often gained applause, sometimes cheers. The troops merely needed a voice, their repressions and grievances the catharsis of a bard's utterance. Nobody really believed that the new city would ever be built.

Which left only art. For him, Ennis, only music. Music had been orchestrating his thoughts as he walked. He had now reached the end of Main Street, the Casemates. On the square there was a rehearsal in progress for the Ceremony of the Keys. The band, brassy as the sun, now burst on him with rich belly-warming clamour. March

and countermarch, pressed khaki drill and blindingly bright instruments, the throb and rattle of drums, the sharp swords of the cornets,
the squeal of clarinets. The drum-major, Ernie Longbottom, jug-
gled with his staff, throwing, catching, spinning, up in the air, down
again, as the copper-bright harmonics flashed in the sun.

Ennis walked out of the sun into the cavern of the dining-hall of
the Docks Operating Group. There they waited, simian, distrustful,
the hardest men on the whole Rock to handle. They would strike
against route-marches, crown their N.C.O.s with half-bricks, steal
lavishly from the cargoes they unloaded. The waiting sergeants, after
a surly greeting, now left Ennis to it, Daniel to the growlers, and
went off for a cup of tea. Ennis faced them, a crouching fifty or so,
let his heart sink, smiled ingratiatingly and said:

'Gentlemen.' This at once provoked derision:

'We're no bloody gentlemen.'

'Chase me up an effin gumtree.'

'Hark at him, Horace.'

'Gentlemen, he says.' Ennis cried:

'Those of you who can read, and that can't be many, must have
seen the term "Gentlemen" often outside public lavatories. I use the
term in that sense.' And then, while they were thinking that one out,
he got in swiftly with 'One of the things that must be in the minds of
a lot of us just now is the future of the British Empire.' There were
groans; Ennis hoped they were of resignation. He continued: 'I don't
suppose you have all that much time for thinking about these things,
because you work all the hours that God sends, but –'

'You bet we bloody well do, mate.' This was a squat pugilist of
a docker. 'Nine hours yesterday and not an effin penny overtime.'

'More like bleeding ten,' came dissentient growls.

'But,' said Ennis bravely, 'we all want to make sure that there
aren't going to be any more wars, and –'

A patent-leather-haired gangster with a toothbrush moustache
and a Canadian khaki shirt stood up at once and shouted: 'Who
makes the bloody wars anyway? We didn't ask for this one. What
we all want is to be back home with the missis and the kids, minding
us own bleeding business.' There were animal noises of approval. 'I

reckon,' said the gangster, 'it'll always be the bleeding same. There'll always be wars because them bastards at the top makes money out of them.' Enthusiasm grew fast. Ennis felt the meeting slipping out of his hands. He yelled:

'Just a minute. We can do something about it. We can. We're a democracy and we're members of a democratic Commonwealth. And there's America, too. If only we can carry on teaching the rest of the world –'

'Let Jack have a word.'

'Poor old Jack.'

A heavy near-bald simian with the light of lunacy in his eyes had risen lumberingly to his feet. 'You talk about them Yanks,' he said in a mad quavering voice. 'Look at this. Look at this letter I got from my missis.' He waved the letter in the air, staggering towards Ennis. 'Gone off, she has, with a bleeding Yank. And me sending her bloody silk stockings home, too. And she couldn't have asked for a better husband. She never had no better husband nor I was.' A dreadful lunatic singsong entered his speech. 'God curse the bastard!' he cried. There were noises from his fellows of sympathy and admiration. 'And you talk about us working with *them*. And it's happening all the time back home while we're out here, and we can't do a bloody thing. It wouldn't have happened,' he sobbed, 'it wouldn't have happened if I could have been there. But,' and here he savagely crumpled the letter, showing mad teeth, though false, 'if I lay hands on them, if I lay my hands on them, so help me Almighty God, I'll, I'll –' He went through the motions and noises of strangling two people at once. Ennis had to do something. With an actor's loud sob he cried:

'I know, I know! Do you think I like this, standing up like a bloody stuffed dummy in front of you, spouting yards of tripe about the British Empire, when my heart bleeds for you, yes, bleeds for the lot of you? I know what you've got to put up with, I know, I know.' He wondered whether he was still sane, looking at the tashed gangster newly holding forth in a corner, the demented Jack sobbing inarticulate curses, one of a three-ring circus. 'Do you think,' cried Ennis, 'I don't think this sheer bloody hypocrisy drives you all mad?

Don't you think I'm going mad, too?' And now he had them; the act was going down well; Jack stared in simple wonder; the gangster was silent. 'To hell with this lecture! To hell with these stripes I'm wearing!' He made a tearing gesture at his left arm. 'You don't want the lecture and you don't want me. What you want is a drink.'

He saw, too late, that he had gone too far. The men rose, cheered, knocking over benches and trestle-tables. Somebody burst open the door and raw Mediterranean light rushed in.

'Good old Sarge!'

'He's all right, he is.' They tumbled on to the square, whence the rehearsing band had departed. 'You're coming with us,' said a burly docker, gripping Ennis by the arm.

'No, really, I can't.' He groaned to himself that he had done it again. 'I shouldn't have said that really. I should have –'

'You're coming with us.' Enclosed by dockers, crouching in his walk so that his face and stripes alike should not be seen by the curious watchers, Ennis was trundled along Main Street to a café where an orchestra of ladies was playing. The dockers whistled at these and called the waiters, whom they summoned fiercely, Spanish bastards. Soon Ennis found several bottled ales set before him, others waiting at the bar. That was not it at all, that was not what had been intended, this sort of session could find no place in the annual educational report to the War Office. Meanwhile, the mirrored walls swam with imaged dockers, their noise drowning the music. The tashed gangster was at Ennis's table, saying, 'That speech what you give had sense, the way I see it. Yanks overrunning our country with no more right to be there than they has, by rights, in what they call their own. Because the niggers was the original people of America, that's in books that is, you ask anyone. And the bleeding Government always going on about not enough money for the working man. What's to stop them printing more money, eh? They've got the paper and they've got these printing presses, they could –'

'Yes, yes,' said Ennis, not listening. Merita, flamenco singer, magnificent, a dream of cream flesh and blackbird hair, head high, in traditional costume with mantilla and high-set combs, had appeared on the small stage.

'Read this for me, Sarge,' a small tough docker was whining. 'Letter from my missis, it is. I haven't learned to read yet.' Ennis caught the illiterate scrawl 'That shevin stik has bin a good usband to me' and said, 'Wait, listen, she's going to sing.' He waved to Merita and Merita smiled, proud Spanish, back. She nodded and the ladies of the orchestra nodded. The piano and violins started a three-eight rhythm. 'This,' said Ennis, 'is mine.' There was less noise now, but still too much. 'QUIET!' yelled Ennis. Somebody said, 'Good old Sarge, half-pissed already,' but the order was roughly obeyed. Enough for Merita's gorgeous Moorish wail to ring out in Ennis's setting of a poem by Lorca:

La niña del bello rostro
Està cogiendo aceitunas –

And then one of the dockers, a private with a false left eye, let out a rude noise. Raging, Ennis leapt on to him and the table went over. Merita stopped singing. Ennis was dragged away by many hands, quick at acts of brute strength. The attacked private, also held back, said:

'I'll do the bugger in. I'll have no effing sergeant taking advantage of his effing stripes on me, by eff I won't.' Ennis said:

'You mannerless bastard. You moronic imbecilic animal sod. You mindless get.' Then he pulled himself up in shame. Such behaviour would not be tolerated at the Rock Hotel. This was what was meant by his art getting in the way.

3

'The Major wants to see you,' said Gregg in the outer office.

'I want to see the Major,' said Ennis, not looking at Gregg, looking rather at the envelope with his name on it in the letter rack. He opened it and read: '*Querido Ricardo* –' It was all in Spanish. It was signed, '*Siempre, Concepción.*' Why should she write to him in Spanish? Why should she write to him at all? Ennis translated slowly to himself: 'You have been very discreet in not coming to the house while my father has been at home and ill. But he has been better these last three days. Perhaps you did not know that? I have to see you very urgently to talk. I have something very important to say –'

'All right,' said Gregg. 'March in.' He held open the door of the Major's office.

'Just a minute,' said Ennis. 'I've got to read this.' He read; 'My father is over the border this afternoon but will be back about six –'

'Sergeant Ennis,' hissed Gregg.

'– So I shall be in the house waiting for you all afternoon. You must come. It is very important.'

'Where's that bloody Ennis?' called Major Muir.

'Coming now,' said Ennis, sliding the note into the back pocket of his shorts. In his head echoed '*Muy importante. Siempre, Concepción.*' He marched in and saluted very sketchily.

'Took your time, didn't you?' said Major Muir. 'Now then, what's the story this time, Ennis? I'm just about sick and tired, that I am.'

'Sorry, sir. I don't quite –'

'Ah, don't act daft, man. They've been ringing up from the Docks

Operating Group. Some story about you marching the men off down Main Street to the Universal Café. A lot of nonsense, of course. Not even a bloody idiot like you would do a thing like that. Come on, let's have it.'

'Culture, sir. Music. It was the men who marched me off, sir.' Then Ennis woke up. Erect, he said: 'What happened was that I wanted to demonstrate something to them, sir. Something musical. I needed a singer, sir. So I took them to the UV.'

'Oh, Ennis, oh God Almighty, Ennis. What the hell's got into you these last few weeks? Oh, Jesus wept, what am I going to do with you?' Major Muir wrung his hands. Then he turned fierce on Ennis, saying, 'It's this bloody woman you've got on your mind, that's what it is. Cunt-struck, that's what you are. Oh, God give me patience.'

'Sir.' Ennis stood nicely, classically, to attention, remembering that Laurel was to come out to see a decent conforming sort of Ennis soon. Everything was going to be different. He now said, 'I'm terribly sorry, sir. I'm desperately sorry. I swear that I won't do anything like that again. I'll toe the line, sir, honestly I will. No more attempts at demonstrating culture.' As a sort of earnest of this, he stood at ease.

'So now you're trying to be bloody sarky,' said Major Muir. He sighed long. 'Well, there's one thing, anyway. The war in Europe's nearly over. Perhaps it won't be all that long before I can get buggers like you off my hands.'

Ennis had a swift delirious vision of himself helping to fight the residuary war in Asia. 'No, sir, please,' he said. 'Everything's going to be very very different. I swear.'

'Scared, eh?' Muir grinned nastily. 'Scared of being seen off by the Nips. Dirty little fighters they are.'

'I want to stay with you, sir,' said Ennis. 'I want to work with you. I want to co-operate. Please give me another chance.'

'I can't make you out at all,' said Muir. 'Go on.' He waved both back-hands at Ennis as though clearing smoke. At the same time he made whistling noises through his teeth. 'Git, git,' he said. Ennis drew himself, as in demonstration of good soldier's deportment, to quivering attention. 'And I don't want any dumb insolence, either,' said Muir. Ennis thrust his right arm out in front and brought it back very swiftly indeed, clonking his right temple. Then, all hunched up, he held a pose of humble salutation. He about-turned, he thought, well. Only when marching off did he realise that he had about-turned left instead of right. Muir's twisted mind would take that to be another obscure emblem of defection. In the outer office Ennis spoke to Gregg, saying:

'Sah. Permission to take the afternoon off. Sah.'

'Permission refused. Why do you want it?'

'Dental appointment. Sah. Very bad toothache,' Ennis leaned forward, finger hooked hard in mouth-corner, gargoyling with a sudden show of agony at Gregg. Gregg was not impressed. Gregg said:

'I don't believe you. You had a dental check-up six weeks ago. We all had a dental check-up.' Ennis released his mouth, which plopped back into position like elastic, made certain painful trombone-noises at Gregg, then went out. He was not seriously worried about Gregg's refusal to co-operate. He walked slowly up Castle Road, wondering what the hell had happened, fearing the worst, then entered Moorish Castle barracks and, in the guardroom, asked permission to use the telephone. He was readily granted this and even offered the preprandial apéritif of a mug of stewed tea. He rang up 414B Tunnelling Company and asked that the Unit Vocational and Cultural Officer be informed that the afternoon's lecture was cancelled. He added that Major Muir's personal recommendation was that the period be used for a quiz on winners of classic race meetings, realised at once he had gone too far, then super-added that the Vocational and Cultural Office would be closed that afternoon and that there was no point in anybody ringing up. He spoke in a weary patrician voice, so that the clerk at the other end said 'Sir'. After this Ennis went in to lunch. There was mournful Bayley, also a kind of stewed mutton full of bits of windpipe, to be eaten with raw curry powder added to taste. Ennis couldn't eat much, but he drank thirstily of watered Scotch.

His heart thumping very painfully, he presented himself at the Murillo residence in Irish Town shortly after two. The siesta was on, the very dogs lay with heaving flanks in the sun, the whole town smelt strongly of coffee-grounds and sea-water soap. Concepción herself answered the door. She was wearing a smart Hollywood-style ensemble of white linen and looked very brown and small. Waves of what he knew to be as near love as made no difference swept all over Ennis's body. 'Darling,' he said. She was colder. She said:

'You'd better come in.' She led him to a room he had never been in before, a sort of small sitting-room, close and smelling of dust and garlic. 'Sit down,' she said. It was as though he was going to be interviewed for something. He sat on a worn tapestry chair and said again, 'Darling.' Concepción said:

'I thought you'd better be the first to know. I'm going to be married.' She bit her lower lip and sniffed. 'He doesn't know yet,' she said, 'Nobody knows yet except you. And you've only just been told.'

'Married?" puzzled Ennis.

'I've kept it from you," said Concepción. 'I thought of going into Spain to have something done about it. But that would have been sinful.'

'Oh God,' said Ennis. 'I see. How long now?'

'Well over a month. I didn't tell you. I didn't really know the right words for telling you with, so I said nothing.'

'It's not too late,' said Ennis eagerly. 'There's somebody here, I believe. Somewhere on Line Wall Road or somewhere, I believe. A Mrs Herrera or somebody. We could do something,' he said eagerly.

'That's like you,' she said. 'You always know about sin and where to get the best sin.' She began to cry.

'It's little Juanito who told me,' said Ennis. 'That boy knows everything, God help him.'

'It's no good,' wept Concepción quietly. 'It will only happen again. It will just go on and on. It's best to finish it now. I'm going to be married.'

'No,' said Ennis. (To hell with Laurel and the Rock Hotel.) 'I love you. *Querida. Queridísima.*' He tried to take her in his arms. She tried to resist, but she was very small.

4

A short while later he lay in bed with his arm round her. She had sobbed, but he had comforted her, and the comforting had led to the other thing again, and now she slept quietly in the dull afternoon heat.

He traced the whole thing back. Paolo and Francesca. But they had read no tales of chivalry together. It had all begun with Murillo coming to the office and asking if anyone could give guitar lessons to his daughter. That was the time of the mass return of the evacuees from Tangier, the Canaries, Northern Ireland and (incredible choice of a zone of safety) London. Education had been a problem then. The Christian Brothers had shot back to neutral Eire, leaving denuded schools. So the Army had opened hospitable doors, making all civilians free of its cultural and vocational amenities – first the Educational Corps, next Muir's sourer (with-an-ill-grace) circus. Giving guitar lessons in his spare time did not at first appeal to Ennis, but Murillo whispered that he was willing to pay. His daughter, he whispered, lacked occupation; please help. She had a guitar of her own, a good one; please show her how to play it properly. Ennis played several instruments in a sketchy way – to gain a smattering of them was essential if one wanted to orchestrate well – and he had always approved of the guitar, though he considered the Andalusian way – thrumming consecutive common chords and drumming the sounding-board, shouting the while – to be meretricious and cheap. The guitar should, he believed, be used as a sort of one-hand clavichord; that was the way Segovia used it. He went off to tell Murillo's daughter all about it, no bloody flamenco nonsense, thank you very much.

He found Murillo's daughter very eager to learn and, moreover, to be possessed of an above-average musical intelligence. She was even ready to be given lessons in composition. And so, ever-conscious of the glow of her body and the smell of her thick fine hair, he had patiently picked out the faults in her academic harmony exercises: consecutive fifths, false relations.

'False relations,' she said. 'There are plenty of those in our family.' Witty, too. One day she said, 'My father wants to know how much we owe you. I have had six lessons, and you have said nothing about money.'

Ennis realised that, wealthy as her father was, he could not now ask anything. 'I do this,' he said, 'out of friendship. May I say that?'

Her eyes were bright and frank. 'Oh, yes. It would be nice to be friends. And I will, in return, if you like of course, teach you Spanish.'

So she taught him Spanish – the real Castilian, not the Calpe mush – and he was at first very clumsy, knowing that he must seem to her, with his halting phrases, young and in need of protection. Her laugh, when he had turned an idiom badly, made his heart beat faster.

'No, you cannot say that! Oh, you are so stupid!'

'*Yo no soy estúpido, pero tú eres mu*y, *mu*y, *muy estúpida.*'

'You should not use '*tú*'. That is the familiar form. You should say '*Usted*'.'

'But you say '*tú*' to me.'

'That is different. You are the pupil.'

One day she said, abruptly, 'Tell me all about yourself. About your life story. About what it is like in England.'

'But weren't you evacuated there?'

'No, to the Canary Islands. I should like to go to England. My father said he would take me after the war.'

Ennis told her about his early life in the provinces, about his university days, about the music he had written, the music he wanted to write.

'And girls. You have said nothing about girls.'

'Oh, well. There were girls, you know, of various hues and sizes.

And there was Laurel. Her parents said no for a long time. They thought I wasn't good enough. But we eventually got married.'

'Oh.' She thought for a little while. 'So you have a wife,' she said. And then, 'Why did they say you weren't good enough? You were a man of education and a good-looking man.'

'Thank you.' Ennis blushed deep. 'It isn't a question of education. It's a question of family. You can have the finest education in the world and all the money in the world, but if your ancestors have let you down by not being the right sort of people. It's hard to explain.'

'Has she been a good wife to you? Have you been happy in your marriage?'

"Yes, I think so. I suppose so. You know I haven't seen my wife for over two years.'

'It is like a death, I suppose. You did know, didn't you, that I have been married?'

'No.' Ennis was almost shocked. 'But you're very young.'

'I was married at sixteen. My father always wanted me to marry one of the Gomez family, and so Pepe became my husband. He was a lot older than me, more like an uncle really. I used to call him *Tio Pepe*, in joke, you understand. We had a very nice flat in this house. But then there was the Civil War over the border and Pepe thought he would join in this war. He was not young, you understand, but he was full of *entusiasmo*.'

'Enthusiasm?'

'Yes. He had these ideas about the British Empire being out of date and the Catholic Church out of date too. He had these very boyish ideas about what he called world fraternity.'

'I see. So he fought for the Republicans?'

'Yes. He got shot at without firing a shot, so they said. He was sniped at, that is how they put it, just outside Calasparra. He was foolish but he was, I suppose, very brave. He was killed, anyway.' She spoke dispassionately. Ennis said:

'Do you miss him? I mean, did you love him a great deal?'

She considered this gravely and answered, 'I was never sure. I saw so little of him. In some ways, of course, I miss him.'

On some days there was no lesson at all. The guitar lay sulking, silent, and the lined sheets were empty of notes. They just met at the usual lesson-times and talked. Ennis made a show of teaching if her father ever called in, though he did this rarely. He spent most of his time in Morocco or Spain, with mad intervals of paperwork – lights burning late and employees grumbling – in his office. He was courteous, smiling, rotund, smelling of garlic and good hair oil. He was proud that his daughter should have such musical talent. 'We have always been musical,' he said, in the stressless monophthongal short-vowelled English of the colony. 'Myself, I could sing flamenco as well as any in Andalusia.' He lifted his middle-aged voice in a guttural Moorish wail:

My mother-in-law has been murdered.
Long live gaiety.

He coughed. 'But,' he smiled, 'my daughter has more talent than I, much more talent.'

Ennis told Concepción about his own father. 'He's become a sort of myth now, I suppose. He was a very fine pianist. I associate him with big pounding chords on the piano; the piano used to stagger with the force of them. But he seemed capable of anything. He could mend a watch, for instance. He had big fingers, but they were always delicate and sure. He could drink twenty pints of strong beer. He could eat a whole ham at a sitting –'

'Now you're exaggerating.'

'Am I? Perhaps I am. But he always gave that impression. Massiveness, you know. And he was good at carving sirloins and turkeys. I suppose he was good at making love, too – tender and energetic. I don't know about that, but there seemed nothing he couldn't do well.'

'And your mother?'

'She was on the stage. A very Junoesque woman, though she was billed for a time, in her early days, that is, as The Blonde Venus or something ridiculous like that. She had a mass of golden hair, great thighs and slim ankles. A fair voice, too, I always thought. We were a very musical family. She died just before the war. My father didn't marry again.'

'He did not die long ago?'

'Not long. The Germans attacked our town. Hideous daylight night-long. Perpetual drone of bombers, crack and thunder of bombs. He insisted on doing what he could. I was on leave at the time, ready to help. A jam factory was hit. An iridiscent sea of sweet-smelling glue. The night watchman screaming from a burning bog of jam. Firemen entangled with the hose, cursing at each other, I remember that clearly. My father and I, both helmeted, rubber-booted, went in, wading in stickiness. A beam fell on my father, brained him. My father lying there in the hot obscene treacle. I took him to safety, dragging his bulk painfully by the armpits. But it was hopeless, quite hopeless. A death which posterity might find absurd or disgusting.'

'That must have been terrible. And to think we grumbled about our evacuation. We haven't had any idea of war.'

'You might yet. Here. We all might. Franco waving the Nazis through Spain, from top to bottom, crashing through the border.'

'Then we all take to the Rock.'

'Then we all take to the Rock.' Ennis shook his head, having second thoughts. 'No, it won't happen now. If it had been meant to happen it would have happened before. Shall we look through this exercise?'

'If you wish.' And, heads together, they examined the simple bars she had harmonised for homework.

On other occasions he told her more. He spoke of his own war experiences. The long wait at Cairo before embarking for Crete. In Cairo a mate of his had deserted, though believed murdered in a back-street brawl. This mate's face had emerged, for him, Ennis, alone, one day from a shop door, walnut-juiced and framed in a Bedouin head-dress, winking, saying, 'Don't let on, chum.' Then the voyage to Crete, the shambles there, the ignominious evacuation, the queer drunken time in Alexandria surrounded by fortune-tellers, repatriation and posting to Glasgow where, one winter night, he had been beaten up by one-eyed toughs.

'Why?'

'Oh, I don't know why. Some argument or other about something or other. I was a private then, of course.'

'And what did the fortune-tellers say?'

'I don't quite remember. Tight most of the time, I'm afraid. Something about I'd only really know what I wanted when I got so hungry that I'd have to eat the table.'

'What nonsense.'

'Something about a platoon of pigs with a sow in charge.'

'You *must* have been tight.'

On a February day, the sky heavy with the February rains, he came as usual. They shook hands as usual, but held them longer. There was a curious diffidence, a sense of having nothing to say. They sat down at the mahogany table in the stuffy drawing-room. She picked up her guitar and tuned it.

'That D's a bit sharp.'

She screwed it down. 'Better?'

'Much better.' She played a little minuet he had written for her. It was in E minor, an easy key for the guitar.

'That's coming along nicely.'

'Yes, I thought so, too.' She rested after playing. He said:

'It's queer to think of you as Mrs Gomez.'

'Why should it be?'

'I'd never really thought of you as that. I'd thought of you as Miss Murillo. Murillo's daughter. Murillo's attractive daughter. *Tú eres muy guapa.*'

'Don't say that.'

'*Guapísima.*'

'Don't. I know it's only a foreign language to you.'

With a thud on the roofs the rains opened out, sky sluices emptying, the empty streets immediately awash with the violence of it. The air was a flowing river.

'I can't go just now, not in this,' he said. 'I should have brought my gas cape, I suppose, but I've only this groundsheet. It's not much protection.'

She said nothing. She was just standing there, breathing rather quickly, her head lowered. The rains broke in him. A single stride in his clumsy boots, he held her. His lips were dry, the thirst intolerable. He drank and drank from her mouth; they could not speak, their hearts hammered against the seething rain. Blindly they sought the couch, his own limbs too weak for standing. The gates opened over-quickly, however; he was nerveless, beyond such control. Then spoke the thunder.

The awful daring of a moment's surrender and all the rest of it. Now, this afternoon, an age of prudence faced him, a desert. Concepción stirred in his arms, muttering dream-words of Spanish. He kissed her eyelids gently, looking at his wristwatch. In half an hour he had to teach Elementary Mathematics in a hut on Windmill Hill. Too late for tea in the mess. Where's Ennis today? Oh, one can put two and two together. Still waters run deep. He kissed her on the forehead, gently waking her. Murmuring, she opened her eyes on him.

Oh, love was a state, a moment of inspiration, not a habit. And he knew that love was the name of what he felt now, more real than the hot early evening, the newspaper-sellers' cries of '*Calpense!*', the Engineers playing Gibraltar United on the Naval Ground, the late waking from the siesta. But the very act of loving, all man had for the body's expression of love, destroyed at the moment of climax. Had they been able to maintain that hovering on the edge, the penumbra of love, there would have been no thought of loss. Now they had heaved themselves upwards to the next ledge, only to deliver themselves into Time's hands.

'Darling. I must be going soon.'

'Not just yet.'

'It doesn't mean that we have to lose each other, you know. We can meet, we can go on meeting.'

'No. It will be the end then. I suppose it had to happen. There will be no going back. But I shall have something of yours.'

'I suppose,' he said slowly, 'things can't last. One has to be thankful for things the future can't touch. But I do love you, and I can never be sorry about it. Even though it hurts you. Even though it's a sin.'

'Kiss me.'

Ennis dressed in silence – shorts, shirt, stockings, shoes. He combed his hair in the long bluish mirror. Suddenly the whole thing welled up in him. 'Oh God!' he cried. 'To think of you with that horrible leering slobbering wet fat lump of flesh. And to think of him kissing you, those nasty blubber lips, and those obscene sweaty hands. And to think I've brought all this on you, sold you to a bastard like Barasi –'

Her cold bare arms were around him. 'Don't,' she said. 'It won't be so bad. We must be grateful it's ending this way. No cooling off, no quarrels. We don't have to watch love die.' She chose a dress from the wardrobe, flowery silk. 'He's coming round this evening. Father and he will drink a little, talk about business, tell a few stories. And then he'll ask the question he's always asking. It has become formal, like talking about the weather. Will he be surprised, I wonder, this time, when he gets a different answer?'

5

Ennis and Bayley walked from their billet above Moorish Castle down to the weekly conference, as it was called, in the Fortress Vocational and Cultural Office. Bayley was sucking wetly his first pipe of the day, Ennis mentholating himself with a Wills' Glacier cigarette. Both were silent, preoccupied with digesting the thin porridge and soya links, the metal taste of mess tea haunting their mouths. Ennis was thinking: 'Out, boy, out. Out, out, out. I've got to get away from Bayley. Bayley and life with Bayley are part of the past. Strange to think that life here, which I thought was going to be a mere parenthesis, should have a past, present and future. A fresh clean start, that's what's needed. The future is Laurel's.' Bayley suddenly said:

'I dreamt about Doris last night. Dreamt she was in my arms, with no clothes on, in that bed up there, and I was kissing her and kissing her.'

'Please,' said Ennis, a bit sick. Why couldn't it be called morning sickness? That's what it was, after all.

'You've got no bloody heart, that's your trouble,' scolded Bayley. 'You've got a lump of ice where a heart ought to be.'

'Ah, shut up.'

'You shut up, bastard.'

'What did you call me then?' And then there was Mr Barasi approaching, up early to make more money, the fat slug. He said, panting:

'A word with you, Sergeant Ennis. If you would be so good.'

Bayley walked on, throwing a snarl back. 'I have some news,' said Barasi. 'It is good news for me.' He was always short of breath and the sweat was out early on his forehead. 'I am to be married. Yes, you will be surprised, I know. Mrs Gomez is to be my wife. She cannot have told you yet. It is to be soon, very soon. That is her wish, and of course I am only too ready to comply with it. I have tried so long, and now I must – how would you say it – hook her before she changes her mind.'

'My congratulations, Mr Barasi. I'm sure you'll be very happy.' He felt compassion for the fat slug; they had something in common now; they had been drawn into the same orbit.

'I shall try to make her happy, Sergeant Ennis. And it will be a good thing in many ways, the union of two large business houses. I have, as you know, a considerable establishment over the border. She will have her work cut out to run it. But there is space to breathe over there in Spain. Not like here.' He frowned at one of the slummy ramps they passed, walking slowly – carious yellow stucco, wooden lattices shutting in bugs, stink, babies. Mournful dogs, all muzzled, mooned about among rubbish. 'But,' said Barasi, smiling sadly, 'there is one thing. It will be the end of her music lessons.'

'I suppose it must be.'

'And she was, I believe, a very good pupil.'

Ennis said nothing. Relegate all this to the past, think of the future. If his future was to be here, it would be easier like this. But that was in another country and, besides, the wench is dead.

'I shall be glad for you to come to the wedding, Sergeant Ennis, to drink our health. And there is one thing you could do. It would please her. To write a special wedding march. I should, of course, pay you for it.'

There was no point in putting on the big cloak of pride. People here thought in those terms. Hovering between conflicting cultures – flamenco, garlic, the sour red wine: Coca-Cola, the American cinema myths, the English weekly papers – they stuck fast to the great reconciler, money. 'Thank you,' said Ennis. 'It will be a pleasure.' Already the wedding march was stirring in that compartment of his mind which dealt with musical creation: the three C's of Concepción's name; Barasi – B flat, A, A, E flat – become a Schumannian 'sphinx'. 'A real pleasure,' said Ennis. Barasi beamed, bowed in his podgy way, and walked on with short steps. Themes danced, played, skipped, fell flat on their faces in the mind of Ennis the musician.

In the Vocational and Cultural Office the instructors were assembling. Williams puffed out uninhaled smoke, the cigarette held like a piece of chalk in his freckled banana fingers. He was balder than on that voyage out, burnt to childish red by the rock-reflected sun, shaky also with his nightly whisky carousals in the Garrison Mess. On his chubby wrist was, mounted on a watch-strap, the dull crown of a Warrant Officer Class Two. The other Welshman, Evans, brooded in a corner, morose. Julian Agate was showing Quartermain, the sergeant who had replaced the luckless Tomlinson, a piece of embroidery he was engaged on. 'So hard, my dear, to get exactly the right silks, but it should be terribly gay when it's finished.' Quartermain was a man Ennis knew little about. Paunchy, with strips of lank straw hair pasted over his bald crown, he was full of nervous tics. An involuntary wink had landed him in trouble with decent women but had also gained him some unwanted conquests. His head shook convulsively, his shoulders wriggled, his mouth sometimes fluttered like an eyelid. He was a psychologist, a mine of information on the Unconscious, sesquipedalian in speech. He had a great reputation with the men, most of whom believed he had seen much active service and now wore shell-shock like a medal ribbon, but the fact was that he had spent all his service at work in an Emergency Hospital, helping to bring the shattered men back to intellectual life.

Major Muir came in, accompanied by the saturnine Gregg. There was a shuffle to stand to attention, a stubbing out of cigarettes. When Muir had seen the charred butts returned to their tin boxes, he said: 'Gentlemen, you may smoke.' He looked unusually cheerful, even affable. The piercing eyes reflected the pain he always carried with him, the private hell, but the lines around his mouth were softer. He said:

'Gentlemen, the work we have done here together has been, I hope, its own reward. We have taught many subjects, educated the men in the duties of the citizen, kept them in touch with current events. You have worked 'ard, hard. But don't think that nobody has not appreciated it. War Office is very pleased, and soon will come the crownin', er, recognition. Soon you will see gracing my manly shoulders the insignia of a 'alf-colonel.'

He looked round expectantly. Ennis was, at that moment, as near to feeling proud of his colleagues as he thought he could ever be. The five faces were quite stony. Only Gregg's hatchet face kept its mask of a grin.

'I want you to feel,' said Muir, 'that this is as much my honour as yours.' He rode easily over the Freudian slip. 'As much yours as mine. It is, however, more than a mere honour. The war is coming to an end, as I think you may have had time to notice, and now we are to really come into our own. We are going to expand, both in our work and in our establishment. I have already outlined a scheme to the War Office and they are giving me the okay to go ahead. I think you should know something of what is going to happen.'

Ennis covertly sketched possible wedding-march themes, Agate hummed very quietly as he fingered his embroidery, Williams puffed smoke in a violent diffused cloud, Quartermain twitched vigorously, Evans scowled, Bayley mooned, Gregg went on painfully grinning.

'I shall have two S.O. 3s, two W.O. 1s, two W.O. 2s. The establishment for sergeant-instructors will be very much increased, and as far as possible we will transfer to the Corps promising men already serving on the Rock. It will be up to you to recommend any that you know, especially men with manual skills, builders, bricklayers, carpenters, plumbers, hairdressers, signwriters, draughtsmen and so on. Get in and get them before the Educational Corps does, 'ighly competitive. We might even perhaps have the odd languages man, in particular those that can teach commercial French or German.'

Quartermain was bold enough to say, 'There is, I take it, to be, shall I say, a soft-pedalling on the cultural side? I mean, the vocational rather than the non-vocational is to be stressed?'

Muir figuratively fingered his holster. 'Thousands of men will be leaving the services without a trade or with a trade half-learned or nearly forgot. There is the work of reconstruction lying ahead. We must fit the men for the part they will have to play in it. Also,

Sergeant Quartermain, it is usual to say 'Sir' when addressing an officer.'

'So I understand.'

Muir let this pass, though a flashback of Tomlinson's grave appeared briefly in his eyes. 'Education is a *useful* thing; we must never forget that. The world has to go on. 'Ouses have to be built, trains run, busted pipes repaired. All the rest is really trimmings. I know it is very nice to read poetry and look at paintings, and I would never deny the value of music. I am fond of it myself.'

Involuntarily Ennis muttered, 'Let us have the tongs and the bones.'

'Exactly,' said Muir. 'But life is more than that. I think you know the words of the immortal bard: "Life is real, life is earnest".' He looked triumphantly at his instructors. 'Well, we are to have a policy that is realistic.'

'But,' said Ennis, 'the full life, sir, the total sensibility. Values, civilised living, the contact with the bigger reality. I mean –'

'These big words,' purred Muir. 'We must come down to brass tacks. We must work, not go in for 'igh-sounding theories. Eh, Mr Gregg?' Gregg tortured his face further into a sardonic smirk. 'Oh, and I think I ought to mention that Mr Gregg will be leaving us almost immediately.'

There was a stir of interest. The salt mines? The sweating jungle? The Jap camp and the bamboo rods?

'He has been recommended for a commission, a regular commission. He deserves it, which nobody will deny. He has worked 'ard, hard, 'ere, here, and work –' (here Muir grinned round at everybody) '– always gets its reward.' Gregg, Ennis knew, had been an elementary schoolmaster in Liverpool. His scant knowledge of everything save neat print script and neatly ruled timetables had kept him in the office. His thin voice, apt enough for the telephone, had never been raised in a scrubbed canteen lecture-room, never had to battle against the outspoken Pioneers or obstreperous dockers.

Quartermain said, 'Perhaps I may say, on behalf of all of us lesser mortals, what good news this is. We are all, I think, very pleased that Mr Gregg is going away.' Quartermain twitched round at everybody.

'He should do well, I think. He should make an officer somewhat on your model.' He added: 'Sir.'

Muir chewed all this over; Gregg went on grinning. 'All right,' said Muir. 'The conference is finished.'

Ennis followed Muir straight from the conference-room to his office. His heart had expanded with this news of expansion. ('– Do push yourself, darling – Amy Strothard says it's lovely out there – I should be so proud – the social life –') He asked Muir if he could spare him a few minutes.

'Well,' said Muir, with frightening affability, 'what can I do for you, Ennis?'

'I wondered, sir, if you would consider recommending me for a commission. I'm prepared to sign on for a few years, and, as you're making all your appointments from the Garrison –'

Muir looked at him. 'I take it you're quite serious about this, Ennis?'

'Of course, sir.'

'And what on earth makes you think you could hold down an officer's job?'

'Well,' said Ennis, 'my qualifications, sir. I'm M.A., Cantab. I was working for Mus. Doc. when the war started. I've had plenty of experience. I've worked hard. I'm popular with the men –'

Muir was silent for a space, but his eyes were bright with amusement. At length he said: 'It's quite out of the question. You, Ennis, are, if you want to know, the last person in this whole bloody garrison I'd dream of recommending for a commission. For that matter, despite your seniority, I've absolutely no intention of even dreaming of promoting you to Warrant Officer. There,' he gleamed, 'that's a bit of a surprise for you, isn't it? You're not the kind of man we want in the Corps.' A sort of hard bitter blaze came into the tortured beautiful eyes. He almost snarled: 'Thinking you can come in with us, showing us what to do. With your bit of music and your haw-haw way of speaking. You've never soldiered, you don't know the life, playing up to the men, the blue-eyed boy. Well, by Christ, you're not going to be *my* blue-eyed boy, even though you are –' He stopped, knowing he was about to go too far. Ennis knew what was in his mind. A sudden pity came over him for the twisted body, the ardent temperament, sensitiveness about his longing for women, his body a tortured useless instrument. This interview had taken place before, but only in Ennis's dreams. He had known it well at the time of his leaving the Church, the vision of the gangster-God saying, 'That may be so, brother, you the last repository of values. But I'm in charge here. If I press the button on the wall, chaos will come again. I know Time, I know the mystery of the budding cell, I know the secret of power.' Then the shackled Lucifer was seen with his *Non serviam*, then Prometheus the brave fire stealer, pecked by eagles on the stark rock. Ennis had become a Manichee, at home in a world of perpetual war. It did not matter what the flags or badges were; he looked only for the essential opposition – Wet and Dry, Left Hand and Right Hand, Yin and Yang, X and Y. Here was the inevitable impasse, the eternal stalemate. He took in Muir's words sickly and helplessly. There was no point in arguing. He saluted feebly without waiting for the words of dismissal and felt, blindly, for the door handle.

Outside the door Ennis thought he heard Muir calling faintly, 'Come back, Ennis,' but he marched out of the office, ignoring the curious glance of Gregg. The thing to do was to ask for a posting, but obviously he was not going to get it. Muir would hold him now in an even stronger vice than before. He walked automatically to the little teashop called The Trianon, where his fellows were already sitting, grumbling. Williams and Evans were now on speaking terms again, quarrelling over the reckoning of the previous night's debauch:

'*Fe tales i am y cwrw i gyd neithwr, paham na allu di wneyd yr yn peth heno –*'

'*– Oes gyda fi ddim arian a peth arall yr wyf fi ddim yn leikio dy wmeb –*'

'My dear,' said Julian Agate, 'we thought the old bitch was seducing you. Though I doubt if you're really his type. Sit down now and have a nice gay mug of swill and one of those awful-looking cakes there.'

'You can see what the bastard has in mind,' Bayley was moaning. 'Show, show, and more bloody show. Although,' he brightened slightly, 'I suppose it'll mean a crown for me, being in charge of the woodwork department. Doris will like that. A bit more money. Just fancy, me a sergeant-major.' He now saw himself emerging from the serviental chrysalis to the legendary glory of waxed moustaches, people saying 'Sah!', deference at the bar of the mess: 'What'll you 'ave, Major?'

Williams had now lunged out at Evans, flailing with chubby freckled arms. Evans cracked back, and a table went over. Two R.A.S.C. drivers, concerned, left their tea to stop the fight. 'Too barbarous,' said Julian Agate.

Ennis drank his tea, cutting off thought like a motor. And then, as he watched the copulation of flies on the ceiling, he listened to the emerging of a new theme in his mind. It had formed itself out of the 'C C C' of Concepción and the 'B flat A A E flat' of Barasi. At least, he recognised the germ there. But now a sturdy eight-bar bass was striding up and down, a passacaglia bass, a tune that would hold together the most fantastically divergent variations. He heard clearly 'cellos, basses, two bassoons and tuba. He began to make sketches, letting his second cup of tea go cold. When little Juanito appeared it was almost absent-mindedly that Ennis gave orders for the obscene savaging of Gregg's billet.

6

The same May day brought Concepción's wedding to Barasi, the anniversary of the death of Ennis's father, and the end of the war in Europe. For Ennis it brought many things to a head and an end. For instance, life with Bayley. Life with Bayley had been steadily growing intolerable.

They shared a room in a row of terraced billets above Moorish Castle, a room which, rarely cleaned, full of the junk of two years, unwashed shirts, sweat-soaked socks, rusty razor blades, was a model of squalor. In the adjoining room lived two infantry sergeants, scrubbed and starched, with a decadent obsession with cleanliness. Their bed legs were islanded in tobacco tins of paraffin, so that bugs might keep away; their towels and underclothes were snowy; their young muscular bodies wore, over the tan, the patina of much fresh-water washing in tin bowls. (Bayley had once discovered that the rich brown of his knees was really dirt, but had become discouraged with many stinging attempts to remove it with sea-water from the tap.)

In the early morning, when Ennis and Bayley uneasily stirred, itching, hot, exhausted, the others were often heard to say, as they passed through to the washroom, 'Stinking rotten'. But it seemed so hopeless, the restoration of order, especially when the bugs multiplied, marched across the ceiling, lay in the crevices of the iron bedsteads. Theirs was the world. Occasionally, however, Ennis would be roused to ineffectual action, would carry fresh water up the steep slopes from barracks to billet, plunge his defiled clothing in, but

soon lose heart as the scrubbing tired his arms. Besides, there was the
new work, the *Passacaglia*, waiting to be continued on the crowded
table: there lay his dream of order. But sometimes he was ashamed
of Bayley, sweating in the starched evening mess in his two-months-
unwashed shirt. One night Bayley threw a cigarette end on to this
near-fabulous cerement: it lay on the dirty floor, by the fireplace;
he had needed a brief smoke after paying homage to his wife. The
Bandmaster said (and he was a dream of crispness):

'So he's been trying to get it off with a blowlamp.'

Bayley would throw his rusty razor blades on to the lid of the
disused copper in the washroom, then throw the piece of sea-water
soap they shared on top of these. Ennis, rushing for a quick wash,
rubbed both soap and blade into his hands.

'You silly bastard!'

'Who are you calling a silly bastard? If you haven't got the bloody
sense to look –'

They would snarl at each other in the dining-room. They would
have long not-speaking periods, uneasy hand-shaking truces engi-
neered by friendly arbiters. But the rope was becoming more and
more frayed.

'Oh,' moaned Bayley. 'If only my wife were here, if only she lay
on this bed with me now, with my arms round her.'

'Don't be so disgustingly obscene.'

'Obscene, you call it! Just because you've no natural feelings. You
don't know what love is.'

'Love certainly isn't that.'

'Who are you to talk? You keep your bloody hypocrisy to yourself. Catholic hypocrite, that's what you are.'

'You keep your bloody wife to yourself.'

A tussle, a little panting fight, a hand on Bayley's unwashed throat.
More things fell off the table.

'All right. You be more bloody careful in future –'

'*You* be more bloody careful.'

Another truce was on now, VE day. Bayley kept saying, 'My God,
we'll be going home soon, do you realise? Going home, oh God,
going home. Oh, Doris, Doris, it won't be long now.' But Ennis

lay wretched on his bed, still unmade, a tangle of dirty blankets, his eyes closed, useless desire stirring. The ghost of Concepción's body's scent hovered round his nostrils, he moved in a little agony of thwarted longing.

For him it was a day of corpses: the disfigured remains of his father, the cadavers that lay for the slow work of sorting and interment all over filthy Europe, the lost body of Concepción. He could hardly think of her as alive, rather as a Persephone doomed to enter the house of Dis, laid out for the final enormity, a necrophilic nightmare.

The wedding took place in the Catholic Cathedral, a mere month after Barasi's last proposal. Ennis did not attend, though he stood on the steps of the Library to hear the funeral-wedding march he had written (the organist, apparently, had told Barasi that it was not really suitable for a joyful occasion, but Barasi – proud that original music should crown his nuptials – had insisted that it be played. His ear was not good.) Ennis waited till the cortège began to emerge, and then climbed, through the knots of early drunks, to the billet. It was here, in a torpor shot with dull lights of lust, that Williams found him. Williams sat on the bed and puffed out unswallowed smoke. 'Dick,' he said, 'the whole of effin Europe is liberated except for effin you. Come and get effin drunk.'

Bayley said, though the invitation did not include him: 'I've got to stay here. I've got to write a really long letter to Doris.' And he sat down to it, clearing a space in the muck of the table, puffing his pipe hard. Ennis said, sighing:

'All right. Life's got to go on.' So down he and Williams went to the Garrison Mess, full of smoke, stripes, song. The Garrison Sergeant-Major embraced the Barsets' Bandmaster; the Garrison Quartermaster-Sergeant was upheld by a knot of fantastically specialised N.C.O.s: the Keys Sergeant, the Sergeant in charge of Rock Apes, the lance-sergeant comedian of the Garrison Concert Party. There was much whisky, there were maudlin protestations of endless amity:

'I'll brain whoever it was said you was no effin good, 'cos you're my pal, see, and I don't give a sod who knows it. 'Ere, you, 'e's my pal, isn't 'e?'

Outside the Garrison Mess little Juanito was waiting. 'You get
taxis, Juanito,' swayed Ennis. 'You get many taxis.' There were
rather a lot of sergeants around; the idea vaguely was that everybody
should pay a visit to the First Fortress Engineers. Juanito came back
soon, riding on the running-board of the first of four taxis. All the
drivers were Spaniards; all spoke the foulest soldier's English; none
had even seen – in the words of one of them – the bleeding sky over
England, mate. Sergeants crammed in roaring – Ennis, Williams, a
Scotsman with incipient D.T.s, an infantry pioneer sergeant called,
because of his beard, John Player, an Air Force man in shoes of glacé
leather, a C.S.M. with a wall-eye, a bomb-disposal sergeant with
splayed feet, a young master gunner, a lean quartermaster and a fat
one, others, more shadowy. There was to be a race of four taxis down
Rosia Road. A Sergeant Sayger of the Medical Corps led, shouting
great orders to his driver, at times grasping the steering-wheel so
that, brown hands tugging one way and white the other, there was
such danger that the sergeants behind thumped on Sergeant Sayger's
shoulders, yelling. Then C.S.M. Cloanth, in the front passenger seat
of the taxi behind, himself jammed a foot on the accelerator and,
to the cheers of his fellow sergeants and little Juanito, pushed into
the lead. The taxi charioteered by Sergeant S. Tussin (Intelligence)
swerved (too many contradictory orders, the driver crying, 'Oh,
effin 'ell!') off the road. Then Master Gunner M. Nesthouse made
his driver press hard on C.S.M. Cloanth, but in vain. Ah, lovely
sun on the silver Mediterranean, ah, gleam of the crowded stucco,
the close-set teeth of the crammed houses, the yawning catchments,
the heaven-kissing sphinx of the Rock.

'Watch out for that ape!'

The senior rock-ape, whose name was Scruffy, scuffled across the
road, bear-like, with a silent snarl, tomatoes strapped below his buttocks. And then on, on, with the metallic slap of the driver's hand on
the taxi door warning the rash pedestrians.

In the Engineers' Mess the roaring newcomers were made welcome and little Juanito, unnoticed for a time, stuffed himself on
bread and corned beef in the mess kitchen, then chewed onions as if
they were apples. There were races, the length of the ante-room, to

get at pints of free gin-and-beer placed on the bar. Then there was
a fight between a pale-haired sergeant called McKay and an Irish
staff-sergeant. Sergeant McKay said:

'Ye're no a man if ye're no a McKay.' The Irish staff-sergeant (far-
gone, victory or no victory: he talked nightly in Erse to leprechauns)
said:

'And what in the name of God do ye know about what's a man
and what isn't, in the name of the Lord Jesus? Saxon leavings, the
lot of ye, with your spotted bellies inflated with stirabout and your
lousy shoulders rubbing the dirt off on your scratching-posts with
God Bless the Duke of Argyll.'

'I'm no quarrelling wi' an Irish soak. Away to your bogs and
praties.'

The struggle was intense while it lived. The issue was never clear,
for, among the windmills of threshing stripes, Ennis saw neither
the Irishman nor the Scot. They supported each other in a corner,
drooling a synthetic Celtic lay from neutral America. Separated
out by the R.S.M., the bloodied contestants vied with each other in
round-buying:

'With me.'

'Keep your dirty money to yourself. Here, Jack, crack that bottle.'

The Navy came in, petty officers and chiefs, the beer flowed, the
occasional man passed out. A sergeant with a mummy face and two
rows of ribbons shed everything, stood naked on the billiard table,
micturated in his beer and drank it to applause. A C.S.M. performed
with one of his sergeants an act of obscure origin. Wrapped in blankets, one wailed like a muezzin, the other snaked round in a *danse-
à-ventre*; the whole ended with blankets thrown off, a naked exit in
thrust and recoil. Ennis focused swimming eyes on the Hogarthian
scene: the glassy-eyed C.P.O. swaying by the bar, the naked veteran
capering round the billiard table, the tubby sergeant vomiting into
the open piano, Sergeant Tussin murmuring in his sleep, the arms
raising slopping pints, the songs resolving into strident rival groups.
He said to Williams:

'Going to speak to them.'

'Eh?'

'Going to speak to them. Address a few words.'

'Don't be an effin fool, Dick. We're off effin duty.'

'Must. Things to tell them.' He mounted the billiard table unsteadily and spoke to the unheeding singers, the sick, the unconscious:

'Listen. Listen a moment. War over now. All over Europe lights going on. Lights never off here, but still. Makes no difference. Peace again. Peace, perfect peace. But listen. All over there littered with corpses. Mass bloody butchery. Blue bloody murder. And whose fault? Your fault, my fault, his fault. You.' He pointed a trembling finger at a tottering dishevelled sergeant. 'You killed my father. He did too. Best bloody man ever lived. Worth the whole lot of you put together. And all those bodies flung on the scrap-heap. Thin wasted bodies. Sunk jaws. Matchstick arms, legs. Cages of ribs. Flung on like muck with a muckrake. Repent. Day of Lord at hand. Fire down below.'

'Get him out of here, for Christ's sake,' said the still sober R.S.M. 'We don't want a bloody sermon.'

'Spoilt priest,' said a petty officer cooling his head on a window pane. 'I know. Seen 'em before.'

And then Ennis found himself at Alameda in a beer tent. He was aware of the burning sun, the unbuttoned soldiery and the spilling pints, hops floating like wood-shavings, the end of the free barrels in sight. He puzzled out how he had got there.

'You're a bloody good bloke – Look out, stomach, here it comes – Get his head down – here, watch his bloody boots – you can undress when you get home, mate – Watch out, the Navy's here – Have this with me, Jack, it's buckshee anyhow – Of all the clumsy bastards –'

Above them the wide blue lovely air. Within them the rising tide of euphoria. Before them the heaven of release: home again, Maggy, get up them stairs.

And then Ennis found himself over at Detached Mole, puzzling again, coming to to find his fingers working soberly on a piano, all ranks round him, singing. How the hell had he got there? By what boat from where? 'I've got to get back,' he said. 'I've got to get over to Spain.'

'Where's your hurry?' said a bombardier. 'Where's your glass?'

'I've got to get back, I've got to. Someone I've got to see.' And, almost sober, worried at these amnesiac patches, he insisted on taking the ferry back to the mainland. There was a slight shiver in the air as he and a few gunners climbed aboard. The bombardier said:

'Welcome any time, Sarge. Any time at all.'

'Yes,' said Ennis. 'Thank you. It's this woman in Spain, you see. She got married today. I've just *got* to see her.' And then they chugged over the grey waters.

They reached Ragged Staff, and the boat was being moored by the steps. It seemed to Ennis that there was no great distance from the gunwale to the grey stone slabs of the quay above. He was the senior rank aboard, the men were impatient to be ashore, so, going first, he tried to heave himself up. Feet on the gunwale, hands on the quay, he prepared for the pull. But then the boat lurched, without warning, away and, to his blank surprise, down he went. The cold green oozy murk belched open to welcome him. He went straight down, the fathom of his height, then another, then another, with a splash and a glug, to the stillness of the men's surprise, blank as his own, then the calls, the cries from above, the gurgling in green water, fathom by fathom down out of the light, the oozy coffin embracing him, his heavy boots, soaked clothing, down, down.

In the close green world time was suspended, and events were laid out on a checkerboard: Concepción in bed, Laurel at home polishing her nails, his father opening a bottle, the line '*Wer reitet so spät?*', a chord of superposed fourths. He was happy as he gurgled in the water-air, in his element, he thought for a moment, prayer for a happy death, sin somewhere else, die in harness.

Then he slid up the embracing body of the water, towards the now alien light, towards braining himself on the boat's bottom, but this now slid away from the quay-side. He struck air with a splutter, green tangled in his hair, his clothes heavy with what was now the obscene defiling of the other world, the water.

'Take it easy now, don't rush.'

'Here you are, grab.'

The helpful faces crowded above, hands held out for him, *tendebant manus*. He was hauled aboard, a lonely fish. *Souvent pour s'amuser les hommes d'équipage.* The équipage of two lean Spaniards with berets was concerned about his watch. '*Reloj, reloj,*' they cried. They tore it from his wrist, washing off the oil eagerly from the crystal, dipping it again and again in the pan of water in the bow. The men were now ashore, away quickly. Where were ye Nymphs when the remorseless deep Clos'd o're the head of your lov'd *Lycidas?* The Spaniards handed back his cleansed watch, passport to time reclaimed. Had ye bin there – for what could that have don?

He mounted the steps, his heavy boots squelching, spitting out oil, his clothes clinging like an unclean familiar. The boat set off to the *ulteriorem ripam* and he was left alone. He shivered towards a hut where there was a private of Movement Control standing.

'Telephone?'

'Yes, Sarge. Did you fall in, Sarge?'

He rang up Fortress Headquarters and asked for the transport pool. Everybody seemed to be off duty today. No, wait. A car, yes, a car, immediately, Ragged Staff, yes, A.V.C.C. business. Authorisation? Christ, man, I've just fallen in the bloody water.

He waited, tasting thick oil. He felt for a cigarette, but the soaked packet was full of fat swelling tubes, the tobacco a mush in the dirty water.

'Have you got such a thing as a cigarette?'

'Sorry, Sarge. Don't smoke.'

Even this man left him now, as though he were too defiled to stay with, and Ennis waited alone. He went on waiting. He rang up Fortress Headquarters again, again he asked for the transport pool. Nobody apparently had done anything about anything. Christ, man, I'm bloody freezing. They'd send a car right away.

At length he crawled into the back of one, the driver solicitous but relishing the prospect of report ('Bloody sergeant damn near drownded'), and crouched with his head down, unseen from the streets. But he heard the smashing of windows, the insulting of shopkeepers, everybody happy. They sped up to Moorish Castle.

Bayley lay on his bed as Ennis dripped in, raising his head and pipe in surprise however at the sight of the living sea-corpse.

'What the bloody hell?'

'Fell in the water.'

Hollow laughter mingled with the splash of the sea-water tap. Ennis, naked, sluiced away vile weeds, green fronds and bladders, bathed his sticky head.

'Ha, that's a bloody good one, that is.'

Shivering, Ennis sought dry clothing. But he groaned deep when he discovered that he had his only other two shirts soaking in a bucket of water (a new attempt at cleanliness to celebrate victory). He lay on his bed, coughing up slime and gobbets of oil.

'I take it you're not going to leave the washroom in this state?' said Bayley, stepping gingerly through pools of dirty water.

'For God's sake give me time. That wasn't a particularly invigorating experience.' Ennis felt homesick for the comfort of Concepción's arms, or Laurel's. 'You might be a bit more sympathetic,'

'Your own bloody fault, I'd say. Clumsy as hell.' Bayley was getting his own back: Ennis had never been sympathetic about Doris far away, the broken marriage bed.

'Never mind.' Ennis spat up more oil. 'Do something for me.' And again oil. 'Lend me a shirt.' And more oil yet again.

'A shirt? Lend you a shirt? Ah, that's a good one.'

'I've got to have a shirt. The only alternative is to wear battledress.' More oil. 'And we're not allowed to wear battledress. Not at this time of the year.'

'So,' said Bayley nastily, 'you propose to go out again, do you? To get drunk again, I suppose. To fall in the water all over again, drunk, and then come asking to borrow shirts.'

'No,' said Ennis. 'Not to get drunk. To go over the border and – Oh.' He realised that he couldn't, that he hadn't a pass, that, anyway, this was the first night of the *luna de miel*, that one doesn't go visiting married women on the first night of the *luna de miel*, that one doesn't do that even in England, let alone in hot-blooded Spain. 'Oh,' he said again.

'And that's all over,' laughed Bayley. 'No more guitar lessons. If that's what they were. I've heard it called a lot of things in my time –'

Ennis spat out more oil and looked at the little shining gob on the floor as though it were a coin he had tossed. 'Right, Mr Bayley,' he said. 'This is the end. This is definitely the bloody end. You can share this room with the bugs in future. You can stew and simmer in your own dirt. You can wipe your bottom with your shirts, that's all they're fit for. You can sacrifice to the goddess of love in peace.' Another gout of slimy oil.

'What do you mean by that last remark?'

'Oh, skip it. I'm moving out.'

'Move out, then,' said Bayley. 'And bloody good riddance. I've put up with enough from you, you bastard. Go and set up shop with some other little rock-scorpion. With some other little garlicky whore.' He collapsed then and started to snivel. 'Oh, Doris, Doris.'

Ennis put on socks, shoes, and battledress. He began to pack. He knew where he was going. He was finished with the old life, finished with the dead. He was going to reform.

7

'I've got to get a job,' said Ennis.

'Right away, dear?'

'Oh, hell, it's a long story.'

Ennis was now living with Julian Agate. Tomlinson had formerly shared that billet on King's Bastion, waving impassioned arms nightly at the still dancer, prophesying revolution, the birth of a new order from blood and fire, but Quartermain, his replacement, had preferred to join the Welsh. This was not because Williams and Evans seemed *simpáticos*, but because Quartermain was professionally interested in primitive social groups. Thus there had been for some time an empty bed in the clean little billet, and now it belonged to Ennis.

'My dear! The state of your underwear!' Julian had shrilled; as Ennis unpacked his kit, his books, his manuscript paper. 'Really, that little slut Bayley hasn't been at all a savoury influence. I must take you in hand.'

And indeed he did. He became a mother to Ennis, insisting – while Ennis snivelled and streamed with a cold out of his baptism – on his going early to bed, giving his soiled linen – 'it has a really *bitchy* smell' – to the Spanish daily help to scrub, to scour, to iron, watching over him while he washed in the morning.

'Behind the ears, now. Come on now, swill thoroughly. Your hair! Really, I shall have to tub you myself.'

It was a changed life, a fresh beginning. Julian hummed gaily to himself as he swept the rooms in the morning, dusted the little ornaments, settled his Picasso and Cézanne reproductions square on the walls. He performed pirouettes and entrechats, lilting the 'Jewel Song' from *Faust*:

'Whoops, the joy! Tralalala – LAH – lalala – *lah*.'

They drank their coffee together, no longer in squalid little shops where 'my dear, they only speak Garlic', but in mirrored palaces full of bronzed staff-officers. Here they talked with Julian's friends – the infantry lance-corporal (unpromoted) whom Ennis remembered from the voyage out, a civilian dockworker with stage ambitions, a lance-sergeant of Engineers, and other, peripheral, acquaintances who spoke the common idiom.

'The little *slut*, he knew he could get round me that way.'

'So there I was in my pelt, positively *stark*, when he came to the door. But was I put out? Not a bit of it, dear.'

'But they would *not* come to order. They had made up their horrid little minds to pay me out. So then I got *really* angry. "Stop it this instant," I positively shrieked. "If you want to behave in this thoroughly sluttish way," I said, "then you must take what comes." My dear, you never saw such faces. The whole platoon sulked and sulked. *Including* Corporal Haskins.'

'Tooty-frooty. A little arms drill with m' squad.'

'How gay. Be good, you old whore.'

Julian would inspect his room-mate's turn-out before they went off together to report at 0830 hours to the Vocational and Cultural Office (a recent innovation: 'Now,' said Major Muir, 'we're getting back to peace-time. We're going to tighten up.') or to coffee, or to the cinema, or to their occasional little dinner parties. He would repolish Ennis's cap-badge or the brasses of his web belt. 'Mustn't look slummy.' On Saturday afternoons they went off for a shilling bath at the town bath-house, Julian carolling from the next-door cubicle as he vigorously puffed on the talcum:

'Whoops, the joy! Tralalala – LAH – lalala – *lah*.'

Ennis now found himself with less work than before. This was partly because the emphasis in high Army Vocational and Cultural policy was growing increasingly vocational. But also he found ways of getting out of evening classes. He would volunteer to enrol students in classes in the subjects he taught but actually dissuade the earnest seekers after knowledge ('I'm afraid this isn't much in your line, you know. Besides, don't let it go any further, but the instructor's no good.') When a class did, in spite of his efforts, get started, he soon killed it, chiefly by frightening the students or insulting them. Thus he and Julian had much evening leisure. Julian himself was now considered competent only to pretend to teach illiterates. The grey squat semi-morons who came to him ('Illiterates will report to Sergeant Agate at Line Wall Road A.V.C.C. Centre' said their notice boards) languished at their brisk slim teacher in sheepish wonder.

'Their manners, my dear,' said Julian to Ennis. 'Sitting there with their caps on. Now I just walk down the aisles, pull them off their great empty heads, and throw them in the waste-paper basket.'

The little dinner parties they held were gay with talk, foot-touching under the table, covert hand-holding. As they sat at the snowy table in the Winter Gardens Restaurant, digesting a meal that was as near civilised as one could hope for in the early days of European peace, smoking, chaffing, giggling over coffee, Ennis often felt almost happy. The world of women was far; the cool flutes of the epicene voices were soothing him to a strange peace. Badinage, discussion about the arts, homo anecdote – these were better than moaning over lost Concepción up in the dirty billet, antiphonal Doris-lorn groans from dirty Bayley. Also, he began to listen to Mozart records in the rooms of the Music Society, and his own work, the *Passacaglia*, flowed limpidly and urbanely now, losing the clotted turbid qualities that had disfigured its first draft.

Yet, as he and his room-mate sat together in their billet, Ennis composing, Julian embroidering silk or darning socks, a sudden wave of desire, of a sort of intolerable homesickness for Concepción would come over him. This was especially when the heat of inspiration, by some deep law of sympathy, provoked sexual heat. Excited as a new theme appeared or an old theme began to develop new possibilities, his pulse would start to race, and his nostrils would be suffused with that maddening smell of musk, his ears would tickle with the softness of her loosened hair. She was, so little Juanita had reported, now in Madrid with Barasi, on a prolonged *luna de miel*,

Barasi tasting *delícias* of marriage, his hairy fat belly wambling, his dentures out. God, how lubricious the language could be, with its 'uuuu' mouthings, its baring of the teeth for the 'eeeeee'. Then, as he copied out a line, again and again and again down the score, the whole orchestra hammering out the theme in unison, the mood would pass, the cool epicene atmosphere he lived in would slide on to his brow again like a phylactery.

Julian would sense these occasional gusts of old desire. He would say, without looking up from his needle and silk, 'Did she mean a great deal to you, my dear?'

'Yes. Oh, I don't know. I don't think I know what love means. I want her sometimes still, very much, but whether I would have been willing to – well, change everything, organise a divorce, take her home with me, I just don't know.'

'They don't last long,' said Julian, 'not out here. The sun ripens them too soon, my dear. They soon look like old dried raisins, or like horrible fat swollen gourds.'

'She wasn't so young, Julian, not by their standards, anyway.' Thinking of her, in the breathless evening heat, his heart thumped again, his breath came more quickly. 'But she was very lovely. I speak of her as though she's dead,' he added. 'Curious.'

'In a sense she is.' Julian went on with his embroidery. 'She'll be swallowed up soon enough in that old world across the frontier, my dear. She'll revert. A British subject technically, but the South well- ing up more and more. Mantillas on holidays and saints' days. Not much call for using English. That nasty growing barbarous tide from the West will hold off there a little longer, that's one blessing.' The needle had jabbed lightly in his thumb. 'Curse you,' he said scolding, 'you horrid little thing.'

'You see it all from the outside,' said Ennis. 'You must have a nice cosy feeling when you see us eating out our viscera over a woman.'

'I don't know, my dear. I've suffered too, you know, one way or another. Love, God help us, is a very big and painful province.'

Ennis was seeing, projected on to the bare staves of his manuscript paper, Concepción in a cold England, shivering over the fireless grate, jaundiced-looking against the snow, Concepción in the fish queue, the 'bloody foreigner' in the English village, the 'touch of the tar brush' from the tweeded gentry. He foresaw the ex-prisoner-of-war Luftwaffe pilot, flaxen, thick-spoken, absorbed into the farming community, playing darts with the boys ('That were a bloody good one, Wilhelm'), Concepción and himself in the cold smoker-oom ('That foreigner that there Mr Ennis did marry'). Finally he saw Laurel meeting Concepción, Laurel slim and patrician, sunny hair glowing under the floppy hat, over the flowered frock, at some garden party: 'But she's terribly sweet; that accent is *most* attractive; such an unusual, such a perfectly fascinating biscuit-coloured complexion; I'm sure we shall be *great* friends.'

These musings brought him back to Laurel, as usual. He tried to analyse the sense of unworthiness that orchestrated his thoughts of her. He was aware of his base stock, of her family's condescension to him, of the aura of success that hovered like a Bond Street perfume round the circle of relatives and friends: the brigadier cousin, the boyish subalterns in smart regiments, the banker, the brain specialist. Something always went wrong socially with him. A Lancashire over-correction would disfigure a vowel at the dinner table; it was so charmingly ignored by the family, who breathed out Received Standard as they breathed in air. Asked to play one of his own works on the Bechstein, he would, in a flurry of wrong notes and false continuations, stop half-way through: 'I'm afraid I can only remember that much. If I had the score –' 'But it's really charming. I should *love* to hear the whole work. Now, bridge, anyone?'

Sexually, he supposed, it had been the same. 'Really, you *are* impetuous.' And yet the initial impetuosity often expired in an inner constriction, an inexplicable deflation. 'Never mind, it'll be all right some day.' Only for that brief death-filled leave before embarkation, did they come to life together. That was because death was in the air; there was no time for the leisurely saunterings of prose, only for the machine-gun rattle of poetry, epigram, the gnomic utterance.

And now? He was lying on his bed in the hot airless afternoon, re-reading the latest airmail letter from Laurel. She had been quiet for three weeks; now she was loud with the same old music: 'So sorry to hear about your major's attitude, though the censor seemed to have cut right out a good deal of what you had to say – Incredible that he should take that attitude – Derek is much younger than you and he's a full colonel – Perhaps the Army just isn't your line, darling – There must be other things you can do – My nerves seem just shot to pieces – I envy you your sun – Years since I saw the Mediterranean – Do try – I do believe in you, really – Mark Winfield says he likes some of your music very much – Met a most interesting American general – quite literary – talked about California – sounds most attractive – longing to see you – Your most loving wife –'

Julian was practising an entrechat. 'You should have seen me, dear, in those days. The flowers they sent, the champagne. One dirty old roué stole one of my practice slippers, the nasty old finchist. You must write me a ballet, you really must. Something bright and clockwork, hard clean lines, like Satie. And now, some tea, don't you think? Hm? Richard, you just don't pay attention at all. I thought I'd got you out of those horrible moping habits.'

'I've got to get a job,' said Ennis.

'Right away, dear?'

'Oh, hell, it's a long story. It's my wife, you see. She wants to come out here. The European Peace is making her very, very tired. Muir won't have me in the Army. What else is there I can do?'

'Oh, lots of things. Really, Richard, I *do* think you go about with your eyes closed. Now you leave it to Uncle Julian. You shall be introduced to some nice, nice people who will be ever so useful. There's that old cow Withers, for instance. He needs help, he told me so.'

'British Council?'

'Oh, dear me, no. Honestly, my dear, you are *ignorant*. Withers is in a much more chic organisation. It's called the Commonwealth Council for the Development of the Appreciation of the Arts in Colonial Territories. You remember, my dear, when we were all at bay, waiting to fight for our *honour* – 1940, as I remember, was the year – this was one of the things that was started. It was supposed to worry the Boche, and I suppose it did. Well then, Withers would be positively *overwrought* if you offered yourself. He'll just *melt* when he sees you, dear, if you turn on some of that charm that you're *determined* to hide from everyone but me. You're such an old bear, you know.'

They strolled out together into the sunshine, strong as a blow in the chops. The sea purred up at them, but they turned the corner, making for Main Street. Then the Rock pounced on them, as usual, with a roar of reflected heat. They entered a trim little teashop.

'Maria,' said Julian, in a clear governess voice, 'we'll have some really *hot* tea and some of those nice little cakes there. No, not those with liver-coloured stripes, those with oodles of cream in them. And here's where we're going to sit.'

'*Si, señor.*' She turned on Ennis the glow of a full bosom, the rich red of an Andalusian mouth, beaded bubbles winking at the brim. Ennis, aware of his hidden charm, responded, with a creak of rusty engines.

8

Meanwhile, Major Muir's dream of a new order was coming to rapid life. Very much the S.O. 2 (though impatiently waiting to be S.O. 1), he sat flanked, a presiding magistrate, by his new S.O. 3s, a couple of ex-gunner lieutenants. Ennis knew them both well by sight. One, Captain Appleyard, was a willowy, querulous public-school master of a man, given to High Anglicanism and calling the instructors by their Christian names. Ennis foresaw eventual teas and frank tasteful little talks about masturbation. The other, Captain Dance, had become semi-articulate through long service as a teacher in an elementary school, followed by lonely communings with the novels of J.B. Priestley on isolated gunsites. He was small and his teeth protruded wetly. He talked much about 'bods' (the final indignity: the stripping off of soul and instincts, the reduction by apocope to puppet status) and would sometimes say, when an instructor had handed in a report on time, 'There's a good bod. Off you go.' There was much jargon now, the cold baked meats of the infantry: 'Button that up.' 'Put them in the post-war picture.' 'Get your finger out.'

As for the instructors themselves, there seemed more now than the original cadre could count: plumbing instructors, accompanied, in the teashops by mates of lesser rank; one-eyed Glaswegian sergeants, expert in bricklaying; greasy commercial artists; morose teachers of shorthand and book-keeping. Of the few that Ennis and Julian and Quartermain had recommended for transfer, none had been accepted. This was not surprising, as the candidates had mostly been quiet-spoken humanists, deeply but not eloquently concerned about the transmission of values, likely to feel, anyway, uncomfortable in the expanding world of Muir. Even the smell of garrison education had changed. The office had formerly smelt faintly of school – ink and new exercise books; now it was rich in the odour of size and cement. One trampled brick dust, kicked buckets of whitewash.

Bright helpful pamphlets flowed from the War Office, along with books to build a sumptuous Vocational and Cultural Library. Here was a guide to the use of a Chinese dictionary, here a seven-volume study in the history of Historiography, there a treatise on Florentine incunabula. These were destined to lie in ever-thickening dust, to be sold off at last to Foyle's in job-lots for a copper or two, unless the prudent and conscientious were to take his chance now, to risk the small sin in the face of the duty of pious conservation. Thus Quartermain sent off weekly parcels of books to his home in Chichester, and Julian made a large collection (which many came to visit) of volumes of art reproductions. Not to have done this would have been a kind of quietist vandalism.

As for the Warrant Officers, Williams had had to be promoted to the rank of W.O. 1, and he sat now in the outer office, unhandy with the telephone, starting a new file for every letter that came in. Bayley smirked through his pipe smoke, casting covert glances perpetually at his new crowns, at home at last with a woodwork department. Promotion had made him cleaner, the need for order in his tool cupboard inducing the sense of a cognate need in his billet and personal toilet. But with the other two appointments authorised by the new establishment, Muir had done the unexpected and humiliating. He had sent home for a couple of ready-made Warrant Officers, the one a confirmed inebriate, in whose eyes had shone a terrible joy at the prospect of cheap whisky; the other a near-bald heavy-shouldered Liverpudlian, whose stutter limited him to office work but whose left-handed scrawl was unreadable.

And so the great machine was assembled and lumbered, hissing and cranking, into life. In the unit Vocational and Cultural offices the men were catechised:

'What do you want to be when you're demobbed, Goddard?'

'Please, sir, a wheel-tapper's harker, sir.'

'Oh, Christ. All right, next man. And what do you have in mind, Auchincloss?'

'My post has been left open for me, sir. Senior Lecturer in Anthropology at Camford.'

'Well, surely you could do with a brush-up? I'll see if they're running any courses in Anthrop – whatever it is. All right, next man.'

The weekly Vocational and Cultural conferences were now very impressive. They were held no longer in Muir's offices but in the ballroom of the Winter Gardens, a place formerly sacred to Tombola. Ennis always expected the session to begin with Muir shouting, 'Eyes down, look in.' But instead he plunged straight into animated discussions about timber, bricks, grinding machines, dumpy levels, angle collet fixtures, de-burring, jobber's drills. He was now in his element, at home in a world of tangibles. Excitement shone from the suffering eyes as the organisation of new technical classes was discussed, the ordering of new tools and materials.

'Well, you see, sir, this here tooling steel is worth getting. I mean, you can use it for reamers, taps, gauges, broaches and what not.'

Ennis felt out of it. Admittedly he still had a number of lectures to give, classes to run, but these represented a mere cultural annexe, a nursery where the children, otherwise likely to be underfoot, could be kept out of the way while the big party went on. Besides, the Army Educational Corps, still shyly carrying on in the shadow of its mountainous upstart younger brother, was responsible for most of the *easy* stuff. But, if Muir had become caught up in a mystical world of forges, kilns, and carpenter's glue, Captain Appleyard kept his pale-blue eyes fixed on the slopes of the snowy hill of culture. He had not been a very successful teacher in his day, so he now aspired to the Inspectorate of the Ministry of Education. He began a series of fantastic courses in pedagogics.

'It would do you a great deal of good to attend this two-day course on the Use of Visual Aids,' he writhed. 'Sergeant Batts was a projectionist in a large West End cinema (come closer and I will whisper its name) and he ought to know his stuff. I myself shall demonstrate the use of the epidiascope and the film strip projector, also, of course, the flannelgraph (hideous hybrid that, but a most useful device, especially for the very young).'

'But,' said Ennis, 'I'm a musician, sir, an auditory type, as Quartermain would call me. Besides, I don't think I approve of this visual bias that's creeping into education. Our civilisation is, surely, based on the ear – the dialectics of Socrates, Shakespeare and his illiterate audience, the peripatetic sermons of Christ –'

'Richard,' rebuked Captain Appleyard, 'there's no need to be blasphemous.' He looked at Ennis with an eye of indulgent reproof, sixth-form master checking clever but brashly iconoclastic scholarship candidate. 'Besides, my degree is in History, and hence I know more about those things than you do. The eye is more important than the ear and has always been. I agree with this little War Office pamphlet. 'Men learn through their eyes,' it says.'

'All right,' said Ennis with some heat. 'To hell with music, to hell with literature. Roll on the era of ideograms, cartoons and television for all, a golden age for the deaf and the *voyeur*.'

'Richard,' said Captain Appleyard sharply, 'I don't like that truculent tone. Remember who – to whom you are speaking. You will attend this course. That is an order now. Oh, don't you see how I detest giving orders? You just *make* me do it.'

Mornings and afternoons were now bright with films and slides and the projection of photographs, sometimes upside down, sometimes curly with the heat of the epidiascope. Ennis and Julian emerged at teatime drunk with harsh images, thirsty for the sound of Mozart.

'I had an idea,' said Julian, 'that that little bitch Appleyard was having a tiny crack at you, my dear, in that last grotesque demonstration of his.'

'What was that?' asked Ennis. 'I wasn't really looking.'

'It was a film strip on the Instruments of the Orchestra. Honestly, Richard, you just don't *attend*, do you?'

'I was sketching out this bit of fugato,' mumbled Ennis, showing Julian the scrawled back of an envelope. 'It was difficult in that darkness.'

'Well, anyway, there it was, dear, crawling all over that unwashed buggy bed sheet he uses as a screen. The Appleyard oozing, no less, about the glorious *bigness* of double basses and the comparative *tee-niness* of violins.'

A little fanfare lit up Ennis's brain. 'An orchestra, you say? An orchestra here?'

'My dear, what is the matter with you? You gibber like the more moronic of my *dear* illiterates.'

'Why shouldn't we have an orchestra here?'

'You shall have whatever you like,' said Julian indulgently. 'But, first, we have to take a dish of tea with that old *prostitute* Withers.'

'Withers?'

'Oh, you're sometimes *naughty*, Richard. The queen of the Commonwealth Council for the Development of the Appreciation of the Arts in Colonial Territories. The time has come. I have told him *all* about you, and he is positively agog. I have helped him a lot, you know, serving tea and dripping charm all over the customers. The grant they get is simply enormous, and he definitely needs an assistant. He told me, so I know, dear. He stroked my thigh when he said it, nasty old thing. He's hardly my type, of course, but you now, you're *different*. You could burn him up with those fierce dark eyes of yours, and he'd just *love* being held off.'

So they went to have tea with Mr Withers. He lurked in a cool little backwater, set off from the clamour of the garrison, the stink of the overcrowded tenements, the rowdier of the shore-leave sailors. A Palladian façade welcomed the thirsty seeker after culture, a trim forecourt crowded with plane-trees. Within were deep carpets, an air of Augustan leisure, eggshell teacups, tasteful reproductions of the less extreme modern painters, and, presiding over the island paradise, Mr Withers himself, urbane, with a greying goatee, an aseptic white suit, a long amber cigarette holder. Ennis asked right out and bluntly about the possibility of a job.

'Well, now,' said Mr Withers, one elegant leg crossed over the other, 'I can't say, I just can't say at all. Do have another of those petits-fours. They are so difficult at home, ages, simply ages before any kind of authorisation comes through, but we shall be very glad, we shall be very glad indeed, of any little help you can give us now. We have quite a varied programme ahead of us this season. Young Rodney Bakeless

– a sick-berth attendant: you may know him – is to give readings from the poets: an awfully nice boy, quite wasted. And we are to have *The Importance of Being Earnest*. And the Wrens are to do something about an exhibition of paintings. I have almost certainly got something started, in spite of the almost pathetic shyness of these dear people out here. But we have a mission, you know, to give them the best, the very best, of culture. You can certainly help, my dear Ennis, with your music and your other great gifts. No, my boy, I have heard, I have heard much about you. I think there is still a little tea left in the pot.'

'An orchestra,' said Ennis. 'Why shouldn't we have an orchestra?' 'Why not indeed? There used to be one, you know,' said Mr Withers. 'You, my dear Ennis, must look around. I am sure there are all sorts of fiddlers and flautists only waiting to be smoked out of their holes.'

Anyway, Ennis helped. Nightly to the hospitable halls of Mr Withers came the shy middle-class of the colony – Mr and Mrs Nuñez and their daughter Charito, the Opissos and the Levys, the Disfrutadas and young Bertie Cornada – all the wanderers between two worlds, despising the animated passionate poor relations over the border, anxious to be absorbed into the really alien universe of their boyish masters. The English slang they used seemed always to be a little out of date: 'good show' and 'wizard' fell painfully from their lips. But Mr Withers always made them feel at home, his polished English diphthongs skimming like kingfishers over the turbid dark water of their round oh's and trilled ar's. They were fed earnestly with culture. Ennis and Julian recited, to their polite incomprehension, the execution scene from *The Duchess of Malfi*, Ennis a growling Bosola, Julian pathetic as the Duchess. A woman major of the Medical Corps, plumply shaking along with her castanets, performed Spanish dances, roguish eyes over an artificial flower in her powerful white teeth, a final Standard English '*Olé!*' as she stamped the last step of her zapateado, a huge hip thrust provocatively at the stony watchers.

Ennis gave piano recitals, and at one or two of these he had a curious illusion that Laurel, or her double, was somewhere in the audience. This unnerved him, producing wrong notes, but at the end, bowing to the mild applause, he saw that the vision was a mirage. He was not so disturbed at his string orchestra sessions. Mr Withers had been right: there were fiddlers on the Rock, with fiddles of all sizes, and it was not long before Ennis was rehearsing *Eine Kleine Nachtmusik*. But one evening, while the swarthy musicians were tuning up, Mr Withers came slyly up to Ennis and put an arm around his shoulders, saying:

'You're doing wonders with them, dear boy, really you are.' Expensive scent, hot breath in his ear.

At times like this he sickened of the atmosphere of his new life and, music being associated with it, sickened of music. He hungered for strong meat again, he sweated for a woman; what had so recently been soothing became nauseating. He would go off on his own, removing his sergeant's stripes, drinking with sappers, gunners, infantry privates in their canteens. Here the monotonous obscenities were like a precious ointment. He would sit too in a beer shop near Buena Vista with a Scottish sapper and a Military Police lance-corporal. Their earthly talk, their thoroughgoing heterosexuality, he breathed in like northern sea air.

But the old hunger for Concepción, who was now, so little Juanito said, living in Spain, keeping in order the huge house of Barasi, concealed from the eyes of men with the veil of purdah, a tradition borrowed from the Moors, ached and rankled. Taking a class in the heat of the afternoon, the sun baking the roof of the Nissen hut, would be painful when young girls of the colony were present. These, having missed much schooling during the diaspora, were allowed to sit, bright subtropical flowers, with the repressed and sweating students of the units. Bending over them to correct their work, Ennis would inhale the heavy cheap perfume, the musk of their glowing flesh, catch the innocent smile of a dark eye, and inwardly rage. He took to spending evenings with Williams, in cafés where one was encouraged to buy coloured water for the dancing girls, for the reward of a close provocative bosom, a hand suffered to encircle a thickening waist, the palpating of a white-powdered arm, a rare snatched kiss. From buying physical release across the border Ennis still shrank. He continued to think in terms of what he called love.

Returning late after these mild carousals, he would be greeted with a reproof from his room-mate. 'Really, whoring again. Too barbarous. I really thought I was civilising you. I declare you're just as bad as the rest of the rough soldiers.'

'Quiet, you old bag.' Ennis would drop off to sleep, lit with hallucinatory images of plump bodies, proffered juicy fruit, love in the sun. His manuscript, neglected, lay dusty and glass-ringed on the table; fireflies flickered about it, tiny flames in the blue Andalusian night.

9

Then Ennis was thrust back into remembering what he was here for. On August 5th Hiroshima was blasted, with over seventy-eight thousand dead. (They were to see it later in the hot cinema, pungent with the smell of orange peel, full of the healthy sweat of white-decked sailors, the huge mounting stalk blossoming into white-hot smoke at its crown, spreading and spreading, a ghastly flower; they were to hear the unctuous booming of the soundtrack: the sun's energy tamed to an essentially peaceful end. They that live by the sword shall perish in freak light-storms, weird mock-photography, cerements of parched oven-stinking skin, delayed-action diseases, the proliferation in dark silent tracts of unearthly cancers.) On August 8th Russia declared war against Japan and, the following day, was perhaps present in spirit at Nagasaki when seventy-five thousand were blasted. On the 14th Japan surrendered unconditionally. On the 15th everybody got drunk.

Williams was at last revealed as a scientist. The shreds of skin of other subjects he had been ordered to teach, coat over coat of over-painting, fell away, and Williams Science appeared, bald and shining. 'Here,' he said, 'you have your effin protons, your neutrons effin here, there your effin electrons. It is effin easy.' He was revealed also as a prophetic poet. 'In theory, mind, in effin theory only, mind, there is no effin reason why the whole effin 'orld should not go up in effin smoke, reduced to heat, light, and effin sound.'

Well, thought Ennis, at last there was nothing to fear. At last he was free. Now he must really think of the future. But first was the

duty to get drunk. There was something ghoulish about the celebrations. In the intense heat, sweating over their beer, men seemed to be
trying to shake off the smell of burning rubber, seemed in their febrile
stickiness trying to avoid the fall of bits of charred skin. Julian went
off with his friends to play hide-and-seek in the Alameda Gardens.
Ennis went the rounds of the messes with Williams. He drank much
but came back to the billet sober and fired by an urge to work. Now,
for some reason, it seemed more than ever before a solemn duty
to get that *Passacaglia* finished. He moved the table from the bedroom to the washroom, taking the moth-haunted lamp with him. He
locked the door and, through the night, chain-smoking, refreshing
himself occasionally with gin and water, he sat, his fingers getting
inky and sore, his pen racing up and down the manuscript paper,
bringing his complex score to a conclusion.

At dawn his work ended; he ruled the double bar, he wrote his
name and the year and month of the finishing of the task. The original scheme had been much modified. The strong eight-bar theme had
served as bass, as inner part, as fugal subject, always there, holding
fast to its original key despite wanton modulation; but in the last ten
pages of full score there had appeared a subtle and gradual disorgan-
isation. The theme had limped, struggled against violent dissonance,
been broken up to appear as its own mocking ghost. And then, as
coda, it had emerged as the tune of a threnody, a slow-moving march
dedicated to all the dead, fading to a quiet statement of the inverted
theme on the oboe, accompanied only by the dull thump of the
basses.

Dawn. His throat was raw. He could hear the Spanish workmen
trudging to the docks, the harshest of roosters cocoricoing in someone's backyard. He stretched, unlocked the washroom door, and
went into the bedroom to find Julian gracefully asleep under a gay
coverlet. He shook him roughly. 'Come on, you old queen. Work to
do. The call of life. Wake up, you bastard.'

Julian came to consciousness. 'My dear. So impetuous.' (Laurel's
words.) 'The middle of the night. Really –'

Ennis shook him again. 'Come on, now. Have a cigarette. Have
some gin. Listen, Julian, we've things to do. I've finished the

Passacaglia. By Christ, I'm going to impose my pattern on this place. We're going to have a concert of the works of Richard Ennis.'

'A concert, dear?'

'Yes. We'll show these philistine sods something about organisation. We'll build up an orchestra, we'll publicise, we'll fill the Engineers' Hall. I shall conduct. In tails, too. And you shall dance.'

'Dance? After all these years?' Julian lay back with grace on the pillow, exhaling cigarette smoke with great delicacy.

'Yes. I've got a short piece for flute and strings. You know Ferrers, the squinting man in Radar? Well, he plays the flute. He can do the solo. You can work out choreography. I have in mind something like Nijinsky's faun. But my music is not imitation Debussy. It is definitely *not* pastiche –'

'All right, dear. Nobody said it was.'

'I'll play it for you this morning.'

Before breakfast Ennis had devised a programme: a comedy overture that had, in fact, been suggested by *The Importance of Being Earnest* – witty, but short and easy, full of open-string work; his 'cello sonata, which had been long in the possession of Corporal Gibbard (there had been a quarrel between Ennis and Gibbard over a year before, but that could now be patched up); a group of Spanish songs, mostly Lorca, which Merita, the café singer, already knew well; a suite for strings; a piano sonata he could play himself; the newly finished *Passacaglia*. And, of course, the real draw – the visual act, the *pas seul* on the spotlighted stage.

Mr Withers was delighted. 'My dear boy,' he said, 'we, our organisation, must sponsor this. Publicity is my strong suit. *Such* a good idea.' And he stroked Ennis's thigh. But Ennis could not stay for thigh-stroking; he and Julian had to go round the Rock looking for instrumentalists. Actually, there were plenty of wind players: the R.A.F. out by North Face was infested with saxophones; the Salvation Army ran a band; the Barsets bandmaster, who, for some reason, had always felt sorry for Ennis, was willing enough to help. He also said:

'Give me your scores, and I'll get these lazy buggers copying parts.'

Three days after VJ day, Ennis was able to make out a list of wind men and percussionists. There was so much brass available that he decided to add to the score of his *Passacaglia* – following the high example of Berlioz – parts for brass bands to left and right of the orchestra. Also he rescored his string suite for brass. Of string players he had only thirty, but Mr Withers wagged his goat beard over the telephone and found two more bass players.

A week after VJ day, Ennis was able to call his first rehearsal. There was no doubt, he thought, facing his orchestra in the Engineers' Hall, about the purely visual appeal of such an army – the buttery gleam of French horns (four of them); the sharper silver stab of the trumpets and trombones; the dull polish of the violins, violas and 'cellos – that rich wood the visual counterpart of the sound of Brahms. There was only one oboe, but there were four flutes; there was only one bassoon, but there was a bass clarinet; the 'cellos were thin but could be enriched, when need be, by a discreet addition of tenor saxophones; there was no harp, but a piano would do there. Really, all problems yielded to the ingenuity of the *practical* musician. Elated, Ennis thumbed his nose at Major Muir and his cohorts of automata. He said:

'Ladies and gentlemen, take it back to Letter D. Horns, you need to re-tune, you're blowing sharp.' The oboe intoned an acidulous A. Meekly, the cornists adjusted. 'Now,' said Ennis, 'this next part must be sung. It says '*cantando*'. Sing it, strings. Sing it, horns.' Somebody began to sing. 'No, no,' said Ennis. 'Sing it with your instruments.'

'My dear,' said Julian, thin as a wand in his practice-suit, 'you're quite the little slave-driver. Now watch me. Now you'll see what Monte Carlo raved about.' He had devised a tasteful little *pas seul* based on the legend of Narcissus. When the time came, mirrors would be needed, also careful lighting. Meanwhile Corporal Gibbard was making sense of the 'cello sonata, and Merita, plump and throaty, was rehearsing the settings of Lorca. With the merest hint of microtones she wailed:

La niña del bello rostro
Està cogiendo aceituna –

All the decline and fall of Moorish Spain was in that wail: Ferdinand and Isabella's centralising forces tramping slowly south, the ruined columns of countless Alhambras, the burning of translations of Aristotle in neat Arabic script, the sundered lips of Islam and Iberia, the ghost of the music of a proud robed race, its empire buried under the remorseless drift of the sand.

So it seemed, in his more romantic moods, to Ennis. And, listening to her, he fretted at the limitations of written notes. The music he wanted to write was, he realised, as elemental as water splashing or rocks falling, as brutal as the grind of heavy chains, something which would strike at the diaphragm. His own works dissatisfied him profoundly. Exciting in the initial conception, the first burst of the theme, they soon began to sound tame in his ears. Yet they were the best he could do. What would his audience think? No, thinking was not the point. Could he move them, hit them in the diaphragm?

He would soon know. Every available hour was now given to rehearsal, and, as he entered the Engineers' Hall, his heart swelling at the thrilling noise of the tune-up – the acid oboe A, the arabesques of the warming-up wind, brass blasts, hollow fifths of the strings, thump of the kettledrums – he felt the resurgence of the confidence he needed. What the hell did any of them matter? – Muir with his machines, Laurel with her sweet gentle nagging, the oiled Barasi paddling with his damned fingers. Here he was doing more than imposing mere authority: he was building a city of sound, a universe of ultimate meaning. Other ambition seemed petty in the face of this.

'Back to Letter H. No, the bar before. Howkins, that's not a triplet, it's a crotchet and two quavers. Now, everybody. This is the final statement of the theme. Give it everything, everything you've got, everything.' And so slam into it.

Mr Withers had seen to the printing of the programmes, with Ennis's own analytical notes. Posters, press-wet, arrived from the *Chronicle* offices, inducing, with their large red blazoning of his name, a new feeling of unworthiness. '*Domine, non sum dignus*,' he muttered under his breath, as, in the past, when the ciborium had come to him, he had declared his house unfit for the divine visitant. Was he perhaps unworthy of this, too – not the little fame, but the

pentecostal bestowing of the ability to create? Had one to give something back? One gave labour, the sweating for hours over the scoring
of a single bar, but perhaps there was something else, something
timeless, something commensurate with the divine gift. For some
reason the word *hubris* kept coming into his mind. Did the gods
decide on the nature of the payment?

He borrowed a dress-suit from a member of the Garrison Concert
Party. A month had gone by since VJ day, and the gods had been
quiet. Let them, he prayed, be quiet just two days more. With a thud-
ding heart he raised his right hand for the final rehearsal (he didn't
use a baton). The orchestra crashed into the Comedy Overture. A
too-early entry from the first clarinet, a bubble from one of the
horns – no other major faults. Merita wailed her songs: she at least
would hit their diaphragms. The brass suite bounced and glowed
along. The 'cello sonata, save for two wrong notes from Ennis himself, went without a hitch, though Gibbard streamed with a cold.
Julian danced charmingly to the little rhapsody for flute and strings.
Finally came the *Passacaglia*.

As, bound by the strong eight-bar theme, the variations –
romantic, dissonant, straightforwardly melodious, humorous, malicious or martial – were spun in brief life on the warm night air, tears
came to Ennis's eyes. 'My God,' he thought, 'this will show them.
I'm bigger than the lot of them, blast their eyes. I'm bigger than the
Rock, I'm bigger than Muir, this is the only power I want.' Now,
after a welter of dissonance, the theme was twisted, underwent an
agony of mutation, and then came the final threnody – the plaintive
citrous oboe theme, the quiet divided bass chords, the fading to
silence – *niente*, the end.

Exhausted, he and Julian walked home together. 'Quite frightening, my dear, really. I felt quite wet when those horrible uncouth
trombones lunged out. But I danced superbly, I know I did. And,
remember, if the hall is filled, it will be with my admirers. Of that
I'm quite sure.'

So came the day of the concert. With it came the expected – the
hurling of the hammer at Ennis. In the afternoon he had a class in
Elementary English. He cancelled it: he wanted to rest. Lying on his

bed, sweating with heat and excitement and fear, he was summoned to the Major's office.

Drunk with the possibilities of technology, Muir had mechanised his office to a degree that made the head swim. A harsh buzzer, the flash of an orange light, told Ennis to enter. In the office were flood bulbs trained on to glossy white charts, maps of classes; blue bands of light showed what classes were in progress. Flanked by his two captains, Muir, the spider, the octopus, sat, waiting to greet Ennis. He said, purring:

'Ennis. Aren't you supposed to be teaching now?'

'I cancelled the class, sir. I gave them some private study. I meant to tell you.'

'If you didn't feel well enough to take it,' said Muir, 'you should have informed the office and reported sick in the usual manner. What's the matter with you?'

'Nothing, sir. I – well, I have this concert tonight.'

'A concert? Yes, I've been hearing something about a concert. I've seen your name on posters in various places. A concert, eh?' He was most affable. 'And you thought you'd have a bit of a rest, eh? Conserve your energies for the concert, eh?'

'Yes, sir. I thought you wouldn't mind –'

'If you took the afternoon off?' Muir purred. 'Well, now, Ennis, this business has been taking up a lot of your time, hasn't it? Some of the students have not been very satisfied with the quality of the instruction they've been getting from you. Perhaps you didn't know that, eh?'

'Nobody's said anything –'

'Oh, but they have, Ennis, they have.' He turned, smiling, to Captain Dance. 'Dangers of over-specialisation, eh? We were talking about that only this morning.' Captain Dance gave a *gamin* grin, showing wet teeth. Muir turned back to Ennis. He said, 'One thing you've got to learn in the Army is that you're on duty twenty-four hours a day, and that the work of the Army comes first. Your own private pleasures don't count.' He clicked his fingers very loudly. 'Not that much they don't.'

'But this,' said Ennis, 'is a cultural activity. It's education, it's –'

'It's for the glorification of Ennis, that's it, isn't it, Richard?' broke in Captain Appleyard brightly. 'You're a scholar. You know all about *hubris*.'

Muir waved *hubris* aside. 'Never mind about him. The point is, and I'm sorry if it's going to cause you any inconvenience, Ennis, but the point is, Ennis, that Sergeant Woods is ill, really ill, and there's nobody but you and Agate free tonight. There are three classes in Elementary Shorthand. I should think that's more in your line than in Agate's.'

'But, sir,' said Ennis, 'both Agate and I are involved in tonight's concert. We've rehearsed. We've put a lot of work into it. It's got to go on. We can't cancel it now.'

'I take it Withers is backing this?' Muir turned to Dance. Dance nodded. 'Nobody said anything about cancelling it, Ennis,' said Muir. 'I think it's a very noble effort. But you just won't be there, Ennis. You'll be taking three classes in Elementary Shorthand instead. Duty comes first, you know. The Army's a very 'ard, hard master.'

'I'm sorry, sir. I don't want to disobey orders –'

The three officers looked at him keenly, leaning forward with great interest.

'But, you see, sir, this just *has* to come first. You can see that, can't you, sir? I can't back out. It can't go on without me.'

'Pride, Richard,' said Captain Appleyard. 'Nobody's indispensable.'

'But *I* am. As far as this is concerned, I mean. I'm conducting, I'm playing the piano.'

'Look 'ere,' said Muir, breaking in rudely, 'we're not going to argue. I've given you an order. Are you going to obey that order?'

Ennis paused for a moment, his Church and Army training battling against Prometheus and Satan. Fire broke out in him. He said, 'No, sir, I'm not. I'm sorry, believe me. I don't want to behave like this –'

'That's your last word?' said Muir. Appleyard squirmed. ('Oh, Richard, Richard.') Ennis said nothing. Muir said, 'Right.' He pressed the buzzer on his desk. Williams appeared. 'Are Sergeant Meredith and Sergeant Laughton out there still?' asked Muir.

'Yes, sir,' said Williams.

'Right. Tell them to stand by.' Muir turned to Ennis. 'Ennis,' he said, 'consider yourself under close arrest.'

10

'Paranoia,' said Quartermain, his face twitching, his turtle neck thrusting out between carapace and plastron. 'Megalomania. He's turning into God. *Deus fio*. But at least the Roman emperors were humble enough to think in terms of an expanding pantheon. Also, they waited till they were dying. Christianity's done a lot of harm to types like him. It's all or nothing.'

They were walking down from the Military Hospital. Julian was in there, lying among lilies, recovering from a broken ankle bone. It was some comfort to Ennis to know that Julian had executed his Nijinsky leap down Castle Steps at the very moment of his own agonised choice in Muir's office. That particular item of the concert would have had to be cancelled anyway, he thought.

'And people like you encourage him,' said Quartermain. 'Lapsed Catholics are the most dangerous of all religious types. You all become very stoical. Nero had his Seneca, remember. God suddenly leaps out at you and you're not trained to wrestle. You think: "Yes, it is in the pattern of things to submit, but within, somewhere hidden along the grey corridors, is the real me, the quintessential self, which the evil deity can't touch." You're a bloody fool,' he added with an involuntary twitch of the left eye which made all that he had said seem ghoulishly facetious.

'It was a valuable lesson,' said Ennis. 'The gangster-god at least quenched my will. He reminded me that the will is evil and ought to be quenched.'

'And the music,' said Quartermain. 'He quenched that, too. Some people might have liked to hear it, but you kept it from them. You Catholics make me sick, saving your own measly little souls at the expense of other people's. You could have given the concert again. You still can. Not that it matters to me, of course. I don't like music.'

They were walking down Rosia Road, approaching the Y.M.C.A. 'Shall we go in there?' asked Ennis. 'I could do with a cup of tea.'

'Their tea is too full of the milk of human kindness,' said Quartermain, 'straight out of a tin. How I detest these jocular Christians, with their sweaty table tennis and hearty pipes. The Padre on Duty will give a little chat to the boys. Jolly hymn-singing and a few manly prayers. God likes a chap to be decent and keep his body clean. Confessions will be heard in the shower baths.'

'You've got it in for everybody, haven't you?' admired Ennis.

'And what if I have?' Quartermain twitched pugnaciously. They entered the canteen. 'Char,' said Quartermain. 'A cuppa char. And a wad.' He grimaced and writhed his way to the counter and brought back to the slopping table two cups of very weak milky tea.

'What I can't understand about you," said Ennis, 'is why you yourself are so damned submissive. The more megalomaniacal Muir becomes, the more you seem to like it.'

'It's not Catholic masochism, anyway.' Quartermain's twitching lips goldfish-twittered towards the teacup rim. 'It's scientific curiosity. His ecology must not be disturbed, he must go on and on and on to his limit. I thought of writing a little paper about him.'

'You scientists,' said Ennis. 'You'll never raise a hand to strike down a Caligula or a Hitler. Your excuse is always the scientific interest of the abnormal. "We need morbid types to justify the existence of morbid psychology." You make me sick sometimes.' He said this without rancour.

'I think it's GPI,' said Quartermain. 'The cerebral tissues are breaking down fast. In any case,' he turned to Ennis, 'he is, after all, one's superior officer. One can't do more than submit.'

There was, it seemed, going to be a lot to submit to. Compulsory P.T. and arms drill, morning assemblies, weekly reports on the progress of individual students. There was, all over the garrison, a tightening-up. 'The men mustn't get slack, mustn't have time to grumble.'

The release scheme was operating slowly. The men said, 'The bloody war's over. We didn't ask to be bloody peacetime soldiers.' There was some talk about leave, but, so far, only talk. Some men were being sent on courses which, of course, meant leave, but this only exacerbated the chronic grousing of the others. 'Always sniffin' round the C.O.'s arse, he were.'

'In other words,' said Ennis, 'he's God.'

'Oh, shut up about God!' cried Quartermain angrily. 'You blasted renegades who don't believe in divorce. Separation, sensual itchings for the once beloved. Why the hell can't you make a clean break?'

'Hell,' said Ennis, 'is the operative word. That's one thing that goes on existing. They threw it overboard, but they never argued it out of existence. It'll rise to the surface again one of these days,' he said. 'You mark my words. Like,' he said, with shameless mixing of metaphors, 'a submerged splinter.'

'I'm not interested,' said Quartermain, twitching all over. 'These things are relevant to one's studies in so far as they're manifestations of the religious mind, but the question of their objective existence, or, if you like, ultimate existence, is a bore. So shut up about them.'

'I'm sorry,' said Ennis. 'I thought that the psychology behind my residual faith might be interesting to you.'

'It's not.'

'Your own behaviour is very interesting,' said Ennis. 'It's dawning on me that perhaps your science isn't giving you all the answers you want.'

'What exactly are you talking about?'

'Your subject isn't anchored to values.'

'That's stupid, and you know it. Truth is itself a value. According,' said Quartermain hastily, 'to your people, anyway.'

'What I mean is,' said Ennis, 'are you finding some states of mind inexplicable in terms of your own science? Is the machine behaving like a human being?'

'I'm not a Behaviourist,' said Quartermain. 'I don't go for all this watching dogs' mouths water. I'm interested in the mind.'

'Ah, the way of introspection,' said Ennis. 'What do you find in your own brain?'

'I don't,' shook Quartermain, 'see why I should answer what I consider to be impertinent questions. My mind is my own affair. In any case, I've got to go and give a lecture now.'

'Your mind isn't open to the investigator?'

'Look here, you needn't try your apologetics on me. Sort out your own position first. You're the one who needs a bit of introspection. Anyway, I'm off now.'

So, mused Ennis, Quartermain was finding faith, was he? He watched the psychologist twitch his way out of the big tearoom, winking horribly, working his neck muscles with vigour. The wind blows where it listeth, but perhaps Muir, image of God, perhaps the Rock itself, solid, ubiquitous, were both helping. 'But I,' thought Ennis, 'with these dregs, these leavings –' He sighed deeply. No faith in anything, it seemed. Not even in art. There remained charity. There remained hope.

Ennis got up, walked out on to the terrace, out on the road. In the upper foliage of the South Gate apes were gibbering. Under the arch-way he saw Muir emerge, solitary in the back of a staff car, preceded by two building instructors, helmeted, on motor-cycles. Ennis threw him a salute. He began to climb one of the ramps; he was going to see Mr Withers. But then, outside one of the dirty yellow hovels, he came upon Bayley. This was embarrassing: they had not spoken since their stormy sundering. Bayley had clasped in his arms a small dirty child who was babbling fragmentary Spanish. He was saying heavily, '*Si, si, si.* You are *mi niño*, that's what you are.' A wrinkled grandmother croaked approval from the open door; from the open door garlic blew out in acetylene blasts. Dogs were all about, a for-lorn gang of them, muzzled, some wearing their muzzles at the alert. It was difficult for Ennis to slip by. Seeing him Bayley spoke first.

'Hallo, Ennis.'

'Hallo, Bayley. How are things?'

'Oh, not too bad, you know. I've got over it now, I think. What happened about Muir putting you on a charge?'

'A reprimand. But, of course, that wasn't the real punishment.'

'No.' There was silence. Bayley lowered the child to the ground, awkwardly. Its knickers evidently needed washing.

'How are things in your department?' asked Ennis. 'Plenty to do, you know. It's kept my mind off things.'

'And how are things at home?''

'Oh, the wife's getting over it, too. She was very upset, of course. It nearly killed her.'

'What did? What happened?'

Bayley looked with a mixture of reproach and wonder. 'You didn't hear? Nobody told you?'

'No.'

'He died. Young John. My son.' Bayley's eyes became moist, his hands trembled a little. 'My only son.' Ennis did not know where to look. Real grief was a knife-edge, not a bath. He waited for the inevitable. 'And I never saw him. I was never able to hear him say "Daddy".' Bayley's long-nosed mournful face began to distort round a crumbling mouth.

'I'm terribly sorry, John. It's shocking, I know. But time heals, they say.' He apologised quietly to himself.

Bayley turned on Ennis as on a murderer. 'What do you know about it?' he said. 'You've never known what love is. You've never loved anybody in your life. Except yourself.'

Ennis kept his temper. The grief-demented must be humoured. 'I think I know a little about it,' he said. 'I'm sorry, just the same. What was the trouble?'

'It was all the doctor's fault. Whooping cough. He never looked after him properly. And Muir wouldn't let me go home. Things might have been different if I'd been there.' The sad eyes looked unseeingly at the bay, empty of shipping.

'But, you know,' Ennis ventured, 'it isn't as though you'd ever seen him. I mean, it's easier for you than for her.'

Bayley turned on Ennis again. 'Death,' he said. 'Love. You don't know what death is and you don't know what love is. It would do you good,' pronounced Bayley, 'to learn what death is like, the death of someone you love. Oh, oh, my little boy.' He wiped his eyes with a grubby handkerchief taken from his field-dressing pocket. 'I try hard,' he said. 'I try and think about my work, but it doesn't help much. I've been very lonely up there with the Barsets. It's not at all as I thought it was going to be. The sergeant-majors don't treat me as one of themselves. So I spend all my time in my workshop, making things.'

'What kind of things?'

"Oh, toys. Dolls. And a play-pen.'

'To take home?'

'Yes. For the children. We shall really get down to it when I get home, Doris and me. That was only like a false start.' Bayley was already throwing off grief's cheap rags. 'We're both young. We can have a lot. And we love each other.' He smirked in triumph at Ennis. 'We know the meaning of that word.'

'But I'm sorry, just the same. It was a pity.'

'Yes. I'm making dolls with jointed limbs. The men are keen on that, too. We might start some puppetry soon. Lots of them, all dangling about on strings.'

'I've got to go now. Come and have a drink sometime in the Engineers' Mess.'

'I don't drink much now. Thanks all the same.' And Bayley turned his eyes to the sea, Doris, love, home.

Mr Withers welcomed Ennis with tea and loud affability. He said, 'I don't suppose you'll feel much like discussing that horrible business, my dear boy.'

'I'm sorry it happened,' said Ennis. 'For your sake as well as mine. It must have made you look a bit foolish.'

'It was unfortunate,' said Mr Withers, pouring the tea. 'I had sent off my quarterly report. I had anticipated a little. I had said that the concert had already taken place. It was only a matter of a few days, you see.'

'Nobody will know,' said Ennis. 'Nobody will bother.'

'The whole business was most unfortunate.'

'Perhaps,' said Ennis, 'when I'm out of the Army you'll be able to rely on me a little more. Though, of course, I can't really be blamed for what happened.'

'Yes, yes, yes.' Mr Withers seemed rather embarrassed.

'You mean you think I *can* be blamed?'

'No, no, what I meant was that the whole thing was most unfortunate. And, my dear Ennis, you'd put so much work into it. You'd worked really hard. Not only for the concert, of course. It's a pity it's all got to end.'

'What's all got to end?'

'You know, my dear boy, I had great hopes of your coming to work for us. I thought we might have got on so well together.' He gave Ennis a meaning look. 'But, I'm afraid, the hopes of both of us have just been rudely dashed.'

'Oh,' said Ennis, 'you mean I don't get the job?'

'I forwarded your application to headquarters in London, together with my own strong recommendation.' Mr Withers fanned himself with fanning ribs of Chinese ivory, paper-delicate. A sweet subtlety of expensive hair oil was wafted towards Ennis. 'They didn't,' said Mr Withers, 'react quite as I expected.'

'You mean,' said Ennis, 'that *I* didn't react quite as you expected.'

'It's a bitter disappointment to me,' said Mr Withers. 'I felt we were going to get on so well, especially when we knew each other better.' He poured out more tea for Ennis. 'The whole thing's quite inexplicable, my dear boy,' he said. 'Except, of course, for your school. I think that just might have had something to do with it.'

'I don't see that. After all, Cambridge –'

'I know, it's absurd, my dear Ennis. It would have made, one feels, just that difference. They're so terribly keen on a good school background. They're sending out, I believe, an old Wykehamist. Please understand I had nothing to do with it. He's probably not a patch on you, my dear boy. But what can one do? One's hands are completely tied.'

'My real trouble, I suppose,' said Ennis, 'is that I'm incapable of love.'

'Why ever should you say that, my dear Ennis? You've put so much into your work here. I'm sorry you won't be carrying on with it. I'll miss you a great deal.'

'But love is the big thing, isn't it?' said Ennis. '*Amor vincit omnia.* Thank you for everything, Mr Withers. I'd better be on my way.'

Mr Withers took a pinch of snuff from an exquisitely chased eighteenth-century box, with grace, elegant in white. He said nothing. Ennis escaped quickly from the civilised sanctuary. There was hope left, of course. There was always hope.

11

Major Muir had to go to the War Office for a conference and, it was whispered, to collect pips to add to his crowns. In the clear light of a Mediterranean autumn day they watched the silver aircraft ascend into heaven. But he left aspects of his soul behind. Also, he had promised, there was no fear of his not returning.

Captain Appleyard was now in charge. 'It would be a good thing,' he had once suggested, 'if we could all start the day together, in prayer and song, dedicating ourselves, as it were, to the tasks that lie before us.' So now, after breakfast, every morning, the instructors paraded in the ballroom of the Winter Gardens. Captain Appleyard would appear, imagining himself in the flowing senatorial robes of a Master of Arts, thin legs below the dark gown, and intone a hymn number. It had been suggested that Ennis should play the accompaniments to the hymns.

'You're the obvious choice, Richard. You're our musician. You'll do that, won't you?'

'You call this a non-sectarian service, but this hymn book looks suspiciously like Ancient and Modern.'

'Well, they're non-sectarian hymns, Richard, sung by all Christians.'

'They're not sung in my Church.'

'Aren't they? Still, we're all singing in praise of the same God, you know.'

'I disagree.'

'Now I think you're just being awkward, Richard. You're almost making me order you to play.'

'You know as well as I do, sir, that you can't do that.'

'Can't I? Oh, dear. Well, I shall just have to ask somebody else, shan't I?' And he went off huffily.

Ennis abstained from the service on conscientious grounds. But he had to wait outside the ballroom doors till Captain Appleyard had finished his prayers and then attend the secular part of the assembly. This was partly routine – standards of personal cleanliness in the Garrison regrettably falling; caps F.S. to be exchanged for berets; trips over the frontier to be limited owing to danger of V.D., and so on – but Captain Appleyard never failed to end with some pious exhortation designed to fill the breasts of his instructors with an urge to work yet harder, to remember their high mission, to see themselves as holy bearers of light.

'I want you all to remember, while our Major is away, that he is in spirit still with you, even, in a sense, watching you. He has never betrayed you – do not you betray him.' So the steady deification went on.

When the instructors had been dismissed, Captain Appleyard had a word with the prefects. 'Mr Fazackerly,' he said once to the stuttering hefty regular, 'some of these classrooms would be happier places to work in if the walls were decorated with appropriate designs, murals and so on. Do you think the instructors might be persuaded to do something about it?'

'Some of them are very b-b-b-burr, sair,' agreed Warrant Officer Fazackerly.

'Leave it to them, I think. Give them a little scope. They may quite enjoy doing it.'

So the bewildered technical staff endeavoured to rise above the aesthetic level of bosomy callipygous pin-ups. With them the scheme was a failure. But Ennis, Julian, and Quartermain all thought it an excellent idea. In the classroom allotted to him, Ennis covered a whole wall with a crayoned representation of the Rock, above which a large octopus crouched, tentacles extended to every cranny. The face of the beast was recognisably that of Major Muir. On the other available wall he painted Muir as Thor, fig-leaved, brandishing a thunderbolt. Captain Appleyard was dubious about these frescoes.

'Surely,' he said, 'there's a certain element of satire in them.'

'Not at all, sir,' said Ennis. 'As you yourself undoubtedly know, the octopus has always, in the folklore of Southern peoples, been a father totem. This symbolises the paternal solicitude which our Major has for the intellectual welfare of the Garrison. As for the other – well, is he not the all-powerful, the all-fruitful, the rain-sender, the maker of water?'

'I beg your pardon?'

'He makes the barren places fertile, sir. The water of the spirit, you know.'

'Yes. Yes. I think this is perhaps going a little too far. I'm not quite sure whether the Major will see it like that. I'm not quite sure whether this was a good idea at all.'

'We're all agreed that it's an excellent idea, sir. Sergeant Agate is very clever with the brush. He's been working on a theological motif, too, sir. It's really most attractive.'

Julian had in fact executed, in a charming rococo style, a series of small panels dealing with the loves of Zeus. The god was depicted as descending on Leda, Danae, Europa. The face of Muir crowned the body of the swan, the huge frame of the bull, and glinted through the shower of gold. In each case the copulation was presented in frank detail, but any suggestion of the pornographic (though in the strict etymological sense the paintings were all of that) was mitigated by the pennant labels attached to the ladies: Art, Science, Technology.

'Rather sweet, don't you think, sir?' beamed Julian. 'So traditional this use of allegory, old-fashioned you might almost say, but I think it comes off, sir, don't you?'

'Will it come off?' asked Captain Appleyard, anxiety growing in his pale blue eyes.

'Come off, sir?' screamed Julian. 'After all this work? It was your idea, sir, remember that. To think of the labour that's gone into our efforts. And poor Sergeant Quartermain has done a *beautiful* mural, too. The Creation of the World, with the Major saying, "Let there be light." I hope you're not changing your mind about the whole idea, sir?' said Julian, softly, threateningly.

'I don't know, I don't know,' breathed Captain Appleyard. 'I thought it would be such a surprise for him, too.'

'It will be, sir,' said Ennis. 'You can be quite sure of that.'

But the work was wasted. Denimed men with whitewash buckets restored the classrooms to their former inoffensive drabness. A great opportunity, it was felt, had been missed by Captain Appleyard.

One morning he dangled coyly over the heads of his torpid congregation kingly crowns, august coats-of-arms. 'Promotion for some of you,' he said archly. 'Mr Williams and Mr Bayley will be going home soon. The Major watches you all the time he is away, remember. Work gets its reward. Work hard, chaps, and these things shall be added unto you. Unto two of you, anyway.'

What caused a genuine shudder, worse than could have been occasioned by any hell-fire preaching at these morning services, was the announcement about P.T. 'We must keep ourselves fit,' said Captain Appleyard. 'It is fatally easy to become sluggish in body, and that makes us sluggish in mind. There is a lot of quite unjustifiable discontent brewing now in the Garrison, and what could be a better means of killing it – or, better still, preventing it from coming to birth – than physical exercise? When our bodies are active we do not brood or make ourselves miserable over silly things. We shall all be going home sooner or later, so why should we not be content in the time that is left to us here, instead of brooding and grumbling? Plenty of P.T. and games will help us to look at life with a less jaundiced eye. And surely –' Here he gleamed coyly. '– Surely we all want to go home with healthy bodies? Our wives expect it, you know.'

Our wives expect it, do they? Still keeping his eye firmly on what more than a fit body his wife expected, Ennis arranged an appointment with the Head of Civilian Educational Services. Dr Bradshaw, a gaunt and intellectual man, was rather encouraging. He said:

'I think there might well be a place for you here. The fact that you are a Catholic helps, of course. I take it you are a good Catholic?'

'Oh, yes,' said Ennis.

'I need an assistant,' said Dr Bradshaw. 'I need somebody who will be able to relieve me of the work of organising supplies, who can arrange courses and do a certain amount of school inspection.

Evacuation hit the colony very hard, as you know. Why, there are children here who have forgotten any English they ever knew, and some who were too young ever to learn any at all. The ignorance of most is abysmal. And when we consider the indifferent teacher material we have in the colony, well – Yes, you must be definitely considered. I shall speak to the Director tomorrow.'

Ennis felt elated. He could now write to Laurel and tell her that everything was fixed. There was the problem of accommodation, of course, which was terribly short, but – But Laurel got a letter in first. It arrived, in fact, on the day of his interview with Dr Bradshaw. It was an airmail letter. It said:

My dear Richard,
Rather an astonishing thing happened the other day. I was having a drink after work with Roland Lydgate who, as you know, is a captain in your mob. We were sitting in the upstairs bar of the Café Royal and another officer came in who Roland knew. He introduced me, and it turned out to be your Major! Well, this was quite a surprise. He was very different from what I expected, and we got on quite well. In fact, as we had *you* in common, he arranged that we should have a good long talk so he invited me to have dinner with him. Despite his being a bit of a cripple – but then Byron was too, wasn't he? – he is really a good-looking man, with lovely eyes. He has done very well too to work his way up in the way that he has done. Anyway, he astonished me by saying that he really has a very high regard for your abilities, but it pained him to think that you didn't use them as you should. He said that you could have been an officer now if you'd only put your back into things and not fooled around. Those were his words. What did he mean by that? He wouldn't say too much. Have you been fooling around? I have, as you know, no objection to your taking a girl to the pictures now and then, but I got the impression from your Major that something a bit more serious has been going on. If this is so, why haven't you told me? I thought there were to be no secrets between us. He said he would have promoted

you ages ago if you'd paid more attention to your work. This is all very disturbing. Be honest with me. I've always been honest with you. I'll be honest with you now and say that I did let him take me home, and I thought it might help you a little if I didn't push him off too much. Write at once now, for I am *really* disturbed and annoyed with you. Love from Laurel.

Well, thought Ennis, was it really so terrible to be cuckolded or certainly half-horned by a god? It was in the nature of things that this should happen, foreseeable in the carpet's pattern. He lit a cigarette, lying on his bed, the still rich but weakening sun flooding the room, the flies buzzing, the motes dancing madly in the beam. He sat up, found his pen – its nib ruined with too much music – and an airmail letter form. He wrote:

Dearest,

Muir is a bigger rogue and liar than you'd think. If you prefer to believe him rather than me that's just too bad. I told you before – though I wonder now how much the censor left in – that he's formed what seems to be a quite unreasonable dislike and distrust of me. He told me that he'd never consider me for promotion, and I left it at that. If you want me to crawl to him, well, I suppose I could, but it's a little too late to do that. Besides, I have some news which may please you, if you're still capable of being pleased with anything connected with me. It looks very much as if I'm going to get a job with the civilian education people. The pay's not all that much, but I think the prospects are all right. I'll tell you more when I have more news.

As for the other thing that Muir's been hinting at, well, honestly, the whole thing's absurd. I gave music lessons to a Mrs Gomez, a widow, but now once more a respectable married woman who lives in Spain and whom I no longer see at all. It was quite innocent, but Muir, touchy about the possible breath of scandal injuring his ambitions, read more into it than he ought to have done. We were friendly, but only friendly. I never mentioned it because I didn't think you'd be interested. I've been really ridiculously faithful – sexually my timber is so dry that the merest spark would set it off – and I'll remain faithful till I see you again. It's you I love, darling – please believe that. I will write again soon. Your loving husband, Richard.

Little Juanito was hovering round the billet, leaning in at the open window, as dirty as ever but, as Julian was constrained to admit, awfully sweet. 'Who you write letter?' he asked.

'To my wife,' said Richard. 'Take it along and post it.' He handed over the limp blue missive, also a gift of sixpence.

'What you write in letter?' asked the knowing urchin. 'You write true or not true?'

'That's no business of yours,' said Ennis. And then, 'You know billet my boss? Big boss, boss with crown on shoulder?'

'*Yo sé.*'

'He come back soon. You go and make one hell of a mess of his billet. Set fire to blankets, break windows. I give you half a crown.'

'Oh, bloody hell, no. *Hombre*, I get bloody dead if I do that.'

'You can't trust anyone,' sighed Ennis.

12

He stood, his lecture finished, high up on the Rock, watching the apes in their isolated sanctuary. His gloved hands held the motorcycle bars, his head sweated inside its helmet. (They all had motorcycles now, a further stage in the mechanisation of Muir's army.) The apes were soothing to watch. Their pattern of life was simple, their language and gestures unambiguous, their inhibitions few. A heavy-dugged mother ape was extracting scurf from the scant fur of a mewling youngster; the patriarch of the tribe masturbated with no sign of enjoyment; the younger apes, with squeals and snarls, copulated, changing partners periodically in a lumbering dance. It was a good life, even though they no longer had the freedom of the city's shops, the small thrills of terrorisation. They had their regimental numbers and their rations, and their only duty was to be fruitful, to bless and protect the Rock with their kind *in saecula saeculorum.*

'I could watch them for hours, couldn't you?' said a woman's voice behind him. Ennis turned, and his heart failed for a moment. Yellow hair, straight slimness, wide mouth. He checked himself, about to cry her name. Now he could explain the mirage at the piano recital, could exorcise the small nagging phantom. 'I heard you play once,' she said. 'I think it was you, wasn't it?' She frowned an instant, peering. 'Yes, it was you. It seemed such a pity about the concert.'

'Yes.' She was bare-legged, sandalled, in a simple summer dress. 'It *was* a pity. You'll forgive my starting just then. I thought you were somebody else, somebody who couldn't possibly be here,' said

Ennis, taking off his helmet and running a hand through his wet hair.

'Oh.' It was difficult, in the harsh light of the upper Rock air, to see the colour of her eyes. 'I liked your recital,' she said. 'I'm sorry I had to leave before the end. I had to get back to the Wrennery, you see.'

'Of course.' He dealt the next banality. 'You like it here?'

'I hardly know. I've not been here very long. I like to walk around, you know. Though there doesn't seem to be very much to see, does there?'

He felt the inevitable veteran orange-sucker's desire to show off the Rock, a relative he did not like but must not be disparaged before strangers. 'Oh, you'd be surprised at the flowers that grow here. It heaves with narcissus in spring.'

'I'm not greatly interested in flowers. I like music, though. I wanted to discuss your piece with you, the sonata you played.'

'Oh, that was nothing.' Come now, no false modesty. 'What I mean is, I wrote it some years ago. It isn't the sort of thing I'd want to write now. I think very little of it, as a matter of fact.'

'Why did you play it then?' Laurel's trick of the disconcerting ego-puncturing shaft. 'I liked it very much, but I'm only a listener. It seemed quite new and original, but very violent. Or when it wasn't violent it was sad. Were you trying to express something, you know, something that had happened to you?'

People, thought Ennis, are never content to take the work of art as it is. They always want to know what it's *about*, especially when they're women. Still – 'Well, you see,' he said, 'it doesn't quite work that way. You don't create anything with any real conscious intention. Your unconscious throws up a theme and a faint glimmering of its possibilities, then you get another theme, or even a whole crowd of them, and you're being more or less ordered to get down to work. Then you're so concerned with the labour of hammering the work out that you haven't time to think about expressing emotions and ideas and so on.'

'Yes.' She looked out over the bay, shrunken below them. 'Of course, I know nothing about the actual writing of music.'

'Do you play an instrument?'

'Well, no. I had piano lessons, but that was a long time ago. At school. But I do try to create something. I write a little verse.'

'And isn't it the same there? I mean, aren't you concerned primarily with the business of finding the right word or rhythm, letting the meaning take care of itself?'

'I don't know. I hadn't really thought about it.'

It was hard to tell her age. A slight darkness under her eyes might mean anything. Her body had lost the jaunty sinuousness of extreme youth: it had the slight suggestion of rigidity, a very slight suggestion, that Ennis always associated with virginity protracted a little too long. Yet there was grace there. She moved her arms in odd quick gestures of emphasis when speaking. Her hands were small, the fingers rather stumpy, but the continuum from hand to wrist to arm was smooth and beautifully turned. The resemblance to Laurel, fading somewhat now as he became used to her, yet shot out from her face in unexpected flashes – on a particular shaping of the lips for a sound, and now in the rather wry smile.

'I told you that about the verse as though I was proud of it. I'm not really. It's awful stuff, but – oh, you know, sometimes I feel I've got to try and set something down, keep it there for good, fix it. Things pass so quickly.'

'Yes,' said Ennis. 'Look, we're talking very seriously, but I don't even know your name. Not that it matters, of course, but you know mine, I think. At least you seemed to show that you do.'

'I do know. Sergeant Ennis – Richard Ennis on those posters. Mine's Grantham, Lavinia Grantham, Leading Wren Lavinia Grantham.'

Ennis gravely shook her hand. Meanwhile the apes shamelessly gibbered and moved like tireless machines their lascivious haunches. For some reason, now noticing them again, Ennis heard the opening lines of *De Rerum Natura* spilling through his brain in soft fragments: '– *Te quoniam genus omne animantum concipitur* –' Was that right? A quick memory of the smell of his sixth-form days dived up weakly towards the light, vanished.

'This is a great pleasure,' said Ennis. 'Look, I don't know whether you propose going down into town or not. I must, I'm afraid.

Would you care to ride pillion? This road's terribly hard on the shoes.'

'I'd vaguely thought of getting some tea somewhere. That would be kind.' And so she got up behind him; her hands rested lightly on his ribs; he could feel their touch through the thin khaki drill. He coasted down the steep road to the first bend, down the next hill to the next bend, the bay coming slowly up to meet them. The wind of the free-wheel passage killed his words.

'What did you say?'

'You must show me some of your poetry –' They sped down, bend after bend, soon coming to the yellow close-set houses, noiselessly entering the town that was waking up for the evening.

'If you could drop me here –'

'We must continue our talk about aesthetics,' said Ennis. 'And I should like to see some of the things you've written.'

'That would be nice. The talk, I mean. I don't think you'd really like my stuff.' She was rather off-hand, showed now, in the warm garlic-smelling passage where he dropped her, that cool aseptic English charm which, he always thought, was like a clear note from which all the harmonics had been eliminated. 'Thank you for the lift,' she said. He waved a gauntleted hand as he kicked the engine to life; then, making for the motor-cycle park at the foot of Castle Steps, he saw her after-image turn into the stock picture of Laurel which his mind wore like a medallion.

Lying in bed that night, he felt desire stir in his tired body. It was undifferentiated desire; voluptuously, fragments of his body's memories of women coalesced, separated again. As always now, when he let himself bathe masochistically in the almost intolerable heat of the vision of climax, it was Concepción who appeared, as at a magical invocation. But this new one hovered somewhere above, outside, suggesting a new kind of appetite and satisfaction of appetite, piquantly taunting in an image that, because it was almost that of his wife, had a peculiar and quite irrational aura of sin. He escaped into sleep.

He looked for Lavinia Grantham in the next few days, casually, in the streets and shops, in the gilded restaurant where he drank coffee with Julian, half-hoping not to see her, fearful and excited at the dangerous prospect which it would be so prudent to shun. When he went up to lecture to the Italian prisoners in the Detention Barracks on Windmill Hill, he kept looking, with a faster pulse, at the fastness of the Wrennery, wondering if she would appear among the trim white summer uniforms. But he knew that, in this cramped community, he was bound to see her again soon.

It was not, however, for another week that she re-appeared in Ennis's orbit. Ennis, on Saturday afternoon Main Street, was in the Rock's sole bookshop, leafing through the few new volumes of interest – *Animal Farm*, *Four Quartets*, *The Unquiet Grave*, *Brideshead Revisited* – when he saw her. She was buying notepaper, dressed in the simple frock and sandals of their first meeting near the summit, and again this almost perverse likeness to Laurel flashed out as she greeted him. It was, he thought, as if some devil had tried to take on Laurel's likeness for the purpose of leading him to some region of easy temptation: something was subtly wrong with the impersonation, he felt.

'I've been carrying these about for days,' she said. 'You did say you wanted to see some of them. I thought at first of dropping them into your office, but then I knew we were bound to run into each other.' She handed Ennis a little sheaf of manuscript. He caught a glimpse of bold blue ink, firm rather masculine writing, unlike Laurel's.

'Couldn't we discuss these now, somewhere?' asked Ennis. 'Perhaps you'd like some tea?'

'I must get back. Thanks all the same.'

'Can I get in touch with you?' asked Ennis. 'Am I allowed to phone? What I was going to suggest,' he said quickly, having just thought of it, 'was perhaps our having dinner together. Perhaps some day next week. I'll have had time to read them. I'll be able to tell you properly what I think.'

'All right.' She looked at him with an appraising steadiness, unexpected, irrelevant in the context of a proposed discussion of poetry. 'What evening?'

'Wednesday? Would that be all right? Unfortunately, I work most other evenings.'

'I'm not sure. I'll send you a note.'

'Please do.'

She was travelling back up the hill in a duty truck. He walked with her to the rendezvous, more aware now of her tallness, her slim, cool, almost glacial Englishry. To read the poems, he hoped, would lead him to the fire that must lie beneath all this, would suggest the essence that, though perhaps carefully encased in layer after layer, he knew, since being married to Laurel, must at length yield to probing fingers. As the truck started off and she gave her rather wry smile of valediction, he thought of Concepción by contrast. His body had always responded to the mere sight of her, in the street, in the stuffy drawing-room where he had given his lessons, been aware of her, manifested desire in a slight sweat, a twitching of the hands, a constriction of the larynx. But with this Lavinia Grantham desire presented itself, as it were, in the form of a geometrical proposition that must ultimately be reached only after working through the rest of the book: it was a conceptual thing.

He took the poems to a small tea shop, empty save for a couple of R.A.M.C. privates talking about the meaning of life, earnest, moustached, pipe-smoking. He ordered a glass of coffee from the proud Andalusian beauty who blasted garlic at him, then, not knowing at all what to expect, began to read through the sheaf of verse. The poems were all very short.

To Endymion

The moon awaits your sleeping: fear to be kissed.
Tepid her light unblenching, but will twist
Your features to strange shapes; though blind, those beams
Get in the mind's slime monsters for dreams.

'Sergeant Ennis.' The voice was familiar. He looked up impatiently to see Barasi waddling into the shop from behind the counter. He wore white which, through its crispness, suggested the defilement of a day's sweat; the thick glasses threw at Ennis a swift image of the passing figures of the street.

'Mr Barasi. I'd no idea you frequented such lowly places of refreshment.'

Barasi sat down at the round marble table, shrugging slightly. 'Business,' he said. 'I must be about to look at the accounts now and then. What little money I possess lies in these small ventures mainly.'

Ennis was able to ask it without much of a tremor. 'Your wife is well? You had a pleasant honeymoon?'

He smiled. 'Most pleasant. Madrid was at its best. I spent much money, but with no regrets. We had, I think, as good a honeymoon as it is possible to have. I, of course, am old and she is still young.'

'And how is – Mrs Barasi? Or should I say Señora Barasi?'

'She is well occupied. My house is large, I have many servants, she has much to do. Please, you must think of her as *Mrs* Barasi. Though we live across the frontier we are, nevertheless, British subjects. She is very well and – I may tell you as a friend, I think – she has made me very happy.'

'She is a good wife?'

'Yes, yes, but in another way she has made me very happy. I have always wanted children. There is the business; I shall not live for ever. She is to give me a child. A son, I hope.'

'That's good news,' said Ennis. 'I do hope it is a son.'

'Yes, yes. You must come sometime and see us.'

'That's very kind,' Ennis's eyes strayed down to the sheet on his knee:

She was all
Brittle crystal.
Her hands
Silver silk over steel –

'Well, Sergeant Ennis,' said Barasi, 'you will be going home soon. You will be glad to see your own wife again.'

Her hair harvested
Sheaves shed by summer,
Her grace the flash of the flesh
Of a river swimmer –

'Yes,' said Ennis. 'It's been a long time.'
'A long time, yes. War is a terrible thing.'

That was not nature's good,
Who nothing understands.
Horrible now she should
Use to her own ends.

'Now,' said Barasi, 'I must go. There is always much to see to.' He leaned over Ennis and, with an unexpected and puzzling earnestness, said, 'Do be careful. Do keep out of harm's way.' And then he was gone, waddling swiftly out of the dark shop into the light and colour of Main Street.

13

'And this I like, too,' said Ennis, passing back to her the page of heavy writing. She read it through coolly, he deciphered meanwhile the upside-down lines:

The stoat's cry tears long slivers of the night,
And, luminous, the owl in the rustling fruit
Draws up the sweating lovers by the root;
They warm in water-blankets worlds of fright –

They had been served with a mixed grill by a creased brown waiter; there were golden olive-oil-fried potato slices in a silver dish. Ennis poured glasses of the coarse wine that tasted of iron, blood, earth. 'It would be stupid of me to ask about the personal meaning,' he said. Her yellow hair, sheaves shed by summer, was irradiated by the last of the sun as she bent over her poem. She put into her handbag the blue-written sheets, not replying yet nor looking at him even, and began to eat with a sea-air appetite.

'Please,' he continued, 'I don't mean that it was stupid of *you* to ask what you did about my music; don't think that. But one can't help being interested in the reasons for your writing this verse. In any case, poetry is much more direct; it relates to particular feelings, particular experiences, doesn't it? You can't say that about music.'

'Don't you think you ought to eat your mixed grill?' she said. 'It's getting cold.'

'Yes.' Chidden thus, he trisected a sausage and began to chew a hot segment of the spiced near-meat. '*Salchichas* they call them here,' he said. For some reason he began to feel very happy. It was like a return to civilisation, this dining with a woman, both of them wearing civilian clothes, a bottle of red wine on the white starched cloth, the frequent silent passing of the waiters. A pity, though, that the restaurant was full of noisy troops. A shipload of G.I.s, going home from Italy, had been enjoying shore leave all day. Draped on the corners, squatting on doorsteps, flaunting their purple hearts and tight-packed bottoms through the streets, they had chewed, wolf-called the proud head-high women, sullenly eyed the Rock which, as they knew from the hand-outs, had been ordered by an American insurance company not to be taken by the enemy. Well, the British had obeyed that order. Now the callow Nordic blonds, the blue-jowled Jews, the Bohunks and Polacks lounged at the restaurant tables, calling for meatballs and ketchup.

'Do they?' Her eyes were grey in this light. 'You know Spanish well?' she added, eating more slowly now, the edge off her service-woman's appetite.

'A little.' Ennis cut a small square of grilled ham. 'I had some lessons.' He began to chew. 'I'll teach you if you like.'

'And who taught *you*?' asked Lavinia. She served herself the last of the fried potatoes, saying, 'One of the local women, I suppose.' Ennis couldn't quite understand the slight flavour of malice.

'Yes,' he said. 'How did you guess? There's nothing wrong with that, surely?' He looked at her, puzzled, holding his knife and fork like handlebars.

'Are you really interested in my poetry?' asked Lavinia. 'Are you being honest when you say that you think it's good?'

'I am, really.' Ennis cut and pronged the last inch of sausage. 'I don't understand when you question that. But,' he said, looking up at the aureole, the grey eyes, 'I'm interested in the poet, too.'

'Oh.' A very English diphthong, close, unrounded.

'I mean,' he said quickly, 'naturally one wants to know what motivates the artist, especially if one happens to be an artist oneself. I want to know what makes the artist tick.'

'Especially if it's a woman.'

'Why especially so? All artists are hermaphrodites.'

'Does your wife like being married to a hermaphrodite?'

Ennis was now free of his plate, fork, knife. He looked at her closely, gauging, weighing. 'I just don't understand you. Have I ever mentioned a wife?'

'Was there ever any occasion to?' There were now small wrinkles of amusement round her grey eyes. 'I can assure you, I'm not in the least interested. I was just amused by the hermaphrodite idea, that's all.'

'My wife, when I have one,' said Ennis, skiing down into the lie, 'will find me sufficiently monosexual for all practical purposes. I'm sorry,' he added. 'That was in rather bad taste.'

At this moment two large American sergeants, swaying towards Ennis's table on their way out, stopped, focused their eyes on Lavinia. One of them put his arm round Ennis's shoulder, saying confidentially, 'That's a nice bit of ass you've gotten yourself, mac.'

'How's about joining the Army, beautiful?' added the other, with a flash of gold-pointed incisors. Lavinia smiled. Ennis, feeling naked of all authority in his mufti, got up and said, 'Look here –'

'Okay, okay, we was just being sociable.'

'Goddam civilians grabs all the pussy. Come on, Red. Ain't no room for fighting men.'

And, a last shot fired swayingly from the door, 'Limeys, eff 'em. Goddam corksuckers.'

Lavinia was smiling openly, dimpling, looking very young and pleased. Ennis began an embarrassed bluster: they've no right; bad manners; guests of ours, after all; uncivilised: but she cut this short, still smiling:

'I thought they were rather sweet.'

'Like the Rock-apes?'

'Well, at least they're honest and direct. They didn't ask me about the personal meaning behind my poetry.'

'That's a silly thing to say, and you know it.' The swift mood of pleasure was now completely crushed; he felt bitter and brutal. He wished he were back in the billet with Julian, in the calm epicene atmosphere where lust could be transmuted into creative energy.

Now too he began to sweat as he drank his glass of *vino rojo*, aware that she would be aware of his moist face, and becoming moister in consequence. He felt cloddish, cheap, boorish, just as he had often felt in the presence of Laurel.

'Why can't you be honest?' asked Lavinia, when the old waiter had served them with coffee. 'Why can't you say what you really think about my stuff?'

'I've said what I really think. I think it's good.'

'And supposing you didn't know the author, supposing you'd just picked up those poems by chance – anonymous, lying on the pavement or a park bench?'

Ennis said nothing for the moment. He saw, in the far corner of the now emptying restaurant, Captain Dance sitting with coffee and a book. Priestley, probably. Beethoven's Ninth evoking memories of suet puddings, hot sun on the tarred Leeds road, Ranji in to bat.

'All right.' He lit her cigarette and then his own. 'I do feel that a work of art can be interesting because it may lead to discovery of a personality. I think that reading somebody's poem can be a sort of exploration of the poet. The poems intrigued me. They gave hints as to what might lie behind a very decorative exterior. I want to know you better.'

'In what way? Like those Americans?'

What was the right answer to that? 'No, damn it, you can't compartmentalise. This atomisation of personality is the modern heresy. You're many things, a complex organism, brain, body, heart, and when I say "you" I mean, I think, everything that you mean by it.'

She smiled at him. 'You find it very hard to be honest, don't you? You're so dishonest with yourself it's become a habit. I really think that you believe everything you're saying.'

Captain Appleyard came in, graceful in service-dress, carrying with grace, like some haughty Tudor steward, his staff of office. Captain Dance showed his wet teeth in greeting, but Captain Appleyard came first to Ennis's table, bestowing on Lavinia a courtly bow. 'Positively a conference of the Muses,' he said. 'How are you, Lavinia? We missed you at the Poetry Circle tonight. A very dull talk by Aircraftman Bickerstaff on the Metaphysical Poets, but you would have enlivened the discussion. You, Richard, you should come sometimes, you know.'

'We don't get all that much spare time,' said Ennis gruffly.

'And a very good thing, too,' carolled Captain Appleyard. 'Occupation keeps us happy. Which reminds me. The Major arrives by boat tomorrow. But no longer the Major, of course.' He giggled. 'I must get into the habit of calling him Colonel. I think he will be pleased at the way things have been going in his absence, don't you? And also these new P.T. people are coming, I believe. No more spare time, and no more spare tyres.' He laughed in a girlish cascade; an American with a simian forehead looked up from his meatballs to growl something about 'fairies'. Captain Appleyard tripped over to his colleague's table.

Ennis and Lavinia found the bright street alive with American troops, many bibulous, some quarrelsome, some seething with a fortnight's continence. Military police, British and American, patrolled warily. Inspector McKeogh, of the civil force, shepherded home a tiny tradesman and his creamy wife. Plaintively the small staggering G.I. group, thwarted, called after them:

'Gee, I offered her ten dollars. That's enough, ain't it?'

'Yeah, you hear that, bud? We was willing to pay.'

The proprietor of a beer hall, helped by his waiters, was ruefully sweeping up a mess of broken window. A Filipino lieutenant, who had gone berserk, was fighting with mad teeth against the strong restraining arms of brother officers. A scream from the ladies of the orchestra across the street, the thud of a falling big drum, the harsh thwack of military truncheons was background to the howled song of the swaying gang who kept to the road, not heeding the slapped metal warnings of cars trying to pass. Ennis, his heart faster with apprehension, took Lavinia's bare arm protectively.

'Don't worry about me,' she said. 'I'm not frightened.' But she suffered his embrace of her arm. They passed the large N.A.A.F.I. by South Gate, where bitter quarrels between the allies were proceeding.

'Gee, I didn't say nothing wrong.'

'Say it again. Go on, say it!'

'I only said if your beer was as cheap as your women England would be a darn fine country. Ain't nothing wrong in that.'

Gorbals fighting, beer glasses crunched in faces, tables swimming in beer and blood – these they left behind, starting the steep Windmill Hill climb to her barracks. They said little as they walked, and Ennis was pleased to notice that she, too, breathed more heavily as they trudged up the long road. This made her seem vulnerable. He now firmly placed his arm round her waist. It was not repulsed, but she did not yield to it, she gave no encouragement. Soon the arm felt heavy, useless, boorish, and with something like irritation he dropped it. What should he do at the top of the hill? He realised that he never knew what to do; he always chose the wrong time, never the right, knowing no mean between importunity and forwardness.

They reached the breezy summit, breathing deeply, looking at the lights that stretched below them, all across the bay, hearing the faint gnat-noise of the crowds so far down. Ennis faced a double vertigo, saying:

'Well. Thank you for having dinner with me. I enjoyed it so much. It was so pleasant to be able to talk to a civilised person again.'

'I'm not so civilised,' she said. 'Thank *you*.'

'We must do it again sometime. Soon.'

'Yes. That would be nice.' She held out her hand. Ennis took it. His heart thumping from the climb, from her nearness, from the awful daring, he kissed the warm hand. Then impulsively he clasped her to him and sought and found her lips. She didn't struggle; she remained slack, inert. She accepted the kiss, it seemed to him, dispassionately. Her quick breathing was due to the climb, and his own lips had to leave hers too soon, his blood crying for air. But he kissed her again, and now his blood began to flow downwards, feeding a speedy tumescence. She again took his kiss gravely, with some slight response, but all the time as if she were standing outside, considering the sensation, material for a minor poem.

'I must go in now. It's late.'

'Don't.' He kissed her again, roughly, careless of his evening's growth of beard.

'No.' She broke away. 'Mother will be annoyed if she sees us.'

'Mother?'

'The Queen Wren. Please let me go.'

Ennis obeyed. 'When can I see you again? When are you free? Tomorrow?'

'No. I don't know. I'll let you know sometime.' He grabbed her again. 'Let me go. I *must* go in.'

'Let me kiss you again. *Please*, Lavinia.'

She broke away and ran into the trim barracks without looking back. Ennis felt a brutal mixture of triumph and disappointment as he stood there for a moment. Then he lit a cigarette. Then, with the musical themes that this sort of contact, any sort of conflict, always engendered running through his head, already being considered by him, put into place, heard on various instruments, suggesting form and development, he began the quicker descent to the town.

The streets now were quieter. Only here and there, still to be poked out of their holes by the M.P.s, stragglers from the American troopship lingered. Vows of maudlin friendship were being exchanged with British soldiers, an abortive fight or two glowed and hissed, amorous whispers came from dark shop doorways. The bars were shut; caps, blood, garments, bottles, scattered on the lamplit road, laid a feeble trail towards the North Mole, where the liberty boat waited. Walking towards his billet, Ennis, lost in a mist of thought, lust, composition, started and stiffened to hear an American voice.

'Pardon me, sir.' He was either a lieutenant or a captain, the two small bars on each shoulder not yielding their colour in this lamplight, young, dark, moustached, sober, soft-toned. 'Do you happen to know if there's any place where I could still grab me a drink?'

'Well –' Ennis felt like a drink himself. He knew a little club in Irish Town. He was not a member, but he was not normally unwelcome there.

'I certainly could use one,' said the American. 'Been kind of a tough evening.'

'Are you in the Military Police?' asked Ennis.

'That's right. Got an hour to wait before the last boat picks up the drunks and corpses. Just handed over to my sergeant.'

'Come along,' said Ennis. 'It isn't far from here. I could use one myself.'

'That's fine. Captain Mendoza's the name.'

'Sergeant Ennis.'

'Glad to know you, Sergeant.'

Ennis knocked at the small door gently, once and then again. Soon, the door half-opened, a bulky silhouette peered out.

'*Quién?*'

'*Soy yo, el sargento inglés, con un amigo americano. No borachos.*'

'You're telling me we're not drunk,' said Captain Mendoza. 'At least, *I'm* far far far from being drunk.'

'You speak Spanish?' said Ennis.

'I *am* Spanish.' Frank, the fat steward, known to many local women as '*El Burro*', served them with gin in a room that was empty of other customers. On the walls were the inevitable pin-ups of elongated bathycolpous steatopygous houris, a febrile dream.

'And what was it like in Italy?' asked Ennis. The captain revealed himself as handsome in his dark way, upright with large eyes and a crest of crisp hair. He said:

'The usual sort of hell. Don't get me wrong: we didn't see all that much fighting. But *la pace*, as they call it, is all stinking drains, bug-ridden hovels, women selling their bodies for corned beef. Some of our men have been lousy with gonorrhea; we've left a fair number of syphilis cases behind, too. That's Europe for them.'

'You'll be glad to get home,' said Ennis. And then, frustrated, senselessly malicious, he added, 'Mom and the icebox, the colonial church with one bell, the drug-store on the corner. Aseptic America.'

'Hell, that's not it.' He drained his gin and placed their two glasses for more. 'You ever read Henry James?'

'Yes, one or two of his novels. *The Ambassadors* –'

'What's your line? What do you do out of uniform?'

'I'm a musician of sorts, a composer.'

'Hell, you should understand.' Out of his pocket he brought a new clean cellophane-wrapped packet of Camels. 'Europe's dying, all right. I majored in History. I guess I've some sort of background. Europe used to be a kind of mythical world, like Homer. Nothing counted till America, not really. Oh, we read all the books, knew we hadn't a Shakespeare or a Cervantes, but the past was kind of artificial, like something on the movies.' Ennis and he drew on their Camels. 'Now it's different. As I see it, decay is a kind of life. To keep moving, to keep living anyhow – that's better, I guess, than reaching out for a dead sort of perfection.' He gulped his gin and tonic with a desert thirst. '*Otra vez*,' he said to Frank, '*por favor*.' And then to Ennis, 'Maybe you just don't see it. The really big day's coming soon. Though I guess you ought to see it. You've a Catholic sort of face.'

'How can one tell?'

'It just sort of shines out. You are a Catholic, aren't you?'

'In a way. Lapsed. Renegade.'

'You heard of Pelagius? Morgan, his real name was. Greek and Welsh for "Old Man of the Sea". He's been called the great British heretic. He didn't hold with Original Sin.'

'I've heard of him, vaguely.'

'He was the father of the two big modern heresies – material progress as a sacred goal; the State as God Almighty.' He spoke glibly, as though perhaps he had often lectured on this subject to his men. 'One has produced Americanism, which is only a mental climate. America's not real, it's an idea, a way of looking at things. And then there's Russia, the end-product of the Socialist process. We're both the same, in a way. We both offer supra-regional goods – the icebox and the Chevrolet or the worker, standardised into an overalled abstraction at a standardised production belt. And you, my friend, are going to suffer. Work, for the night is coming. You're going to get one of us, sooner or later.' He drank his gin in a gulp. Ennis, fingering his last ten-shilling note, ordered more. He said:

'I'm a European. But there's a great deal I've admired in America. Whitman, for instance. There's nothing more stirring than that democratic vista. The world all before them, where to choose –'

'Hell, you should know better. He was a Pelagian. No, he went a bit farther back. He was a true prelapsarian, he'd never eaten of the fruit. He saw himself as Adam, and that's another aspect of Americanism you'll never understand. A lot of us haven't just rejected Sin; we just haven't reached it yet. My Sin is just the name of a cheap perfume. But it all comes to the same thing in the end, I guess – Pelagianism.'

Ennis was growing bored. Also his jangling nerves had beaten him into a desire for dead sleep. He said:

'Very interesting. You'll forgive me if I go soon. I shouldn't be out after curfew, not even in mufti. Our own M.P.s are still prowling around.'

'Curfew? But the war's over.' He slumped against the bar. 'No, I guess the war's never over.' He looked up at Ennis and said, 'Where could I get pesetas?'

'What do you want pesetas for? You're on your way home, aren't you?'

'Never mind. Hell, why not?' He spoke to himself, softly. 'I could fall overboard. Nobody would know, not at first, not with that fer-ry-load of corpses. How much of a swim is it?' he asked Ennis.

'What?'

'To round Algeciras way?'

'It has been done,' said Ennis. 'I don't recommend it.'

The captain sighed. 'I guess you're right. Ah, hell,' he said vio-lently. 'Sin. I guess Europe's the last stronghold. I shall be coming back to stay, when I've gotten things straightened out back home. But, hell, why shouldn't she stew in her own juice? Damn little tramp. Goddam little whore. My wife,' he explained in an aside. 'Bread and garlic and bad drains. Harsh red wine. And Sin.'

'Is that why you joined the Military Police?' asked Ennis. 'Because of Sin?'

'That's about it. I never expect too much, so I'm never disap-pointed.' He drained his drink and said, 'Sin is life.' And then he pulled out his wallet and extracted many dollar bills. Frank came over to look at them. 'I guess I could get a lot of pesetas for these, eh?' he said.

Ennis left him. He sought his billet, his footsteps echoing guiltily in the dark emptiness. Julian turned in his sleep and said, 'Whoring again.' Stealthily Ennis crept to his bed. That American was right, really. Right about Laurel and Lavinia and all the goddam rest of them. Still, once started one had to push on. Push on.

14

And to his crowns shall be added a glory as of stars. And to one that walketh under stars shall a crown be given. Muir came back a lieutenant-colonel, and, it was whispered, Captain Appleyard was to be made a major soon. As befitted a deity, the Colonel now hid himself in the clouds of high policy, unseen of the lesser underlings, while Appleyard, in an ecstasy of prolepsis, prepared for himself a high table before the gates of the Lord. Things were looking up.

Among the instructor-rabble, too, there were changes. W.O. Raeburn, the dipsomaniac whom Ennis had never actually met, had been posted back to the Depot. He had few regrets. He had evaded much work and drunk a steady two bottles of whisky a day. Even when in hospital (he had worn his knees down to the bone crawling back to his billet from a party at Trawler Base) a liberal supply of liquor had appeared from many sources and, when that had failed, he had found various raw but heartening spirits in the dispensary. Also, with the slow clanking of the Release Scheme, Williams, Bayley, Evans, and a shadowy number of instructors whom Ennis had never got to know, had lugged their kit and hands of green bananas aboard homeward-bound troopships. With infinite and painful slowness the garrison ascended the ladder of release group numbers, yet the gaps were always filled. Ennis had a high enough number, but he felt very much a veteran when he saw, in the teashops, scarce-bearded youths surveying the barren months ahead, their own astronomical numbers outside the scope of decent human computation.

There were new promotions, new transfers to the Corps. A

plumber W.O. 1 stalked the streets, followed by more than one sycophantic mate. Brick-dust deadened the crowns of a W.O. 2. New sergeants appeared like stripy toadstools – bank clerks, boys with matric, clock-menders, plasterer's labourers. Ennis worried little about all this: the post with the Civilian Education people was as good as confirmed, Laurel wrote more ardently than ever (a cold autumn in England) about sun, wine, sea-bathing. Also he was pre-occupied with Lavinia.

With the shifting of personnel in all the units, life in the garrison became febrile and nervous. Nothing seemed solid and permanent now, and work itself seemed futile. The hooting of the troopship in the bay, farewell parties in the N.A.A.F.I. or the mess begot a murmuring restlessness in those who had to stay behind. There was still talk of leave – PYTHON and LOLLIPOP (Lots Of Local Leave In Place Of Python) – and some men were sent on courses, but the unlucky, biting their nails on their bunks, groaned as they watched the slow sun crawl to the end of yet another mild winter day. Christmas would be here soon; they had thought they would be home by Christmas.

Occupation was the thing: so Appleyard (now at last crowned and gin-anointed) had frequently said. There were, it was true, classes in many subjects, but a lively jolting of the body's juices, which else would scowl in a poisonous sediment, was needful for all. And so, with the ship that brought back Colonel Muir, came the eupeptic athletocrats, replacements for the P.T. instructors who were leaving, but representing a great augmentation of the original establishment. Long based at Primary Training Centres and Military Hospitals in England, the new arrivals sniffed with relish the orange-laden air. One foresaw that their large chests and sinewy legs would take on a preternatural brown when the time for sunbathing came round again. They breathed a morbid fitness, infecting the atmosphere about them with a painfully delicious tang of healthy flesh.

Their leader was Regimental Sergeant-Major Instructor Turner. He was a barrel-chested slim-hipped giant, six feet four in his bare feet. Under his battledress smooth muscles purred. A boxer, wres-tler, rowing man, expert in the propulsion of balls, he was also a dancer (ballroom, Scottish, English folk, Laban) and could sing folk-lorically to his own guitar accompaniment. A professionally friendly smile, learnt on a course at Aldershot, gleamed from his empty eyes and full lips. Hyacinthine hair, clean, clipped, pale, rode above his unimpressive forehead.

He and a quartermaster-sergeant instructor became mess-mates of Julian Agate and Ennis. It was evident from the start that Turner – striding into the ante-room with a cheerful 'Who was the best billiard player before I came in?' – was going to dominate the Engineers' Mess. His loud and cheery voice gave a new taste to the morning porridge, and the orange squash he drank at the bar seemed invested with a potency far beyond wine. Julian, of course, was horrified. 'My dear,' he muttered, when Turner and his crony first marched in, 'look at all that *meat*. I shall definitely turn vegetarian.'

Ennis had foolishly pretended to take Turner's crossed swords (in soft cloth above the fighting cats) for a pair of scissors. He had asked Turner if he were perhaps the new Regimental Tailor. Turner took this well but perhaps resented it inly. Soon came a real crossing of swords. Sitting in the ante-room one day, some time before the bulk of the mess members were due to come in for lunch, Ennis was listening to Delius on the radio. The rich clotted nostalgic chords were engendering gently in him the usual response; ignoble but sumptuous, ravishing, the sorrows of the world (not *Weltschmerz*: that was a different thing altogether) lapped him (he could lie down like a tired child) like warm (and weep away this life of care) bath water. His eyes, behind their dark shells, saw the rank foliage of the Florida plantation and felt the heavy summer of an only imaginable England, a summer that was also primaverally agonising, autumn-ally sad.

Then, harshly, the sounds were changed to the loud laughter of a British factory canteen audience listening to a dialect comedian ('Ee, that tom cat of ours dooz smell. A proper pong. Ah could smell it all last Soonday in't' coostard.') Ennis had hardly noticed the entrance of Turner and his colleague, who were now choosing billiard cues. He now sat up angrily. He said:

'Excuse me. I was listening to that.'

'What, that tripe?' Conscious of fine muscles, Turner chalked his cue. The Q.M.S.I. grinned with many teeth.

'Whether,' said Ennis, 'you think it's tripe is neither here nor there. I was listening to it. I was enjoying it. You might have had the manners to ask if you could change the programme.'

The Q.M.S.I., taking his cue, guffawed briefly, covering the noise with a belch of hunger.

'Well,' said Turner, breaking the triangle of red balls, 'it's a question of what the majority wants, isn't it?' He had a cidery sort of West Country accent. 'Two to one, old man. You're outnumbered, you see. You can see that, if you know how to count. I don't want to use my rank, old man.'

Ennis, saying no more, turned the radio switch back to the Delius. A burst of applause came through. He waited till Turner had potted the black, then a red, then failed on the pink, and said: 'The question of using your rank hardly arises. In the mess we're supposed to be all equal. And if my manners were like yours I'd tell you what to do with your rank.'

'Tut tut tut tut,' clucked Turner humorously. He watched his opponent sink a colour. 'I'm not going to argue, old man. But, if you're talking about manners, how about switching the wireless back to what the majority want?'

'If you want it all that badly,' said Ennis, 'you can bloody well do it yourself.' And then, stupidly, he made a loud derisive noise. He moved, forcing himself to take his time, to the door of the anteroom. Then he heard a cue clatter down behind him, the tiger-patter of swift feet, and then he felt his arm twisted up towards his nape, a slick piece of unarmed combat. He sniffed a somehow *laundered* smell of under-arm sweat, was warmed by hot breathing. Then the pain was excruciating. 'Stop it!' he yelled. 'Stop it, you bloody fool!' He saw, in his writhing to be free, Turner smiling at the billiard table. Turner smiled:

'Let him go, Stan.' The arm was untwisted. 'Now,' said Turner, 'what about saying you're sorry?'

'Sorry,' sobbed Ennis. 'I'm not bloody sorry. You bloody brainless gorillas.' The Q.M.S.I. seemed to take this as a compliment.

He went back to his game, placidly switching back the radio from Wagner (*Die Meistersinger*) to loud community singing. Turner, sinking the yellow, said:

'All right. It doesn't matter. I don't like hard feelings. If anybody has hard feelings towards me it means I've failed. I'm sorry I switched off that tripe. No, it wasn't tripe, it was beautiful music. I didn't realise you were listening to it. I'll ask next time.' He unsighted the ball an instant and gave Ennis a professional smile. And Ennis felt a split-second's gush of gratitude and admiration, this big strong handsome man who could smash him with ease doing the big strong handsome thing, but he froze the warmth quickly and muttered, 'That's all right.' So here was another allotrope of God; the strong could afford mercy, retraction, even self-abasement.

The return to compulsory P.T. parades was a nightmare step back to childhood. Ennis's sleep was often haunted – as a respite from the spiv-God – by images of a sort of casual sauntering into a concentration camp which was school, where, still an adult, he had to submit to crouching in the cage of a child's desk, reciting infantile lessons. The way in was always so easy, but the only exit was through a tortuous labyrinth of corridors which dripped snakes and toads from the ceiling. He always woke sweating from this dream, wondering. His real school-life had not been unhappy, and the memories of its last years – the smell of furniture polish in the old library which was the Sixth-form room, the discoveries in books and the more surprising alcoves of his own mind – dripped an April dew. Now he began to realise that any reversion is evil and that what lies before the magnesium flash of 'now' stinks of corruption.

For the instructors of the Vocational and Cultural Corps there were two early morning P.T. parades every week. The war was over, and yet here was the uneasy smell of recruit days, the sick autumn smoke of Ennis's first week in the Army. Stripped of rank, they exposed their bodies to a curly sergeant in a teddy-bear tracksuit, who leaped and handsprung about to a sinister patter of cajolery. 'Come on, now,' he would cry. 'One more for me. Once again, one for Joe Stalin. Last one now, lads, just one for the King and Queen. That's it. Now, when I say "Dismiss", I want to see you turn smartly to the right, get up high high high on your toes, high as you can, then away and change. Ready?'

The knees-bend-arms-stretch routine was one which Ennis had always found difficult. Crouching in a compromise one morning, he felt the sky darken and, looking up, saw R.S.M.I. Turner looking down, high as a tower. Turner said, pleasantly:

'You look as if you're sitting on the po. Come on, sergeant, do it properly. Everybody else is managing all right.'

'I don't want to do it.'

'Naughty naughty naughty. Of course you want to do it. Let me show you.'

'I don't want to be shown.'

'Temper temper. No tantrums, now. You're on parade, remember.'

'Oh, Christ,' said Ennis, standing upright now but still looking up at Turner, 'it's so bloody childish.'

'Now, look,' said Turner, 'I'm not going to get on my high horse. You know as well as I do that this is disobeying orders. But we don't want any talk about charge sheets, do we? Of course we don't. We don't want any unpleasantness at all. All we're trying to do is make you fit and happy, and all we ask is a bit of co-operation. Come on now, let's see you smile. Have another try.'

Richard stood still for a moment, undecided, then he mentally threw the die, examined its number, and started to walk off. The sergeant-instructor called, 'Hey!' Turner waved his hand, frowning. Then he followed Ennis. 'Tell me all about it,' he appealed. 'What's on your mind? We're only trying to help.' Ennis was almost impelled to lay his head on that confident chest, to sob in a father's arms. He said, loud:

'Why the hell have we got to be organised all the time? Why has everybody got to be God? I want to be left alone.'

'It's for your own good, you know that,' said Turner. He put his huge hand on Ennis's shoulder. 'Why can't you be happy? What's the matter? Have you got something against me? Is it that music business?'

'Oh, hell, that was nothing,' Ennis said. 'It's all this. It's everything. It's all so bloody pointless.'

'All right, everything's pointless,' said Turner, tightening his grip.
'So what? We've got to soldier on, that's all. Out with it, now.
You've got a woman on your mind, old man. You're as thin as a rake.
What's the matter? Has the missis been playing away?'

'Mind your own bloody business,' said Ennis, getting into his
jacket.

'And if it's that blonde Wren,' said Turner, amiable, unruffled,
'don't think twice about her. I wouldn't touch her with my walk-
ing-stick if I were you.'

'What do you mean?' Ennis stared, mechanically buttoning his
jacket.

'She's given me the old come-hither more than once,' said Turner
without complacency. 'Anybody's meat up to a point. Up to a point,
I say. Another kind of P.T., if you know what I mean.'

'Oh,' said Ennis.

'You go off now,' said Turner, 'and get ready for breakfast. Try
and eat more. Try and put some weight on. And, for God's sake,
stop worrying. Women are just not worth it.' He smiled, gave
Ennis's shoulder a final squeeze, then went back to see how the
squad was getting on. Ennis tottered slightly, walking back to the
billet. It was the sort of totter, or sense of tottering, that always
accompanies the carrying away of a shock – an overdraft instead
of the expected credit balance, failure in an examination that had
seemed a walkover. He sat down on his bed, lit a cigarette, and
cursed himself for taking things so seriously. He had now been out
three times with Lavinia, and each meeting had ended in the same
way – the kisses, the increase of ardour on his part, the struggle to
be free, the run back to the Wrennery. From his desk he took the last
poem she had given him.

And his hooves hammer me back into the ground,
The four gospel hammers, till, in that corn death,
I am promised to be queen of the bellied wheat.
I pray a last thanks in my killing breath,
Glad to be ripped, torn of the panting hollow,
While his one eye glows, the angels carry away

The suffocating forge to become the sun,
Who throbs in waves to suck the fainting day.

Julian came in, still in gym kit, fresh as the morning. 'I showed those great louts, my dear. Could they, I ask you, even *attempt* that terrifying leap in *Spectre de la Rose*? They could not. They are just a little abashed. I can see a faint gleam of respect, which – I know the signs so well – will turn to the most *abject* admiration before I am finished with them. They will be bringing me flowers and melons before long, they will be eating out of my hand. The big muscle-bound serfs. I would not employ one of them on the estate. *Not one.*' He dressed with care, putting on between battledress jacket and shirt a delicate but warm fur-lined jerkin. 'You, my dear,' he said, 'have been truculent again. This rebelliousness will do no good, as I've told you time and time again. You must melt them, drip charm over them.'

'Are you going out tonight?' asked Ennis.

'Why do you ask?'

'I'd like to entertain a visitor for an hour or so.'

'Barbarous,' wailed Julian. 'You dirty little thing. Whoring again. I've a good mind to refuse Vincent's invitation and stay in with my embroidery. Filling the room with disgusting female smells. Hairpins all over the place. I'm not tidying up after you, anyway. I just *refuse*.'

15

'I expected a kind of monk's cell atmosphere,' said Lavinia, standing coolly in the middle of the room and surveying it with a woman's eyes. 'What kind of perfume does your friend use?' She admired the reproductions of modern painters, set tastefully on the walls, and the hanging gay embroideries which were Julian's work. She examined the books on the shelves – a mixture of expensive limited editions from the Vocational and Cultural Library, orchestral scores, volumes of verse. 'So you read poetry?' she said, thumbing through a selection of Theophilus Gardner's work.

'I set it,' said Ennis. 'I use it. And here,' he said, 'is a little surprise for you.' He took from the table some sheets of music paper. 'It's a setting, look, of one of your poems. For soprano and muted brass quartet.'

'Oh,' she said. She glanced through the score, slowly mouthing the words:

Pigs snort from the yard.
Above, gulls mew and heckle.
Memory's shadows speckle
The blind, with its swinging cord.

'That's nothing to be proud of,' she said, 'that bit of nonsense. I wrote it as a joke.'

'I set it,' said Ennis, huzzahing within, 'as an act of homage.' Huzzah.

She glanced further through the score, frowning, saying nothing. 'Would you like a drink?' asked Ennis. 'I've gin and a bottle of lemon squash.' He fetched them, also iced water in a thermos. 'The plural of *thermos*,' he said, 'should, I suppose, be *thermoi*.' She still said nothing, but she took the proffered glass. She sat down on one of the two beds. Ennis sat next to her. At length, having drunk deeply, she said:

'Why did you bring me here?'

'I never see you alone. The Rock's always on top of us. We're always in a crowd. I wanted to talk to you.'

'What about?'

'Nothing in particular. Just to talk. I enjoy talking to you. I enjoy just being with you.' Again, infuriatingly, she said nothing. 'Tell me about yourself,' pleaded Ennis. 'I know nothing about you.'

'Mystery,' smiled Lavinia, wryly turning down her mouth, just like Laurel. 'Let me remain a mystery. Say what you want to say.'

Richard swallowed, then swallowed his drink, then launched the trite words. 'I love you, Lavinia.' He said this with the slight sickness in his heart that always accompanied the tearing-up of a score (finally unsatisfactory) that had taken weeks of work. He expected another of her silences, but this time she spoke promptly.

'I suppose I should ask what you mean by that, but I won't. It's a great pity, of course. I'm sorry you said it.'

'I'm not,' said Ennis. 'I've wanted to say it for a long time.'

'You haven't known me for a long time.'

'Oh, that makes no difference. I only wish there were some new way of saying it, some new coinage. I said that disinterestedly, anyway. Please believe that.'

'Said what disinterestedly?'

'That I love you. I suppose, to prove it, I should have waited till my last day here. I love you humbly and with no hope of return.'

'You're never honest, are you? If you'd said, "Look, I love you in the Elizabethan sense – Lady, let me love and lie with you", I'd have respected you for that. Instead, you don't attempt to define. You hand me a word steeped in the treacle of popular songs and presumably expect me to be flattered.'

'I never thought of that. I was saying what I felt. I was selfish enough not even to consider what you might feel when I said it.' Irritable, he took his glass to the table. 'Would you like some more gin?'

Lavinia was standing beside him. 'Put your arms round me,' she commanded. In a shock of surprise, Ennis took her in an embrace, saying:

'I do love you, if that word has any meaning at all.' He then remembered saying that, not so long ago, to somebody else, but now was not the time for thinking about it. He kissed her forehead, eyes, neck. 'Any meaning at all,' he repeated.

'All right, you love me.' He kissed her mouth. She said, 'Let's not have any more talk.' He kissed her again, holding the kiss, waiting for her response. Excitement began to flood his body, welling as blood wells from a razor-cut. He took her, unresisting, over to Julian's bed. They lay, she silent, passive, waiting. He kissed her bared neck, unable to hold back words. 'I do love you, Lavinia. My darling, I do love you.' At the same time, his aloof brain worked out a passage of double fugue. Her dress unfastened down the front. With an unwonted deftness he reached the rose-eyes of her breasts, and she began to speak his name now in a kind of trance, an invocation. Now he came deeper, nearer to the heart of the mystery, his mouth full of sea salt, the taste of electricity, caressing, eating, lashing up the blood in his own veins to the point which, anyway, was approaching of its own volition, the point where the train must run over them, the ship sink, the bomb explode, the cynical faces look on, but this not stop. Minute by minute the evening slid away and the different world of the voices in the street, the rare car passing, the aircraft overhead, the wailing ship in the bay, idly made daisy chains, whittled wood. At the too-close approach of his own scalding crux, he felt her cry of an accepted ultimate covenant, was aware of the opening of the door. He sweated with a shock of incredulity and his heart began to sink rapidly as the flaccid cold of failure crept towards him. He kissed her hot face in an agony of humiliation.

'It doesn't matter. You can't help it, I suppose.' Her eyes were open, sober again. She sat up, starting to tidy herself.

'One becomes overwrought. The excitement is too much –'

'Yes. Give me a cigarette.'

They both smoked in silence. At length she said, 'Who is Laurel?'

'Laurel?'

'It sounded like Laurel. Why did you call me that?'

'Did I? That's curious.'

'Yes. I suppose Laurel is the name of your wife.' She puffed at her cigarette. The statement was made so unemphatically that Ennis was taken aback. She knew. He could not deny it.

'Laurel,' he said quietly and with little tone, 'is the name of my wife. I hate her.'

'Nonsense,' she said briskly. 'I always suspected you were married. I could have confirmed the suspicion easily enough if I'd wanted to. No trouble at all. But it didn't seem worth while. It just didn't matter. Now,' she drank again at her cigarette, 'do you still love me?'

'Of course I love you.' The statement had neither tone nor colour. The sense of failure sat heavily on him, and the sense too of his being quite naked before her: she had seen his manhood collapse, his secret uncover itself, and now she read him in her own translation – a pirated edition which he could never drive from the market.

'I do like you,' said Lavinia, taking his hand as though it were a child's. 'And you are so very young. How old are you?'

'Does it matter?' Ennis let his hand rest, passive like a woman's, in her grasp. 'I'm nearly twenty-seven.'

'And I,' said Lavinia, 'was thirty-two last month. Which makes me *very* much older than you. It justifies my feeling maternal towards you, doesn't it?'

Richard said nothing, but, inflating the collapsed bladder with a force close to hate, took her roughly in his arms and began kissing her. Whatever slept in him did not wake up. She suffered his embrace for a while, then said:

'It's not much use going on, is it? You and I were perhaps merely meant to talk aesthetics to each other.' And then, sitting up and reading her wristwatch, 'I really must go.'

'You're always saying that. It's early yet.'

'There's a meeting of the Poetry Group tonight. I have to give a talk on Shakespeare's Sonnets. If you're so anxious to be with me, you can come to that.'

'I hardly ever see you alone. I want to make love to you.' Flogging a dead. She said nothing, tidying her hair at Julian's mirror, fastening up her dress. 'I know it was foolish of me not to be honest with you, not to tell you about Laurel. But – well, you know how it is.' He raised his hands in a foolish gesture which, preoccupied with her mirror-image, she could not see. 'It seemed irrelevant in the face of the way I felt – feel about you. I didn't want to seem the typical married philanderer.'

'Untypical, then?' She turned, a hair-clip between her teeth.

'You see what I mean – That's just the attitude I didn't want –'

She came up to him and kissed him gently and coolly on the forehead. 'Poor poor Richard. Tumbledown Dick.' She blushed at that. 'What do you want out of life?' she continued. 'You seem to have thrown so much overboard. Where do you think you're sailing to?'

'I don't see what all this has to do with anything.' He sat sulking, but a grin (Tumbledown Dick, indeed) tried to stab through, like a needle.

'You want God, and yet you want to be alone. You obviously worship your wife, and yet you say you hate her.'

'I do, I do. It's you I love.'

'And then there's the question of your art. You call it your art, anyway. I would say that it's more of a hobby, like building Spanish galleons out of matches –'

'What do you mean? What are you getting at? What exactly did you mean by that remark?'

'I had a long talk with Corporal Coneybeare about your music.'

'Coneybeare? That fool? Coneybeare doesn't know the first thing about any kind of music after 1883 –'

'No? Well, he gave me the impression that he knew at least a little. And he is, after all, Professor of Harmony at the Royal College of –'

'Yes, yes, yes. So he's gone back to his old job, has he?' sneered Ennis. 'Lance-Corporal Coneybeare in his demob suit.'

'That's a silly sort of crack,' she said sharply. 'What I was going to say was what Coneybeare said. About your music.'

'What did he say? Not that what he could say about it could ever carry any weight. What was it then?' asked Ennis eagerly.

'He said that you just have no ear. That he could see what you were getting at, but it was rather pathetic the way your effects just didn't come off. He said it's nothing to do with knowledge or experience. It's just something you don't happen to be born with. That's what he said. I, of course, know nothing about music.' She read her watch again. 'Come on, we'd better be going.'

'He didn't have the guts, of course, to say these things to my face.' Ennis's fists were clenched. 'He knows nothing about it, nothing at all.'

'And yet,' said Lavinia, 'some of his works have been broadcast. Have any of yours?'

'Influence,' raged Ennis. 'He knows the right people. It's a conspiracy, it's a –' He swallowed and tried to calm himself. 'His stuff's harmless stuff, the sort of stuff you'd expect from a professor of Harmony. It's dead, correct and dead. Dead, dead, dead.'

'Now,' smiled Lavinia, 'how about telling me you love me?'

'Ah, to hell with love,' stormed Ennis.

16

Lavinia and Ennis walked silently through the streets towards Hospital Steps, she smiling coolly, he like a clenched stick of thunder. By the steps of the Garrison Library they saw a knot of brown dapper civilians, talking excitedly in the slack Spanish of the colony. Ennis knew some of them. One of them, a small man with a clerkly face, thin moustache, spectacles, he had taught for a time. In some class or other. Elementary Book-keeping or something. His name was Rioja or something. This man said to Ennis:

'You, Sergeant Ennis, are on our side. I know you are. In the Matriculation English you have talked much about freedom and democracy.' These two terms, spoken flatly and without accentuation, sounded remote and unreal. 'Though you are English,' said Mr Rioja, 'you will admit that we are in the right. This is our Rock and it is we who should govern it.'

'Come along,' said Lavinia. 'We're going to be late.'

'It is only right,' said Mr Rioja, with gestures. 'India has self-government now. It is the professed and general aim of the British Government to give self-government to all the colonies. We are an old colony. We are older, for instance, than Australia, and Australia has been for a long time a dominion.' He knew it all, by God.

'Come on.' Lavinia tugged Ennis's arm.

'But,' said Ennis, 'it's hardly a country, is it? It's only a rock, a strategic point in the Mediterranean. What good would it be if the British went?'

'No, no, no, no,' said a lined brown man with a twitch. 'We are

British. We would still be British. We would be the British in charge of the Rock, you see.'

'It is small, but it is our home,' said one small fat man, not without dignity. 'As it is, we are not properly represented.'

'Will you speak at our meeting, Sergeant Ennis?' asked Mr Rioja. 'It would mean a great deal. You are, you see, a member of the garrison. The war is over, it is time for reforms.'

'If you don't come,' said Lavinia crossly, 'I shall go on my own.'

Ennis shook his head, protesting his unworthiness, the lack of a sense of reality in this desire for autonomy. Without the naval base, without the garrison-key to the Mediterranean, to the East – Spain would walk in, had always regarded it as hers – Impossible.

'We thought we knew our friends,' said a man like an Arab, keeper of a general store.

'It's not that,' insisted Ennis. 'I *am* a friend, believe me, but it's so, it's so –'

'Oh, come along, blast you,' said Lavinia nastily.

'– So unrealistic.'

'We're really late,' said Lavinia. 'They'll think I'm not coming. Oh, you *are* a nuisance.'

'I don't like all this,' said Ennis, hurrying to keep up with her. 'There've been some very ugly things down here in the town. An R.A.F. sergeant got beaten up by North Face the other day. Did you hear about that?'

'Oh, never mind,' she panted. They began to climb the narrow flight of stone steps. Washing, fat women, garlic, children, the cry of '*Niña*!' 'Yes,' said Ennis. A mess-mate of his, Sergeant Fellowes, a football referee, had been found bleeding in the gutter after the United team had lost a match. A group of Spanish workmen had recently paraded on the Casemates square with an ill-painted banner: 'YOU HAVE WIN YOUR WAR. NOW TO FIGT FRANCO.' 'Yes,' said Ennis, forgetting about Coneybeare and his sexual failure. 'Trouble.' The troops themselves had not been thoroughly purged of the sluggish blood that begets discontent and impatience, despite the P.T., the arms drill, the classes, the E.N.S.A. shows. (A raddled star had sung a song about coming home and been given the bird.) There was murmuring on parade, active disobedience to junior N.C.O.s, open growls and punch-ups in the N.A.A.F.I. There was an atmosphere appropriate to the end of a war.

Ennis, sighing, allowed himself to be led to the poky premises of the Literary Society. This was a break-away from the much bigger voluntary organisation called the Garrison Literary and Debating Society, which was ostensibly concerned with the promotion of cultural activities among the garrison's exiles. There had originally been little groups devoted to the discussion of the arts, the reading of verse, the hearing of gramophone records, but there had also been a political group which, starting as a Cinderella on the margin, thin, ragged, had now fattened unconscionably, absorbing the whining arty groups, or, if they would not be absorbed, expelling them. Most of the members of the political group were disaffected R.A.F. clerks, lance-bombardiers who had failed matric, bespectacled sick-berth attendants who dreamed of a new order. They met to paint a Marxist picture of the current affairs which seemed so remote, usually under the leadership of a leading aircraftman with a slick battery of jargon and a gabbling Lancashire platform voice. There had formerly been Conservatives, Liberals, old-womanish Commonwealth zealots at these meetings, but these had been shouted down so often with cries of 'Reactionary running dog,' 'Fascist butcher' and 'Plutocratic jackal' that they no longer attended. So now there was a Literary Society for the mildly humanistic and a Debating Society for the dialectical progressives, and that was that.

The club-rooms of the Literary Society tonight were full of pipe-smoking tea-drinkers, all talking with gentlemanly anxiety to teach each other. In a small smoky room the five members of the Poetry Group were waiting for the meeting to begin. Conspicuous was Major Appleyard, chummily housemasterish in his flannels and faded blazer. Lavinia was to give a short talk on Shakespeare's Sonnets, it was announced; afterwards there would be a discussion. With pipes ablaze, all prepared doggedly to listen, ignoring her ankles, anxious to learn. Ennis took out a sheet of manuscript paper and began to sketch a fugue. That blasted Coneybeare. What did he know about it, anyway?

Ennis caught odd words and phrases as, in a rather prim voice,

Lavinia outlined the various groups into which the Sonnets could be divided, the chambers of the heart which Shakespeare unlocked. 'The charge of homosexuality – ardour of the sonnets to the Earl of Southampton – no true artist really a hermaphrodite –' (Surely he had heard that term used before, in some similar connection? Was she answering an argument in which he had once taken part himself?)

'There is no doubt,' she said, 'that immense artistic vigour is related to strong sexuality. The revulsion expressed in this sonnet to the loveless sexual act shows Shakespeare's capacity for becoming, against his reason, against his will, intoxicated with physical desire. He knows he will regret it, but it is too strong to resist. All he can do is to purge his brain with these words:

The expense of spirit in a waste of shame
Is lust in action, and, till action, lust
Is perjured, murderous, bloody, full of blame –'

Ennis, fascinated by the coolness of that voice, looked at her as she went on reading. Her legs were crossed and, seeing them, his body responded violently. Belatedly. Damn and blast. He had to leave. The members of the group, wreathed in pipe-incense, looked up at him curiously. Major Appleyard creased his face in sorrow.

It was Major Appleyard who came out of the meeting first. He saw Ennis sitting gloomy there, with an old copy of jaunty *Punch* and a cup of tea. He said, 'It was a pity you had to leave, Richard. I hope you feel better now. You looked quite ashen, you know. Something you ate?'

'Something you can't eat,' mumbled Ennis, with soldier's ribaldry. He saw Lavinia come out now, talking with two earnest young privates, saying, 'A dark complexion would always be out of favour so long as there was a redhead on the throne –' She did not look for Ennis; she went straight to the little tea bar, chattering coolly away. Appleyard said:

'There's something I want you to do for us, Richard. Something that lies, I believe, well within your province. Richard, are you listening?'

'Sorry, sir. What were you saying?' My God, Turner had come in, Turner in a place of culture, Turner too high for the room, stooping under the lintel laughingly.

'We're going to run an Eisteddfod, Richard. There.' He beamed in triumph.

'But I don't know any Welsh, sir,' said Ennis. 'Surely, when Evans and Williams were here –' By Christ, he had gone up to Lavinia. Both were smiling. It was a pre-arranged meeting.

'No, no, no, nothing to do with Welsh. We are going to have a speakers' competition. Different groups or classes, you know. After-dinner speeches, political orations, poetry, that sort of thing. I know you'll approve. Don't you remember saying that our civilisation is based on the ear? I still think the other senses have a claim,' he said archly, 'but a competition like this would stimulate an interest in good speaking. It would certainly encourage some of our instructors to improve in that respect.'

'What do you want me to do?' Lavinia's teacup was poised for drinking. She was smiling, looking up at Turner. Turner was talking quietly to her. She went on smiling. Blast them, blast all women. He would get Turner.

'Lavinia suggested that there might be a Spanish-speaking section. She said you know something of Spanish literature.'

'I don't know much.' By God, he would get him. As for her –

'She says that a certain lady taught you quite a lot.' Major Appleyard smiled roguishly. 'No, no, I will say no more.' He wagged a finger. 'Will you select a couple of Spanish poems for us?'

'I don't know much.'

'Richard, you *are* tiresome. You don't pay attention at all.'

'Sorry, Julian. Sorry, sir, I mean. You said something about poems.' Lavinia and Turner had put their cups down. They were leaving together. Never a backward glance.

'Two Spanish poems. Nothing erotic, mind. Something rather cool-blooded, if that is possible. Richard, what *is* the matter with you? You worry me, you do really.'

Something rather cold-blooded, if that was possible.

17

Another week brought Christmas, carols, fighting, tears, much drunkenness. It was like VE day and VJ day all over again, except that, battledress and not khaki drill being the regulation uniform for tepid winter, crapulous vomiting over one's own, or some other, person could be entered on less lightly. Ennis, maudlinly accompanying the maudlin singers, was a Niobe of gin, sobbing for the Christ-child, snow on the thatched roofs of home, the angelic message of peace. But his heart, with its burden of seven days' hate for Turner, hummed like marine engines, his vessel cruising on no straight course towards a haven of revenge. They sang 'Silent Night, Holy Night', boozing their eyes out round the mess piano. Turner sang too, as loud as any on orange squash.

'I'll get the bastard,' Ennis had told Julian, 'if it's the last thing I do.'

'Why all this?' asked Julian. 'Hatred is too big a compliment, my dear. I thought we'd agreed merely to *despise* him and his muscle-bound morons. Is there anything between you two?'

'I just can't stand him. I've tried to keep it bottled up. Now it's got to come out.'

'You won't stand a chance, you know. He's very large.'

'Never mind. I shall think of a way.'

For the very first time, something went wrong with the conventional room-savaging arrangements that little Juanito, for a consideration, would, with bright eyes and smiling teeth, fulfil. Ennis had given little Juanito a whole half-crown, the whereabouts of Turner's billet, and detailed instructions in English and Spanish. Little Juanito came back to say:

'Bloody hell, *hombre*. I go there, I start bugger up room, he come in. He say what you do, I say you say I bugger up room. He say I not bugger up his room, I bugger up your room. He give me *mucho dinero*.' Little Juanito looked sly.

'How *mucho dinero*?'

'Ten *chelines*.' Little Juanito showed the ten-shilling note with pride.

'I see,' said Ennis. 'So you're going to wreck my billet, are you?'

'Big *señor* he say do that. But,' said little Juanito, 'I not do that. But you say to big *señor* I do that. You play hell with big *señor* because you say I do that. And,' said little Juanito, 'I do sweet effay and have ten *chelines*.'

'I see,' said Ennis. 'The point is that I gave you half a crown to go and wreck this big sergeant-major's billet. When are you going to do this wrecking?'

'Not no more, *maestro*. I go work for big *señor* now. He big man give big money.'

'Traitor,' said Ennis bitterly. 'Bloody Spanish traitor. Give me back my half-crown.'

'Not give back,' said little Juanito. 'I try to do job. I get half-crown for try to do job. He give me ten *chelines* for try to do job. He not let me bugger up his room. You not let me bugger up your room. I not give back ten *chelines*. I not give back half-crown.' In some remote ancestor of Juanito's the cunning Aristotle-reading Moors had injected the steel-wine of logic.

'Go,' said Ennis loudly. 'Traitor. The Spanish were always a treacherous lot of bastards. *Vaya, vaya*.' He waved his arms. Little Juanito slunk off. He reappeared at the open window to say:

'If he die, *maestro*, then I come back bugger up rooms for you like old time.'

'Die? What are you talking about?' But little Juanito had gone.

On Boxing Day Ennis volunteered for bar duty in the Engineers' Mess. This task was normally reserved, on a roster, for the sergeants of the regiment and there was often grumbling because the attached personnel went free of it. Ostensibly a lucrative and bibulous job, it was in fact a nuisance: there were always arguments about prices, and there were sometimes veiled accusations of till-pilfering. Ennis's offer was gladly accepted by Lance-Sergeant Huggins, whose arithmetic was not good and who hated the smell of beer. Grimly this busy night he awaited Turner's appearance in the mess, his clean-limbed order. Turner was to be made very drunk. Ennis did not think this was likely to be a very difficult thing to do. Once Turner was on the billiard table with his crony, he would stay on. He would down his orange squash distractedly, his eyes on the run and the click of the coloured balls. And so Ennis had ready a smooth-tasting mixture of gin, rum, sherry, whisky and brandy – what was money where revenge was concerned? – to doctor the harmless beverage.

His heart leapt when Turner finished his first pint glass and accepted the second, bought for him by Julian. In the middle of the third glass Turner's opponent remarked that Turner's play was not as good as usual. He had missed a sitter.

'Can't understand it,' said Turner, somewhat thickly. 'Can't see as well as usual. Old age creeping up. Hey,' he called to Ennis, 'that orange squash tastes a bit queer. You trying something on? Can't take a joke, is that it? Can't take it when you're hoist with your own whatsit.'

'Petard,' said Ennis. 'I'm afraid I don't understand.'

'You'll understand soon enough,' said Turner. He hiccuped.

'Have some more orange squash,' offered Julian. 'It's a new kind. It's supposed to be rather good.'

'Spostberawthawgood, is it?' minced Turner. 'Isn't he lovely?' he mocked, trying to chuck Julian under the chin. 'Gorgeous, inny?' A very low-class accent, long hidden, was creeping out. 'Booful lil boy,' he said. He swayed at Julian, seeing several of him.

'Back to the game, major,' said the Q.M.S.I., uneasy. But Turner was fast losing interest in snooker. He began to sing and to demand that others sing, too. He went round the mess shaking hands with a gorilla-grip, he shouted, he told perfect strangers what good bastards they were, he shook the floor in a blurred sort of dance.

'He's drunk,' said the young, rather weedy R.S.M., chewing his thin fair moustache.

'Can't be. He only takes orange squash.'

'Are you all right, major?' asked Turner's crony, anxiously.

'Never better,' shouted Turner. 'Christmas spirit. Here.' He lurched over to Ennis at the bar. 'She's all right, brother. On to a good thing there. A man's what she wanted. Got a man now, a real one. Have a drink.'

'Have some more orange squash?' offered Ennis.

'Bloody good orange squash. New kind of orange squash. Blood oranges.'

At the summit of his ecstasy, Turner began to look pale. He tottered, he slurred his speech. He began to stagger, a broken Colossus, to the door. 'I'll go,' said Ennis quickly to Julian. 'Look after the bar for a minute.' And, before Turner's companion could get there, Ennis was at the street door of the mess. To his satisfaction, he saw Turner already lying supine in the gutter, flat out, out like a light, vomit billowing from his mouth on to his pressed battle-blouse. A mean trick, he thought. A bloody mean trick.

'Help me to get him home,' pleaded the Q.M.S.I., the twister of Ennis's arm, the sniggerer at Delius, the gorilla. 'People mustn't see him like this.'

'He's your pigeon,' said Ennis. 'Carrying him is a man's job.' Then he watched, without much pleasure, as the hard-muscled physical trainer staggered off, the snoring Turner wreathed about him in a fireman's lift. When would one outgrow apple-pie beds, booby traps? Only, presumably, when men outgrew anti-personnel obstacles, commando knifings. The Army was one vast prep school. But this revenge was neither sweet nor bitter; it was just nothing.

'You can expect the worst now, my dear,' warned Julian that night, as they undressed to go to bed. 'It was not a very clever thing to do, was it?'

'This,' said Ennis, fingering an anthology of Spanish verse, 'was a present from Concepción. Poor Concepción. Poor poor Concepción.' He sniffed.

'Now,' said Julian briskly, 'we won't have you feeling sorry for yourself, will we? Because that's the only person,' he said brutally, 'you ever *have* felt sorry for.'

'Yes, yes,' snivelled Ennis, 'I know I'm no good. Listen to this.' And he began to read, with a fair Castilian accent, from St John of the Cross:

En mi pecho florido
Que entero para él sólo se guardaba,
Allí quedo dormido,
Y yo le regalaba
Y el ventalle de cedros aire daba.

'Lovely, lovely,' said Julian, now neatly and fragrantly in bed. 'What does it mean?'

'It means, it means – Let me see. "In my blossoming heart, which kept itself entirely for Him only, there He stayed sleeping, and I regaled him, entertained him, and the fan of cedars gave us air."' He got ready to sob again, then reminded himself of Julian's astringent watchfulness. But, reading through the lines, he had felt the mystical content vanish and the musky scent of Concepción's body intoxicate him again. He imagined himself lying with her, in a confusion of incense, the oriental spices of the Canticles, the cedars of Lebanon. He knew where his home was: back in the Church, with his child and Concepción's dressed in a white First Communion frock (the child, of course, was a girl; a son would only be himself again); his home was here, the Mediterranean, the womb of history. No, not here on the Rock, where Turner and Laurel-Lavinia could find their English-Protestant element (poor old Turner), but over there, over in the land of bullfights and religious processions. He did not love Laurel; he did not love Lavinia. They were out of his world, an older world than that of the braying Oxford vicars, the cold embraces, the cold climate. His heart went out for an instant to that American – what was his name? Pereira? Mendoza? – who too had homed, pigeon-like, towards that past that would soon be fumigated out of existence.

'To sleep now, my dear,' said firm Julian. 'The holiday's over now, such as it was. Tomorrow we are lashed once more to labour.'

'I've got to find another Spanish poem,' said Ennis. 'Miss Appleyard wants them tomorrow morning first thing.' He chose, while Julian – who had drunk more tonight than he normally allowed himself – sank elegantly to sleep, Lorca's '*La Casada Infiel*'. The faithless wife, eh? Romantically, he saw himself as the faithless husband, snatching sweet fruit from civil war's blasted branches. The woman who lay with him in the warm aromatic night was, of course, Concepción.

Aquella noche corrí	*Sus muslos se me escapaban*
El mejor de los caminos,	*Come peces sorprendidos,*
Montado en potra de nácar	*La mitad llenos de lumbre,*
Sin bridas y sin estribos –	*La mitad llenos de frío.*

And, feeling himself riding that best of roads that night, on a saddle of pearl, near-fainting with remembered sensuality that the poem pricked back to life, he himself escaped to sleep.

18

He copied the two poems out before breakfast and took them to Major Appleyard after breakfast. The mood of last night had passed, the old sensations, the old excitement, the image of a fulfilment which had always seemed to be too precious for his deserving. The poems had become words in an alien language, a language he did not really understand. In the office which Appleyard shared with Captain Dance, the ante-room to the tabernacle where the numen resided, the Major was busy with his project, thumbing through the Oxford Books, making lists, humming the Overture to the *Marriage of Figaro*.

'Well, Richard,' he said, 'you know all about Spanish poetry, so I take your word for it. A saint seems harmless enough, anyway, even though he was R.C. Who's this Lorca fellow? Yes, yes, it seems all right. Isn't this something about riding a horse or something?' He read with an air of understanding all, as a child reads a newspaper upside down.

'A sort of riding is the theme of the poem, sir.'

'Good, Richard. Off you go, now. We're busy.'

Captain Dance was deep in the merry Panglossian world of *The Good Companions*. Remembering his position, however, he added, as in sleep, 'Off you go. Good bod.' Ennis, under cover of a truck's backfiring without, made a tight fricative noise with his lips, left. Julian was waiting for him. They walked off together for coffee. Julian said:

'He'll be gunning for you, my dear. He is still on his bed of sickness, but his cronies and henchmen are already muttering. They'll be coming for you, you mark my words.'

'Why me?' said Ennis. 'He doesn't know it was me, unless somebody's told him.'

'Nonsense.' They entered the café. 'It's perfectly obvious to everybody who it was. Perfectly obvious, my dear.' In the mirrored gilt soft-carpeted hall officers coughed, getting over Christmas, opening birdcage-bottom mouths to the mid-morning draught, palates like all-in wrestlers' jockstraps (ha ha) to the rich grateful fresh-ground aroma. Their patrician barks ('What? What?') and changing-room laughs were an astringent music.

Ennis felt a slight tremor of bodily fear. 'But what can he do?' he asked. 'He's not war-substantive. He said so himself. He'd lose his rank if he tried any rough stuff.'

'There are ways and means.' Julian lifted, in an exquisite gesture, a relic from his study of Balinese hand-movements, his full cup of coffee. 'A soft rabbit punch in the dark. A little pain, administered in harmless doses, on the P.T. parade.'

'I'm not attending any more of those.'

'Really? I'd no idea you'd been granted exemption.'

'I haven't. I'm just not going any more.'

'Then,' said Julian, 'they will drag you out of your bed with boisterous laughter. They will throw cold sea-water over you. They'll have a whale of a time.'

'I shan't stay in bed. I shall go to early mass. Nobody can stop me doing that.'

'Oh, yes, they can. A parade is a parade. In any case he'll get you, like the Hound of Heaven. Flee him in the mess, on the pay-parade, in the Alameda Gardens, he'll catch up with you. He'll punish you for your own good.'

'Are we still talking about Turner?'

Julian drained his cup and now turned round, nodding queenily at various acquaintances. A second-lieutenant gave him a sweet smile and a twinkle of reminiscence. 'My dear, what does that man think he's doing?' Ennis followed his gaze and saw that a bulky brown civilian had risen to his feet and was pounding on his table with a heavy glass ashtray. 'Help us in our fight,' he called loudly. 'You soldiers do not want to be here. You want to be home. So do we. We want this to really be our home. We want to rule ourselves. Give us back our Rock.'

'Oaf,' said Julian. 'What do they propose to do? Sell each other imitation Persian carpets?'

The agitator was swiftly escorted to the door by gold-toothed waiters. He shouted to the last. As Julian and Ennis left, they were aware of a curious headiness in the dry winter air, a quality as of things about to happen. Julian said, sighing, 'Sometimes, my dear, I have to reconcile myself to the fact that the whole world is changing. Things will *never* be quite the same again. No more British Empire, God bless it.' He made it sound curiously cosy. 'Even ballet. I have heard; and you may well look pale, of ballets being performed without scenery and in practice tights only, accompanied by a piano, God help us all. In factories in England during the lunch hour, no less. This,' said Julian, 'is what war does for us. Sneerers,' he added, 'and dodgers and wide boys. People crying out for what they call democracy. You, my dear,' he said sternly, 'are substantially to blame. You and people like you.'

'Me?'

'I have heard,' said Julian, 'about your lectures to the troops. Down with privilege and autocracy and so on. Government of the people, and all that Priestleyan nonsense. Before you've finished there won't be a single orchestra capable of playing your music. And there'll be no more ballet.' Julian's reasoning was elliptical but close. Ennis wondered and wondered, entering the dining-hall of the Anti-Aircraft unit where he was to lecture. His subject was the Beveridge Report, the Five Giants, the Rights of Man, etc, etc. He found a certain excitement buzzing among the men; they seemed to have shed their habitual apathy. On Ennis's entrance there was an inexplicable burst of applause.

'Is that right about the meeting, sarge?' asked a wrinkled but age-less gunner with a cavalry bandiness.

'What meeting?'

'The meeting you're supposed to be getting up. We heard about it from the Tunnellers. They said it was tomorrow night, outside the Governor's Palace.'

'That's news to me. What's the meeting supposed to be about?'

'They didn't say. They said *you'd* got something in mind.'

'Me?'

'It's about leave, isn't it, sarge?' said a ginger dwarf of great toughness. 'Leave, and the speeding-up of the Release Groups. That's what I heard from some of the Medicals.'

'I know nothing about it,' said Ennis. 'Nothing at all.'

'Of course you don't,' grinned a cocky Cockney. 'Say no more about it, sarge.'

'Right,' said Ennis. 'No more talk, please. If you want to talk, we'll have ten minutes discussion after the lecture.' And he began to speak about the need for National Insurance against Want, Squalor, Sickness – God, it sounded demagogic, inflammatory. '– We're all human beings with certain basic human needs. The rich man's tooth doesn't ache worse than ours. The poor man's body needs clothing against the winter winds. The aristocrat has no monopoly of the right to a full stomach.' The men cheered him. Every word was tinder. Had that stupid fair-crack-of-the-whip That's-a-point Tomlinson been right after all? 'I'd better say at this juncture,' said Ennis, 'that I'm not committing myself personally to the ideas I'm putting forward. Certain great men have thought out these ideas. They may be right or wrong. It's not for me to say. It's up to you to decide these things for yourselves.' He put too much emphasis on the 'up to you'. The cheers broke out again loudly. 'I think,' said Ennis, 'I've said enough on this subject. Variety is the spice of life. Now I'm going to talk about something entirely different.' (What? The provenance of eggless custard? The difference between a bacillus and a spirochaete? Minor Elizabethan drama?) 'I see we have a piano here,' said Ennis, seeing they had a piano there. 'I'd like to tell you a little about a man called –' (Wagner? William Byrd? Palestrina? Sacheverell Coke?) '– Beethoven.' The men cheered.

'Everybody knows at least a few bars of Beethoven,' said Ennis, sitting down at the piano. 'This, for instance.' He tinkled a phrase from the Minuet in G. 'This, too.' He hammered out the opening

theme of the Fifth Symphony. 'Victory!' called a gunner. 'Victory for the working classes. The upper classes have had their victory, now it's time we had ours.' 'No, no, no,' cried Ennis. He got up from the piano. 'That theme,' he said, 'means nothing. It means itself, no more. The call of the yellow-hammer, the hammering of Fate – these are poetic fripperies. To a musician they mean nothing. Beethoven was a musician, not a fabricator of slogans in sound. Music was his life, he cared nothing for politics. He snapped his fingers at the thunder, he snapped his fingers at Napoleon. He had absolutely no respect for authority. He was a man who would not cringe to the powerful. He was independent, fearless, alone, no base crawler –'
The men cheered.

'Good old sarge!'

'Perhaps,' said Ennis desperately, 'I'd better go back to the Beveridge Report.'

19

'My dear,' said Julian, 'he's actually up. He has risen from his bed of sickness. The longest hangover on record.' It was lunch time next day. And there indeed was Turner, pale, shaky, crawling in to the tinned meat and the dehydrated spuds and greens. Turner accosted Ennis at once. He said:

'It was you who doped my orange squash. I thought there was something fishy about you being behind the bar.'

'I can't be blamed for everything,' said Ennis. 'If you decide to get drunk it's your own affair.'

'You,' said Turner, 'got me tight deliberately. Trying to get your own back, that's what it was. It wasn't funny. A joke's a joke and I can take a joke with the next man, but that wasn't funny. Just because you're bloody jealous. Right,' promised Turner. 'Now it's going to be my bloody turn.'

'Turner's turn,' said Ennis involuntarily.

'That's right,' said Turner. 'You're not a bit bloody sorry, are you? Sheer downright vindictiveness, that's what it was.' He looked at the amorphous jumble on his plate. 'Oh, no,' he said. 'Oh, no, I can't.' And he stumbled very quickly out of the mess.

'You're going to suffer, my dear,' said Julian. 'You're going to suffer terribly for that.'

Turner's crony, the gorilla Q.M.S.I., came up to Ennis. 'You see what you've done to him?' he said. 'By God, you're going to cop it for this.'

'You're putting me off my food,' said Ennis. 'Go back to your own table like a good ape.'

'You've had your time and I'll have mine,' said the Q.M.S.I. 'I'm not saying no more than that.' And he went off.

'How terribly cryptic,' said Julian.

As Ennis walked through the streets in the balmy winter afternoon, he was greeted by odd conspiratorial grins by many soldiers. He had tea in the mess and was surprised when the R.S.M. – who never normally acknowledged his existence – came up and spoke to him. He said: 'I hope you realise you're letting yourself in for a court-martial.''

'What do you mean?'

'You can't do that sort of thing in the Army. You ought to know that. They'll say you were inciting the troops to mutiny. You ought to realise that, chap of your age.'

'Look here,' said Ennis hotly. 'I don't know what the hell you're talking about.'

'You do, you know. They're talking about nothing else in the barrack-rooms. Don't say you haven't been warned.'

'Ah, hell.'

The man of vital integrity is sufficiently armed against – Ah, hell. At six o'clock Ennis went to teach in a Nissen hut in the Alameda Gardens. A class in Elementary Arithmetic. He was astonished to find that his group had swollen considerably. The hut was crammed with men and cigarette smoke. He was cheered as he entered.

'Look here,' he began. 'You're not all in this class. I must ask those of you who didn't register for it to get out.'

'Never mind, sarge,' said one moon-faced private or driver or gunner or sapper. 'We're only the escort. We want to get you there safe and sound.'

'If you think,' he answered, 'that I'm going anywhere, you're sadly mistaken. I'm staying here. I'm going to teach Elementary Arithmetic.' Nobody moved. 'Elementary Arithmetic,' he repeated. 'The fundamental science.' That trembled on the verge of something like radicalism. He said, 'I don't like doing this sort of thing, but it will be my painful duty to put the lot of you on a charge. All, that is, except those who are bona fide students of Elementary Arithmetic. I've given an order,' he said. He looked around. Nobody spoke. They all gazed at him with a kind of affectionate interest, almost with a sort of compassion. 'Right,' said Ennis. 'You must take the consequences of your own act. We must all,' he said, 'take the consequences of our acts. That is life. That is freedom.' Freedom, dangerous word. He turned sadly to go. Immediately there was a clatter of brash wooden benches, the troops were after him. With cheers they impelled him in the direction of the South Gate. 'Don't be a lot of bloody fools!' he cried. He walked quickly, trying desperately to dissociate himself from the growing crowd. He saw various solitary military policemen, undecided, worried, chewing their lips. In sight of the Governor's Residence his eyes swam at the prospect. Small groups of soldiers were hanging about, sheepishly, waiting for some event which would encourage them to coalesce and become a mob. He saw a number of civilians, excitedly chattering. As Ennis appeared with his escort, now somewhat subdued, there was a ragged murmur, one of those sounds that belong to a crowd not as an aggregation but as a new inhuman entity. Ennis remembered his authority, normally so purely nominal, the three faded stripes flashing at last into power. He observed the watching M.P.s. He would clear himself at once. He cried:

'Why don't you chaps go home?' He realised at once that he'd done a fatal thing. At once some of them cheered; the civilians cried: 'Go home!' A tough-looking lean frontiersman of a soldier called: 'That's what we bloody well want. Send us home!' The slogan was taken up – 'Send us home!' – and, in antiphony, the shout of the Gibraltarians: 'Go home!' And then some called: 'Speech, speech!'

'This won't do any good,' shouted Ennis. 'I know you're all fed up, but it can't be helped. We've just got to wait.' There were some new murmurs. 'This isn't the democratic way,' he continued. 'Mob rule gets nowhere. We'll all get home in good time.'

'Go home now!' yelled a civilian. 'We want to go home!' replied the troops. Then one of the excited Gibraltarians did a foolish thing. He picked up a stone and hurled it into the throng of troops. It was not a very big stone, but immediately there was confusion, anger, the imminence of fighting. 'For God's sake, break it up!' pleaded Ennis. 'That's right,' some soldier agreed loudly. 'Break up the Governor's bloody mansion! Down with privilege!' Then the military police moved in.

Swiftly Ennis got away. The redcaps were busy with the fighters. Surely, he thought, panting round the corner to Line Wall Road, surely they can't pin anything on me. I did my best, I tried to stop them. I did, didn't I? He looked at his watch. The best thing to do was to get up to Willis's Farm on his motor-cycle. High up there, at the peak of the spiralling rock-road, he had a German class in half an hour's time. Best get up there now, out of the way. To teach German to the three earnest plodders up at Willis's Farm. As he approached the billet his heart failed for the second time. Parked outside were four motor-cycles additional to his own and Julian's. He knew what this meant. It was too late to worry now. He entered.

In the room he found, as he had expected, Turner, and with Turner were the billiard-playing Q.M.S.I. crony and two rather handsome and lean-looking sergeant-instructors. They were sitting on chairs and beds but they rose almost courteously – the courtesy due to a sacrificial victim – as Ennis entered. Turner towered above the sinewy others, clad, like them, in motor-cycling helmet and gauntlets, looking like Death's outriders in Cocteau's *Orphée*.

'Welcome,' said Turner. 'We've been waiting a long time.'

'Outside,' ordered Ennis. 'This is my billet.'

'We'll go when we're ready.' Turner spoke suavely, seeing himself as something unruffled and heroic. At that moment Julian came in.

'My dear,' breathed Julian, astonished. 'I see the meat has been delivered. To what do we owe this pleasure?'

'Now then,' smiled Turner. 'Your pansy friend might as well be in on this.'

'My dear,' said Julian. 'Are we to be assaulted? How very thrilling.'

'We're giving you a little boxing lesson,' said Turner. 'No extra charge. Part of the service. All right, Ennis, take off your shirt.'

'Much as I appreciate all this,' replied Ennis, 'duty remains duty. I have a lesson to give.'

'So have we,' said the Q.M.S.I. Pleased with the repartee, he looked about him for applause. Ennis moved to the door. No one attempted to haul him back to the room's centre, but one of the sergeant-instructors whisked panther-like to bar the exit and stood with arms folded, smirking.

'Well,' said Ennis. 'You leave me no alternative but to beat the lot of you up. It's a great pity.' This joke, simple and direct, went straight to their hearts. Julian, taking advantage of this relaxation of laughter, now moved lithely and, with a swift and graceful ballet kick, went right for the testicles of the doorkeeper. With a groan this sergeant doubled up, embracing the hurt with both hands, cursing. 'You dirty bastard,' said Turner, making for Julian.

'Away, my dear. I can cope.' Ennis was out through the doorway. Helmetless, he sought his motor-cycle, kicked it into life. Raggedly he steered it into the road, the comforting roar bore him on. Looking through the window in the split second granted by the vehicle's speed, he saw Julian kicking lightly and blithely away, perhaps singing. And then, 'Get the sod!' he heard. They were after him. The crowds were clearing from the streets now, but Ennis, his hair flying, had frequently to cry himself a way clear. He chugged up Castle Road, starting the long climb. He switched on his headlamp. The engine increased its heat. He rounded the first bend. Behind him were his pursuers, steady, calling above the roar their execrations. This needs music, Ennis thought, hurry music, chase music. His inner orchestra began to improvise some – string semiquavers, blasts of brass. He went up and up, the engine burning. On his left below was the vast panorama of the bay, the lower Rock, the vertiginous prospect which had, through the long history of British military occupation, tempted so many overdrawn subalterns. He climbed higher with effort, rounded another bend. The pursuers kept their distance. They would get him.

Well, here it was. The narrow ledge-road that led to Willis's Farm. Who was Willis? Had there really been a farm here? He climbed no longer. He slowed down, braked, switched off his engine, waited. The pursuing roars were dying down now. There was silence. He could see only their headlights shining from the other side of the jutting buttress. Rock. It was just rock. What was the Rock made of?

That was a geological matter. There were so many things he didn't know. Down below, dizzily low, the lights of the town stretched in strings. Look now, a winking light out at sea. Another. And another. Now their tramping boots approached. The avenging what-you-calls. Furies.

'Just one good bloody big punch on the jaw,' said Turner. 'One from each of us. That will do. But first we'll see him grovel.'

'I've got this German class up here,' said Ennis. 'I'll get into a row if I miss it.'

'You won't miss it,' said Turner. 'Though you probably won't be able to do much teaching tonight. Jaw trouble, you know.'

'Look,' said Ennis. 'Let me warn you. Don't try anything here. It's highly dangerous. Look how high up we are. Look at all those lights down there. If you want to beat me up come and do it in the Nissen hut over there. Much more comfortable.'

'Kneel down, Ennis,' said Turner. 'Pray for forgiveness.'

Ennis knelt obediently. As well now as later. He prayed aloud: 'O my God, I am sorry and beg pardon for all my sins and detest them above all things –'

'Bloody mockery,' said one of the sergeants. 'Give it him now.'

Ennis stood up. On his right was the incredible well of the Mediterranean night. 'I'm warning you,' he said. Turner's clenched fist approached. Ennis sidestepped rapidly. Turner struck air and swore. 'Do be careful,' said Ennis. 'Please do be careful.' Turner punched out again with a little grunt. Ennis ducked. Turner got mad and said, 'Bastard.' He launched a killer (hangoverish still?) at the big Southern mild starry winter night. 'Watch it, major,' said the Q.M.S.I. But Turner was too late to watch it. He tried to restore his balance. It was like acrobatic comedy. One of the sergeants thought it was that and laughed. Turner fumbled for a hold, saying, 'Sod it.' His hands wildly played a few rhapsodic bars on the piano of the air between himself and the rockface. Then he did a dance on one leg, wildly pressing at a sort of sustaining pedal with it. 'Oh, Christ,' he said against the starlight, a fair final Faustian statement. Then he went over the side howling, his body bumping against rock, brushing sparse grass, dryly harping at dry leafless twigs. He was going down very fast. His howl grew steadily more distant. Fascinated, they all peered down. It was a hell of a long way down. They imagined a final bump somewhere down there among the town lights. Very far down.

Lost, they all looked at each other. 'That,' said Ennis, 'was an accident. It really was an accident, wasn't it?' The Q.M.S.I. was making very deep retching noises. 'We'd better get down right away and report it,' said Ennis. 'We'd better all stick to the same story. It was an accident. He slipped. He did slip, didn't he?' The Q.M.S.I.'s retching noises became rhythmical, quadruple, crotchet equalling about sixty M.M. The others said nothing. Perhaps already they were thinking about promotion. The work had to go on. 'I'll save your bloody skins somehow,' said Ennis. His leadership was tacitly accepted. In near-silence they freewheeled down as the night thickened.

20

'You've got to go,' said Lieutenant-Colonel Muir.

'Go?' Ennis looked at him. Muir seemed older, greyer, more tortured, more tolerant.

'Yes. They can't pin anything on you, but you make a bad smell in the garrison. When are you due for release?'

'About May or June, I should think.'

'You'll be posted to the Depot. I shouldn't suppose they'd want to give you another job now. You'll just stay at the Depot and get into nightly trouble in the town. It's a big town, full of Americans. It ought to be quite an easy life.'

'But,' said Ennis, 'I had other plans. A job with Dr Bradshaw. My wife was to come out and join me, sir. I wanted to take my demobilisation here.'

'A job with Bradshaw?' Muir's voice climbed through a whole octave. He allowed himself a twisted smile. Contempt or pity or something. He looked through the in-tray on his desk. 'Here it is.' He glanced through the letter, his smile broadening but still twisted. 'Read this. You might as well. It concerns you.' Ennis took the typewritten sheets. 'Sit down if you like,' said Muir. 'No ceremony here.' Ennis sat. He read:

Dear Colonel,

With reference to our telecon of the 29th ult., in which you kindly suggested that schoolchildren over the age of eleven be allowed to enter for your speakers' competition. I have, unfortunately, received a complaint from a religious source which it would, perhaps, be prudent not to specify, about some of the poetry selections. The cleric in question referred to the Spanish poems which had been set, and pointed out that these were in every way unfit for children. I quote his own words: '– The poem by Lorca is, not to mince words thoroughly filthy and depraved. The shameless description of an act of adultery is hardly fit material for adult entrants who possess any notions of Christian cleanliness. The fact that the poem was written by a notorious atheist and anti-clerical does not improve matters. To suggest that school-children, brought up in a Christian atmosphere and conscientiously shielded from vice, should study and deliver the poem in public is criminal. It would not be going too far to say that it is a sin against the Holy Ghost –

'But,' said Ennis's small voice, 'I understood from Major Appleyard – What I was told was – This competition was intended for members of the garrison. Children were, surely, never intended to –'
'Finish the letter,' said Muir.

– Even the poem by San Juan de la Cruz is liable to misinterpretation and becomes a mere outburst of unbridled sensuality if divorced from its mystical context. It is certainly not a fit poem for children.

Ennis showed his teeth. 'Oh my God,' he said. 'Oh, Jesus Christ Almighty.'
'Finish the letter,' said Muir.

– I am asked to register the strongest possible protest about this on behalf of the religious authorities. Your major tells me that Sergeant Ennis was responsible for the choice of the poems. As I proposed recommending him for a place in the Education Service, I feel that it is in some ways fortunate that I have found out, through this thoroughly embarrassing matter –

the gravamen of which is, of course, in no way mitigated – the sort of influence he is likely to have on children.

In the circumstances it seems better that I, on behalf of the various schools for which I am responsible, decline the kind offer you made, and I should be glad if you would regard all entries from the schools already lodged with you as withdrawn.

Yours sincerely

F. A. Bradshaw.

'Writes a flowery sort of letter, doesn't he?' said Muir.

'How can I be blamed for all this?' asked Ennis. 'Major Appleyard didn't make things at all clear. I understood that the competition was for adults only. It's grossly unfair.'

'I can't argue,' said Muir blandly. 'Anyway, there it is. Now, what was this you were saying about a job with Bradshaw?'

Ennis hung his head. Muir stood up and limped round towards him. 'Look here, Ennis,' he said, 'you're not a bad type. You're just one of those poor buggers who always do the wrong thing. Now I don't want you to think that you're being sent home in disgrace. War Office is being told that you're being posted to U.K. because of your wife.' Ennis looked up, hard, at him. 'Yes,' continued Muir. 'The story is that your wife will have a nervous breakdown if you don't live together, if you see what I mean. I met your wife, you know. A highly nervous type, I thought. I don't see any reason why that shouldn't be the truth.'

'What do you mean?' asked Ennis.

Muir ignored the question. 'There's a vacancy for a W.O. 2,' he said. 'You might as well have the benefit of it.' He rang the bell on his desk. 'You needn't look at me as though I've gone daft. You're already improperly dressed. Here's a razor blade.' He slid one across his desk. 'Cut them stripes off,' he said. 'It went up on orders at midday and it's ten past twelve now.' Ennis sliced through the loose stitching, left arm then right arm. He held out the limp soiled chevrons to Muir. 'I don't want the bloody things,' Muir said. 'Chuck them in that waste-paper basket.'

'Is this what you wanted, sair?' W.O. Fazackerly had entered.

'These c-c-c-crowns, sair?' He bore them, shining brass, on a sort of cushion, gulping.

'Yes,' purred Muir. Fazackerly left. 'Here,' said Muir. 'We'll make a sort of a bloody coronation of it. You'd be bound to put the bloody things on upside down.'

'A crown,' said Ennis, looking down at his right forearm. 'A sacrificial king.'

'Two crowns,' said Muir, deft as a tailor. 'Two crowns is ten shillings. When you get home give my regards to your wife. The boat leaves the day after tomorrow.'

Back in his billet Ennis sat heavily on his bed, the unaccustomed glint of metal smirking up at him, what they called the old poached egg on the forearm. What do you think these is, lad? Bloody glow-worms? 'What do I do now?' he said. 'I can't see anything in the future at all.'

'We're going to celebrate, my dear,' said Julian. 'And properly, in a civilised manner. We're going to Hell.'

'What do you mean?'

'We're going over the border. That passport of yours has been gathering dust for months. And before going to Hell it is meet that you consult the Sybil.'

'Is everybody going mad?'

'Only you, my dear. You want to know the future. Mrs Carraway will tell you everything.'

'And who in the name of God is Mrs Carraway?'

'A Queen's Army Schoolmistress. A widow. Surely you've seen her about? Rather a nice old thing. She's taken a house on Castle Road. She's wonderful, knows it all. Cards, tealeaves, palms, the lot. She can read the future like a book. The things she told me! You shall come with me tonight. No, not another word. It's a big opportunity.'

Ennis submitted though, being a Catholic and superstitious, with misgivings. Mrs Carraway proved to live in a damp old cavern of a house. The wind was rising as they sought it, a night of gusty rain blowing up. Mrs Carraway was warm and hospitable, a decent corseted little body with platinum-silver hair, impeccably permed, a

good synthetic accent and the peremptory manner of an old teacher.
It was so nice of them to come and visit a lonely old widow, she said.
She was still only settling in. Sure she would get to know people, but
at first everything was very strange. This was one station she had
never previously visited, except, of course, for a brief afternoon from
the boat travelling farther east. She supposed, however, it would
be like any other. Would they have tea, or something stronger?
Something stronger, then, if she could find the bottle.

She showed them her little treasures: brassware from Benares, an
ivory elephant from Port Said, a musical cigarette lighter from Aden,
Kelantan silver from Penang, wooden effigies of yodellers from the
Tyrol. Then out came her photograph album.

'This, I think, is a very clever and cool-headed snap. Crossing a
field in Hampshire, 1920 I believe it was, the bull started to chase me
just as my husband, rest his soul, had raised the camera. Always as
cool as a cucumber, bless his dear memory, he took me as I started to
run. It wasn't far to the stile. I could run then, you know. How old
would I be? Let me see, now –'

She shuffled more, browning, stained, curling. 'Here's the
Hampton Court maze, where we got lost on our honeymoon. No,
not for long. A couple of hours, that's all. And here's the last photograph my dear son had taken. In the garden it was. A bit blurred, my
husband's hands were shaking. Yes, yes, the decay had set in. It was
bound to happen. The doctor said let him have as much as he likes
now, it could do no further harm. Robert, my son, died in training.
He was just getting his wings. My husband, you see, had been in the
Flying Corps. A great tragedy. He didn't last much longer then. In
the midst of life we are in. It was then that my hair turned white.' She
patted the silver waves complacently. 'But,' she said, 'you haven't
come to hear about my unhappy life. You want me to tell your for-
tune. I'll do my best, but please remember I'm only an amateur. I'll
try the crystal for you in a little while, but meanwhile let's see what
the cards can tell us.' She moved to the sideboard and took from
a drawer a thicker pack of cards than Ennis had ever before seen.
'This,' she explained, 'is the Tarot.'

The Tarot, to Ennis, had so far merely been a literary reference.

'The wisest woman in Europe,' he now quoted, 'with a wicked pack of cards.'

'Some people say it's wicked,' said Mrs Carraway. 'I always say that wickedness is in the eye of the beholder. Now what is it you want to know? Business, a love affair, a lawsuit, a money matter?'

'Yes, please.'

'You can only have one at a time,' said Mrs Carraway. 'Goodness, how the wind is rising.' Draughts indeed knifed them from innumerable crannies, from under the doors, from the badly fitting windows. They could hear thunder rolling over the Iberian plain.

'A love affair, please,' said Ennis.

'So.' She sat at the bare round table. They drew up their chairs. 'Now,' said Mrs Carraway, 'I take the minor arcana and pick out the Cups.' She deftly separated out the gaudy cards, all, number or court, containing chalices, the ace a huge castellar monstrance. She shuffled. Ennis cut. Taking the top four cards of the deck she arranged them, faces down, as the four corners of a lozenge. 'Now,' said Mrs Carraway, 'I take the major arcana. Draw out any seven. Don't look at them. That's right. Now give them to me.' The wind howled piteously under the door. The Iberian thunder approached. She shuffled, Ennis cut. She took the top three cards and arranged them as the points of a triangle, base uppermost, inside the lozenge. 'Now,' said Mrs Carraway, 'I turn them face upwards.'

One by one they appeared. In the outer lozenge the knave, the six, the nine, the ten: an idiot-faced young man on a horse with a chalice in his hand; a whole clatter and gleam of cups. Then came the inner triangle.

Mrs Carraway caught her breath, clicked her tongue against her plastic palate. 'I'm sorry,' she said. Ennis's heart sank. The huge pictures of the major arcana were disclosed. A man hanging upside down from a tree. A tower struck by lightning. The moon, sharp-faced, dripping blood. 'Things have not been going well,' said Mrs Carraway. 'Things will not go any better. That's what the cards say. I see birth, but I also see death. I see failure to run a love affair properly. That's in the past. There's a double meaning here in the six. The destruction of love, or widowhood. That's in the future. Now look at the middle cards. Sacrifice, ruined hopes, hidden enemies. Somebody's death, not yours, but you're involved in it, perhaps even responsible,' She shook her head. 'It's one of the worst I've ever seen. I am so sorry.'

'It's not your fault,' said Ennis.

'And the one you love,' said Mrs Carraway. 'You'll never see her again.' The thunder was heard receding. The wind continued to howl: hollow, hollow, hollow all delight.

'Thank you very much,' said Ennis. 'You've been very kind.'

'I can't leave it at that,' said Mrs Carraway. 'It wouldn't be fair. I must give the powers-that-be another chance. We'll have the crystal now.' She rose and walked again to the dresser, looking again in the drawer, her back to them.

'My dear,' condoled Julian, 'you *are* in a bad way.'

'Perhaps,' said Mrs Carraway, 'we'll get something brighter from this.' She brought to the table a globe of glass, naked, mounted on a red plush stand. She turned out the main light, switched on a table lamp that was shaded with a parchment travesty of Siva. She breathed heavily, asthmatically, over the globe. Her eyes and silver hair glinted in the focus of the light.

At last she said, 'I can see nothing. Nothing.'

'Please,' said Ennis, 'see something. Anything.'

'Wait,' she said. 'Wait, it's coming. Yes. Yes.' The wind fluted, fingering many stops. 'A man. He's wearing a sort of robe. A long robe. It's a minister. It's a priest. In his hands he bears a chalice.'

'Chalices again,' said Ennis. 'Always chalices.'

'He dips his hand into the chalice and takes out a small round white thing. Communion.'

'The Eucharist.'

'He holds it out. I can't see. Yes. Now. His hand is empty.'

'Anything else?'

'Wait.' She paused, breathing hard under the ponderous god. 'No. No. A blank.' She closed her eyes, breathing steadily, opened them again to peer once more into the crystal. 'Nothing at all. Goodness, what a lot that took out of me.' She exhaled a pint of breath.

'Are you sure there was nothing else?' asked Ennis.

'Nothing at all,' answered Mrs Carraway.

'Tell me.' Ennis leaned forward. 'Tell me, who was the priest?'

Mrs Carraway looked at him, wide-eyed, for a moment. 'I've no idea,' she said.

'Yes,' said Ennis, with growing excitement, 'you know. Come on, tell me.'

'Really.' She looked a little scared. 'I didn't notice. It wasn't anybody I recognised.'

Ennis stood up, looking down on her in a sort of triumph. 'It was me, wasn't it?' he said.

'I just don't know,' she answered. 'It might have been anyone.' She herself now got up, wearily. The Rock was a hilly, exhausting place for an old widow.

'Come on, my dear,' said Julian, also rising. 'It's time to go. It was so terribly kind of you, Mrs Carraway. Really, Richard does appreciate it, don't you, Richard?'

They said their good nights and walked slowly back to the billet, cloaked in their groundsheets against the rain. Dim, misty, the Rock loomed above, watching, crouching. 'All it means,' said Julian, 'is that you're going back to the Church.'

'It means a lot more than that,' said Ennis. And then, as they walked on, 'Oh, I don't know. The Rock's always there, I suppose. You spend a Technicolor evening in the cinema, you discuss politics in a wineshop, you make love, you arrange your pack of cards into the most tasteful little pagodas. When you come out into the air you see it, waiting, doing nothing, just existing. It's there, and you're here because it's there.'

They clumped on in silence, down the flowing street, a prospect of drowned lamps. 'Do you believe in all that nonsense?' asked Ennis at length.

'God? Religion?'

'Fortune-telling. Cartomancy, or whatever it's called. Is there anything in it?'

'Well, my dear, it's a bit like the old oracles, I suppose. You know, ambiguous. If it fails on one horn it prongs you on the other. You remember: *Domi ne stes. Domine stes.*'

'We can test it, anyway. That business about never seeing her again.'

'Never seeing who again?'

'The one I love. That's what she said.' He jerked his thumb towards the sybilline house on Castle Road.

They had reached the billet. The Rock had disappeared into the dark rainy night, except for a dim light glowing from its forehead. As they got into their beds, Julian, brilliant in electric-blue pyjamas, said, 'Sleep well, my dear. Your last day tomorrow. Make the most of it.' And after ten minutes of sleepless silence Ennis said:

'That's all I'm fit for, I suppose. Whom art rejected, whom love rejected, God rejected not.'

'Oh, shut up about God,' said Julian crossly. 'Let God and me sleep.'

21

All the year round it is fiesta, the towns and villages gay with the gorgeous colours of traditional costumes, white teeth flash from happy faces blessed by the sun, the wine flows and the romantic old songs are sung. Under the flowery balcony the ardent caballero woos his lady with passionate melody, his guitar twanging to the resonant tenor voice, full of the hot-blooded south, while she coyly twirls a rose, her red-lipped smile coquettishly luring him on, her dark liquid eyes (what tigers of passion, what fires of abandon lurk within!) glowing under the glossy raven hair, the crowning splendour of the mantilla. The night is filled with the lilt of haunting flamenco, vying with the nightingale's song. Then comes another day, full of the glory of the sun, vibrant with the promise of new thrills – the pageantry of some religious procession, the glamour of the bullfight, death in the afternoon. Life, colour, wine, music, the fabulous beauty of the women, the old-world courtesy of the men, fire in their eyes, warmth in their hearts, a welcome to all, the rich civilisation of a proud and ancient people.

Viva España!

'I shit myself,' said the shabby simian little tout, 'on your father,' frustrated greed in his mean eyes, 'your mother,' the dusty creases of his face, 'and all the family.'

'Milk,' said Ennis, evenly.

'God in a lavatory –'

'Ah, go away,' said Ennis in English. And to Julian, 'We don't need a guide. We can find our own way.'

'I think you're making a big mistake, my dear,' said Julian, his hands deep in the pockets of his civilian raincoat. 'If he finds you there he'll create hell. You know these hot-blooded types.'

'There's time enough,' said Ennis. 'I couldn't do it cold sober anyway. Wait till evening.'

They walked on, leaving behind the shabby rococo façade of the frontier, where the ill-uniformed guards quarrelled over the cigarettes that Julian had donated. To the sergeant of the guard, called Dogface by his men, Ennis had given a small bottle of English gin. He had retired at once to a filthy inner room to drink it, dealing out slaps to his snarling subordinates on the way.

'But,' said Ennis, 'I must see her.' Must I? he thought. Was it really prudent? Was it not better to take home the memory of a love that had never decayed, a perfect image, than to see a reality which might, even after so short a time, appal him? And there was his child, surely born by now. He had not seen Barasi for a long time, over a month. Little Juanito no longer came to bring news. He just did not know what had been happening. But the hurt tooth had to be probed to see how hurt it was, and it was perhaps not good to people the world with goddesses.

'It would be a good idea to acquire a couple of whores now,' said Julian primly. 'It would inoculate us, as it were, immunise us from a plague of others.' They walked down the main street, picking their way through a mess of cabbage leaves, avoiding a dead cat – its mangy fur jewelled with rain – as they went. Ragged urchins played with bits of filth – mud dollops, old cigarette packets, abandoned condoms; there were limping, crutched, eyeless veterans of the Civil War begging with held-out boxes and tin mugs; black widows roamed the streets hopelessly; everywhere whores made clicking noises, jerking their heads in invitation. An old man pushed a handcart loaded with rubbish-sacks up a ramp, patiently, weakly, suffering the handcart's pushing back. A younger man without many teeth rode a trick monocycle grimly, a boy taking the hat round.

'This will do,' said Ennis. 'A drink.' The garish little café announced itself with a blare of jukebox music and a fried garlic smell. Outside its windows two barefooted children and an ancient weeping man breathed in the smell, famished. One of the children, skeletal, sexless, begged a penny of Ennis, whining like a caged monkey:

'*Penique, penique, penique!*'

Ennis placed a coin in the thin hand. The other child grabbed the offering, jabbering, padding down the wet street, his cheated companion racing flatfooted after, wailing like a lost soul. Ennis and Julian entered the café, sought a table, their raincoated images looking strangely and critically at them from the dirty-mirrored walls. '*Vino*,' ordered Ennis. '*Vino rojo.*' The waiter breathed caries, peppermint, garlic on them in a sad smile. The place was empty save for shoeblacks, condom-sellers and a group of prostitutes sitting bored in a corner. Two shoeblacks at once took possession of the feet of Julian and Ennis and scrubbed and wiped away, at intervals raising brush and free hand to beat both together, like dead cymbals, in a pitiable bullshit flourish.

'Those two,' said Julian, when the wine had been brought, 'look the least unsavoury.' He indicated a thin-lipped blonde whose black hair-roots showed clear as a patch of acne, and a matronly-looking woman in a very tight skirt, her face a white mask save for full tomato-ketchup lipstick. 'I'll beckon them.' He switched on his stage-smile and lifted and wagged a finger. They all looked, some giggled. One called, hoarsely, 'Siggy, siggy,' with a hand-to-mouth V-sign. The two of Julian's choice came over, sitting down, giggling, rubbing themselves like cats against their clients, raising skirts provocatively, feeling for signs – with pathetic prematurity – of tumescence. 'That will do,' rebuked Julian, in a governess voice. 'You are to behave. Drink some of this nice vino.'

'No jig-a-jig?' asked the blonde. 'Not like?'

'No, we do not like,' answered Julian sternly. 'How much do you require for the doubtful pleasure of your company?'

'*Cuanto dinero?*' asked Ennis. They gabbled eagerly. 'It seems a lot, my dear,' said Julian, as they handed over their torn pesetas (obtained on the black market – a small tobacconist off Main Street). 'Still, presumably they know best.'

'Who,' asked Ennis, 'started this jig-a-jig business? I mean, wherever two races meet, each race thinks it a genuine idiom of the language of the other race. I mean, like "mungie". When Spanish workman and British tommy meet at Four Corners the food in the Spaniard's basket is always "mungie".'

'That, my dear, is Italian *mangiare.*'

'But the Spaniards can't stand the Italians. They would never borrow an Italian word. I have heard, with my own ears, Spanish workmen say: "Italiano poor a' pi'."'

'Meaning?'

'Poor as piss.'

'Poor a' pi',' giggled one of the whores.

'There you are, you see,' said Ennis in triumph. 'Now let's finish this bottle.'

The bottle finished, their spirits – despite the damp cold unspanish day – appreciably higher, they started a café-crawl, their whores clinging to them like sagging limpets. In the shabby streets, down the stinking alleys, they saw the rash, pox, caries of the sick state: the ragged beggars and the policemen patrolling with steel whips. By a vacant lot, heaped with nameless organic putrefaction, tin cans, rags, bottles, merds, metal, stood a Palladian building in peeling stucco. In its dark interior lay huddled figures, tattered shawls drawn round them. 'This,' said Ennis, raising his eyes to the austere and noble Roman lettering, 'is called the Centre of Education and Rest."

They drank steadily. Ennis's blood grew braver, fitter for his mission. A lecherous urge led him to embrace the pallid matronal whore, thrusting a hand down her décolletage. A fat spongy ample palmful, knobbed as by a wart. She giggled, waiting for worse. His gorge rose and he desisted, swilling more wine, handing round cigarettes, becoming popular, speaking more and more fluent Spanish. And then a quarrel began.

The dark young man by the bar came over and whispered something to Julian. Julian shook his head, but the young man persisted. Julian said, 'This man is pestering me, my dear. I don't know what he's saying, but I can guess.' With a swoop the young man was down on him, biting his right ear passionately. Julian screamed. The black-rooted blonde was up on her feet, teetering in high heels, red claws flashing. She drew blood from the dark man's cheek, the smoky air was harsh with rising throaty gabble, the man retreated, the whore followed.

'All right,' cried Ennis. '*No es nada. Venga aquí. Bebe otra vez.*' The blonde returned, displaying twin tunnels of the atavistic in her dark eyes, bearing her loud part still in the jabbering cacophony. Julian groaned and was given womanly comfort. 'I'm bleeding like a pig,' he wailed. 'I'll get hydrophobia. I need medical attention. Look at it, blood dripping on my collar!'

'Perhaps one of these ladies –' suggested Ennis.

'A' righ', wiz me,' nodded the blonde. She swayed off, leading the wounded Julian, hurling a final rattle of execration at his assailant.

'Wait, do wait,' called Julian. 'Don't go away. I'll be back in a minute –'

'I'll wait,' said Ennis. He ordered another bottle. He told the remaining whore how beautiful she was. Her name, she said, was Pepita. She showed her bad teeth often in a ghoulish succession of provocative smiles.

'*Y su pecho,*' he continued. He stopped dead, the flood of literary encomium stemmed by a sudden memory of St John of the Cross and of Concepción. '*En mi pecho florido –*' He said aloud, 'Oh, God. God, God, God.' Pepita looked alarmed, she offered the bottle. Ennis drained his glass, biting bitter lees. The wine was blood, iron, earth, dirty water. 'Lavinia,' he said clearly, 'was a bloody bitch.' He realised that soon he was going to be very drunk. He stood up, looking about him. The place was filling up now, and perched above the fancy dress of civilian clothes were faces he knew – Bloggs, Entwhistle, Carew, Smith, Macdonald, Vosper, others. His legs were gelatinous, but into his arteries beat the fighting strength of whole infantry platoons. He heard greetings.

'Hallo, Sarge.'

''Ave a bash, Sarge.'

'Watch 'er, Sarge. She'll give you a dose.'

'Major,' corrected Ennis loudly. 'Sarnt-major. You think these is bloody glow-worms?' But on his arms were no crowns. He had been demoted to temporary freedom.

'Good old Sarge.'

'Up the Reds.'

'Next stop Moscow.'

Ennis looked down at Pepita. 'Come on,' he said. 'We'll go some-where else. Have a drink somewhere else.'

'*Y su amigo?*'

'He'll find us. Come on.'

They left the smoky den and sought another. The streets were now full of visitors, suppliants at the Venereal shrine, each with his heavy bag of seed to throw on the rotten barren ground. The lights were coming on, and the smell of horse steaks, lemon juice, garlic fed the damp air. In the distance was the Rock, the other side of the moon, warning of the thunder of Britain's history, strange-looking from this foreign angle, strange and familiar, like the mufti-clad troops.

The café they now entered was a little hell of heat and fairy lights. Sweat was issued to each fresh entrant like rose-water. The amplifier, raucous with its bullfight march, itself was a source of sweat. Here were more prostitutes, rubbing up to the unwary soldiers, galvanis-ing their plucked painted skulls into a grimace of proffered abandon. Shirt-sleeved barmen drew sticky chocolate liqueurs out of kegs, mopped the drenched counter, while the coloured light-bulbs cast infernal gleams on the hot excited faces.

'Hell,' said Ennis loudly. '*El invierno.*' His voice was muffled in the blanket of heat and people. '*Crede?*' he asked Pepita.

'*No credo,*' she grinned. Ennis shuddered slightly, hearing Latin not Spanish, hearing what sounded like a liturgical expression of negation. In hell they speak tortured Latin, he thought. He heard the jukebox change its record, and all the whores began to sing, in their harsh Andalusian voices, a popular song, '*La Casa de Papel*'. The house of paper, highly inflammable.

Pepita, becoming drunk and amorous, leaned on him, an arm round his waist. Shall I? he thought. But that could be deferred. She was hungry, she said. Ennis suddenly realised that he was hungry also. He realised that, what with one thing and another, he had not really eaten for two days. 'What have they got?' he asked. They had huge salty prawns and small hard-boiled eggs. He seemed to have seen that waiter before. That waiter nodded to him, winked, made a shushing sign. Who the hell was it then? They also had frogs' legs fried Valencia style. Pepita and Ennis were served with platters of unleavened bread, on them slices of broiled bull flesh (there had been a *corrida* less than a week before) and chopped olives. You were not supposed to eat the bread, said Pepita. You were merely supposed to use it as a kind of miniature table. '*Mesa?*' repeated Ennis, puzzled. All sorts of things were stirring in his mind. He ate the *mesa* of unleavened bread hungrily, feeling not less but more drunk. 'Mendoza,' whispered the waiter. 'You remember me.' He spoke soft American.

'God,' said Ennis. 'Captain Mendoza.'

'Shhhh,' said Mendoza. 'I told you I'd do it. I'm home at last, boy.'

'How *did* you do it?'

'I was drowned,' said Mendoza, winking. 'Next week I move on to Cordova. I've got a really good job waiting for me there. I'm going to sing.'

'Sing?'

'Yes, I can sing. In four languages. I told you I'd do it, boy. I'm free.'

'Free.' Ennis nodded. 'I'll come with you,' he said. 'I can play the guitar pretty well.' A sort of open road beckoned – Don Quixote's, with cork-trees and wine cooling in a goatskin, acorns, cheese as hard as a brick. 'By God, I will,' he said.

'You do that,' said Mendoza. 'We'll beat them all yet.' And then, in response to a drunken soldier's wave, '*Pronto, señor.*' He went away. Ennis did not see him again; had he really seen him at all?

Pepita wanted to eat prawns. She showed Ennis in pantomime what shellfish do to a man, giggling the while. They now drank a fierce coarse brandy, grew thirstier and returned to wine. He was aware of the sweat pouring from his forehead, of a damp shirt and a handkerchief soaked to translucency. He began to talk more, without reserve, discovering that Spanish was easier than English, for English came out slow, blurred and stuttered. He decided that he'd forgotten English, that he was being drawn into the net of Europe, that he'd –

'By Christ,' he said, 'I won't go back. I'll stay. I'll damn well stay. Concepción can play the guitar as well. Concepción can sing.

Mendoza, you sod, Mendoza!' But Mendoza was nowhere to be seen. 'I'll stay,' he said to a younger whore than Pepita, one with a fresher voice, a clearer skin, and an upswept mass of lacquered hair. 'I'll get lost. I'll disappear. They won't find me again.'

'Here,' said a rough voice. Ennis recognised a sergeant of the Royal Engineers. 'My bit of stuff, if you don't mind, mate.'

'Deference,' said Ennis carefully, swaying forwards, backwards. 'Address with due deference. Superior in rank.'

'You come one inch nearer and you'll get my effin fist in your face.' Ennis swayed forward. Pepita grabbed his arm, tried to impel him towards the door. The voices, dimmed for a fight, began to swell up again.

'Murderer,' said a voice near Ennis. 'Bloody murderer. You chucked him over the side. You threw him from the top of the Rock, you murdering bastard.' He couldn't see who it was. Pepita pushed him outside. An uncertain moon was riding the air. In the dim lamplight the beggars waited, whining for pence. An old crone held out a stick of an arm and opened a ruined mouth. Down the street a child with a bright foxy face asked for alms. A policeman appeared from the shadows, waving a steel whip. He chased the child down an alleyway. 'Love,' said Ennis, unmanageable now, zigzagging from wall to gutter. 'Town of love. Love is everybody's business. Listen.' He stopped and addressed Pepita and the cobbled street, the rare passers-by and the lamplight:

Then let us love, dear love, like as we ought.
Love is the lesson that the Lord has taught.

And then, 'Spenser,' he said. 'Mild Spenser. Called from Fairyland.' He was off in the direction of the plaza, leaving her behind, staggering but making speed. She cursed after him, shrilly, shouting, '*Dinero!*' As he went zigging on, a cool chamber in his brain told him there was purpose in his hurry. He had an appointment, someone to see, it was urgent. He remembered, he called to a hovering tout:

'*La casa de Señor Barasi.*'

The man sidled up, pointing across the plaza. '*Allí, maestro.*' He switched the pointing hand into a lowly begging posture. '*Mi esposa muy enferma – siete niños – poco dinero –*' Ennis thrust a crumpled note into the dirty begging-cup of a hand, staggering on to his goal. The man did not leave him, but hung on, keeping up his whine. As they passed an open drinking-shop Ennis could hear a flamenco singer, the pulse of guitar chords. The session was warming up. Hands clapped, the swirl of a skirt was shadowed on the wall, lit by an unseen oil lamp. He stood, undecided, watching, listening. The chant finished, the major chord rang out on the guitar. He saw the wine poured, the mobile mouths opened animatedly, the guitar set, as though to cool, just inside the open door. Ennis crept up on the guitar and, with drunken swiftness, grabbed it. He half-expected the instrument to emit some throb of protest, but it didn't. Why he took it he could not decide. It seemed needful somehow, a talisman, a weapon, the protective symbol of his craft.

'*Aquí, maestro.*' The tout, who had not interrupted his long plaint to comment on the theft, pointed eagerly. '*Poco dinero mas – Muy pobre –*' Ennis surveyed the house. Large, balconied, it stood in a mess of hovels, a queen feigning to ignore the surrounding squalor. It was in darkness. She would be in bed, then. He would wake her. He set the fingers of his left hand to the guitar frets and strummed in a rough chord. He intoned, improvising in Andalusian style:

Concepción! Concepción! Concepción!
Ti quiero mucho, muchísimo.
Soy yo, Ricardo!

The lyrical merit of this chant was non-existent, the musical hardly less so, but it had the merit of directness, simplicity, immediate intelligibility. Yet from the dark house came no response. Ennis began to sway up to its waft, seeking the gate, crying, 'Concepción!' Behind him came people, chattering hotly, ready to strike. One voluble young man, his mouth golden in the lamplight, grabbed for his guitar, a robbed indignant guitarist. There was a woman, all fire, with high Spanish combs and ten red talons. 'A joke only,' said Ennis, bowing. '*Una broma.*' He bowed lower, unsteadily. 'Señora Barasi,' he said.

'Señora Barasi?' They were quieter then, shrugging and making frog's mouths. An old man, curiously like Ennis's father as he might have been had he lived to be an old man, came down the middle of the road, prophesying loudly, his hands raised to heaven.

'In Madrid, perhaps?' said Ennis.

They shrugged again. In Madrid, if it pleased him. Anywhere. Certainly not here. Ennis felt a sort of relief and a strong thirst. '*Bebed*,' he invited, '*todos, con migo.*' And so they went back, all friends, to the wine shop. Accepted by all, drawn into the dark stream, Ennis bought wine. He was dishevelled. He had lost his raincoat somewhere. His tie was under his ear. But he had money still, a little handful of dirty paper.

'*Salud.*'

'*Salud, salud, salud.*'

'The position,' said Ennis, in wild Spanish, 'is this, ladies and gentlemen. Out there, beyond that border, is the new world, the world that is emerging out of the ruins of our war for which your war was but a preparation. Don't let it infect you. Keep to your dark squalor and illiteracy. True, you are not free. True, you are living under the tyranny of a dirty big he-goat (*cabrón*). But, with the help of God and His holy mother, he shall soon be drowned in a resurgent undulation of brave hearts. I, for my part, will stay· here with you. I will help you in your fight.'

Ennis wondered at the silence, the eyes uneasily watching a point beyond his back, the mouths and index fingers combining in a 'shhh' gesture. He turned to see a uniformed man, belted, holstered. A woman beyond this uniformed man spat surreptitiously. The man looked about him, upright, contemptuous, drinking a glass of clear spirit. '*Quién?*' asked Ennis. Nobody answered. He tottered up to the uniform, bottle in hand. '*Un vaso, señor?*' he suggested. '*Con migo?*'

'*Gracias, no.*' The man's left cheek had a long scar. He was a proud disdainful man. Ennis fancied he smelt stale blood. He saw himself as the hero of a film about fascist oppression, the foreign saviour, snapper-of-fingers at torturers in black uniforms. He raised his glass. '*Libertad*,' he proposed. '*Muerte a los tiranos.*' The man said nothing, holding his glass, staring at the rows of bottles behind the bar, the bullfight poster. '*Franco*,' said Ennis, without heat, '*es un puerco*.' A little murmur began among the onlookers, grew. '*Muerte a Franco*,' suggested Ennis. '*Viva la libertad*.' He then, having no more words, emptied his wine on to the floor.

The uniformed man was already blowing a whistle, his hand was to his holster. The fat barman was pleading. '*Es un ingles. No sabe nada*.' The voices rose higher, all eyes on the emerging revolver. Ennis rushed to the door. This was absurd, only a film really. The whistle shrilled. Ennis ran into the arms of three policemen. He was surrounded by an unintelligible hubbub, a rapid counterpoint of hot speech. Faces were alight, the crowd growing. Ennis saw himself in prison, the cold dawn, the firing squad. Worse – rubber truncheons, steel rods, castor oil. He struggled, shedding the luxury of another language, shouting: 'I'm English, blast you, English. It was only a joke.' Then, pathetically, '*No es que una broma*.' The arms tightened, the frog-march about to begin. He yelled, 'Help!'

Then, to his relief, a relief that – as though he were some character in an American war novel – nearly loosened his sphincter, he saw a familiar face. It was Barasi. The greasy podgy nose, the thick glasses, the swollen body in a black raincoat, stabbed his heart like a vision of home. 'Mr Barasi!' he called. Barasi did not answer, hardly looked at him. The speed with which the tangle was untied, notes were passed, shoulders patted, rapid speech modulated from the acrimonious to the tolerant and amused, was incredible. The police were off, smiling, saluting; the uniformed official with the whistle cracked a last joke, stuffed hundreds of pesetas in his pocket, cleared the crowd, smiled at Ennis, clicked his heels, saluted and was gone. Barasi and Ennis were left alone.

'Well, Sergeant Ennis,' said Barasi, sadly, 'I am sorry that we meet after so long in such circumstances. Young men should not drink if they cannot control their tongues. It is lucky I was near.'

'I'm grateful,' mumbled Ennis. 'I was a damned fool.'

'It is nothing. I too was young once. Come with me.' He put his podgy hand on Ennis's arm. 'Some coffee will do you good. I own most of the cafés here. This one is less dirty than most. Let us go in.'

He steered him into a grim hole loud with sucking, tawdry with gilt and plush, and led him to a corner table. The shirt-sleeved waiter came obsequiously running, taking the order with bows.

They sat silently for a time. Ennis sipped the bitter black coffee, warming both hands on the white belly of the cup.

'Grief, too,' said Barasi at length. 'That will drive a man to do stupid things.'

'Grief?' Ennis looked at him. Barasi was not the kind of man to know grief.

'My wife,' explained Barasi.

'Oh,' Ennis nodded. 'Your first wife.'

'Yes, my first wife, too. That is in the past, though. Time softens all pain, as it will soften this. But she was so young. It is hard not to grieve. And the child, too, the child that was not born.'

Ennis stared, incredulous. 'Who are you talking about?'

Barasi stared back. 'You know. It was in the newspaper. My wife. Concepción. You heard about that.'

Ashen, his hands arrested with the cup to his chin, Ennis answered inaudibly, 'No.'

'A miscarriage, the doctor called it. He was a good doctor. English. No expense was spared. And yet I blame myself. I must be responsible. She was carrying my child. It is a bitter thing to remember.'

'You must try to forget.' Ennis paused, his mouth, despite the hot bitter draught, very dry. He framed the word '*muerta*'. He shook his head hopelessly. 'I knew nothing about it, never heard.' He wondered what was the right emotion to feel. He was empty, drained.

'So *there* you are. I've looked everywhere, simply *everywhere*. It was most unkind, it was a filthy trick.' Julian stood before them, a Van Gogh bandage on his ear, a little dishevelled, very indignant, ignoring Barasi, pouring shrill wrath on Ennis. 'You said you would wait. You promised. I seriously thought you were in grave trouble. I have not had *one* minute's peace, worrying as I did. I shall never come here again, *never*.'

Barasi smiled wanly. 'I will go now,' he said. 'Goodbye, Sergeant Ennis. We shall not meet again, I believe. I have heard stories, but

– never mind. Keep out of trouble.' Ennis rose, shook his hand, thanked him. Compassion, self-pity, alcohol made the moisture dazzle his eyes. He said good-bye.

'Knocking around with horrible fat slugs like that 'said Julian, sitting down, 'and I don't know what else besides. Really, it's too much. You might have spared a thought for me. The time I've had. It was horrifying.' He looked Ennis straight in the face. 'Do you know what she did?'

'No,' said Ennis, a cigarette staining his fingers.

'My dear, she raped me, positively raped me. There is no other word for it. She had me down on that horrible stinking bed. The strength of the woman!'

'Yes?' said Ennis.

'You're not listening. I don't think you're interested. You don't seem to care *one little bit*. Surely it was up to you to come and look for me, instead of swilling that disgusting gut-rotting stuff with that obscene whore. You just don't care. I shall say no more.'

'I'm sorry,' said Ennis, dropping the unsmoked butt-end in his coffee cup. Hisssss. 'Tell me what happened.'

'She had the strength of fifty,' said Julian, animatedly. 'She had me down to my buff, to my veritable *pelt*. And then! I really can't describe all the horrible *obscene* things she devised. I was appalled, petrified! I shall go into a monastery, my dear. If this is *love*, as they call it, I've had all I want, and more. All I want to do now is to go home. Moreover,' he added, 'she took all my money. Every penny. The embarrassment,' he wailed, 'when I ordered a reviving glass of something, and there was nothing in my pocket but the lining.' He poked Ennis in the stomach. 'I blame *you*,' he said. 'You should have looked after me. Never again,' he stated emphatically. 'Never, *never* again.'

Two policemen appeared at the door, making coaxing whistling noises, flicking at their contraband wristwatches. 'Good God,' exclaimed Ennis, suddenly awake to time, peering at his own watch, the calm impersonal recorder of the burning minutes of so many experiences, so many parachronic discoveries, 'I didn't realise how late it was getting!' And then: But I'm not going back, he thought.

I'm going to stay here. I'm going to see Mendoza again and Mendoza and Concepción and I are going to travel north, strumming and singing and earning our black bread and wine and cheese and acorns. He slumped ready for tears, but Julian thumped him briskly.

'Three minutes to go,' urged Julian. 'We can just about make the frontier in time. We must *fly*.'

They flew. But there were soldiers still lurking in the shadows, moaning in the sordid ecstasy of approaching detumescence: they were going to be in trouble, really they were. Ennis and Julian flew through the evil shadows, past the toothless, chinless, ragged alms-begging crones, the children still alert for pennies. They flew, their feet unsure on the shining greasy cobbles, to the rococo folly of the gate, the proscenium-arch of a cold inferno, down the long shining neutral stretch to the little island where they must, first, show their passes and then, if they had used Spain as Spain was mostly used, wash out their prepuces. Thence on, slowly, panting, down the road to the deserted town. The moon shone moistly on the Rock.

'The descent,' said Julian, 'is so easy. But to return involves over-much labour. It isn't worth it.' Their over-worked lungs were easing now, and the sweat on their faces was dry. 'A town of the dead,' he added, looking back to the receding lights.

'Of the dead,' agreed Ennis, dully. 'Necrophilia. Copulation with corpses.' They walked on. '"Say, dainty nymphs, and speak, Shall we play Barley-Break?" That was also called "Last in Hell".'

'Concepción is dead,' said Ennis.

'Concepción?'

'Dead.'

Julian said nothing for a long time. When he spoke, it was not to the purpose. He pointed to the troopship that lay at anchor off the North Mole. 'You'll escape from it all tomorrow, my dear,' he said. 'A new world, I believe. Wide boys, drones, a cult of young hooliganism. State art. Free ill-health for all. Lots and lots of forms to fill in. The *Daily Mirror's* increasing circulation. Nostalgia among ex-flying types, sick for the lost mess games. Returning corporals killing their wives. Bureaucracy growing like a cancer. Reality will seem very unreal over there.' As they approached Line Wall Road, he said, 'A great weight will have been taken off your mind.'

'I must learn to grow up,' said Ennis. 'I can't put it off much longer.'

22

A crapulous breakfast (porridge, tea, soya sausages) in the grey dawn. A sleepy good-bye to Julian, who put up his cheek to be kissed. The unhandy fastening of pack straps, tightening of the cord of the kitbag. The truck speeded through the early streets, passing ('Goodbye! Good-bye, you bastards!' called the troops) the small cafés where Spanish workmen sucked up the broken rolls of batter which they had drowned in coffee. A donkey or two brayed a five-octave-dropping good-bye at them. The air was fresh as they waited on the Mole in ragged formation, watching the growing sunlight butter the ship's flank. A whole battalion was embarking and 'Stop grunting, you pigs!' yelled a fat sergeant to his platoon. 'Bloody pig himself,' muttered an orderly-room clerk to Ennis. 'Sowe by name and pig by nature. Oink, oink, oink.' Names were called, Movement Control rustled lists importantly. As the lighter edged to the quay, a staff car arrived from Garrison HQ, the driver waving a bunch of airmail. It was given out. There were two for Ennis, one from the BBC, the other from Laurel. This latter he stuffed into his field-dressing pocket. He knew the handwriting so well, even the content. He weighed the emotion that would follow surprise at his unheralded appearance: would disappointment cast out delight, he wondered, or would the solidity of his body in her arms make up for the failure of the plans she had dreamed? He tore open the letter from the BBC. They thanked him for the score of the *Passacaglia*; they doubted if they could find a place for it in their programmes; it was being returned to him by surface mail. He boarded the lighter with the rest of the men, and soon the ship became not a goddess but a hulk one could enter.

Only when his kit was stored and he stood at the rail, did he think to open Laurel's letter. The self-conscious crown on his forearm flashed in the sun as he dove for the thin blue slip. Over the side, in the dirty bilge water, he saw the choppy boats of the banana-sellers, crying from another world. He tore open the letter's folds, glued with her spittle, and read. It was not easy to take in the meaning at first, so he read again, his sore eyes blinking, his face bunching into an incredulous frown.

When you get this I shall be gone – I know you will be happy enough there with your little Gibraltese (is that right?) girl-friends. He has been asking for so long and I thought it would be easier now that you and I have become almost strangers. No trouble about immigration formalities and suchlike. I am officially going to work for him. You can divorce me on grounds of desertion. It's three years, I think, not long to wait, really. America sounds wonderful, no shortages, no aftermath of war. He has been very kind. He is sending you a cheque for five hundred dollars which should tide you over for a bit. I know you'll settle down all right. I shall hear your music some day soon, I hope. I shall always think of you, it was lovely, really. You'll soon get over me –

Over me, over me. A grotesque memory of himself and Laurel in bed together on a hot summer night. Leave, 1942? Threshing bedclothes and bodies. Well. The Sybil could only prophesy in riddles. There was no future to worry about as yet. The empty flat was somewhere in a time-world beyond; there was the voyage which was the real future. Eat up all this first, like a good boy; no next course till you've finished what's on your plate.

'Well, look who's here! It is you, isn't it?' Ennis turned to see a big blonde Wren smiling and frowning at him. She'd hardly changed at all since that voyage out how many years ago? Plumper, browner, not less desirable. Ennis smiled and said:

'Yes, it's me. How are things in Aden?'

'It was Cyprus,' she pouted. 'I'm on my way home from Cyprus. I thought you wouldn't remember, somehow.'

'I remember,' said Ennis warmly. 'Could I ever forget?'

'You're different, somehow,' she said. 'Thinner, like, and older-looking. Oh, and you've got a thing on your arm. What does that make you?

'A sergeant-major,' said Ennis. 'Sort of.'

She simpered. 'Did they give you that for telling lies?' And then: 'I've got to dash now. I'm on my way to rehearsal. We're putting on a show tonight to welcome all you Gib lot aboard.' She waved and winked. 'See you after.'

He smoked a cigarette. The voyage was half taken care of. Images droned through his brain without sequence as he stared steadily at the bay. From among the drift of his mind a theme emerged. With a tiny pulse of excitement he heard its possibilities. A string quartet, obviously. Last movement. There must be another theme logically anterior to this one; that would make the first movement. No real sonata form, no great length. Economy. Absolute unity of construction. On the back of Laurel's letter he drew five rough lines and noted down what he heard.

By the time he had found some manuscript paper, losing his way often before he recognised his own deck, the cabin he was to share with a wall-eyed company sergeant-major of Pioneers, the ship was under way. Dinner smells gushed from hatchways; the clank and throb of the ship's heart beat out a new kind of time, the time of the voyager.

'Yoo hoo,' cooed the blonde Wren. 'They've rehearsed my bit. They said I could go.'

'Come and see my cabin,' said Ennis. 'It's awfully nice. I share it with another man, but he's giving his men a pep-talk or something.'

'I oughtn't to, really,' said the blonde Wren, giggling. Afterwards Ennis stood, all alone, at the stern. (She had to go and see her Queen Wren, or something.) The themes pricked his mind, asking to be released, but he knew that this slow agonising exultant process of useless creation would have to wait a little longer. He stood looking along the ship's wake at the dwindling past. It shook impotent fists, trying to assert an old power, but it knew that it was becoming too small to be anything but ridiculous or lovable.

He watched for a long time. There still the tiny human beings squeaked and gibbered, and their passions and convictions buzzed like gnats. The beetle-donkeys squeak-brayed, and the toy milch-goats dropped microscopic tumbling black berries. The ants committed small brittle corpses to the ground. It was so small and distant, that world that had been as close as sweat or tears and big enough for nightmares. He watched and watched till it vanished, leaving only the haunting of certain voices which would fade soon enough. At last the sea's lips opened to receive the morsel. The Rock sank, englutted to the fading of slow chords, raising not a bubble.

Appendix 1: Anthony Burgess, Introduction to the first British and American editions of *A Vision of Battlements* [1965]

A Vision of Battlements was, is, my first novel. I wrote it in 1949, three years after leaving the scene where it is set – Gibraltar. There, as a sergeant and subsequently a sergeant-major, I had spent the second half of my six years' war service. When I wrote it I had no intention of setting myself up as a novelist. My profession was that of a training college lecturer in Speech and Drama, and my ambition was to be known as a composer of serious music. 1948–9 had been, musically, a busy time for me. I had written various things for use – a piano sonata and a piano sonatina, a little concerto for piano duet and percussion, some realisations of Purcell songs, a polytonal suite for recorders, orchestral incidental music for *Murder in the Cathedral*, *The Ascent of F6*, and *The Adding Machine*. When the Easter vacation of 1949 arrived, I was empty of music but itching to create. And so I wrote this novel. It filled up the vacation, kept me out of mischief, and also satisfied a vague curiosity I had always had: could I, for good or ill, compose an extended piece of prose without getting bored? There was another, submerged, motive for writing, and that was to see if I could clear my head of the dead weight of Gibraltar. I had lived with it so long that it still lay in my skull, a chronic migraine: a work of fiction seemed the best way of breaking it up, pulverising it, sweeping it away. But to my surprise, the act of recomposing the Rock and of reconstructing the artificial life that was lived around it served only to call back pain and loneliness that refused to be exorcised. I pushed on to the end, but then made little effort to seek publication. The typescript travelled to Malaya and Borneo with me, then back to England, always pushed into drawers but – so loath is the artist to waste anything – never actually condemned to destruction. Sixteen years after its composition, I find it possible to read the work with little personal pain and not as much artistic depression as I might be expected to feel. And so it is at last published.

I had better say at once that the personal pain has little to do with the content of the story. No character is based on any real person living in Gibraltar at the end of World War Two. The names and personalities and events have more to do with Virgil's *Æneid* than with remembered actuality. 'Ennis', who tries to blue-print a Utopia in his lectures and create actual cities in his music, is close to 'Æneas', 'Agate' to 'Achates', 'Turner' to 'Turnus'. Lavinia is Lavinia, Barasi is Iarbas, his name anagrammatised. Concepción is Dido, a dark-skinned widow loved and abandoned. The use of an epic framework, diminished and made comic, was not mere pedantic wantonness, nor was it solely a little tribute to James Joyce; it was a tyro's method of giving his story a backbone; it was also a device – failed, alas – for taming the Rock by enclosing it in myth, which is bigger than any chunk of strategic geology. I have had to tame the Rock, an emblem of waste and loneliness, by other means – by revisiting it in middle age and finding it very much shrunken. My wife went with me, and that helped to put the Rock in its place.

One other point. Richard Ennis, my composer-hero, has made other appearances in my works, particularly in *The Worm and the Ring*, also – as a memory or name only – in my Malayan books. He means a good deal to me, because he is a failed composer, but readers may see in him an anticipation of a particular type of contemporary hero, or anti-hero. In point of public appearance, he limps after the known and established rebels; in point of creation he comes pretty early. It's as well to remember that the Welfare

State rebels were anticipated by the Army rebels, especially those who, stuck and frustrated, waited in vain for the siege of rocky and invincible Troy.

Appendix 2:
Anthony Burgess, 'Gibraltar'

In *Essays Today* 6, ed. by William T. Moynihan (New York: Harcourt, Brace & World, 1968). First published in *Holiday* magazine, February 1967.

A rock of preposterous size, with a town crowded around it. A bit of geographical Spain – sun and balconies and yellow stucco – but with British-looking bobbies in the streets, and pounds, shillings and pence in the emporia. The claustrophobic atmosphere of a besieged garrison, but also a sense of immense width: on a fine day from the top of the Rock you can see the time on the town clock in African Ceuta; from Moorish Castle you can find – like a lost coin – the bull ring in Spanish Algeciras. The biscuit-coloured beauty of the girls, the gold-toothed business drive of the men. Baroque processions on Corpus Christi; an Anglican cathedral in the form of a mosque. Sherry from Jerez and tepid, bitter beer from Burton-on-Trent.

I know three Gibraltars. In 1943, I stepped ashore as an army sergeant, resigned to a kind of barrack incarceration that would end only with the defeat of Germany. Gibraltar was a grim garrison then, equipped for siege; the women and children had been sent off to safety; the lights that shone there (as they shone in neutral Spain) were a mockery of peacetime. Another Gibraltar has supervened since then – the pleasure town I visit in middle age. The third Gibraltar is neither a garrison nor a centre of tourism: it is a bone of contention that history will not bury. The Spanish yap for it, the British hold it down with an uneasy paw. It is a colony doggedly persisting in a world that has shed the colonial principle. To the stay-at-homes who read of it in the newspapers, it is a mere political abstraction, smelling not of oranges and garlic and seawater soap but of trouble. Gibraltar is used to trouble.

For most of us, the Rock exists as a metaphor long before we see it as a reality. In everyday speech it goes on standing for strength, integrity, impregnability; and, to the comfort of the British, those qualities have been reflected from that mass of Jurassic limestone onto the occupying and colonizing power. But with the coming of the atomic age, no chunk of strategic geology can impress as in the old days of cannon; the metaphor celebrates a fossil. We have to think ourselves back into an age of imperial glamour to be moved by Wilfrid Scawen Blunt's lines:

Ay, this is the famed rock which Hercules
And Goth and Moor bequeath'd us. At this door
England stands sentry. God, to hear the shrill
Sweet treble of her fifes upon the breeze,
And at the summons of the rock gun's roar
To see her redcoats marching from the hill!

The rock gun may still roar, but it no longer frightens. The redcoats have changed to khaki, and they would not harm a fly. The fifes are drowned by the jukeboxes in the Main Street cafés. And there is no point in guarding a door when the roof already has been blown off.

But, denuded as it is of the connotations of military and naval power, the Rock is still imposing – whether, as the massive full stop of the Iberian peninsula, it looms on the road from Granada, or, like palpable thunder, towers over the ship's deck. Its dead weight of limestone has always been there – the northern Pillar of Hercules, matching Mount Abyla in Africa across the strait; the end of the known world for the Romans; the point where prehistory cracked into the antediluvia and postdiluvia ages, for it was here that the Atlantic rushed in to make the Mediterranean. As a sheer *thing*, a tough entity slapped down in southern Andalusia, it continues to excite wonder. More than two and a half miles in length – from the grim, broad face, looking northward to Spain over the flat *campo*, to the winking light on its southern tail – it sprawls like a living organism.

I say 'living' advisedly: it does not give the impression of a dead thing. Its body is fissured and arteried; it echoes with galleries and caverns yielding fresh water. Its skin teems with flowers and herbs in the spring, after the rains and before the long, dry heat. The Rock has its native stone pine and wild olive; Africa and Europe meet in the richness of its imported flora – palmetto, cactus, algarroba, cypress, orange, lemon, mimosa, pepper tree. Few birds make their home there, but many lodge on the Rock's heights during migration, taking a breather before tackling the shortest sea route to Africa – kite, honey buzzard, osprey, snake eagle, goshawk. And if there are few resident mammals, these at least include the only Barbary apes living wild in all Europe: they are a kind of heraldic marvel.

Nobody is sure how the Rock apes got there. It was once believed that they were a prehistoric survival, a leaping and gibbering reminder of the time when the strait was a bridge and Spain and Africa one territory. Another theory suggested that they crawled from the African hills by a submarine route, a tunnel leading from the Barbary Coast to Saint Michael's Cave in the body of the Rock. But none of the fossil bones found in Gibraltar are simian. The apes belong to a time remote enough but still historical. They travelled by ship with the occupying Arabs: they are among the things the Moor bequeathed us.

Tourists visit them now in their home on the Upper Rock. But not so long ago they were regarded as one of the less attractive of the Moor's bequests. I remember the time when they roamed the town freely, stealing from kitchens and even ships' galleys, terrorizing women, children and banana vendors. Not only those. Descending one afternoon from Moorish Castle to Main Street, I found a fierce ape defending the narrow stone stairway. It snarled. I decided it would be more prudent to take the longer route down to sea level, so I walked half a mile to some steps off Castle Street. There I found another fierce ape defending the narrow stone stairway. It snarled.

In 1900, when the apes were counted, it was discovered that there were about two hundred of them snarling all over the Rock. Their numbers declined, however, and the jealous Spanish put about a saying: 'When the apes leave the Rock, the British will leave too.'

It is good politics to pay heed to popular superstitions. Just before the First World War, the whole population of apes went on the Governor's payroll. A non-commissioned officer was put in charge of them and made responsible for their rations (there is not enough natural vegetation to feed them) and general well-being. When, during the Second World War, the superstition smouldered again, Winston Churchill himself gave orders that the survival of the apes – threatened by the urgent building of new fortifications – should be assured through the making of special enclosures and the importation of fresh stock from North Africa. Now they flourish modestly on the Upper Rock, in two packs of about twenty each. The Spanish have forgotten their old saying: they are relying on more rational pressures to get the British to move out.

It is unfair to put simians before people, but this is what most visitors to Gibraltar do. They snap their cameras at the apes but not at the Gibraltarians, whom they do not find very interesting. The visitors buy carpets and wrist watches and duty-free whisky from the Gibraltarians, but do not go in search of old Gibraltarian customs. This is because there are none. The poorer cousins across the Spanish frontier erupt in romantic passion, internecine enmities, flamenco and bullfights, but the Gibraltarians are chiefly dedicated to the careful making of money.

To be disappointed in their failure to demonstrate the temperament of Spain is to misunderstand their ethnic makeup. They speak Spanish – a rough Andalusian dialect, deficient in the s-phoneme, so that *España* becomes *E'pañia* – but they are not Spanish. They are Genoese, Moroccan Jewish, Portuguese, Minorcan, garrison-English-Irish-Scottish, and they call themselves, rightly, British. There is, inevitably, some Spanish blood, but this has been induced rather than imposed: traditionally, young Gibraltarians go over the border to find brides. No Gibraltarian can point to a Spanish father. Spanish is the mother tongue, but the father tongue is English. It is a kind of English nurtured in classes on bookkeeping and the economics of trade; it is somewhat flavourless and totally unliterary. Figurative English of even the most prosaic kind is not well appreciated. Teaching in Gibraltar at the end of the war, I asked a class of earnest adults to write a sentence that would illustrate the proverb, 'Too many cooks spoil the broth.' Most of them gave me something on this pattern: 'There were many cooks in the kitchen and they were all trying to make broth. But it was not good broth, and this proves that too many cooks spoil the broth.'

They call themselves British and are happy to leave the administration of their external affairs to Britain. There was a time when they acquiesced in the military dictatorship (wholly necessary in a fortress) that their Governor represented, but – though the Governor remains – they moved toward full internal self-government after the War, complete with a freely elected legislative council. That they do not wish to go farther, choosing total independence of Britain, is a puzzle and a vexation to those progressives who believe that colonialism is, *ipso facto*, a bad thing. To the Gibraltarians, colonial status has never been a matter for shame. Now, with the Spanish eager to embrace them and reclaim their city as part of the motherland, they cling more than ever to the torn and dusty skirts of Britannia.

But why do they prefer the Protestant English – with whom they have little in common except a liking for tea, chipped potatoes, football and parliamentary government – to a neighbour with whom they share a language, a religion and even a cuisine? The answer is to be found in a history that is spatialized in the ramps and passages and alleys and bastions called after long-dead heroes of this tiny raj, in the ceremony of locking the city gates against the intruder, in the contours of a city little changed since the days of siege, but that is – in the British manner – a force at least as live as the jukeboxes and the casinos and the new funicular railway that takes you to the top of the Rock. Nothing is forgotten. It is, indeed, impossible to forget the history of twelve and a half centuries, since the relics of that history refuse to be tidied up, cast out, overlaid. The ruins of the Moorish Castle are still there. Any local schoolboy will tell you that the name of his Rock is derived from *Gibel Tarik* – the Mountain of Tarik ibn Zaid, who in 711 took over what the Romans had called Calpe (the Spanish-language newspaper of Gibraltar is called *El Calpense*). Spain captured it in 1309 and the Moors retook it in 1333, holding it until 1462. But the story of Spanish-Moorish wrestlings, the eventual driving out of Islam from a Christian peninsula, means less than what happened in 1704, the date that marks the true beginnings of British Gibraltar.

The War of the Spanish Succession was being fought. Admiral Rooke bombarded Spanish Gibraltar and forced the governor to surrender. Taking over the town, he invited its inhabitants to live peacefully – no tribute exacted – under the British flag, but all except about a hundred Spaniards fled to the mainland. Thus what the Spanish now urge strongly – the fact of a national continuity on the Rock – is very hard to support. The Spanish were asked to stay, but they got out. Moreover, by the Treaty of Utrecht, which was signed in 1713, Spain surrendered the fortress to Great Britain 'to be held and enjoyed absolutely with all manner of right for ever.' But that was not to be the end of the story. A mere thirteen years after the treaty was signed, the Spanish attacked the fortress and were repulsed. A more serious effort was made in 1779, when Britain was at war with both France and America. That year saw the beginning of the Great Siege, in which Gibraltar discovered her strength and her patriotism.

The whole story is in the epic-film tradition, though no film has yet recorded this astonishing four-year feat of endurance and defiance. Blockade and bombardment from without, smallpox and scurvy and starvation within – the pattern of suffering is familiar. When Lord Howe, with a fleet of thirty-four ships, trounced the combined French and Spanish fleets of forty-two, it was the end of Spain's claim to Gibraltar. Until now. But now Spain does not harry with cannon: she merely closes her frontier to wheeled traffic from the Rock.

It would be untrue to say that, ever since the Great Siege, Spain has filled the role of Gibraltar's natural enemy. It is rather that Spain has continued to stand for trouble of one kind or another, while the Rock has always symbolized stability and security.

Whichever side was destined to win the Spanish civil war in the 1930s, it was bound to make an uneasy neighbour for colonial

Gibraltar – the dictatorship of the proletariat or the dictatorship of the Falange. Hindsight has shown that Franco never once intended to involve his people in the Second World War (to have suffered the rehearsal for it was quite enough), but his equivocation made for six years of British uneasiness. There were spies in the ragged frontier town of La Línea; there was the known existence of the 'Ferdinand and Isabella' plan for the German conquest of the Rock – with, of course, Spanish assistance. We soldiers pushed on with our tunnelling, cramming reserve larders with corned beef and baked beans; the guns were kept oiled and their teams alert. The work was wasted, but how could anyone know that?

In the twilight of Franco's rule, Spanish demands for sovereignty over Gibraltar have a ring less sinister than demented. Imperial Spain is supposed to be dead, replaced by a decent middle-class country more concerned with production schedules than baroque dreams. Franco is seventy-five; it looks like a last mad flourish.

The Anglo-Spanish talks go on intermittently, but the British will not flout the principle of self-determination, which – in the case of the Rock – means a determination to remain a British colony. Meanwhile, Spain conducts a mean policy of frustration and harassment. Some Gibraltarians have not seen Spain for as much as two years. There are restrictions on the passage of commuting Spanish day labour to the Rock. Communion wine and medical supplies are confiscated. When the two territories should be cooperating for their common prosperity, the niggling acts of vindictiveness anger and irritate, entrenching both Britain and Gibraltar more firmly in a common attitude of intransigence. Concessions have been offered to Spain (full consular representation on the Rock is one of the latest), but total cession is – in the face of the determination of 25,000 Gibraltarians to remain British – quite out of the question.

But Gibraltar has its fears. Harold Wilson is no Winston Churchill; 'loyalty' may have become a tarnished term. There are murmurs about the possibility of Spain's being granted the freehold of the Rock, while Britain pays for a lease. And there are voices – such as that of Major Bob Peliza, chairman of the Pro-Integration with Britain movement – that use Churchillian language. Peliza says he would help to burn Gibraltar if ever Spain took over. Integration might mean something like county status for Gibraltar, with the burden of British taxes (income tax on the Rock is, at its highest, the equivalent of twenty cents to the dollar), but with full representation in the Parliament at Westminster. At present, Gibraltar's relationship with Britain is one of 'free association': it is the kind of 'British' compromise that comes naturally to a British people.

The English have, since the war, looked to Spain as the best and cheapest source of holiday sun and whisky. Now they are not too happy about lolling on Franco's beaches. An ill wind may turn into a prosperous breeze for Gibraltar, and it will blow more balmily with the foreign currency restrictions that Britain is imposing on its holidaymakers. Gibraltar is exotic, but it is in the sterling area: *chelines* and *peniques* sound like strange currency, but they are only shillings and pence. The sun is strong in summer, and winter feels like an English May. Drink and cigarettes are cheap. The range of tourist attractions is growing. You can play roulette (French and American), baccarat, craps and blackjack at the casino; you can charter a yacht for a fortnight; you can drink at Harry's Trafalgar Bar and dine at the Sombrero on Cornwall's Parade; you can buy fine wines from Saccone and Speed; you can buy fine watches from Morillo and Co Ltd; you can see *son et lumière* in Saint Michael's Cave, reaching it by one of Bland's Cable Cars. North Africa is only a twenty-minute flight away.

I can do without the catch-*penique* delights. I lived in Gibraltar for three years of my youth, and while I resented that enforced expatriation, I learned, with a steadily diminishing reluctance, to love the bizarre blend of disparities. The policemen wore London uniforms and spoke excitable Andalusian. Taxi drivers, forbidden by law to sound their horns, made far more noise with a hand slapping on the outside of the door. Main Street had a city gate at either end, but in the bay rode the shipping of the whole free world: the contractive and the expansive nicely balanced.

The people I know in Gibraltar are mainly the people I knew before, twenty-three years ago. I trained them in the Gibraltar Defence Force or watched them preparing to take over their fathers' shops. They are amiable, undistinguished, living in council flats and running small cars. They drink not in the smart bars but in small, dark wine-shops in the winding side streets, passages, alleys and ramps. They follow the progress of their football team, Gibraltar United, and watch soap opera on television. They read the *Gibraltar Chronicle* (one of the oldest of all English language newspapers) but also *El Capense*. Their bilingualism imparts a special flavour to the town – an English cucumber sandwich rubbed with Mediterranean garlic. The idioms of their Rock Spanish have never been eternalized in literature. They have little taste for serious art, and their view of learning is utilitarian. Still, they are far from frivolous. Their patriotism is vital and quite un-self-conscious. They are hurt when Englishmen mistake them for Spaniards.

Gloomy at British ignorance, they are also resentful of Spanish arrogance. The Spaniards have recently been vilifying them as a racial hotch-potch with little history and no culture. Perhaps the Gibraltarians recognize this as a just revenge. The menial tasks of the Rock have traditionally been done by Spaniards, and the Gibraltarians have naturally tended to flaunt a certain superiority. But many of them have sucked in a love of Spain with their mother's milk; they know the language, they appreciate Spanish opera and flamenco; they used to go to *corridas*; they celebrate religious feasts with the same gaudy piety as animates Algeciras or La Línea de la Concepción. They want the best of both worlds, and perhaps they feel – with their Spanish superstition – that their wish has always been opposed by history.

They take me to the Prince of Wales Club or the club in Irish Town, and I take them to the bar of the Rock Hotel. It breathes an air of the raj, and I remember that, as a noncom, I was never allowed in during the War; it was for officers and their ladies. These friends of mine – Chris Holgado and Charlie Murillo and Joe Seruya and the rest – were never of the officer class: there clings to them, despite their modest prosperity, a hint of the ruled and not the ruler.

They may live in a couple of tiny rooms, for space is hard to buy in this crammed town – even for millionaires (of these there is never any shortage in a crown colony). The walls will be decorated with sad and tasteless little hagiographs – Saint Anthony and the Virgin Mary and the Sacred Heart. The living room will smell of frying and garlic: the Spanish wife, running prematurely to fat, will draw Joe or Chris or Charlie out of his proud Britishry into that other, now inimical, *ambiance*. The daughters will be doing their homework – perhaps arithmetic set by their nun teachers, out of textbooks printed in Dublin. Rich-haired and prematurely nubile, the girls will present a problem soon: Gibraltarian males, with a perhaps wise instinct for exogamy, used to look across the frontier for wives. But it is hard to get over there now and start the rites of courtship. Even in the business of matrimony, the Rock must look to its own resources.

In a world that abhors untidiness and anomalies, that wants self-determination to mean African nationalism, and colonialism to be as archaic a concept as mercantilism, Gibraltar is a disfigurement, a sort of rocky callus. There are times when an Englishman, putting off the worn mask of chauvinism, can sympathize with Spain. England would be unhappy – as the Spanish are always telling us – if Land's End were an outpost of Germany. Britons to whom Gibraltar is one of the last of the anachronistic red spots on the map may see the plausibility of jettisoning a territory that has no further military or naval value. But there remain these 25,000 other Britons. They remind us that ordinary human beings are perverse, and that they thrive on the untidy. The anomaly of Gibraltar must give the tourist a certain quiet aesthetic joy; aficionados of human variety would be sorry to see it Hispanicized for the sake of tidiness. But apart from all that, there is this unique race of people to whom it is a home and who – *con valor churchiliano* – are ready to defend it. It has been defended before, many times.

It is a good home, despite the ships that spill out hordes of strangers. It has no farms and little water; there are bugs and brown scorpions and the occasional sun-blotting cloud of the levanter. The peaceful civilian barks his shins on bastions and gun emplacements. But it has the domestic coziness of a city like Dublin, where everybody can know everybody else. James Joyce brought the two cities together in *Ulysses*. He never saw Gibraltar, but he found the right words for it: 'the sea the sea crimson sometimes like fire and the glorious sunsets and the fig-trees in the Alameda gardens yes and all the queer little streets and pink and blue and yellow houses and the rosegardens and the jessamine and geraniums and cactuses.' It is like that.

Appendix 3: Anthony Burgess, 'Rock of Ages'

In *Guardian*, 9 November 1966, p. 18.

I returned from Gibraltar a few weeks ago. I had been paying the Rock one of several brief postwar visits, more in the nature of toppings-up a longish experience of the place, or gulps of reassurance that it was still there, than greedy raids on Saccone and Speed of the SPQR tobacco-shop. Having spent three wartime years in the garrison, I can never be merely a visitor.

I don't know whether I like Gibraltar or not, but it became an aspect of my private mythology, and I can claim a minor part in its history. I taught Matric Spanish to slim dark youths who are now plump business men; I helped to train recalcitrant conscripts in the Gibraltar Defence Force; I also worked on the *Gibraltar Chronicle*.

The Spanish pincers were on the frontier on this last trip, but they had plenty of tightening still to do. Nevertheless, here were enough irritations, even within the gates. In a bar of a Gibraltar hotel I called a waiter politely – '*Camarero, por favor*' – and got abuse in return. Even my English breakfast, Spanish-cooked, was a deliberate yolk-smashed cold-fat-swimming lampoon of an English breakfast, like a desecration of the flag. Nobody can be happy about the Spaniards; but I found myself also becoming not too happy about the Gibraltarians. This is not a prelude to siding with Franco, a hypocrite who has his fair share of colonies in other people's territory. If the Gibraltarians wish to remain British then nothing must stop their singing 'God Save the Queen,' trading in £ s d, and being protected by biscuit-complexioned bobbies.

The trouble is that this is about the limit of their Britishness. They speak English, but only on that denotatory level which is wholly adequate for commerce and local legislation. They know nothing of English literature and have not themselves produced either a poet or a novelist. Their primary language is Andalusian Spanish, but not even in this have they asserted a cultural identity (the story of the Rock is a magnificent epic subject, and it can only properly be celebrated by a Gibraltarian poet). Their songs, dances and cuisine are Spanish (tea and chips are for visitors only); they watch Spanish television and used, when they were able, to go to bullfights.

Of course, the proximity of a noble, rich, and ancient civilisation, an ineluctable influence, has meant the relegation of anything England could give to a margin of triviality. And there is also the matter of an educational system that has mainly been in the hands of Irish Catholics. But, whether the Gibraltarians like it or not, they are already a cultural appendix of Spain. Sometimes one must think that their Britishry is, in spite of patriotic shouts, a very negative attribute. That is why I should like to know what the general response would be to a genuine integration with Britain – complete with all the taxes. As for a wholesale transference of the population from there to here, on Tristan da Cunha lines, one remembers that the wartime evacuees were not too happy about the cold and the privation: to be British is well enough if that means a subtropical climate and nugatory income tax.

I am deliberately being cruel now, but it is time that the Gibraltarians were whipped into taking stock of themselves. The privilege of British citizenship entails certain duties, not one of which the Gibraltarians seem willing to fulfil. The West Indies have enriched British civilisation, even just by adding a fresh temperamental strand to it. The Gibraltarians produce pertly pretty girls and spoiled handsome youths, but all are of an immense insipidity. They have neither art nor craft; they have not even any ambition that is not wholly commercial. Unless they take colour from their vivid neighbours they are a wishy-washy people. They cry their identity, but this is merely a reflection of British military history.

Perhaps the Rock itself is to blame, that inhibiting mass of dead geology. It might be better for the Gibraltarians if they no longer lived in its skirts. If Franco so desperately requires Spain to be a geographical entity (prelude to a demand for a unified Iberian peninsula?), let him take the Rock and give Tenerife to the Gibraltarians. They might do very well there. How well they will do in Gibraltar when it really comes to the crunch one cannot really say.

During the war they were reluctant to be soldiers. They might do heroic work at the barricades, should these ever need to be manned. One hopes so. One likes to think well of the British.

Appendix 4: Anthony Burgess, 'Everyone's Free … Except Me: One Man's View from the Barrack Room'

An edited version of this article was published in the *Daily Mail* on 8 May 1985 (p. 25), to commemorate the fortieth anniversary of VE Day. The original typescript, titled 'A Day It Would Be Nice to Forget' and reproduced here, is in the collection of the Anthony Burgess Foundation.

On 8 May 1660 the British monarchy was restored. On 8 May 1811 the Duke of Wellington trounced the French at Fuentes de Oñoro. On 8 May 1921 Sweden abolished the death penalty. 8 May in any year is the feast day of Wiro, Flechelm and Otger, whoever they were. That 8 May 1945 was VE Day sometimes eludes my memory.

I had got drunk the night before in anticipation of the rejoicing. When I woke very late and very ill, a Welshman named Ben Thomas was breathing smoke over me and saying: 'The whole of fucking Europe is liberated except fucking you.' He was a regimental sergeant-major and I was a warrant officer class two. We were in the barracks at Moorish Castle, Gibraltar and had been there for over two years, ready to stop the Germans marching in from Spain, with the kind permission of General Franco, and taking over the Rock. The Germans never did march in, and it was too late now. General

Franco had played fair and neutral, ever the Christian gentleman. We had, in a sense, been wasting our time.

It was too late for the Germans, and it was too late for breakfast in the sergeants' mess. Ben Thomas and I struck sparks with our boots all the way down the steep road from Moorish Castle to the Casemates and had a cup of char and a wad in a café run by a moustached Spanish matron. The café was called the Trianon and was very dirty. Rough soldiers, already drunk, jeered at us because they no longer feared our rank. We promised them immediate transportation to the mysterious East, there to fight the Nips. The war, as Ben Thomas said, was not yet fucking over.

No, it was not. The rejoicing seemed premature to those of us who had a wider than European view of things. We did not know what horrors applied nuclear physics was preparing, and we assumed that the Japanese would fight to the last Kamikaze pilot. The war in Europe over, we were now made available for fighting in the jungle and expiring of beri-beri in Changi or somewhere. We feared the little yellow men; the Germans, though Nazis, were at least white. We left the Trianon and went to get drunk in the Garrison sergeants' mess.

There some remarkable specialisations were represented, all already drunk – a master gunner, the drum major of the First Dorsets, a pioneer sergeant with a beard (the only rank in the army not required to shave), the glum comedian of the Garrison Concert Party, the editor of the *Rock Magazine*, an Irish engineer sergeant fighting leprechauns. They were all drenching palpable concern, especially the regulars: these had been jumped up in rank with the war; now, with peace, they would have to revert. Those of us who were not regulars had our own worries. There was a release scheme based on a coordination of age and date of joining up: troops would trickle back to civvy street so as not to swamp the labour market. I had worked out that I would join the trickle in May 1946 (this proved exact). Another year with only Japs to fight. Let's have another drink.

I was 28. I had joined the army at 22. I would be 29 by the time I got out, perhaps older: was not Winston Churchill already warning of the need to maintain a large European army to face the Soviet menace? Winston Churchill was not popular with the conscripts; the regulars naturally liked the idea of a large army – who the enemy was was neither here nor there. What I tried to swill away now was the realisation that I'd missed nearly a whole decade of my life. I'd learned nothing except how to read company orders and do as little work as possible. What the hell was I to do in the real world where people worked for a living and even got sacked? Let's have another drink.

There are times when you drink only to get more sober. This happened to Ben Thomas and me on VE Day in the Alameda Gardens, where beer tents had been set up and there were snarls because the barrels were beginning to run out. Then Ben Thomas began to have visions. He saw all the European dead marching to the tune of *Cwm Rhondda* towards a bonfire. The long repressed preacher in him started to come out and he assured the drinkers that hellfire awaited them: couldn't they smell the stink of the everlasting conflagration that seethed under their bootsoles? I determined to get away from liberated Europe and visit fascist Spain.

I had fairly free access to Spain. One of my jobs had been to dress up as a civilian and spy on the transfer of British money to enemy agents. I dressed up as a civilian now but found I had no pesetas. There was a CQMS whom I particularly disliked. He, I knew, had in his quarters a large number of contraband wristwatches. I broke his table drawer open (splintery cheap wood anyway) and stole four. He had plenty more; he would not miss them. I exchanged these watches for a handful of pesetas with a barman on Main Street known as *El Burro*. Then I walked to the frontier, handed over the mandatory gift of two tins of issue Victory cigarettes to the unshaven Spanish guards (Orwell was to remember those cigarettes in *Nineteen Eighty-Four*) and then entered La Línea. There was no VE Day here.

I fought off the whores, mostly war widows or the wives of political detainees, and drank alone and sadly in bar after bar. Then I drank less sadly. I offered a drink to a member of the Guardia Civil. He refused. I took offence. I said, in impeccable Andalusian: 'You spurn my hospitality because I belong to the forces that have, passively, alas, in my case, broken the forces of Italian and German fascism, leaving the stinking goat of a caudillo that you presumably idolise alone in Europe. His time is coming, mark my words.' The policeman blew his whistle and two others appeared. I was taken to a Spanish lock-up. I remained there for three days.

Spanish lock-ups in those days were very filthy affairs, full of uncleaned vomit and stinking of Spanish urine, which is more aromatic than the British variety. There did not seem to be any catering facilities, but I shared a cell with a middle-aged Andalusian who, whatever his crime, was well-liked by the police, who permitted his little daughter to bring in garlic sausage, cheese, brick-hard bread, and *vino tinto*. These he shared with me and taught me flamenco songs like 'My wife has run away. Long live gaiety'. After three days Ben Thomas managed to get to me. He pointed out the irony of my celebrating the death of fascism by being shoved into a fascist jail.

I got out on the plea of bad Spanish misunderstood by the Guardia Civil. I also said that I had been trying to get away from VE Day celebrations, which indiscreetly jeered at the downfall of a brother caudillo, and was drinking in Spain in memory of a great Anglo-Spanish victory over Napoleon's peninsular army: 8 May 1811, at Fuentes d'Onoro. When I got back to Gibraltar I faced big trouble – three days absence without leave on foreign territory. From this I learned that, despite VE Day, the war was not yet over. Or, put it another way, I was still in the army.

Appendix 5: Anthony Burgess, 'First Novel' [1993]

In *One Man's Chorus: The Uncollected Writings*, ed. by Ben Forkner (New York: Carroll & Graf, 1998).

In the 1930s I was a published poet of modernist tendencies. In 1940 I won a large prize for a short story. Nevertheless, my ambitions were never really literary. I wanted to be a great composer.

This ambition continued until 1953, when, as an English master at Banbury Grammar School, I had a few musical works locally performed but no hope of national acclaim. Devising the libretto for a possible opera, I discovered a capacity for writing dialogue which went beyond the strictures of musical form. It induced me to write a novel; this did not indicate a switching of ambition: it was merely a relief from the scratching of musical notes.

At that time I rather admired the work of Graham Greene. He was published by William Heinemann, and so it was to Heinemann that I sent the typescript of this first full fictional effort. To my surprise, I received a letter from Roland Gant, the Editor in Chief of the establishment, inviting me to visit him. Schoolmasters in those days were so badly paid that I could not raise the rail fare to London. But it happened that at the time I had applied for a post in Malaya and was summoned to a meeting at the Colonial Office. I was sent a travel warrant and so was able in the same day to confront two new futures – one as a colonial officer, the other as a published novelist.

Gant liked my novel. He found it funny. This rather surprised me, as I had always seen myself as a creature of gloom and sobriety. He said, however, that it was not suitable as a first novel: it had the quality of a second novel. Would I now kindly go home and write a first novel and present it for the consideration of Heinemann?

I did this. The novel was entitled *The Worm and the Ring*; it had a dank Midlands setting and was suffused with Catholic guilt. Gant was extremely annoyed and very reasonably rejected the novel. As there was to be no first novel from my pen, there was to be no second novel either. Both typescripts were doomed to languish.

The fictional ambition was not to be fulfilled then, but the colonial one was. I went to Malaya as an education officer but had the novelistic ambition newly thrust upon me. Malaya had to be recorded before the British abandoned it to self-rule. I felt that Somerset Maugham had never done this adequately and not even Joseph Conrad had known the inner working of the Malay mind sufficiently well to delineate it. I got down to the planning and plotting and eventual composition of my *Malayan Trilogy*, later to be entitled, following Tennyson, *The Long Day Wanes*. Heinemann was the publisher. That original contact had borne fruit, though of an unexpected tree.

When I was invalided out of the colonial service in late 1959 I was forced into being a professional novelist in order to keep my wife and myself. With the kind of novels I wrote, and still write, this was not easy. My advances were much the same as what D. H. Lawrence had received in 1912, and my royalties were negligible. It was necessary to write much and to publish much in order to attain an income of something like £300 a year. It was inevitable that I try to publish those two rejected novels of 1953. The typescript of *The Worm and the Ring* was grossly disfigured by its tropical residence, so I retyped it and daringly submitted it to James Michie at Heinemann. This time it was greatly liked; Roland Gant thought it was masterly.

There remained the other novel, the genuine first. This was entitled *A Vision of Battlements*, and its setting was wartime Gibraltar. The title had a double reference. It meant the great Rock itself; it also meant one of the symptoms, according to a family medical dictionary, of migraine. I suffered from migraine throughout my army service, but medical officers never considered it a genuine ailment. I suffered it especially in Gibraltar – something to do with the heat of the sun, the stress of duty, above all sexual frustration.

A Vision of Battlements could have been autobiographical, but was not. Its hero is an army sergeant named Richard Ennis, who resembles his creator only in his army rank and his musical ambition. In North Carolina in 1971, a university professor gave a learned lecture on this book (now, evidently, published) and discovered that the name of my hero was a palinlogue: R. Ennis is sinner backwards. It signified the load of Catholic guilt which I have never been able wholly to eliminate from my work. But this was entirely uncon-scious wordplay: I had chosen the name Ennis because it was Celtic for an island and stood for isolation; it was also as close as I could get to the name of Virgil's hero Aeneas.

In fact, I had followed James Joyce in using a classical matrix to support my first lengthy exercise in fiction. The Virgilian refer-ences were often merely facetious. In the very first paragraph Ennis announces himself as belonging to the Arma Virumque Cano Corps, instead of the Army Vocational and Cultural Corps, a thin disguise for the Army Educational Corps. Ennis has to have a love affair with a Gibraltarian Dido, widowed in the Spanish Civil War. He has to pay a visit to hell, which is Franco's La Línea. As Aeneas has his faithful Achates, Ennis has his faithful Agate, a homosexual ballet dancer. The Virgilian references are not all pure fancy. Aeneas the Trojan has the task of founding the Roman empire. The Catholic and half-Irish Ennis has two tasks – one imposed upon him by the British Army, the other springing out of his own musical ambition. In an age of chaos he wishes to create great music that mirrors the cosmos. The army tells him to teach the troops how, through freshly developed democratic techniques, to build a Utopia.

This is not a bad novel. Written at the age of thirty-five, with a background of wide reading and a certain verbal talent, it had to have some virtues. Why then did I not rush it into the hands of Heinemann and request its publication as my nth novel? Well, I was overloading Heinemann with freshly minted fiction, from *The Doctor Is Sick* to *A Clockwork Orange* and old stuff had to be nudged out. In 1964 I sold *A Vision of Battlements* to Sidgwick & Jackson whose fiction list at the time was very skimpy. It was proposed that the Victorian custom of publishing illustrated fiction should be revived, and my novel appeared with comic illustrations by Edward Pagram. This turned out to be not a good idea: the text was diminished by the drawings and the book not taken seriously. It was never paperbacked and so failed to reach a genuine reading audience.

The situation in the United States was different. There the book appeared without illustrations and was taken seriously by *Time* magazine. It reached a paperback audience and ended up as a subject for university dissertations. I was in New York last December and found copies of the work around. In Britain it was permitted to sink like a stone.

I should very much like to see the book back in print. Indeed, there are a number of books of mine that I should like to have introduced to new audiences. Roman poets like Horace could, when they wrote, boast of having achieved something *aere perennius* – more lasting than brass. In Shakespeare's sonnets we find the same proud blazon. Nowadays an author of any seriousness accepts that his/her work must be liquidated in order to make room for the mere phantom books of Jeffrey Archer, Barbara Cartland, and those devisers of best-selling adjuncts to television commercials. This is unjust, and injustice can be partially remedied by the occasional reprint. My wartime vision still has something to say to the world.

Notes

21   **Wren**: a member of the Women's Royal Naval Service, known, following its initials, as the WRENS. The acronym was first recorded in *The Times* on 5 January 1918 (*Oxford English Dictionary*).

21   **Ennis**: The name is a corruption of Virgil's Aeneas. Burgess points out in *Little Wilson and Big God* (pp. 363–4) that Richard Ennis, shortened to 'R. Ennis', spells out 'sinner' in reverse.

21   **Arma Virumque Cano Corps**: 'Arma virumque cano' ('Arms and the man I sing') are the opening words of Virgil's *Aeneid*.

22   **Dunkirk**: Dunkerque is a coastal town in northern France, near the border with Belgium. Dunkirk was the scene of the evacuation of British forces between 29 May and 3 June 1940.

22   **Crete**: the Battle of Crete, in which British, Greek and Commonwealth forces were overwhelmed by German paratroopers, took place in May 1941. The British surrendered on 1 June.

22   **Yankland**: British slang for 'the land of the Yankees', or America. See Jonathon Green, *Chambers Slang Dictionary* (Edinburgh: Chambers, 2008).

22   **epicene**: 'having the characteristics of both sexes' (*OED*). Burgess's immediate source for this word is probably Ben Jonson's play *The Epicene, or The Silent Woman* (1616). Christopher Ricks's essay on gay and bisexual characters

in Burgess's early novels was published under the title
'The Epicene' in *New Statesman*, 5 April 1963, p. 496. For
Burgess's discussion of this essay and the questions it raises,
see *You've Had Your Time*, pp. 66–70.

23   **Tabs**: theatre slang for 'tableau curtains' (*OED*).

23   **piano player**: Before he went to Gibraltar, Burgess (like
Ennis in the novel) had spent time as an army pianist, working for the Entertainments Section of the 54th Division,
nicknamed the 'Jaypees' after their commanding officer,
General John Priestland. See Burgess's discussion of the
words 'pianist' and 'pianoplayer' in his autobiographical
novel *The Pianoplayers* (London: Hutchinson, 1986): 'My
dad always called himself not a pianist but a pianoplayer [...]
Pianoplayer gives you the idea of him and the instrument
being like all one thing, jammed together. In the pub, in the
cinema, at the end of the pier in Blackpool he was always the
pianoplayer' (p. 12).

23   **Aeolus**: 'Aeolus, in Homeric legend, was appointed ruler of
the winds by Zeus, and lived on his Aeolian island' (*Brewer's
Dictionary of Phrase and Fable*, 14th edition, 1989). In James
Joyce's *Ulysses*, the chapter set in the newspaper office con-
tains numerous references to Aeolus. For Burgess's com-
mentary on the 'Aeolus' chapter in Joyce, see *Here Comes
Everybody: An Introduction to James Joyce for the Ordinary
Reader* (London: Faber, 1965), pp. 114–25.

24   **sonata for violoncello and piano**: Burgess himself completed a 'Sonata for Violoncello and Piano in G Minor'
on 21 August 1945. This is his earliest surviving composition. He mentions the cello sonata in his interview with
Jim Hicks, 'Eclectic Author of His Own Five-Foot Shelf',
in *Life* magazine, 25 October 1968, pp. 87–97. The second
movement of the sonata, a funeral march, carries a dedica-
tion: 'For the Dead: 1939–45'. The manuscript of the sonata
has an epigraph from a sonnet by Gerard Manley Hopkins:
'The shepherd's brow, fronting forked lightning owns / The
horror and the havoc and the glory.'

25   **Proteus**: In Greek and Roman mythology, Proteus was the son of Neptune or Oceanus, famed for his ability to assume different shapes at will.

25   **P.T.**: Physical Training. *OED* records the first usage of this initialism in 1922.

25   **Sloane Square**: a fashionable square in the Royal Borough of Kensington and Chelsea in London. The New Court Theatre, later renamed the Royal Court Theatre, opened there in 1888.

25   **Deucalion's flood**: 'When Zeus, angered at the evils of the Bronze Age, caused the deluge, Deucalion built an ark to save himself and his wife, which came to rest on Mount Parnassus' (Brewer).

25   **games of solo**: solo whist. Also known as 'heart solo' (OED).

25   **Petrouchka**: Petruchka (the French spelling is 'Pétrouchka') is a character in the ballet of the same title by Igor Stravinsky (1882–1971), first performed by the Ballets Russes in Paris on 13 June 1911. The role of Petruchka was danced by Vaslav Nijinsky (1889–1950). Burgess wrote and presented a documentary film about the modernism of Stravinsky and James Joyce, *Making It New*, directed by Eric Nielson and broadcast on Swedish television in 1982.

25   **Diaghilev**: Sergei Diaghilev (1872–1929), Russian-born founder of the Ballets Russes and producer of Stravinsky's *Petruchka*. He worked closely with Nijinsky, who confessed his strong dislike of Diaghilev in *The Diary of Vaslav Nijinsky* (New York: Simon and Schuster, 1936).

26   *Saes*: the English (Welsh).

26   *hwyl*: 'An emotional quality which inspires and sustains impassioned eloquence; also, the fervour of emotion characteristic of gatherings of Welsh people' (*OED*).

26   **Tomlinson**: 'Tomlinson' is a poem by Rudyard Kipling ('Now Tomlinson gave up the ghost at his house in Berkeley Square'), published in 1891 and quoted by Burgess in *Little Wilson and Big God* (p. 352). The narrator in *Byrne*, whose name is also Tomlinson, claims to live 'not in Berkeley

Square' but 'in a room in Islington' (p. 147). Eric Partridge notes in his *Dictionary of Slang and Unconventional English* (1937) that 'Berkeley' or 'Berkeley Hunt' (as a variant of 'Berkshire Hunt') is rhyming slang for 'the *pudendum muliebre*'. Burgess had read Partridge with close attention, and it is possible that he intends the name 'Tomlinson' in *A Vision of Battlements* as a veiled insult against a former army colleague.

26   **swaddy**: a soldier (British army slang). *OED* records that by 1918 'swaddy' had been superseded by 'squaddie', but the word was revived during the Second World War.

26   **He clenched his fist**: He gave a Communist salute. Burgess mentions the wartime rumour of an imminent 'British Revolution' in *Little Wilson and Big God*, p. 295.

27   **Venus came from Cyprus**: an allusion to 'Fairest Isle', an aria sung by Venus in the opera *King Arthur* (written 1684; performed 1691) by John Dryden and Henry Purcell: 'Venus here will choose her dwelling / And forsake her Cyprian grove.' Burgess includes Dryden's poem and Purcell's melody in *They Wrote in English*, his anthology of English literature (Milan: Tramontana, 1979), vol. 2, pp. 169–70.

28   **Andromeda**: She was chained to a rock but was rescued by Perseus, who married her (Brewer).

28   **many cigarettes**: Burgess states in *Little Wilson and Big God* that he regularly smoked eighty cigarettes per day on Gibraltar (p. 304). He also claims to have introduced George Orwell to Victory cigarettes (p. 334). For more detail on Burgess's smoking habits, see Andrew Biswell, *The Real Life of Anthony Burgess* (London: Picador, 2005), pp. 107, 125–6, 264, 277, 321–2.

30   **Concepción**: She is named after the Immaculate Conception of the Virgin Mary, whose feast-day is celebrated on 8 December. Concepción is intended to be a version of Virgil's Dido.

30   **Paolo and Francesca**: Dante and Virgil meet Paolo and his lover Francesca in Canto V of the *Inferno*.

31   **Barasi**: This character is loosely based on Virgil's Iarbas, of which his name is an anagram.

31   *yo tambien soy católico*: I am also Catholic (Spanish).

31   *martellato*: hammered. 'Of notes: heavily accented and left before their full time has expired; percussive' (*OED*).

31   **R.S.M.**: Regimental Sergeant-Major.

32   **U.S.S.**: United States Ship.

32   **jolly jacks**: 'Jack' or 'Jack-Tar' is British slang for a sailor (*OED*). First recorded in 1781.

32   **Major Muir**: Burgess modelled this character on Captain (later Major) W.P. Meldrum, his commanding officer on Gibraltar. See *Little Wilson and Big God* (pp. 298–9) and *The Real Life of Anthony Burgess*, pp. 95–7.

32   *Penique*: a corruption of 'penny', the smallest unit of currency. Before the decimalisation of British currency on 14 February 1971, one pound was worth 240 pennies or pence.

33   *Oqué*: a Frenchified corruption of the English word 'okay'. Not recorded in *OED*. Burgess uses 'oqué' again in his posthumously published novel, *Byrne* (London: Hutchinson, 1995), p. 109.

33   **A.C.I.**: Army Council Instruction.

33   **W.O. 1**: Warrant Officer, class one. According to the *King's Army Regulations* of 1912, 'The position of warrant officers is inferior to that of all commissioned officers, but superior to that of all N.C.Os' (cited in *OED*). Burgess's roman numbers for classes of W.O. and S.O. have been replaced here by arabic numbers following correct army usage.

34   **N.C.O.**: non-commissioned officer.

34   **Warbox**: a slang term for the War Office (*OED*).

34   **Pioneers**: 'an infantry group going with or ahead of an army or regiment to dig trenches, repair roads, and clear terrain in readiness for the main body of troops' (*OED*).

35   *Cabrón*: coward, bastard (Spanish).

35   *Naranjas*: oranges (Spanish).

36   **Casemates**: the name of a fortified barracks building in Gibraltar.

37   **tinned M. and V.**: tinned meat and vegetables (UK forces' slang); 'a familiar expression for the tinned meat and vegetable ration' (*OED*). First recorded in 1925.

37   **heavy duff**: a boiled or steamed sweet pudding, usually containing fruit (*OED*).

37   **Alex**: Alexandria.

37   **Economic Recovery After the War**: Working for the Army Education Corps in Gibraltar, Burgess delivered a series of lectures on this subject, to audiences of British troops and Italian prisoners of war. His lectures were based on a series of eighteen *British Way and Purpose* pamphlets published by the Directorate of Army Education between November 1942 and February 1943. A 'consolidated edition' of *The British Way and Purpose* was published as a hardback book in 1944.

38   **Maybe he get dose in Tangier**: British forces slang of the 1940s. Green defines 'cop a dose' as 'catch a venereal disease' (*Chambers Slang Dictionary*).

38:   **V-2**: the V stands for 'Vergeltungswaffe' (German: 'reprisal weapon'). The V-2, successor to the V-1, was a type of German rocket bomb, also known as a robot bomb, first used against the British in 1944 (*OED*).

39   **the perils of hypergamy**: Geoffrey Gorer wrote, in an article on contemporary fiction published in the *New Statesman* on 4 May 1957: 'The curse which is ruining, in fantasy if not in their own lives, these brilliant young men of working-class origin and welfare-state opportunity is what anthropologists have dubbed male hypergamy.' Hypergamy means sexual intercourse with a partner of higher social standing. For further discussion of Burgess's use of this word, see Christopher Ricks, 'Rude Forerunner', *New Statesman*, 24 September 1965, pp. 444–5; and Biswell, *The Real Life of Anthony Burgess*, p. 103.

40   **bolshie**: an abbreviation of 'Bolshevik'. The figurative meaning here is 'left-wing, uncooperative, recalcitrant' (*OED*), first recorded in 1918.

40   **And so perhaps we can look forward**: Ennis's speech mimics the uplifting rhetoric of 'British Way and Purpose' lectures.

40   **Ceremony of the Keys**: The ceremonial locking of the gates of the garrison and Old Town in Gibraltar takes place twice each year, in April and October.

43   **What you want is a drink**: Burgess retells this story in exactly the same words in *Little Wilson and Big God*, p. 307.

44   **a poem by Lorca**: The poem is 'Arbolé, Arbolé' ('Tree, Tree') by the Spanish poet and playwright Federico García Lorca (1898–1936). The lines quoted here translate as: 'The girl with the pretty face / Is picking olives'. Burgess has mis-transcribed the second line, which should be 'está cogiendo aceituna'.

44   **mindless get**: mindless bastard, idiot or fool (Green).

46   **Cunt-struck**: 'obsessed with sex, or with a particular woman' (Green). This expression is much stronger than 'effing' and 'eff' on page 44, and it provides further evidence of Burgess having revised *A Vision of Battlements* after the unsuccessful prosecution of *Lady Chatterley's Lover* by D.H. Lawrence in October 1960 (Regina versus Penguin Books Ltd) made it possible for novelists to spell out vulgarisms and obscenities in full.

46   **Nips**: the Japanese. Military slang of the 1940s; now considered offensive.

47   **sea-water soap**: a soap designed to lather well with sea-water. Also known as marine soap or sailors' soap.

49   **Segovia**: Andrés Segovia (1893–1987), a Brazilian-born classical guitarist and arranger.

50   **false relations**: a musical term, meaning 'the separation of a chromatic semitone between two parts' (*OED*).

50   **not the Calpe mush**: 'Calpe' is the old Spanish name for Gibraltar.

52   **a very Junoesque woman**: 'resembling Juno in stately beauty' (*OED*). Juno was the wife and sister of Jupiter, and the queen of heaven (Brewer).

52   **The Blonde Venus:** Burgess claimed that his own mother, who had retired from singing and dancing on the music-hall stage some years before her death in November 1918, had been known professionally as the Beautiful Belle Burgess ('a pleonastic title'). See *This Man and Music* (London: Hutchinson, 1982), p. 11.

53   **I took him to safety:** The story of Ennis carrying his father from the burning factory echoes the episode of Aeneas carrying Anchises from the ruins of Troy in Book 2 of the *Aeneid.*

54   **a platoon of pigs with a sow in charge:** In Book 8 of the *Aeneid*, Aeneas receives a prophecy that he will see a sow with thirty white pigs under a tree, as a sign that he should found a city there.

54   *Tú eres muy guapa*: You're beautiful (Spanish).

54   *Guapísima*: Very beautiful (Spanish).

55   **then spoke the thunder:** a quotation from *The Waste Land* by T.S. Eliot (line 399). The fifth section of the poem is titled 'What the Thunder Said'. Burgess made a complete musical setting of *The Waste Land* in 1978, for performance at Sarah Lawrence College in the United States.

55   **The awful daring of a moment's surrender:** a quotation from *The Waste Land*, part 5 (line 403).

57   **a Wills' Glacier cigarette:** Glacier cigarettes were advertised on their packet as being 'menthol-cooled'. The firm of W.D. and H.O. Wills also produced a brand called Woodbines, smoked by Burgess's father, a tobacconist by trade.

57   **soya links:** the soya sausage was, according to *OED*, 'the staple diet of the British in the Mediterranean campaign' during the Second World War.

58   **But that was in another country:** A quotation from *The Jew of Malta* by Christopher Marlowe (c.1590). Burgess's immediate source is the poem 'Portrait of a Lady' by T.S. Eliot, which uses this line as its epigraph. See Eliot, *Collected Poems 1909–1962* (London: Faber, 1963; new edition, 1974), p. 18.

59   **Julian Agate:** Agate corresponds to Achates in the *Aeneid.*

His name also resembles James Agate (1877–1947), the flamboyant Manchester-born author and diarist, who was the theatre critic of the *Saturday Review* and the *Sunday Times*. Although James Agate was briefly married, he was indiscreetly homosexual.

59   **Emergency Hospital**: Burgess had worked as a medical orderly at an emergency hospital in Winwick, near Warrington, in the early part of the war.

60   **Freudian slip**: In the 1970s and 1980s Burgess wrote six episodes of a television series about the life of Sigmund Freud, and a novel, *The End of the World News* (1982), in which Freud features as a character. He also wrote a film script about Daniel Paul Schreber, whose autobiography was the subject of one of Freud's case histories, and a libretto for an opera about Freud.

60   **S.O.**: Staff Officer.

61   **Let us have the tongs and the bones**: an allusion to Shakespeare, *A Midsummer Night's Dream*, IV.i, in which Bottom, asking for music, says: 'Let's have the tongs and the bones.'

61   **Life is real, life is earnest**: a quotation from the poem 'A Psalm of Life' by Henry Wadsworth Longfellow: 'Life is real! Life is earnest! / And the grave is not its goal; / Dust thou art, to dust returnest, / Was not spoken of the soul.'

63:    *Fe tales i am y cwrw i gyd neithwr*: Dialogue in Welsh. 'Fe tales [dialect for "dalais"] i am y cwrw i gyd neithwr [dialect for "neithiwr"], paham na alli di wneud yr un peth heno –' ('I paid for all of the beer last night, why can't you do the same thing tonight –')
'– Oes gyda fi ddim arian a peth arall yr wyf fi ddim yn leikio [dialect for "hoffi"] dy wmeb –' ('I don't have any money and another thing I don't like your face –').

64   **R.A.S.C. drivers**: Royal Army Service Corps drivers.

65   **end of the war in Europe**: Victory in Europe was declared on 8 May 1945.

65   **iron bedsteads**: Burgess retells the story of how he set fire to

his iron bed every week on Gibraltar to kill the fleas and lice in *On Going to Bed* (London: Deutsch, 1982), p. 43.

66   **two-months-unwashed shirt**: Standards of personal hygiene before and during the Second World War were surprisingly lax. Kevin Jackson writes, in his life of Humphrey Jennings, that English intellectuals of the 1930s changed their clothes no more than once a week. See Jackson, *Humphrey Jennings* (London: Faber, 2004), p. 180.

66   **VE Day**: Victory in Europe Day. The date of the German surrender in the Second World War on 8 May 1945.

67   **Persephone doomed to enter the house of Dis**: Persephone was the wife of Pluto and queen of the infernal regions known as Hades or Dis. Virgil mentions Persephone in Books 4 and 6 of the *Aeneid*.

67   **the whole of effin Europe is liberated except for effin you**: Burgess used a version of this line in a newspaper article commissioned to mark the fortieth anniversary of VE Day: 'The whole of fucking Europe is liberated except fucking you.' See Burgess, 'A Day It Would Be Nice to Forget', typescript dated 17 April 1985 (International Anthony Burgess Foundation); published as 'Everyone's Free ... Except Me' in *Daily Mail*, 8 May 1985, p. 25.

68   **incipient D.T.s**: delirium tremens. 'A species of delirium induced by excessive indulgence in alcoholic liquors, and characterized by tremblings and various delusions of the senses' (*OED*).

68   **John Player**: Player's Navy Cut cigarettes featured a picture of a sailor with a beard on the packet.

68   **glacé leather**: smooth leather with a high polish.

68   **C.S.M.**: Company Sergeant Major.

68   **catchments**: natural drains for rainwater.

69   **stirabout**: porridge made by stirring oatmeal in boiling water or milk.

69   **God bless the Duke of Argyll**: 'a jocular expression used when scratching one's skin, from animals scratching on posts supposedly erected by the Duke of Argyll' (*Dictionary*

of the Scots Language). Green records the legend that 'posts were erected around the duke's various estates; primarily for the benefit of sheep, they were adopted by verminous shepherds.'

69   **praties**: potatoes.

69   **C.P.O.**: Chief Petty Officer.

70   **All over Europe lights going on**: On 3 August 1914 (the day before Britain entered the First World War), the Foreign Secretary, Edward Grey, said, in an interview with J.A. Spender, the editor of the *Westminster Gazette*: 'The lamps are going out all over Europe, and we shall not see them lit again in our lifetime.' Burgess has reversed Grey's famous utterance to reflect a new spirit of peacetime optimism. See Spender, *Life, Journalism and Politics* (London: Cassell, 1927), vol. 2, pp. 14–15.

70   **Day of Lord at hand**: A quotation from the King James Bible (Isaiah 13:6): 'Howl ye; for the day of the LORD is at hand; it shall come as a destruction from the Almighty.' Osbert Sitwell includes this passage in his libretto for William Walton's cantata *Belshazzar's Feast* (1931), and Burgess frequently alludes to this work in his novels (including *Tremor of Intent* and *Earthly Powers*).

70   **Fire down below**: A traditional sea shanty: 'Fire in the cabin, fire in the hold, / Fire in the strong room melting the gold. / Fire, fire, fire down below, / Fetch a bucket of water, / Fire down below.'

70   **buckshee**: free, gratis (Green). A corruption of 'baksheesh'.

71   *Wer reitet so spät*: A German poem by Goethe: 'Wer reitet so spät durch Nacht und Wind?' ('Who rides so late through the windy night?'), set for male voice and piano by Franz Schubert in 1815 under the title 'Der Erlkönig', and known in English as 'The Elf King' or 'The Alder King'.

71   *tendebant manus*: A misquotation from Virgil. 'Tendebantque manus ripae ulterioris amore' ('And they stretched out their hands in longing for the further shore'). The source is Book 1 of the *Aeneid*.

71   *Souvent pour s'amuser les hommes d'équipage*: The first line of Charles Baudelaire's famous French poem, 'L'Albatros' ('The Albatross'). 'Often, to amuse themselves, sailors / Catch albatrosses, vast birds of the seas'.

72   **Where were ye Nymphs**: A quotation from 'Lycidas', John Milton's 1638 elegy for his friend Edward King, who had drowned at sea: 'Where were ye Nymphs when the remorseless deep / Closed o'er the head of your loved Lycidas?' See Milton, *The Major Works*, ed. by Stephen Orgel and Jonathan Goldberg (Oxford: World's Classics, 2003), p. 40.

72   **Had ye bin there – for what could that have don?**: a line from Milton's 'Lycidas'.

72   *ulteriorem ripam*: See note on 'tendebant manus' above.

76   **'Jewel Song' from *Faust***: Marguerite's aria, otherwise known as 'Air des Bijoux', from Act 3 of the opera *Faust* by Charles Gounod (1859). The libretto was written by Jules Barbier and Michel Carré. The first line of the song is is 'Ah! je ris de me voir si belle' ('Ah! I laugh to see myself so beautiful').

76   **Tooty-frooty**: Slang: the meaning here seems to be 'Goodbye'. Possibly a corruption of the French expression 'À toute à l'heure', meaning 'See you later'. Green also records 'tooty fruity', meaning 'homosexual' or 'effeminate'. Not in *OED* or Partridge.

78   **fat belly wambling**: 'wambling' is 'to roll about in walking' (*OED*).

79   **touch of the tar brush**: 'a derogatory term used to describe someone who supposedly has a degree of black ancestry' (Green).

79   **Received Standard**: 'The standard form of English pronunciation [...] traditionally based on educated speech in southern England' (*OED*).

80   **nasty old finchist**: a swindler (*OED*).

80   **Satie**: The French composer and pianist Erik Satie (1866–1925).

80   **Boche**: the Germans (derogatory). First recorded in 1914 (*OED*).

81   **beaded bubbles winking at the brim**: a quotation from John Keats, 'Ode to a Nightingale': 'O for a beaker full of the warm South! / Full of the true, the blushful Hippocrene, / With beaded bubbles winking at the brim.'

81   **such an old bear**: 'a gruff, irritable person' (Green).

82   **J.B. Priestley**: A popular English novelist, playwright and broadcaster (1894–1984). He was the author of *The Good Companions* (1929), *Time and the Conways* (1937) and *An Inspector Calls* (1945), among many other works. Burgess regarded Priestley's 'Out of Town' novels, *The Image Men* (1968) and *London End* (1968), as two of the best books written after 1945. For Burgess on Priestley, see his review of Vincent Brome's biography, published in the *Times Literary Supplement* on 21 October 1988, p. 1163.

82   **bods**: Bodies. A slang abbreviation.

82   **apocope**: 'the cutting off or omission of the last letter or syllable of a word' (*OED*).

83   **Foyle's**: a large bookshop on Charing Cross Road in London, founded by William and Gilbert Foyle in 1903.

83   **wheel-tapper's harker**: a railway worker who listened to the tone of a hammer being hit onto the wheel of a train, to check its soundness.

84   **epidiascope**: 'A magic lantern made to project images of both opaque and transparent objects' (*OED*).

85   **flannelgraph**: 'A sheet of flannel to which paper or cloth cut-outs will adhere, used as a teaching aid' (*OED*).

87   *The Importance of Being Earnest*: a play by Oscar Wilde, subtitled 'A Trivial Comedy for Serious People'. First performed on 14 February 1895.

87   **English slang**: 'good show', meaning a good fight or battle, is British military slang from the First World War; 'wizard', meaning 'excellent', is English school slang of the 1920s (Green).

87   *The Duchess of Malfi*: a Jacobean tragedy by John Webster, first performed at the Globe Theatre in 1613 or 1614.

87   **zapateado**: a flamenco dance which involves stamping of the heels and toes in imitation of castanets (*OED*).

88   *Eine Kleine Nachtmusik*: A composition for chamber ensemble by Mozart, written in 1787. For Burgess on Mozart, see his formally experimental novel, *Mozart and the Wolf Gang* (London: Hutchinson, 1991).

88   **Nissen hut**: a tunnel-shaped hut made of corrugated iron with a cement floor.

90   **Hiroshima**: The United States bombed Hiroshima on 6 August 1945. Burgess later wrote a long poem about the atomic age, published under the title 'Sonata in H' in the *Banburian*, 12: 2 (May 1954), 5–8. For a discussion of this poem, see *The Real Life of Anthony Burgess*, pp. 112–14.

91   **cocoricoing**: An allusion to Eliot's *The Waste Land*. 'Co co rico co co rico' occurs at line 392 in the part 5.

92   **Nijinsky's faun**: a reference to *Prélude à l'après-midi d'un faune* (1894), a symphonic poem by Claude Debussy. The piece was choreographed by Nijinsky for the Ballets Russes and performed in Paris on 29 May 1912.

93   **VJ day**: 14 August 1945, the day on which the Japanese army ceased fighting. They formally surrendered on 2 September 1945.

93   **settings of Lorca**: See note to page 44 above.

94   **Chronicle**: The *Gibraltar Chronicle*, a newspaper founded in 1801. Burgess contributed a number of film reviews to the *Chronicle* in 1946.

95   **Comedy Overture**: possibly a reference to the *Comedy Overture* written for brass band in 1934 by the English composer John Ireland (1879–1962).

99   **Deus fio**: The dying words of the Roman emperor Vespasian (AD 17–79): 'I believe I'm turning into a god.'

100   **the milk of human kindness**: A line from Shakespeare's *Macbeth*. It comes from Lady Macbeth's soliloquy in I.v.

100   **A cuppa char. And a wad**: British slang, meaning 'a cup of tea and a bun' (Green).

100 **GPI**: General Paralysis of the Insane. 'A late manifestation of syphilis in which there is inflammation and atrophy of brain tissue' (*OED*).

101 **C.O.**: Commanding Officer.

102 **The wind blows where it listeth**: from the King James Bible (John 3:8): 'The wind bloweth where it listeth, and thou hearest the sound thereof, but canst not tell whence it cometh, and whither it goeth: so is every one that is born of the Spirit.'

105 **Wykehamist**: a former pupil at Winchester College, an elite private school in Hampshire, England.

105 *Amor vincit omnia*: A line from Book 10 of the *Eclogues* by Virgil, meaning 'Love conquers all'.

107 **Ancient and Modern**: *Hymns Ancient and Modern* is the title of a hymnal used in the Church of England, first published in 1861.

108 **Caps F.S.**: The Field Service Cap, known as 'Cap FS', was introduced into the British army in 1894. It was a 'peakless folding side-cap made of khaki cloth' and fitted with a regimental badge (Imperial War Museum). Cap FS was replaced by the General Service Cap in 1943. Burgess writes in *Little Wilson and Big God* that he preferred to wear a peaked cap known as a 'cheese-cutter' (p. 245).

108 **callipygous**: 'Designating a person who has well-shaped or finely developed buttocks' (*OED*).

108 **he painted Muir as Thor**: Mocking the pagan gods in the *Aeneid*, Burgess suggests that Major Muir has acquired a god-like status. See also the reference to Muir 'hurling the hammer at Ennis', a metaphor which also gestures towards the god Thor (p. 95).

114 *in saecula saeculorum*: a phrase from the Latin Vulgate Bible, meaning 'unto the ages of ages'.

116 *De Rerum Natura*: 'On the Nature of Things' (Latin). A long philosophical poem by Lucretius, written around 50 BC.

116 *Te quoniam genus omne animantum concipitur*: 'through

you every kind of living thing is conceived' (Lucretius, *De Rerum Natura*, Book 1).

118 *Animal Farm*: a short novel by George Orwell, published by Secker & Warburg in August 1945.

118 *Four Quartets*: A sequence of landscape poems by T.S. Eliot, originally published by Faber & Faber as letterpress pamphlets and collected in a single volume in 1943. The four poems are 'Burnt Norton' (1935), 'East Coker' (1940), 'The Dry Salvages' (1941) and 'Little Gidding' (1942).

118 *The Unquiet Grave*: Subtitled 'a word cycle', this influential book of pensées, aphorisms and quotations by 'Palinurus' (Cyril Connolly) was published by Horizon in 1944 and reissued by Hamish Hamilton in 1945. The title is taken from an old English folk song: 'The wind doth blow today, my love, / And a few small drops of rain; / I never had but one true-love, / In cold grave she was lain.'

118 *Brideshead Revisited*: a novel by Evelyn Waugh, published by Chapman & Hall in 1945.

120 **She was all / Brittle crystal**: a poem by John B. Wilson (Anthony Burgess), published in a magazine called the *Serpent* in 1939 when he was a student at Manchester University. For a note on the history of this text, see Burgess, *Revolutionary Sonnets*, ed. by Kevin Jackson (Manchester: Carcanet, 2002), p. 12.

123 **G.I.s**: enlisted members of United States armed forces. G.I. is an abbreviation of 'government (or general) issue' (*OED*).

123 **Bohunks and Polacks**: derogatory terms for Hungarians and Poles (OED).

124 **Limeys**: American slang for Englishmen or the British.

126 **fairies**: American slang for effeminate or homosexual men (*OED*).

126 **N.A.A.F.I.**: The Navy Army and Air Force Institutes, which run canteens and shops for members of the British armed forces.

127 **If your beer was as cheap as your women**: Burgess uses the same line in *Little Wilson and Big God*, p. 277.

127   **Gorbals**: a notoriously violent slum district of Glasgow. The novel *No Mean City* (1935) by Alexander McArthur and H. Kinsley Long is set in the Gorbals.

127   **awful daring**: An allusion to part 5 of *The Waste Land* by T.S. Eliot. The full line is 'The awful daring of a moment's surrender' (line 403).

128   **M.P.s**: Military Policemen.

129   *Quién?*: 'Who?' (Spanish).

129   *Soy yo, el sargento inglés, con un amigo americano. No borrachos*: 'It's me, the English sergeant, with an American friend. We're not drunk' (Spanish).

129   *El Burro*: the donkey (Spanish).

129   **bathycolpous**: large-breasted.

129   **steatopygous**: 'Having a protuberance of the buttocks' (*OED*).

130   **Pelagius**: a fifth-century monk who denied St Augustine's doctrine of original sin. Although none of his writings has survived, the views imputed to him are the subject of Augustine's anti-Pelagian tracts. For Burgess on Pelagius and Augustine, see his novel *The Wanting Seed* (London: Heinemann, 1962), pp. 8–19.

130   **And you, my friend, are going to suffer**: an echo from W.H. Auden's sonnet, 'Yes, we are going to suffer, now', from *Journey to a War* (1939); reprinted in *The English Auden: Poems, Essays and Dramatic Writings 1927–1939*, ed. by Edward Mendelson (London: Faber, 1977), pp. 256–7.

130   **work, for the night is coming**: a Canadian hymn from 1864. Words by Anna Coghill and music by Lowell Mason: 'Work, for the night is coming, / Under the sunset skies; / While their bright tints are glowing, / Work, for daylight flies. / Work till the last beam fadeth, / Fadeth to shine no more; / Work, while the night is darkening, / When man's work is o'er.' The text is based on John 9:4 ('I must work the works of him that sent me, while it is day: the night cometh, when no man can work').

130   **Whitman**: For Burgess on Walt Whitman, see his essay 'The

Answerer' in *Urgent Copy: Literary Studies* (London: Cape, 1968), pp. 48–53.

132   **And to his crowns shall be added a glory as of stars**: a mock-heroic imitation of biblical discourse. The King James Bible has 'Thou shalt also be a crown of glory in the hand of the LORD, and a royal diadem in the hand of thy God' (Isaiah 62:3).

132   **high enough number**: Burgess explains the postwar demobilisation scheme in *Little Wilson and Big God*: 'The War Office issued a pamphlet outlining the release scheme. More important than the words was a numerical chart. There were two coordinates – age and length of service – and these met in a numbered release group [...] Of course, the release numbers were unattached to any calendar date: 25 got out of the army before 26, but nobody knew when this would be. My own number was 30, and I was not to be released until May 1946' (p. 317).

132   **scarce-bearded youths**: An allusion to Shakespeare's *Antony and Cleopatra*. In I.i, Cleopatra says to Antony: 'Or who knows / If the scarce-bearded Caesar have not sent / His powerful mandate to you.'

133   **boys with matric**: Boys who have passed the school-leaving examination (*OED*).

133   **PYTHON**: the code name of a scheme operating at the end of the Second World War, under which members of the British armed forces were entitled to a period of repatriation after a long term of overseas service (*OED*).

133   **athletocrats**: Members of the athletic elite or aristocracy. This word appears to be Burgess's coinage. Not in *OED*.

133   **Turner**: As Burgess points out in his introduction to the 1965 edition, he has translated Turnus, the warrior-antagonist from Virgil's *Aeneid*, into the character Turner, a Physical Training instructor.

134   **Laban**: a system of dance notation invented by Rudolph Laban (1879–1958), a Hungarian-born choreographer.

134   ***Weltschmerz***: 'A weary or pessimistic feeling about

life' (*OED*). The first UK edition misprints this as 'Weltschmwerz'.

134 **and weep away this life of care**: a quotation from 'Stanzas Written in Dejection, Near Naples' (c.1818) by Percy Bysshe Shelley: 'I could lie down like a tired child, / And weep away the life of care / Which I have borne, and yet must bear.'

134 **primaverally**: Not in *OED*. The adjective 'primaveral' means 'taking place in early spring'.

135 **Q.M.S.I.**: Quartermaster Sergeant Instructor.

136 **spiv-God**: British slang. Green defines a 'spiv' as 'a flashy, sharp individual who exists on the fringes of real criminality, living by their wits rather than a regular job'. *OED*'s earliest citation is from 1929.

137 **sitting on the po**: sitting on the toilet. From the French 'pot de chambre', meaning a chamber pot (*OED*).

139 ***Spectre de la Rose***: A short ballet by Hector Berlioz, based on a piano piece by Carl Maria von Weber, and first performed in Monaco in 1911. Nijinsky danced the part of the Rose. The piece is derived from the poem of the same title by Théophile Gautier.

140 **Theophilus Gardner**: A fictional poet. No author of this name appears in the catalogues of the British Library or the Library of Congress.

141 **Lady, let me love and lie with you**: This does not seem to be a genuine Elizabethan poem, but Burgess may be thinking of the play *Philaster* (c.1610) by Francis Beaumont and John Fletcher, in which Pharamond says: 'Love me, and lie with me.' See Beaumont and Fletcher, *The Maid's Tragedy*, ed. by Arnold Glover (Cambridge: Cambridge University Press, 1905), p. 94.

144 **Tumbledown Dick**: The nickname of Richard Cromwell, the son of Oliver Cromwell and Lord Protector of England, Scotland and Ireland, who fell from power suddenly in May 1659, having spent less than a year in office.

144 **music after 1883**: Richard Wagner died in February 1883, a few months after completing his final opera, *Parsifal*.

147   **E.N.S.A.**: An acronym of Entertainments National Service Association, formed in 1939 to entertain members of the British armed forces.

147   **given the bird**: jeered, mocked or hissed off the stage. Theatre slang (Green).

149   **The expense of spirit in a waste of shame**: The first line of Shakespeare's Sonnet 129.

151   **Niobe**: 'a weeping woman' (*OED*). Niobe was the daughter of Tantalus in Greek legend, supposed to have been changed into stone while weeping for her children.

151   **a whole half-crown**: a coin worth two shillings and sixpence.

152   **sweet effay**: A corruption of 'sweet FA', meaning 'sweet fuck all'; sometimes euphemised to 'sweet Fanny Adams' (Green).

155   **St John of the Cross**: San Juan de la Cruz, a Spanish Catholic mystic and poet (1542–91). His poems were published in 1618.

155   ***En mi pecho florido***: The lines quoted in the text, from 'Song of the Ascent of Mount Carmel' by San Juan de la Cruz, translate as 'In my burgeoning heart, which kept itself wholly for Him alone, there He stayed asleep and I entertained Him, and the cedars were the fan that made the breeze.' See *The Penguin Book of Spanish Verse*, ed. by J.M. Cohen (London: Penguin, 1956; 3rd edition, 1988), p. 221.

156   ***La Casada Infiel***: A poem by Lorca. The title means 'The Faithless Wife' or 'The Unfaithful Wife'.

156   ***Aquella noche corrí***: The eight lines of the poem translate as: 'I ran that night / On the best of roads, / Mounted on a young white mare / Without bridle or stirrups [...] Her thighs ran away / Like caught fish, / Half full of fire, / Half full of cold.'

157   **numen**: 'divinity, god; a local or presiding power or spirit' (*OED*).

157   **Panglossian**: resembling the character Dr Pangloss in Voltaire's *Candide* (1759); 'unwaveringly or unrealistically optimistic' (*OED*).

157   *The Good Companions*: A best-selling novel by J.B. Priestley
      (1929). A film adaptation, directed by Victor Saville, was
      released in 1933.

158   **war-substantive**: confirmed in a rank for the duration of a
      war.

158   **Hound of Heaven**: a reference to the poem 'The Hound of
      Heaven' by Francis Thompson (1859–1907), published in
      1893.

159   **wide boys**: Green defines 'wide boy' as 'a minor villain,
      often dabbling in get-rich-quick schemes'.

159   **Beveridge Report**: Written by the economist Sir William
      Beveridge and titled *Social Insurance and Allied Services*,
      this report was published by His Majesty's Stationery Office
      (HMSO) in 1942. It led to the creation of the British Welfare
      State and the National Health Service.

159   **The Five Giants**: The five giants were 'the five giant evils
      of society', identified by the Beveridge Report. They were
      Want, Ignorance, Disease, Squalor and Idleness.

160   **National Insurance**: Established in the UK in 1946,
      National Insurance is a scheme providing assistance and
      financial support for people who are unemployed, sick or
      retired, funded by compulsory contributions from employ-
      ers and employees.

160   **William Byrd**: English composer (c.1540–1623) and Catholic
      convert. He was a friend of the composer Thomas Tallis
      (d. 1585) and the poet Robert Southwell (1561–95), both of
      whom were admired by Burgess.

160   **Palestrina**: Giovanni Pierluigi da Palestrina (1525–94), an
      Italian composer.

160   **Sacheverell Coke**: Roger Sacheverell Coke (1912–72), an
      English composer.

163   **You've had your time and I'll have mine**: The second
      volume of Burgess's autobiography is titled *You've Had
      Your Time*. Asked about the origin of this title in a broadcast
      interview with John Dunn, Burgess replied: 'This is what
      they say in the army, in the morning at reveille, when the

corporal comes into the barrack room and says: "You've had your time and I'll have mine. Out of them wanking-pits!"' (*The John Dunn Show*, BBC Radio 2, 31 October 1990). *OED* defines 'wanking-pit' as a bed.

165   **Death's outriders in Cocteau's *Orphée*:** The film version of *Orphée*, directed by Jean Cocteau and based on his stage play of the same name, was released in September 1950. Burgess often watched French films with his friend Moyna Morris when he lived in Banbury, Oxfordshire, during the period when he wrote *A Vision of Battlements*. See *The Real Life of Anthony Burgess*, pp. 137–45. The reference to Cocteau's film means that *A Vision of Battlements* could not have been completed earlier than 1950, despite Burgess's claim to have written it as early as 1948.

167   **avenging [...] Furies:** In Roman and Greek mythology, the three Furies were the goddesses of vengeance.

167   **final Faustian statement:** An allusion to Christopher Marlowe's play *Doctor Faustus* (c.1593), on which Burgess wrote his undergraduate dissertation in 1940. Before he is dragged off to hell by the Devils, Faustus says: 'My God, my God, look not so fierce on me!' See Marlowe, *Doctor Faustus*, ed. by Roma Gill, 2nd edition (London: A & C Black, 1989), p. 68.

168   **about sixty M.M.:** Sixty minims per minute. A moderate tempo.

172   **before going to Hell it is meet that you consult the Sybil:** This section of the novel echoes the episode of Aeneas consulting the Sybil and descending into Hell in Book 6 of the *Aeneid*.

173   **In the midst of life we are in:** 'In the midst of life we are in death.' A line from 'The Burial of the Dead' in *The Book of Common Prayer* (1662).

173   **This is the Tarot:** Burgess owned an English translation of *The Tarot of the Bohemians* (1914) by 'Papus', a pseudonym of the French hypnotist and occultist Gérard Encausse (1865–1916). In the 1960s Burgess wrote an unpublished

short story about cartomancy, 'Chance Would Be a Fine Thing', broadcast on BBC Radio 3 on 13 October 2010.

174: **The wisest woman in Europe with a wicked pack of cards:** Ennis is quoting from *The Waste Land* by T.S. Eliot (part 1, lines 45–6).

175 **Siva:** 'The third deity of the Hindu triad, to whom are attributed the powers of reproduction and dissolution' (*OED*).

176 *Domi ne stes. Domine stes*: a Latin pun. The two sentences mean 'Do not stay home' and 'Master, stay.'

178 **caballero:** 'gentleman' (Spanish).

178 **death in the afternoon:** the title of a book about bullfighting by Ernest Hemingway, published in 1932. Burgess wrote an illustrated biography, *Ernest Hemingway and His World* (London: Thames & Hudson, 1978). He also wrote and presented a television film about Hemingway, *Grace Under Pressure* (directed by Tony Cash, London Weekend Television, 1978).

180 **jig-a-jig:** sexual intercourse (slang). Burgess may have found the term in the novel *Magnolia Street* (1932) by the Manchester writer Louis Golding. A 'jig-a-jig joint' is a brothel (Green).

181 **merds:** *OED* defines 'merd' as 'a piece of excrement, a turd'. From the French 'merde', meaning shit.

182 *No es nada. Venga aquí. Bebe otra vez*: 'It's nothing. Come here. Drink again' (Spanish).

182 **hydrophobia:** aversion to water or difficulty in swallowing liquids. A symptom of rabies.

183 *La Casa de Papel*: 'The Paper House' (Spanish).

185 **Then let us love, dear love, like as we ought:** from *Amoretti*, a sequence of love poems in sonnet form by Edmund Spenser, published in 1595. The first line should be 'So let us love, dear love, like as we ought.'

186 *Aquí, maestro [...] Poco dinero mas – Muy pobre*: 'Here, master [...] A little more money – Very poor –' (Spanish).

186 *Ti quiero mucho, muchísimo. Soy yo, Ricardo!*: 'I love you very much. It's me, Ricardo!' (Spanish).

187   *Bebed todas, con migo*: 'Drink, everyone, with me' (Spanish).

187   *Libertad. Muerte a los tiranos. Franco es un puerco*: 'Liberty. Death to tyrants. General Franco is a pig' (Spanish).

188   *Es un ingles. No sabe nada*: 'He is an Englishman. He doesn't know anything' (Spanish).

190   **parachronic**: A parachronism is an error in chronology, similar to an anachronism.

191   **Say, dainty nymphs, and speak, Shall we play Barley Break?**: from Thomas Morley's part-song *Now Is the Month of Maying* (1595). *OED* defines 'barley-break' as 'An old country game, varying in different parts, but somewhat resembling *Prisoner's Bars*, originally played by six persons (three of each sex) in couples; one couple, being left in a middle den termed "hell", had to catch the others.'

191   **drones**: non-workers or idlers.

193   **HQ**: headquarters.

193   **BBC**: the initials of the British Broadcasting Corporation, the state broadcaster of radio and television programmes, established by royal charter in 1927.

196   **milch-goats**: goats which yield milk.

196   **englutted**: swallowed (archaic). The most recent citation for this word in *OED* dates from 1814.